Advance praise for The T

"The Twelfth Stone seamlessly introduces the reader to the world of faerie, to the myths and legends of both the Irish and Scottish traditions. A faerie tale with a modern twist and a moral hidden within, Jana Laiz illustrates the links between our behavior towards our environment and the resulting damage that can occur, conveying the need for her readers to be aware of their actions and how it is possible for them to have an effect on their own future. I love this book!"

Deirdre Scanlan, Former Lead Singer, SOLAS, Irish Band

"Celtic faerie-lore comes to life in *The Twelfth Stone* by Jana Laiz. When a twenty-first century girl comes face to face with the world of faerie we need no coaxing to follow along. Magical and authentic, heartbreaking and joyous, this is a book for everyone who knows the power of a dream."

Kat Goddard, Children's Department Buyer at The Bookloft, Great Barrington, MA

"I can see the beautiful faeries on the wide screen and hear the rhythmic music of Scotland and Ireland in the halls of movie theaters everywhere."

Irena Mihova, Award Winning Producer, Running the Sahara

"Unputdownable! I love this book! Once I entered this world I did not want to leave. A magical, exciting, original adventure. You are sure to love it."

Alison Larkin, *New York Times* Bestselling author of *The English American*

"I reveled in this book the same way I reveled in Tolkien the first time I read him. The fully developed characters, the evocative imagery, the tension on our hero's journey is enchanting and exciting. The story invites the reader away from this world and into one that gives hope for the future of our planet if only we would *believe*!"

Ann-Elizabeth Barnes, co-author "A Free Woman on God's Earth"

Published by Crow Flies Press

THE TWELFTH STONE

Copyright © 2011 by Jana Laiz

ISBN 978-0-9814910-4-2

Library of Congress Control Number 2011906278

Printed in the United States

Visit us on the Web! www.crowfliespress.com

JANA LAIZ

The Twelfth Stone

Crow Flies Press
The Berkshires, Massachusetts

Also by Jana Laiz

Weeping Under This Same Moon

Elephants of the Tsunami

co-author of *"A Free Woman On God's Earth"*

To Zoë
for believing...

JANA LAIZ

The Twelfth Stone

Chapter 1

"I willna marry him. Never! Ye canna force me!" shouted Rionnag defiantly, with more courage than she actually felt.

"Aye, I can and I will and there's naught ye'll be doing about it!" her mother thundered.

"Then I'll leave before ye put yer marriage shackles around my neck!"

"Ye'll be going right to the altar, that's what! Do not think to defy me! Ye will not disgrace us or yerself!" When her mother spoke like this she knew there would be no argument.

Rionnag tossed her head back and stormed to her room. Let her mother think she'd won the battle. She would wait for night and the moon and then she'd slip away. Her parents had arranged this marriage when she was born, but according to custom, she couldn't meet the groom until the wedding day. How unjust, how despicable, how utterly

1

medieval!

"Mòr, come and brush my hair," she ordered her maid whom she knew hovered outside the door. It always made her feel better to have her long hair stroked. The door, which had been ajar, was flung open and Mòr entered unceremoniously. "If ye wouldna be sae defiant, yer mither wouldna be in such a state all the time." The maid, who had been in charge of her since the day she was born, had no qualms about speaking her mind to the girl.

"Do ye not think my situation intolerable?" Rionnag demanded.

"Aye, that I do, but that has naught to do wi' it. I understand what yer feeling, but yer mither will never bend in this matter." The maid removed the foxglove cap from Rionnag's fair head and began brushing her silken hair.

"Well, she'll soon see that I am not so easily forced," she replied with a gesture indicating the conversation was at an end.

Mòr on the other hand was not so eager to end it. "Listen to me, my girl, I love ye as if ye were my oon..."

"I wish I was," Rionnag interrupted.

"Let me finish. Ye are the daughter of a queen and king and in matters of marriage, it is yer duty to obey yer parents. I ken ye dinna love the lad, but in time ye may..."

"Love him! Mòr, I have never even met him!"

"Och, child, I hear tell he's a fine lad. Handsome too!" she winked at the girl trying to lighten the situation.

"I dinna care for looks. That's no the point of the matter. What of my choice? Nay, I willna go through with it," she declared, throwing herself down on the bed. Mòr sat down beside her, patting her back. Rionnag's statement was true. She cared nothing for looks, and Mòr knew this because for all the girl's beauty, she hadn't a vain bone in her body. Rionnag was the bonniest of all the lassies in the hill, the envy of many. Her hair shone golden and curled naturally at the bottom, her eyes were the darkest violet with an amethyst cast to them. They shone as if there were tears welling just below the surface, but Rionnag's sure smile indicated that if there were any tears, they were tears of laughter. That smile formed on a full mouth was the object of many a lad's fancy.

Mòr stayed until she thought the girl was asleep and quietly left the room. As soon as the maid was gone, Rionnag opened her eyes and looked around her chamber. The gnarled wooden bed with its webbed canopy and blanket of spun silk was the place she liked best to dream. Sweet peas, violets, and periwinkles grew in profusion on their covering of soft green, perfuming the air. Her birch chair in the corner was where she spent many hours curled up with a book. She would miss this place, but her mind was made up. When the moon rose, she would leave.

There was a light knock on the door and without waiting for a reply, a striking looking man entered. His hair was ebony, his eyes, indigo. He wore a robe of the finest velvet. Upon his head he wore a crown of gold, encrusted with blue stones that matched his eyes: Tanzanite stones, for power. He looked fiercely at the girl, but then his look softened to one of fatherly love.

"Why do ye give yer mither such trouble, my love?" he asked.

"Oh, Faither, I dinna want to marry!" she cried. "Why must ye force me to do this?"

"Rionnag, my daughter, this is a matter of the Seelie Court. Ye are a princess of that Court, and ye must abide by its rules. This marriage has been arranged since before ye were born and if ye do not go through with it, there'll be trouble from the court."

"I care not what the court does!"

"Child, ye must remember, it is not only the court that

3

will be affected if ye do not wed. All of Faerie will feel it." He hesitated before he went on, weighing his words carefully. He looked at his wild-eyed daughter, the blessing of his life, and yearned for her to be a child again. But this, the year she was to be wed was upon them and this marriage was ordained.

"Ye'll not be far from here when ye wed. I'll see to it. But Rionnag, ye have been told the truth of what is happening to our world. The dark forces are gathering as the old forests are destroyed, as the earth is befouled. Come, look." He took her by the hand and led her to the casement. She could see the encroaching gloom, the dark shadowy tendrils creeping around bush and briar. She turned her head away, but her father gently turned it back, forcing her to take another look at what was happening, even within the royal lands. She pulled away once more, pushing aside all thoughts but how unfair this marriage was. Her father took her face in his hands.

"Lassie, I am that sorry to say, Faerie is fading. Yer marriage with the Prince of Ireland's Deena Shee Court will strengthen the pure side, and perhaps save our way of life. It is a great responsibility, overwhelming perhaps, but do not fret. I shall still be King for some time, and yer mither will still be Queen. So please, do not rile us again. Next time, I will not be so understanding." With that he kissed his daughter on the top of her head and left the chamber.

"Acchh!" she spat out. She had barely heard a word he said, her ire was so high. How could her loving father not budge? Why must she be of royal blood? Who cared what the Seelie Court did? Her resolve became stronger as she waited for the rising of the moon.

From her bed, she looked out and listened to the familiar sounds of twilight. The birds were chattering their goodnights to one another. She saw the outline of an owl fly past and heard the muffled scream as he took his first victim. Finally, after what seemed like hours, the moon peered from behind the great Rowan tree outside her window, spreading dappled light throughout the forest. This might be her only chance. She thought about her father and felt a pang of remorse, but it dissipated quickly as her thoughts turned to her future. She took one last look around her room, and then opening her iridescent wings, lifted herself out of the window. She landed high on the branch of the familiar Rowan and crouched for a few moments to listen. Tonight, there were no other sounds. No music, no bells, nor pipes, nor fiddles. No songs, nor voices carried on the soft breeze. How fortuitous.

Her heart tripped erratically in her chest as she left the branch and headed for the old ring. Remembering the ominous shadows, she looked behind her nervously as she made her way to her destination. She had found it only days before, nearly hidden among the overgrown brush. The old stones were tumbled and worn, standing in their circle of power. It was obviously a rarely used ring from the distant past, but one that none would think to look for and her essence would be long gone by the time they might discover it. She had only gone through a ring once with her father, a long time ago, when she was a wee thing, but that was a popular ring that was used every feast night. Her father had wanted to show her the other side, its beauties and dangers. It had been All Hallow's Eve then and easy to get across, unlike this night, which was no feast night. Rionnag had never forgotten the colors and the way the light fell there and it seemed the perfect place to go to escape the cruel fate that awaited her.

She followed the path from Rowan to Oak to Birch to Ash until she found the spot. A hedgehog gawked at her then hurried away. A Pixie spy? No, just a hedgehog, she told herself. The ring was just as she had left it. No one had disturbed it. The stones in their circle of power were worn with age. Moss and fallen leaves covered them, and the fey symbols were made illegible by time. She circled above the ring several times trying to give herself the resolve to follow through with her plan. Rionnag had no idea where she would come through on the other side, but it had to be better than a forced marriage.

Taking a deep breath, she whispered the old words to herself, magical words she had learned from her mother's lexicon of spells. She'd had to memorize them quickly. Her mother would have been in a rare state had she found Rionnag with the book. Only those adept in wielding power were entitled to use that book, and Rionnag was neither ready nor skilled enough. Now, as she eyed the ring, she prayed she would remember.

The words were old, older even than the ancient tongue she spoke. She had to practice them until they were strong in her mind. Any mistake could prove dangerous, even fatal. Taking a last look around, then collecting her courage, she made the old symbol, recited the spell, and stepped through the ring.

The coyote stood like a sentinel below her partially opened window as he had done so many nights before. The curtain shifted and he saw her peering out, catching his yellow eyes in her blue-green stare, her long brown hair moving in the light breeze. The clouds raced past the moon putting the coyote in and out of shadow. Perhaps in greeting, perhaps warning, he howled into the night, his eyes fixed upon hers. A large cloud covered the moon and he was gone, melting into the darkness, leaving no trace he had ever been there except the faint echo that lingered on the breeze.

Chapter 2

Fiona sat at her desk, her long tangled brown hair draped around her like a cloak. She ran her hand over the carvings on the desk that read like Braille, of past history. "Jimmy + Sue 4ever," probably whittled with a pocketknife and then filled with ink for eternity. "Mr. F. is a dweeb," written lightly in ink in case the said Mr. F. happened to see it, though with his coke bottle glasses, he'd never even notice. While Mr. Fisher droned on and on pointing to the board with his famous pointer, Fiona wondered where Jimmy and Sue were now. Were they married or maybe only in tenth grade? Not that she cared, but it was something to think about.

"...explain the geographic features of *Chiner* that made governance and the spread of idears and goods difficult and served to isolate the country from the rest of the world."

Mr. Fisher pointed to the board with his pointer, scratching it against the old slate blackboard creating hair-raising screeches, like fingernails gone mad. The entire class grimaced in unison.

"Who can locate *Chiner* on this modern map of *Asiaer*?" Mr. Fisher said monotonously. The class snickered at his pronunciation. The students looked blankly into their books, silently praying he wouldn't pick on them. Fiona could not believe that he actually asked them to locate the biggest country in Asia. She had tried to participate in discussions before, even bring up topics that might actually be relevant, but Fiona was not Mr. Fisher's favorite and he was more often than not condescending toward her. Plus, Fiona hated the way he butchered the English language, her name especially. She draped her hair into a more enclosed cavern around her, shielding her. This time it worked.

"Colleen, come up to the map and show us." Poor Colleen. She was the shyest girl in eighth grade and could hardly stand to be noticed by her few friends let alone the entire class.

Fiona, though, breathed a sigh of relief. Through her hair, she watched with pity as the poor awkward girl shuffled her way to the board, her cheeks reddening with each step. Fiona, hidden beneath her cloak of long hair, changed her position, turning her attention to the window and out into the schoolyard. The day was one of those perfect autumn days where the sky was so blue it almost looked painted on. How could that color exist in nature? Fiona wondered. The New England maple trees were not quite at their peak, but they were getting close. Soon the hills would be ablaze with rich hues of red, yellow and orange, which of course meant the dreaded tourists would take over the little town, causing her grandmother to curse under her breath about traffic and lines in the supermarket.

In contrast to the blue sky, the birch standing alone in front of the building looked stark white, breathtakingly so. Fiona called it the Wounded Birch. Someone long ago had tried to cut it down, but for some reason had stopped, resulting in a long scar across its middle. As Fiona continued staring out the window, her gaze became unfocused and then, as with all her daydream experiences, this one began in a flash and she was immersed in it. Only an empty body sat in the classroom, no longer listening to the teacher or the yawns of the class. Now she was standing inside a circle of otherworldly beings, caught up in a lively, whirling dance in the schoolyard.

"It's Fiona! Come Fiona! Dance with us!" She smiled broadly, though slightly confused, wondering how the *beings* in the daydream knew her name. Although she daydreamed constantly, she only had vague recollections of where she'd been and what she'd done in them when she came back to "reality," though these beings did look somehow familiar. Did they know her? Did she have a relationship with them? The thought made her nervous about the possibility she was losing her mind. But that thought had no staying power in this world as her hands were held and she was pulled into the dance. She could make out the sounds of fiddles, whistles and drums. She couldn't see the musicians; she was whirling too fast. Her hair streamed around her, no longer mousy, instead a beautiful thick rich auburn, like her mother's. And her vivid blue-green eyes with their orange rings around the pupils shone even more brightly. Her full mouth was open in a wide smile, crinkling her face and making her few freckles stand out. Had she seen the change, she would have wondered and been pleased, but as it was she could barely see her companions.

She felt the beat of the drums, reminding her of the time her mother had taken her to a pow-wow. Those drums had made her want to move and never stop. She felt the same way here. Above the sound of the drums the music sounded

Scottish or Irish, similar to what her mother played at home, *all* the time. Like a jig or a reel, the fast-paced beat made her breathless. Other kids her age were listening to rap, hip-hop or whatever was popular, but she really preferred the sounds of fiddles, harps, and pipes. She never admitted this to her mother, but when Fiona heard music from Scotland or Ireland, the feelings it evoked made her feel as if her insides were being torn. At other times the music made her smile so wide it amazed her.

The music stopped and she looked around at her companions. The hands holding hers had no human shape, but were warm and alive nevertheless. To her left was a smiling coyote-like face on a boy's body, hairy hands holding hers. His eyes sparkled and shone like topaz as he caught her gaze. By some magic, his coyote face changed to that of a boy and stayed that way for a long moment, Fiona's eyes unable to look away. She caught her breath. Gorgeous, she thought. Fiona thought she might have seen him before. Maybe she had danced with him. She tried to remember. He smiled, his canid features returning and she felt herself blush shyly under his gaze. She turned away and looked to the being on her right; a beautiful female *something*, but what, Fiona couldn't tell. She was taller than Fiona's five feet two inches by quite a few more. Her face was bronze, her hair wild and nearly white, and where her feet should have been, she had hooves. Around her long neck she wore scarves the color of cantaloupe and from her pointed ears a tumble of turquoise earrings dangled wildly, the color perfectly matching her eyes. Fiona looked down at her own clothes, realizing how shabby they were compared with her otherworldly companions. Her standard outfit was army pants with big side pockets, where her soprano recorder lived, baggy flannel shirts to hide her developing figure and black high-top sneakers, most of which were purchased at

11

the local thrift shop or army-navy store. Just now, though, she wished she were wearing something prettier. But no one here seemed to mind what she had on.

Without warning the music started up again, this time faster and louder. Her partners whooped and hollered joyously and she let go all inhibitions and whooped and hollered as well. Around and around they went, faster and faster until she was laughing tears, reminding her of galloping on horseback. Whenever her mother took her riding and they cantered together Fiona would burst into laughter. She had always been a natural on a horse. In the beginning, she had felt embarrassed by her own abandon, but when she watched her mother's joy, she too, would let go, tears streaming as her laughter and the wind combined in raw happiness. It was the only time she knew her mother to laugh so freely. It had been a long while since she and Maggie had ridden together. Today's dance gave her the same exhilarating pleasure.

"...Fion*er*, Fion*er*, answer the question. Who made the first major contact between East and West with the conquest of Central Asi*aer*!! Fion*er*!" Fiona was back in her seat instantly, inwardly fuming at being interrupted from her joyous experience. Barely audibly she said, "Alexander the Great!" and audibly under her breath she said, "And it's Fion*aah*!"

"Fion*er*, you will move your belongings and take a seat behind Colleen." The sudden renewed attention turned Colleen's otherwise pasty face beet red.

"But Mr. Fisher, I knew the answer!" Fiona protested. Without the distraction of the trees, birds, and the occasional vivid daydream, she didn't think she could make it through eighth grade.

"I'll have no more of this constant gaping out the window! When you can pay attention to matters in class, perhaps you can return to your regular seat," Mr. Fisher said harshly.

"But..."

"Now!" he shouted, the veins on his neck getting thick, his face blotchy.

Fiona, thoroughly humiliated to know every eye was on her, grabbed her belongings and dumped them unceremoniously into the desk behind Colleen. She slammed herself down into the seat and draped her hair around her face once again.

"Go to Mrs. Reed now if you can't control yourself."

Fiona jerked her head up. What now? I did what he told me, but it's never enough, is it? She wished she had the nerve to snap back at him, but instead, head down, pretending to be invisible, she made her way out of the classroom.

Fiona walked alone down the hall to the guidance office. She knew what the guidance counselor would say. She had said it many times before. "Now Fiona, you used to be such an exemplary student. I'd better speak to your mother... Blah, blah, blah..." While Mrs. Reed lectured, Fiona sat and revisited her schoolyard experience. The topaz eyes returned to her memory and she smiled slightly. Lunch detention, big deal. She never had anyone to eat with anyway.

She took the long route back to class, and hesitating at the door, peeked in the window. The entire class looked like they were bored out of their minds. She took a deep breath and strode in, taking her old seat. Mr. Fisher gave her the nastiest look he could muster, but made no attempt to move her. Instead he walked over to her desk and threw down a test from the previous week that was riddled with red marks. Without even looking at it, she shoved it into her emptied desk and then, as if her eyes were magnets and the window the pole star, she turned her gaze to the world outside once more and could swear she saw two brilliant eyes staring at her from behind a rock. She looked again, but they were gone.

Chapter 3

The colors changed slightly as Rionnag stepped through the ring. Although it was dark, she was sure she noticed the change. She looked around and could make out bittersweet vines clinging to the branches of a nearby tree, the burnt orange, brighter somehow. The dusky sky was deep blue, yet the silver moon had a different brightness, as if a light from some far off beacon shone upon it.

All was still. She waited. Maybe this old ring had lost its power, she thought. Even as the thought entered her mind, her hair was lifted off her neck as a gentle wind began to blow. The leaves swirled around her and she began to sway with the breeze. Rionnag closed her wings tightly and grabbed onto one of the stones. This proved to be a mistake as sparks flew and an intense heat burned her hand as she touched it. She immediately withdrew her fingers, blowing on them to stop the burn. Her eyes widened in fear as the wind rose to a feverish pitch and, with nothing to hold on to, she was tossed about like a rag doll in the mouth of a vicious beast. She tried to grab onto a nearby branch, but it eluded her.

Her mind raced. What had she said as she entered the ring? She tried to repeat the words the way she thought she had said them, but her mind was flying about like the rest of her. From a distance she heard banshee screams, and put her hands to her ears to still the sound. Muffling the screams only made them more terrifying and she cried out for her father.

She seemed to be whirling in a vortex, closing her eyes tightly as she was tossed about, uncertain that she wanted to open them again. If the sights were anything like the sounds, she was sure they should remain shut. Her stomach heaved as the wind and whatever force she had created with her spell threw her helter-skelter until she thought she might be sick. This was nothing like the first and only crossover experience with her father, an experienced traveler who had been through many times. Rionnag was completely inexperienced and had picked an unused ring, perhaps left unused for good reason. The banshee sounds got louder until she thought she would go mad with fright. Her eyes and fists were clamped tightly shut, her thoughts incoherent. She felt hot tears streaming down her face, but could not wipe them away. She tried to take a breath, but there seemed nothing to draw in. She tried frantically to steady herself, but there was nothing tangible to hold onto. Instead, she hugged herself with all the force she could muster and buried her head in her arms.

Then, as abruptly as the screams had started, they ceased. All became quiet. The wind died to a slight ruffle and for the first time she dared to breathe. Pulling in a calming breath, releasing her grip around herself, her features relaxed and she opened her eyes.

She was flying past objects she didn't understand, a ribbon of hard black where the earth should be, tall structures where there should be trees. She felt cushioned as she moved along and almost began to enjoy this strange ride when all at once, with the force of a blow, she stopped and fell. She cried as pain ripped through her shoulder.

Rionnag lay where she had fallen, drifting in and out of consciousness until her pain subsided and she could open her eyes again. She looked up at a startlingly blue sky, more vivid and crisp than anything she had ever seen before, except once, long ago. She remembered her father's voice. "Look at the way the light falls here, vibrant, aye?" Her gaze drifted over to a white birch, stark in contrast to the sky. It reminded her of home and her corner chair. She brushed the thought away and moved gingerly to assess any damage. As she sat up, her shoulder throbbed dully, but the pain was manageable. She looked around.

She was sitting in a grassy patch by a large rock surrounded by ivy, yet the path near the rock was grayish black and hard, like one continuous stone that curved about. An enormous brick and wood structure stood to her left, and she felt tiny in its shadow. To her right, fast moving objects, shiny and colorful, sped by. This was not at all like the place she had gone with her father long ago. It was all very confusing. Nothing seemed familiar except the birch, but even that looked strange, a livid scar across its middle. A wave of nausea swept over her. Rionnag gripped the rock.

Thinking she could make out conversation she peered over the rock to look. There, at the base of the birch tree, was the strangest assortment of beings she had ever set eyes on, and she had seen her share of odd. She strained to listen.

"... yes, this is the original place, the spirit home, where our forefathers dwelt," whistled a female with a pointed face, reminiscent of a possum.

"Before the destroyers came, cutting down our homes with their metal teeth and dumping poisons into our rivers. Then, all was one place, one land, one heart," interrupted another, this one a male with the jowly features of a bear, his face changing before Rionnag's eyes, from human to bear and back again.

"Yes, and our folk tried to teach the destroyers how to care for the Mother. How to take only what they needed and to thank the Great Spirit for all they took," an otter woman said, her deep, throaty voice gurgling like a bubbling brook.

"But times changed and we were massacred. We fled, put up curtains of protection, so we could survive. Not many did, but enough so that we could still reach our human brothers and sisters, had they the ears to listen," returned the possum-woman.

"Perhaps they will finally understand on the coming feast night. Don't dwell on it, friend, let's dance," the otter-woman spoke, then rose, giving her turquoise ring-clad hands to the companions on either side. "Come." The colorful animal-like beings stood tall and began to move in a circle of hands, feet, hooves, feathers and fur.

And then Rionnag heard it. Music. It echoed the music of home, but was different somehow. Perhaps it was the heavy drumbeat that distinguished it from the music she knew.

She lowered her head and hid for a moment, but was too curious not to look again. On second glance, she saw a girl, or so she thought amidst the bizarre assortment of creatures. She'd only seen them in books, but was fairly certain this was a human girl. If Rionnag hadn't felt so ill she might have smiled seeing the girl's face change as she looked around her, her mouth making a perfect circle and her eyes becoming equally round. But the girl didn't look frightened, only surprised, as if this was an unexpected, yet not unwelcome trip. As the girl's partners on either side grabbed her hands, her face lit up and her eyes shone like firelight. Rionnag couldn't take her eyes off the girl and watched, mesmerized by the rhythm of the dance. For no reason she understood, she felt drawn to the lass. Perhaps it was just the fact that the girl was the only being she recognized; yet she sensed a connection between them. She resolved to find out more about her.

Without warning, as abruptly as she had arrived, the girl was gone. The others paused momentarily, but continued their fast paced jig.

Rionnag watched the dancers, waiting for the girl to reappear, but as the rhythm changed to a slower beat, still the child did not return. Rionnag looked around for the lass, her only link with anything remotely familiar in this place. Her gaze lit on the enormous structure nearby and she was relieved when she saw the girl's bright eyes looking out from a window. For a moment their eyes met and then once more, the girl was gone.

Feeling unsure, her heart beat quickly in her chest, her breathing grew labored. Calm yerself, her inner voice spoke, but it was hard to obey. Focus on the girl. For some reason she didn't understand, the girl was familiar to her and she knew she had to stay fixed on her. Without something recognizable to put her attention on, she might get lost in this alien place forever. But where had the lassie gone? Rionnag felt faint and sat down on the grass. The connection to the earth centered her and she was able to take a full breath. Steadying herself, she remembered that she alone had done this, had ventured into the unknown, and had to be brave. She told herself she would wait by the rock until she saw the human girl again and would then follow her. Closing her eyes, she called on her Source to give her strength and its comforting light appeared in her mind's eye. She whispered the ancient word that gave her courage in trying times and repeated it, this time singing it in one long, melodic note. Then her exhaustion got the best of her and she dozed.

Chapter 4

Fiona thought the day would never be over. She spent most of it daydreaming about her whimsical experience. Had it been real in some way or just the product of her very active imagination? Were the dancers real? If so, who were they? And what a dance! Had she danced with them before? Could she dance with them again? She thought it had to be real because none of it was fading from her mind like her nighttime dreams often did. These memories remained.

School let out, but today was Fiona's recorder lesson, her favorite part of every week. Ms. Green, the high school music teacher ran a recorder ensemble and though Fiona was the youngest, only in eighth grade, she was so far advanced she was made first soprano. To Fiona, the whistle was magic. Hers was made of golden pear wood and played crystal notes, sharper than a flute and to her, sweeter. She carried it everywhere. It was always with her, either in hand or in one of the big pockets of her baggy pants.

After the hour rehearsal, Fiona headed to the elementary wing of her school where her grandmother was still in the first grade classroom where she had been substituting.

"How was school today?" Gram said cheerily as Fiona entered the brightly decorated classroom.

"Terrible as usual," Fiona replied.

"How was your practice? Better I hope?" Gram smiled at her granddaughter.

"Yeah, it was really good."

"C'mon, let's blow this Popsicle stand. We're going out for pizza tonight!" her grandmother said. Gram grabbed her filled-to-the-brim book bag and the two headed for her ancient VW beetle.

"Pizza? What's up?" Fiona asked as they headed out into the twilight. Gram lifted the hood of the beetle and threw in her book bag. Fiona yanked open the creaky passenger door and climbed in.

"Well, your mother is spending most of the day marching at the rally protesting the proposed cement factory. Then she's got to do inventory and restock, so she'll be working late tonight. I thought I'd take you to that new pizza place in town. How about it? We'll order extra cheese. Don't tell Maggie!" Gram tried to sound sly.

"Sounds great," Fiona said without much energy.

"Boy, hold back the enthusiasm!" Gram scolded.

"I'm sorry, Gram, but I have so much homework and wish I was back in elementary school. Mr. Fisher is such a creep."

"Hey, give the guy a chance."

"Gram, you know Mom and Aunt Kat couldn't stand him either! They said he was boring then, well now he's worse, boring *and* nasty! He sent me to Mrs. Reed. She said she was gonna call Mom, or you."

"What dastardly deed did you do to make him take

such drastic measures?" Gram teased.

"It's not funny. I was just looking out the window."

Gram shook her head. Fiona softened and smiled at her grandmother, knowing she'd let her tell what had happened in her own time. Today had been one of the worst yet. It wasn't just about being interrupted, it was everything. That stupid father-daughter dance for starters. Her school district had it every year right before Christmas and it caused her no end of distress. She couldn't understand why it was such a big event in her school. Hers wasn't one of those posh, private schools that had fêtes and balls, just a regular public school, but for some reason, this stupid dance was a tradition. She scowled as she recalled the catty conversation.

"So, Jen, what are you going to wear to the dance?"

"My mother bought me a green velvet dress. I told my dad to wear his tuxedo." Shannon had glanced over at Fiona, a smirk on her face. She had continued talking to Jen, but her eyes kept darting in Fiona's direction. *"My dad is going to get me a corsage, isn't that great? Is yours?"*

And then there was honors English class where they were reading scenes from Shakespeare's King John. She could just make out the slightest of whispers and glances aimed in her direction whenever Phillip *the Bastard* was mentioned.

Fiona sat in the passenger seat, gripping her recorder in her hands, her fingers pressed down on the holes, creating impressions on her soft skin. She looked unhappily out the window. It was not quite five o'clock, and already nearly dark. Fiona hated these dark days, she loved the summers when the sun would be out until nearly nine. Darkness so early didn't seem natural and felt depressing. She was tempted to share today's daydream with her grandmother, but would feel too guilty about not telling her mother, and there was no way she was about to tell her mother *that*.

Gram started the engine, turned on the lights and pulled out of the school parking lot. The moths had returned with the unusually warm October evenings and they were out early, doing their kamikaze stunts into the headlights. A large one crashed into the car. Fiona hated to see them get smushed on the windshield. It made her sad and a little sick to see their once lovely winged bodies pasted to the window and then smeared back and forth as the wipers tried to clean them off.

The car stalled. "I've got to bring this car to Ray's. Again," Gram said, pumping the gas pedal. She turned the key and it roared to life once more. They moved forward about three feet and the car stalled again. Gram slammed her fist lightly on the steering wheel, put the car into neutral and started it up again. Throwing it into first gear they jerked ahead.

"Ouch!" Gram said as another moth hit the windshield. Fiona watched from the passenger seat as the intermittent wipers spread the remains of the poor moth across the glass. Gram tried spraying wiper fluid and put the wipers on high speed. It only made it worse. Now neither of them could see clearly. The car stalled again as yet another moth crashed into the windshield. It hit the passenger's side and Fiona watched the thing slide down the glass, frantically, almost as if it was trying to hold on.

Fiona jumped out of the stalled vehicle. She ran to the front of the car and there, clinging to the bumper for dear life was something not quite resembling a moth, one luminescent wing possibly broken. Fiona bent over to give closer inspection and she and the "moth" exchanged shocked glances. Still crouched on the ground, out of Gram's sight, Fiona tenderly lifted the hurt creature, placed it gently in her jacket pocket, and quietly, got back into the car.

"Fiona, what do you think you were doing?"

"Um, I was trying to save the moth," she said, her heart pounding quickly.

"I hate being the cause of death for all those moths, Fi, but it's impossible to stop them from going toward the light."

Fiona rolled her eyes. "Now you sound like Mom!"

"I mean the physical light bulb of the car, not the heavenly light calling us all home!" she said, dramatically.

"I knew what you meant." Fiona tried to sound casual but her heart was racing. She had an inkling of what was in her pocket, though thinking she was crazy to even think it. But after what happened in the schoolyard this morning, and her memories of it more vivid than ever before, maybe, just maybe, her waking life was merging with her dreaming self. Or maybe she was going nuts. She wasn't sure what was possible at this point.

"Young lady, do not get out of a moving vehicle again, please," Gram scolded, interrupting her musing.

"It wasn't moving."

"That's beside the point," she argued as the car stalled for the fourth time. "Arrgh! He said he fixed it. I'm going to have to borrow Maggie's truck, not that it's any better!"

"Yeah, whatever," Fiona said, turning to the window. She remained quiet for the rest of the ride home, every now and then making sure that what was inside her pocket was still there. She tried to look but the car was too dark. The normally short ride home seemed to take forever, the car stalling twice more by the time they finally pulled into the long driveway. Fiona practically flung herself out of the moving vehicle.

"Hey!" was Gram's brief response, but Fiona was already out of the car and in the house, leaving Gram shaking her head. She bounded up the stairs two at a time and entered her room, quickly shutting the door, and stood against it catching her breath. Turning on the light, she peeked into her pocket to make sure the creature was still there. It was.

She breathed deeply and looked around her cozy, cluttered room. Her old four-poster bed was pushed up against the wall by the window, a handmade quilt draped over it. A large dream catcher hung above the bed, the feather stirring as a breeze came through the partially opened window. On the windowsill behind the desk, there was a collection of rocks her mother had given her, presently covered by dusty math papers.

The walls were covered with posters of her favorite bands alongside framed pictures from her great-grandmother's fairytale book. They had been in her mother's room when she was a child.

In the corner was Fiona's most beloved object, her Victorian dollhouse: a painted lady. Her mom had built it before Fiona was born, and painted it lavender with accents of pink, green, and gray. Each room was filled with furniture, some handmade, some store-bought. Maggie, Fiona's mom, prided herself on finding terrific buys in flea markets and tag sales, and though Fiona no longer played with the house, her mom kept adding little accessories every now and then. Her latest find was a miniature breadbox made of tin with a door that really opened. Fiona loved it. Although she felt too old to play with dolls, she still enjoyed rearranging the furniture. But to Fiona, the best things in the dollhouse were the tiny paintings on the walls. One year her mom had been on a painting kick and she'd copied the fairytale pictures that lined Fiona's walls, into tiny dollhouse-sized ones. She'd bought miniature brushes and spent each Sunday painting them in exact detail. Fiona had loved to watch quietly as her mother worked. She'd been only a little thing then and any chance to be with her beautiful mother was a joy. When the pictures were done they turned out amazingly like the originals. The real pleasure for Fiona was that her mom had made them for *her*. But that had been before she lost herself to the shop.

Fiona took another deep breath and reached into her jacket pocket. Nervously feeling for what she had placed inside, her fingers immediately found what they sought. Carefully she gently took the thing in her hand and lifted it out of her pocket. She stared at what lay on her open palm.

It had to be, she thought. She'd seen enough pictures of them all her life, and though one was lying right there on her upturned hand, she was beginning to think she was hallucinating. Faeries were in books, weren't they? She knew her mother believed in them, as well as in native spirits, crystals, standing stones, and who knew what else. That's why she'd never tell her mother about her daydreams. Not anymore. She used to, but Maggie would get so serious, tell Fiona she had "the gift," whatever that was and basically freak her out. So she kept her experiences to herself.

She stared at the being in her hand. Fiona's first impression was that it looked like a Luna moth and it was about the size of one. She guessed it was about five or six inches, and though she thought Luna moths lovely, the being in her palm was exquisitely beautiful. It was definitely female. She was lovely: long, golden hair spiraling around her tiny, delicate face. Her petite ears came to a dainty point. Her eyes were closed tightly, as though she were frightened. She wore gauzy luminous material to cover her body, and Fiona wondered if she was cold. She had wings, but Fiona couldn't make them out in any detail; the creature was holding her arms about herself.

After gazing blankly for quite some time, Fiona realized the faerie or whatever it was, was hurt and needed help.

She put her face close to it and whispered gently, "It's

27

all right. Can you hear me? I won't hurt you. Can you understand English? Will you open your eyes?"

The creature opened one eye and then the other, and looked directly into Fiona's. The eyes were deep and brilliant; were they purple? Fiona straightened and held her slightly shaky hand a few inches further away.

"Aye. We speak English if we must, but the old tongue is what we speak." Her voice, much to Fiona's surprise was not a tiny voice, but a voice rich and mature.

"What's the 'old tongue'?"

"Ye'd call it Gaelic, I suppose. It's nearly dead now above the hills, but below, it's our tongue to be sure."

"What hills and who are 'we'?" Fiona asked.

"Ye ask a right many questions," the creature said with an indulgent smile, laced with pain. "But have ye never seen a faerie, bogie, sprite, nor pixie?"

"I *knew* it!" Fiona said out loud to herself. To the faerie she said amazedly, "No, you're the first."

"Aye, that is who we are. We live under the hills, in the old forests, in the night and on the other side."

"The other side of what?"

"Just the other side," the creature said, and Fiona left it at that.

"Which are you?" Fiona couldn't help but ask.

"Faerie, of course. And ye are a *lassie*, am I right?"

"Yes, I'm a girl," she said. "Haven't you ever seen one of us?" Fiona asked a bit surprised.

"Nay, only in books. I notice you've got a strange way of speaking English. Could ye tell me where I am? Am I in Wales?"

"You're in Massachusetts," Fiona explained.

"What's that, then?" she asked, a look of confusion on her face.

"Massachusetts, you know, in the United States of

America."

The fairy put her tiny hand to her mouth in astonishment. "Do ye mean to tell me I landed clear across the water?"

"Where *did* you come from?" Fiona was fairly certain it was Scotland, but at this point she wasn't sure about anything.

"Glen Et..."

The two were interrupted by the sound of the front door slamming shut. "Helllooo! I'm home!" Fiona's aunt called.

Moments later they heard her light footsteps coming up the stairs. "C'mon Fi, I hear we're going out for pizza! You ready?"

Fiona knew her aunt would barge in without knocking and looked frantically around the room, trying to figure out where to hide the faerie from the other members of the household. Her eyes fell on the dollhouse. It was the perfect place. She placed the faerie gently on the piano bench in front of the dollhouse's petite baby grand and went to the door. Before her aunt reached the knob she opened it a crack and said, "I'm not hungry. You guys go." She shut the door and stood against it looking into the dollhouse.

"Come on, Fiona," said Aunt Kat, pushing the door open. "This is our chance. I want to go out! Maggie's working late and I'm tired of tofu and brown rice. I want..." and she looked slyly around the room pretending the place was bugged, "... pepperoni tonight!" Fiona raised her eyebrows, knowing full well that her aunt wanted nothing of the kind.

"Ok, well, at least extra cheese!" she said theatrically.

With Maggie and all her health foods, it was a treat to go out and eat junk food, especially without being under Maggie's critical eye.

"What's with you tonight, Fi? I thought you'd jump at the chance," Aunt Kat pressed. Fiona knew she'd better agree and practically shoved her aunt out the door.

"Okay, okay, but I get to have root beer! Deal?"

"Absolutely!" her aunt agreed happily.

"Fine!" Fiona said, trying to sound normal. Sometimes Aunt Kat could be so cheerful it was annoying. But Fiona couldn't help but be cheered, not only by her aunt's infectious grin, but also because she had discovered a miracle tonight. She felt a surge of excitement. She'd go to Cristiano's and then she'd come back and learn more about a mystery that until now had only been part of her imaginings. On the way down the stairs she paused, finding a reason to return to her guest, "I forgot my jacket; be right back." She dashed up to her room again.

The faerie was sitting, apparently uncomfortably on the little bench. Fiona bent down and said in a quiet voice, "I've got to go out. Will you be all right here for a bit by yourself? Are you in pain?"

"Aye, my shoulder does pain me. Perhaps ye can look at it when ye return."

"I'll definitely do that. Here let me move you to a more comfortable place," she said and gently lifted the faerie, placing her upon the miniature sleigh bed.

"I'm really sorry I have to go out, but Aunt Kat and Gram'll get suspicious. It's pizza, you know."

The faerie gave her a puzzled look but Fiona didn't have time to tell her about pizza just then. She started to leave, but stopped short, remembering her jacket and grabbed it off the back of the chair. She hesitated, trying to decide whether or not to turn off the lights. Against her environmentalist mother's orders, she left them on, and closed the door firmly behind her.

Chapter 5

The Seelie Court was in an uproar. After her argument with her daughter, Queen Catriona had gone to the hollow hill in which the Season Room was housed to oversee the creation of rain in arid lands, sunny skies in cool places and snow in the northern climes.

Two faeries were standing in front of a huge crystal dome, heads together, frowning. One of them looked up as the queen entered. Quickly bowing low, she signaled to the other faerie to curtsy. Rising at the queen's wave of her hand, they politely gestured for her to come and look into the orb. The images were that of swirling clouds and dark raging skies. "Yer majesty, if ye please, we are having the most awful time. It seems the UnSeelies have been creating storms such as we've never seen before, making it difficult for us to adjust the weather as it should. We dinna ken what to do."

"This was bound to happen! Those humans! How many

times have we tried to tell them! As they befoul the rivers and lands, both worlds are being destroyed. The UnSeelies are becoming more powerful as they revel in wreaking havoc and mayhem. The humans do not know it, but they are giving sustenance and power to the most vicious entities on this side!!" raged the queen.

They had heard this speech before. The malevolent side of Faerie was rising and it was now harder for the Seelie Court's faeries to complete their responsibilities.

Faerie had once been filled with lively, mischievous beings, full of beauty and delight. The forests had been alive with sparkling sprites flitting from tree to tree. Yet, the destruction of the old forests and the rivers, the mountains and the seas were bringing to life the basest, the lowest, and most malevolent and virulent form of faerie the world had ever seen. Merriment was vanishing, beauty replaced with ugliness.

The two court faeries had looked to their leader for answers. She had none they could understand. The Queen paced the floor, hands knotted behind her back. "I know what had better take place, and no mistake!" The two faeries looked at one another, eyes wide. They were ignorant of what had gone on within the palace, and though the queen was often given to fits of anger, they knew she was a good and kind ruler. They waited for her instructions but none came. Instead, she stormed out, leaving them shaking their heads in dismay.

The child could be so defiant, Queen Catriona thought, remembering their stormy conversation. She returned to Rionnag's chamber to put some sense into the girl's head and found the room empty. She guessed exactly what had happened and the anger that normally was kept under tight rein escaped and the wind began to blow with a terrible force. The queen flew to her own chamber, her fury turning her otherwise beautiful face to that of a crone, teeth bared and snarling. Unfortunately, Mòr, who had been waiting to bring the queen her supper, bore the brunt of her rage.

"She's gone! Find her, I tell ye! Find her! How could this happen in MY house?" she screamed.

Mòr, cowered in the corner and waited for the tantrum to subside. Soon enough the queen regained her composure. Her hair was wild and the wind still churned, but the worst was over. Mòr brushed herself off and bowed deeply. "Yer Majesty, when I left her chamber she was asleep. Dinna fret, I'll find her and bring her back."

"Och, Mòr," she said, her anger subsiding into sadness laced with worry, "Why must she be so defiant, so willful? She shall not make me lose face. How could ye not have seen this coming? Nay, how could I not have seen it? I pray she is safe. If my sister should hear, och, I shudder to think!"

Her daughter's marriage had been arranged long before Rionnag was born; in fact it had been arranged generations before. It was a tradition that if there was a daughter from the Scottish Seelie Court and a son of the Irish Deena Shee Court, born during the same reign of a king, they must be wed to bring the fairies of Scotland and Ireland together. In the past there had been arguments, power struggles, even battles between the two Faerie realms. The wise ones had decreed that the two houses joined by marriage would prevent such hostilities, and now, time was of the essence. The earth was in jeopardy, and the two houses joined could help strengthen Faerie and perhaps change the course of action the humans were taking. With the Irish faeries' skills in storytelling and the Scottish faeries' advanced magical techniques, the hope of both courts was that the unification might bring about change for the better.

It hadn't happened in many generations, but finally a daughter was born to Scotland and a son to the Irish Royal family. There had been much rejoicing at the birth of both babes, but as custom demanded, they were not to meet until the wedding day.

No, Rionnag's marriage was destined and take place it would, the queen affirmed to herself. Any change could affect the future of the faerie world, and things in that world were changing far too quickly. Faerie was in trouble and this marriage was more crucial than any previous nuptial. Queen Catriona shuddered to think what would happen were it not to take place. It might be the one way to strengthen both sides enough to fight the darkness that was threatening like the distant thunder of an approaching tempest.

If the queen of the Deena Shee should hear of Rionnag's disappearance, she could declare war. The Irish queen's son would not be so disgraced. Rionnag had no idea how serious this was.

"This is just the opportunity my sister Barabel wants. Should this marriage not take place, my sister could ally herself with Queen Deirdre in an attempt to unseat my court. That Rionnag, she shall be punished! Mòr, go, go and find her before my sister's henchmen do!" Queen Catriona cried. Mòr made her way awkwardly out of the chamber as the queen slowly rose from the divan and went over to the looking glass. She sat on a high stool and smoothed the despair from her face and arranged her fury-swept hair into some semblance of order.

King Niall burst into the chamber, passing Mòr and her assistant, Jinty. They could see he was aware of the situation, his kingly robes flapping wildly as he stormed about. Catching his breath as he did every time he looked upon his wife, he said urgently, yet gently, "Where is our daughter? I just went back to talk with her. Why is she not in her chamber?"

The queen took both his hands in hers and said, "I did the same and found her gone."

"Where did she go? Did she take her horse?"

"Nay. I just sent Mòr to find her."

"My dearest, do ye think Mòr is capable?" he asked doubtfully with a hint of impatience.

"She's known the lassie forever. She knows all her hiding spots."

"Ye do realize what will happen if Barabel finds out."

"Believe me, I am aware of my sister and her treachery. I swear she will pay dearly if she harms a hair on my lassie's head. But that child is so defiant. Och, Niall, what shall we do? She'll fight this marriage."

"She can not have gone far. When I find her, I will speak with her again. She'll listen."

"That's what ye said before."

"Aye, but I was not grasping the seriousness of her feelings on the matter. I appreciate her position, but she must understand that she's no ordinary faerie. I thought I had made her see the responsibility she bears. I'll make her understand."

"I would not want our Irish Queen to hear a word," the queen said, putting her finger to her lips.

"Nay, we'll keep this to ourselves as long as possible. I'll give Mòr a wee bit of time, but I'll send my troops if I must," said King Niall.

"Aye," the queen agreed. The king kissed his wife's hand and looked fiercely into her eyes. Their gaze lasted a long moment. The queen still caught her breath at his striking appearance. How lucky she was to have been able to have had a choice in her marriage. She felt rather like a hypocrite, but this was different. This marriage must take place.

King Niall gave his wife a long look filled with concern,

then kissed her, bowed and swept out of the chamber.

Mòr and Jinty had been hovering outside the door, eavesdropping. The king moved past them without a glance.

"Ye'll help me find her, Jinty, aye? Ye ken what will happen if we fail," Mòr told her assistant.

Jinty groaned in response, for she knew exactly. Mòr, her hand to her ample bosom, said, "We *must* find her. If that Queen Barabel hears of this, she'll send those odious henchmen after oor lass. We must find her before they do."

Jinty, a solemn and frail sort of faerie, nodded her head; lime curls bobbing, and rolled her golden eyes in understanding and fear.

The two went into the Princess' room to look for any clues as to her whereabouts. Nothing was out of place. The girl must have been planning this for some time. They left the chamber and searched the area around the hill, in the gnarled hole in the great Rowan, under the fern canopy, on the rock, by the burn, but there was no trace of their princess. They flew deeper into the old forest.

Jinty, who up until this time had scarce uttered a sound said, "I feel she was near."

"Och, Jinty, there's naught here but some stones and leaves. I dinna feel her and I've been wi' her since she was wee. I'd surely ken if she'd been by. Noo come!" Mòr declared as she stumbled over a stone and into what she realized was a ring. The magic must have lingered from when the princess had used it only hours before, because the leaves began to swirl and Mòr got caught in a whirlwind. "Help me, Jinty!"

Jinty grabbed Mòr's fat hand but instead of pulling her out of the ring, Mòr pulled Jinty in and they both began to whirl as the magic of the ring did its work. They held on to each other in fear. Neither had ever been through, had never wanted to leave their familiar world to venture into any other. They both said a faerie spell to themselves in a vain attempt to put an end to this terrifyingly and unexpected turn of events, but it was too late and moments later, they were well on their way to the other side.

Chapter 6

As the old beetle pulled away from the house Fiona looked up to see the light glaring from her window. A definite 'no-no' in her family. Gram noticed it too.

"Oh, Fiona, you left your light on. I hope we get home before Maggie."

"Do you want me to go up and turn it off?"

"No, but I'm really not in the mood for the environmental lecture," Gram said, her annoyance obvious.

"Do you want me to turn around?" Kat asked from the driver's seat.

"Forget it," said Gram. "Next time Fi, remember, okay?"

Fiona grunted affirmative from the back seat. She agreed with and defended all her mom's conservation and ecological ideas, but man, Maggie could be radical. She had turned the family into fanatical recyclers, composters, and water savers, which was great. But just accidentally throw a banana peel into the trash instead of the compost or leave a light on and she'd freak!

Fiona loved her mother but sometimes wished she could ease up. Go out on a date, watch T.V., something! Once when they were fighting she had thoughtlessly wished aloud that Aunt Kat was her mother instead. Her mom was sad and distant for days after. Fiona had finally put her arms around her and apologized, but Fiona wasn't completely honest with her apologies. Ever since she became owner of the shop, Maggie rarely had time for Fiona and this made her angry. Fiona wondered if she'd be as resentful if her mother ever met a man. Even though Fiona often helped out after school, Maggie was so determined to be successful that she often worked long into the night. And tonight, once again, she was working late. Maggie was one of the organizers of a rally protesting a cement factory that was trying to infiltrate its way into a town twenty miles west of their little village. Her mother was on the bandwagon to stop it from coming in and spewing mercury and other poisons into the air, threatening the health of anyone within a fifty mile radius, not to mention building the proposed smokestack that would tower over three hundred feet high. Fiona was proud of her mother, but she often wondered whether Maggie thought her own daughter was as important as her many causes.

Gram tried to make up for it, always being there when Fiona got home from school. She was the cookie-baker and sweater-knitter, giver of hugs and kisses; altogether she was the ultimate grandma.

They got to Cristiano's and ordered a large pie with extra cheese and Fiona reminded her aunt about her promise of root beer.

"A promise is a promise," Aunt Kat said, looking at Gram whose eyebrows were raised at this request.

"Sure is!" Fiona said with satisfaction.

As they sat and waited for their food to arrive, Fiona drummed her fingers on the table nervously. She really wanted to hurry this up and get back to her room.

"What's up with you tonight, Fi?" Aunt Kat asked. "A little nervous energy there or are you planning on taking up the drums?"

"Nothing," she said in a rude tone. Softening, "It's just... I've got lots of homework tonight and I really want to practice my new Bach piece."

"Hey, now, we don't get to do this often, so would you mind enjoying yourself? You sound like Maggie."

"Actually I don't. Mom would have to practice yoga moves or turn over the compost," she said, her sarcasm evident.

Aunt Kat changed the subject. "How was your ensemble this afternoon?"

"It was good. Really good. Better than the rest of the day."

"What was so bad about the rest of the day?"

Fiona knew she'd better tell them about her detention, so she carefully told her tale, omitting the parts about dancing with creatures from another dimension.

"I hate Mr. Fisher! He's so freakin' nasty!"

"Oh, give the guy a chance, Fi," her aunt winked.

Fiona did not think it amusing in the least. "Aunt Kat, you and Mom had him when you were in high school and he's worse now. Why couldn't they make *him* retire?" The last comment was directed at her grandmother.

Gram gave Fiona a sympathetic look. She knew exactly what her granddaughter meant. Why Gram had been forced out while Mr. Fisher remained was a mystery. Gram knew the politics of the system and it seemed that sometimes the ones who should leave stayed interminably. Gram, who had adults coming up to her thirty years after having had her in first grade, giving her flowers and writing her poems thanking her for being a truly wonderful teacher, had been forced to retire.

"Ooh, smell that!" Gram said, changing the subject as the pizza arrived.

Gram breathed in the aroma of the pizza as if it were a long lost friend and while she cut hers with a knife and ate it piece by piece with a fork; Kat held it in front of her and pulled on the melted cheese to see how long it could stretch. Fiona couldn't help smiling at her aunt's good mood and followed suit with her own piece.

"Hey, Ms. Harris!" a teenage boy said as he came by. Fiona could see by his red cheeks he was in love with his teacher.

"Hi, Will!" Kat smiled through a mouthful of cheese.

Fiona shook her head. She knew her aunt was the most popular English teacher in the high school, but these boys in love with her made Fiona roll her eyes at how seriously pathetic they were.

She ate one slice quickly and began drumming her fingers again. At the next table sat a couple of punk-looking boys. Fiona recognized one of them. It was Jason, one of Maggie's employees in the shop, and Fiona thought he was pretty cool.

"Hey, Jason," she waved.

"Hey, Fiona! Hello Ms. Harris, Mrs. Harris," he said politely.

Gram smiled. She'd once had a bit of trouble thinking this kid with the eyebrow ring, the black boots, and the pink streaked buzz-cut could be so polite. She leaned over and whispered, "I'm embarrassed to say this, but when I first met Jason I really was a little afraid of him."

"Jason's cool. I was thinking of doing that to my hair,"

41

Fiona teased. Gram raised her eyebrows.

Aunt Kat smiled and said, "And this is why I love teaching high school so much. You see a guy like Jason and you might think, 'Now there's a kid crying out for attention,' but, you know, he's one of the brightest and nicest kids I know. I'm glad he'll be working when Maggie goes away."

Gram gave Kat a meaningful look when she mentioned Maggie's departure and Fiona caught the exchange immediately. It took Kat a moment to realize what the look meant. She thought maybe she was speaking too loudly, but then she realized her mother was trying to shut her up about Maggie leaving.

"Gram, it's okay. I get it. Mom *has* to go do her yoga thing, and anyway, she's missed every one of my Halloweens. I'm way too old for it anyway. I'm *so* over it," Fiona said.

"Well, *I* was there, wasn't I?" Gram sounded a bit dejected.

"Yeah! Me too!" Kat added.

"Oh, of course you both were!" Fiona touched her grandmother's arm lovingly. "It's just that she's never taken me trick-or-treating. Not even when I was really little."

"Fi, you know she really needs these yoga retreats," Gram said.

"Yeah, whatever," Fiona mumbled, putting her hands together sarcastically in the traditional namasté form.

"C'mon Fi, don't get all snarly!"

"*Snarly*? Is that even a word?"

"You know what I mean. Your mother works very hard."

"Why are you always defending her? Did she ever even think of taking me once? I wouldn't mind missing a week of school! And why not ask me to go with her to the cement protest? I'm just as against it as she is! Just forget it!

Can we go now? I'm really full," she said, visibly upset.

"Oh, Fiona."

Fiona put her head down on the table.

"Are you feeling all right?" Gram put her hand to Fiona's forehead.

Fiona gently brushed Gram's hand away and said, "I'm fine. I just want to get back before Mom."

"Oh, is it the lights? Forget it, Fi, Maggie will just have to deal with it if she gets there first," Aunt Kat said.

That thought did not reassure Fiona one bit. She knew what would happen if her mom got home before they did. She'd go straight up to Fiona's room and turn off the light. Well, that wouldn't be so bad, she thought, but what if she looks around? What if she finds *her*?

Her aunt, calling the waiter over through a mouth full of cheese, interrupted Fiona's thoughts. "We need our root beer, please!"

"No, Aunt Kat, forget it, I'm not thirsty," Fiona said.

"You forget it, honey! I am thirsty and we're staying, so chill out!" Kat enjoyed talking like her teenage students, and actually, it was one of the things that made her so popular. As the honors English teacher, she wasn't particularly strict about "proper English," citing the fact that Shakespeare himself created many of the words we use today, and who knew, maybe one of her students would be the next Shakespeare. In fact, she and her students often made up words to try out. Fiona recently tried to use a new word in Mr. Fisher's social studies class, but he didn't get it at all and thought she was being rude. It was only October and how Fiona wanted to be done with school!

As they drank root beer and ate pizza, the place started to fill up with teenagers, mostly seniors, many of whom either had Kat as a teacher, or wished they did. The girls waved and the boys looked longingly.

Fiona looked at the clock above the pizza oven. Seven-fifty-five. She no longer had any appetite and there was only one piece of pizza left. Remembering her tiny guest, Fiona pretended to fiddle with the slice but actually tore off a tiny piece and wrapped it in a bit of greasy paper.

"Fiona, do you want that piece or not?" Gram asked, watching Fiona mangling the slice.

"No thanks, you have it," she said.

"I think I'll just do that!" Gram said, stabbing her fork on what remained. "Not a crumb left for Maggie," she added guiltily.

"As if she'd eat it anyway!" Fiona said. They gulped down their root beer while putting on their coats and headed home.

Chapter 7

Rionnag thought the girl had smelled like autumn air. She lay back against the pillows and closed her eyes. She breathed deeply. Yes, crisp autumn air. Rather comforting, really.

The girl had asked so many questions, too many to deal with when her wing was in such pain. She wished Mòr were here to comfort her and brush the hurt away. She did not want to be alone. What was this "pizza" they were so concerned about? She hoped the girl returned soon.

"I am daft, that's what I am," she said reproachfully to herself. As she sat against the soft pillows, she looked around the tiny room. Her eyes fell upon images of her own kind. They were pictures on the dollhouse wall, obviously drawn by someone who had intimate knowledge. The rings were exact, in every detail. The Shee, or faeries themselves were very like. Was the girl the artist? No, she couldn't be, because she had wanted to know what Rionnag was. If the girl had drawn these images, she certainly would have known. Yet the girl was accepting and apparently unafraid. Obviously this human girl had some knowledge, as the memory of the child dancing with those fey creatures came back to her.

The chamber felt cozy and safe and she snuggled down in the bed, trying not to jostle her wing, which she hoped was not broken.

She fell in and out of a light sleep. When she was fully awake the girl had not yet returned. Glancing at the large window she saw the moon high. Had hours gone by? She realized that it was her empty stomach that had awakened her. What did they take here for nourishment? Would there be honeysuckle? Just the thought had her stomach gurgling. She looked around, wondering where humans might have something to eat in such a place as this, but she saw none from where she sat and did not want to venture out of her relative safety to find out. The girl said she wouldn't be too long.

Well, if she could not eat, perhaps she could evoke the scent. And with her focus hard upon it, the room was filled with an overwhelming scent of honeysuckle. She leaned back and breathed deeply. This would have to satisfy her for the time being.

Chapter 8

Queen Barabel paced the entrance to her hill, watching for her spies to return. Her spider-webbed cloak swept the ground, stirring the elf-like elementals huddled by her feet. One glance made them quiet down and wait for instructions, watching her expectantly. Her vivid ochre eyes stared at them unseeingly for a moment, burning into them until they had to turn away. She stopped, dug her talon-like toenails into the ground, and with one swift movement, flicked a rock hard against the wall. The rock shattered, sending dust flying through her cloak, onto her black gauze shift.

She had sent her agents to the Seelie Court to watch for events concerning the marriage that was to take place this Beltane between the Scottish princess and Irish prince. She had been filled with rage since the betrothal was announced; in fact she had been incensed ever since the two were born. *She* had wanted an alliance with the Irish Deena Shee. The Scottish Seelies knew of Barabel's misdeeds too well, but the

47

Irish knew her not at all and she recognized were it not for the impending marriage, *she* could charm her way into the Irish court, gaining the power she longed for. In her mind, only her sister's brat, Rionnag, stood in her way. How she hated Rionnag, hated all children for that matter.

The King and Queen of the Seelie Court were far too powerful for her to overthrow, and try as she might to think of a way to get rid of Rionnag, her fear of Seelie wrath remained too great an obstacle. Ultimately they were the most powerful of all the trooping faeries, and for all their righteous ways, would fight to the bitter end when provoked. No, she would have to bide her time.

Her pixie informants had heard of the princess' unwillingness to wed and this was just what Barabel had hoped for. Should there be no marriage, or better yet, a blatant defiance to the marriage, then Barabel would be able to play her long-awaited role, that of commiserating confidante to Queen Deirdre. There she could slander and malign her traitorous sister and the entire detestable Seelie Court. Who were the Seelies to disgrace the Deena Shee? In Barabel's fantasy, the Irish queen would declare war on Catriona's court, eliciting Barabel's assistance. This would surely raise her status and enable her to usurp her sister. To have the Deena Shee as her ally would give her the influence she craved. Belonging to a lower court, she could never hope to compete with her sister, whose impeccable goodness made her sick. Looking disgustedly around at the brilliant day, she returned to her room and continued pacing its darkly carpeted floor.

She stopped once to admire herself in the murky glass that hung by her divan. Her eyes changed color to suit. Just now they went from pallid yellow to emerald, flashing heatedly. She turned her face at an angle, mentally noting her fine nose and flawless complexion. She shook her mane of raven hair sensually over her shoulders and continued her pacing.

Before long, there was a knock on her chamber door. "Enter," she said haughtily.

"M'lady." Before her stood what appeared to be a hedgehog, but soon transformed into a small elfish creature, pointed ears, beady, bright eyes, and a turned up nose. The pixie bowed low before her.

"Rise. Now tell me what news."

"M'lady," the spy said in a hoarse voice. "She has indeed run away."

Queen Barabel's eyes lit with maniacal glee. "Details, and quickly."

The pixie told of Rionnag's hasty, moonlit departure. Queen Barabel rubbed her long hands together. "Bring Fearghas and Ceallach to me at once. Ye ken where to find them. And here, take this." She thrust two gold coins at the creature who bowed low again, and went off.

Barabel waited impatiently for her two henchmen to appear. Within moments, the hideous bogies stood before the queen. Her back was to them, but she needed no announcement to tell her they had arrived. Their stench was enough to make her take notice. Before they could see what she was doing, she inhaled in large swallows, the putrid air giving her a surge of power. They didn't know the effect they had on her, and they must never find out, lest they gain an advantage over her. So thinking, she pulled out a lace handkerchief and held it to her nose, pretending to be offended by the odor. She knew that to the virtuous Seelies, the pungent smell coming from these two would cause fits of nausea and dizziness, but she drank it in like the warm calf's blood she enjoyed so well.

Queen Barabel turned to face the two and hid a grimace. Though their reek empowered her, their appearance made her steady herself every time she did business with them.

They stood barely as high as her voluptuous chest, and since they lived in the darkest part of the forest under the loam, their rotting garments were coated with turbid muck, and it was not certain if they were wearing clothes or if filth merely covered their skin. The larger of them bowed low, sweeping his soggy arm at the queen, exposing a large fungus growing from his armpit. The queen cringed as she smiled a wan greeting.

Their faces were greenish brown and erupting with pimply red patches like poison ivy. The shorter of the two scratched furiously on the side of his head, crusty skin and strands of wiry hair falling to the floor in clumps. Their eyes burned like hot coals as they waited for instructions.

"Find the princess of the Seelie Court and when ye do, bring her to me at once. Do not touch a hair on her precious head! I want her alive," the queen demanded, and then continued, "Do not disturb her chamber, but take something with her scent. And whatever ye do, do not get caught!"

"There's the issue of payment, yer majesty," Fearghas, the shorter one, grunted.

"It'll be the usual fee. Now go!" Queen Barabel shouted, their appearance nauseating her thoroughly.

"Och, that will nae do. 'Tis a more delicate job than we've done for ye in the past. We demand double oor normal fee. Each." The larger one drew himself to his full height, sticking out his barrel chest defiantly.

The queen's eyes flashed for a moment and then she smiled sardonically behind her handkerchief. "Ye will be paid what ye ask when ye bring her to me and war is declared on the Seelie Court."

The two looked at each other and began speaking in a tongue incomprehensible to the queen. After a heated discussion the shorter one said, "Yer Majesty, we want half up front, half when we finish the job."

"Ye greedy fools! I can get Redcap to do the job for a pint of goat's blood! Do ye want the work or no?"

The two conferred once more.

Queen Barabel interrupted, her tone growing more hypnotic, "Ye ken, there are rewards I can give ye in addition to gold."

Scabby tongues hanging like begging dogs, they visualized what she could do for them, and so announced in unison, "Aye, aye, we'll do the job." And they departed the chamber empty-handed, leaving Queen Barabel with the revolting scent of methane, as was their trademark. Drinking in large gulps of the noxious odor still permeating the air, Queen Barabel could hardly contain herself. She knew these bogies would do her bidding if the reward was high enough, and for success in this assignment, she would pay well.

She had captured her own husband so she could reign and become a queen. The flower liquor she had placed on his eyes to cast the love spell on him so many years ago had barely faded, and he remained enchanted, never suspecting her treacherous nature. This suited her, though it also increased her contempt for him. She had reveled in her royal status for some time, but she wanted more: more recognition, more troops, more status, more *everything*. She wanted what her sister had. She hated that her sister was not only the queen of the highest court in the land, but also the younger of the two. Barabel was the eldest and should have been given status because of her rank, but after their mother had held her sweet, second, precious babe in her arms, Barabel was thrust aside. Although her beauty was heralded, their mother had sensed her inherent wickedness early on, and was apprehensive of her. Her baseness likely came from her father's distant blood ties with Annis, an evil faerie famed for luring goats, lambs and young children into her cave, then devouring them alive. When Catriona was born, her mother focused all her energy on raising *her* to be a queen.

When the powerful Stag King, the object of Barabel's deepest desire, asked for her sister's hand instead of hers, Barabel went into fits of rage and resentment that grew stronger over the centuries. Only by destroying her niece's marriage to the Irish Prince would she get the vindication and revenge she craved.

If her virtuous sister ever suspected the activities in which Barabel engaged, she might bring the law down on her head, so she performed all her unsavory deeds in secret. She took human babes out of their cradles and replaced them with changelings. She thrilled at crossing over to the other side, capturing mortal men and making them her servants until she thought fit to sacrifice them to the banshees on All Hallows. She surrounded herself with them, using them for her pleasure, teasing and toying with them until they were either her complete slaves or they were begging for their sorry lives. She delighted in seeing the expression on their faces when they realized they were captive in Faerie. Her man-stable was growing; in fact she was certain it was the largest in Faerie.

Her tithe to Hell would have to be paid this year, as it was every seven. Which of her consorts would she chose to sacrifice? She must decide before the day arrived.

She hoped her bogie henchmen would be quick about finding her niece. She would hold the wench until after the planned wedding day when she would offer friendship and revenge to the Irish Queen. By then Queen Deirdre and King Eamon would be so up in arms at having been disgraced, they would accept Barabel's offers of alliance. All she needed to complete her plan was her niece. She knew her sister would have search parties after her precious daughter already, so her two henchmen must be swift.

Fearghas and Ceallach left the Queen's chamber brimming with eager anticipation. The only thing that could make this assignment more pleasurable would be if they could have the wench for themselves, but as it was, they could do a bogie's harm to any that got in their way. The prospect made them both salivate. They licked their chops in anticipation.

Bogies and faeries did not usually mix, but in Queen Barabel's realm, it was different. Fearghas and Ceallach preferred to work for their own kind, but Queen Barabel paid well and obviously this job was serious enough for her to double their usual fee. Upon delivery of the niece, they would be generously rewarded, perhaps with a tasty human babe taken from the cradle, or maybe a whole herd of sheep taken from the other side by sprites and pastured in the Court's fields.

They left the lower court and made their way to the high Court of the Seelie's. They would have to shape-shift when they neared the grounds. Even that would help only marginally to disguise them, for their foul odor stayed near them no matter what shape they took, making their presence obvious to anyone with an olfactory sense.

They neared the large hill that housed King Niall, Queen Catriona, and Princess Rionnag and took on the shape of two gray wrens, bland in color, inconspicuous. The two "birds" watched carefully as a troop of guards made their rounds, and then quickly found and flew into the lass' chamber searching for any clue or sign she may have left, revealing her plans. How they wanted to tear the place apart, but this was no ordinary assignment and they knew they had to cause no suspicion. Should the king or queen learn they'd been hired by the queen's sister to find their precious daughter, they would react by declaring war on Barabel. They would destroy the wicked old darling and that would mean no pay and no more work for them. Nay, they'd leave the chamber as they found it and instead, follow the princess' scent, like two bloodhounds.

With his beak, Fearghas ripped a tiny piece from the silk coverlet from where the princess slept, to have her scent, and then the two flew out of the chamber onto the great Rowan tree. The tree did not care for the energy they emitted and with a disgusted shake of its limbs, threw them off. They hit the ground hard, returning to their original shapes on impact. They were snarling as they picked themselves up, immediately shape-shifted once more, and followed the path the faerie had taken.

From what the Queen's pixie spy had told them, the place from which she departed wasn't too far from where they were. The Princess' scent was strong and smelled disgustingly like lilac, the two thought, as they flew off in hot pursuit of the runaway bride.

Chapter 9

Maggie looked at her watch. Nearly eight. She counted the register quickly, wanting to get home. She had spent most of the afternoon at the cement factory protest march and had to come in and take care of some inventory business and close up the store. She'd been working late nearly every night this month in preparation for her trip and she knew Fiona was feeling the effect of it. And so was she. Her daughter was growing up and Maggie was missing it. She couldn't believe her daughter was fast becoming a young woman. Though nearly forty, she still felt like a teen herself and still looked young. Her hair hung in long, dark auburn braids. Her blue eyes were bright, their black pupils always large, and a light dusting of freckles covered her smooth face. Today she wore a heavy hand-knitted sweater, baggy pants and sparkling handmade beaded earrings that matched her eyes.

She cleaned up the shop, always liking to leave things

just so. A Solas CD playing a beautiful ballad about two hearts beating as one, echoed across the shop. Standing quietly listening, she felt the music so deeply a tear slid down her cheek. She brushed it away. She looked down at the large pendant hanging around her neck from a leather thong. "It won't be long," she whispered to no one. She closed up the shop, got into her old pick-up, and drove home.

As soon as she pulled into the driveway she realized her family must be out. All the lights were off, except for the one in Fiona's room.

"Oh, that girl!" she said aloud.

She got out of the truck and went inside. The old farmhouse was warm; the fire from the large woodstove in the farm kitchen had been banked and was heating the house nicely. She hung her coat on the iron hook by the front door, took her boots off replacing them with woolen clogs and went directly into the kitchen and put some water on for tea. The mail was in a pile on the table and she picked it up and went through it. Mostly the usual bills, but the return address of a local development company made her curse under her breath. She immediately threw that one in the recycling bin. She then headed upstairs to shut the light in Fiona's room. As she walked up the narrow stairway, something made her stop. Her head cocked to one side, she sniffed the air, and realized that it was the unusual smell that brought her to a halt. It was a strong scent, like flowers and honey. She thought it strange, as no one in her house used perfume, nor were there any fresh flowers this time of year. It was coming from upstairs and it reminded her of another scent she couldn't quite place. The sweet fragrance evoked a longing so strong she couldn't brush it aside. She walked slowly up the wooden stairs, following the scent-trail into Fiona's room. She stood in the open doorway and inhaled, trying to place why this seemed so familiar and why it caused her to feel as she did.

She looked around for burning incense, but found nothing. She observed the room, its cozy clutter, Fi's stuffed animals on the bed. She went over to the desk where a framed picture of Fiona at about age three in a lion costume holding a plastic pumpkin stood. She picked it up, and looked at it. She had missed every one of Fiona's Halloweens. One day she'd tell her daughter why, but not yet. "Oh, little one, if you only knew..." She gave the picture a light kiss. From downstairs the teakettle whistled sharply. She put the photograph back, turned off the light, shutting the door as she left.

Chapter 10

Rionnag was dozing, the pain in her shoulder reduced to a dull ache. The scent of the honeysuckle had staved her hunger for the time being, allowing her to rest. Still the child had not returned. Had something happened to the girl? Would anyone come back at all? She began to become somewhat anxious. Thoughts of regret and guilt began to quilt her in despair. She tried to shake them off, but her thoughts kept returning to her dear father. She remembered her frenzied flight from home, how she landed, possibly doing damage to her wing or shoulder. She prayed the injury would not be permanent.

Rionnag closed her eyes tightly, not wanting to remember. She just wanted someone to help ease her pain, and more importantly give her something real to eat. She heard a sound from some other part of the house and sat up expectantly, relieved, assuming it must be the girl. Footsteps came up the stairs. The door opened. It was not the girl. A human woman stood in the doorway, her head tilted to one side, a look of puzzlement on her face, sniffing the air and breathing deeply, as if she, too, smelled the sweetness.

The woman, who looked very much like the girl, came into the room and looked around. For a moment Rionnag froze in the bed, praying the woman would not see her. She willed herself invisible, but who knew what was possible in this strange place?

She thought of pulling the covers over herself, but was fascinated by the human woman whose energy felt both strange and familiar at the same time. There was a powerful feeling of regret in the air, filled with longing. Rionnag thought the woman was beautiful, her hair was long and reddish-brown like the girl's, her eyes deep and shining, yet sad somehow. She was sure this must be the girl's mother. She wanted to call out, something about this woman making her want to lend comfort, though she had no idea why. The woman was slender and moved in a graceful way, though her mouth was pulled down in an expression of sorrow. Rionnag would like to see the woman smile, imagining how her bright blue eyes would sparkle and her spotted face would crinkle, but the woman remained somber, which seemed to add to her drama and mystery.

Rionnag watched the woman move to an image of a tiny human child. She thought it strange to hear the woman whisper something to the image as if it could hear and then even more strangely kiss it. She would have to ask the girl about this custom.

Rionnag thought she heard the words "...if you only knew..." and then a sharp whistling sound was heard and the woman abruptly left the chamber, extinguishing the light. Rionnag was left alone in the darkness.

Chapter 11

They pulled in and Fiona could see that the lights in her room were off. Maggie's cream-colored old pickup was parked in the driveway. Fiona wanted to utter one of those phrases she knew would only get her into trouble so she kept her mouth shut. She might as well relax now; it was too late. Either Maggie had seen what was hiding in her room or she hadn't. Gram, seeing Fiona's expression, took her hand and squeezed it. "Your mother isn't such an ogre," Gram whispered in her ear.

They went inside. A strong scent of flowers pervaded the entryway.

"Maggie, what perfume are you wearing tonight?" Gram yelled towards the kitchen.

Maggie came into the hall with a slight smile on her face. "I was going to ask you the same question." To Fiona, she said, "Hi, darlin'." Fiona stiffened as her mother grabbed her in a tight hug. Her mother let her go, giving her a hard

60

look.

"So where were you guys tonight?" Maggie asked.

"At a lecture on the evils of dairy products," her sister said solemnly.

"Ah, and what did you get out of it?" Maggie grinned, softening.

"It was very informative. We learned all about mozzarella and parmesan and how they can be addictive when consumed in large quantities." Kat tried to sound serious.

"We stayed for the lecture concerning the evil drink, root beer," Fiona added.

"Did you pick up any literature on the subject?" Maggie asked.

"No, we were so full of information, we left without taking anything. Maybe next time," Gram said.

"Ah," Maggie said.

Fiona tried to get up the stairs unnoticed.

"Fiona," her mother called, "You left the lights on in your room."

She rolled her eyes, "Give me a break," she muttered under her breath. To Maggie she said, "Sorry, Mom, I'll shut them off," knowing full well her mother already had already done so. She walked slowly up the stairs hoping she could actually proceed without another interruption. When she heard Gram talking to her mom she ran swiftly up the stairs. Her room was in shadow when she opened the door. She switched on the light and hurried to the painted lady dollhouse. There was no movement. She looked on the bed where she had put the faerie. Nothing.

"Oh, my God," she whispered.

Then she saw a tiny rustling from under the miniature blanket and breathed a sigh of relief. She reached over and gently pulled the coverlet off her guest.

"Mind my wing, will ye."

"Sorry. Are you all right?" Fiona asked.

"Time seems somewhat different here, but it does seem like ye have been gone awhile."

"Sorry I took so long. I couldn't get out of there 'til now. How's your wing?" Fiona asked, trying to decipher the faerie's accent.

"Och, it pains me to be sure," she said.

"Let me take a look at it." The faerie slowly sat up and turned so that Fiona could look at her bruised or broken wing.

Fiona gently touched it, carefully taking it between two fingers, examining it. Though it looked translucent, it was solid. Gauzy yet unrippable, and unbelievably beautiful.

"It doesn't look broken, but I haven't seen too many broken wings before. I tried to set a bird's broken wing once."

"I'm no a bird and that's a fact," the faerie said, somewhat miffed. "Well, it may not be broken but it pains me, as does my shoulder. Perhaps ye could wrap it up."

"Sure." Fiona looked around the room for something small enough to wrap it. She spotted a tiny umbrella; the kind from the Chinese restaurant that they put into fancy drinks. She'd had it for a long time. It was bright blue and pretty dusty. It was tucked into the crook of her old teddy bear's arm. He really didn't need it. She popped off the bright blue parasol and wiped the dust off the stick. Then she looked around for something to wrap around the splint. "Poor Mr. Ruggly," she said as she took the ribbon from around the teddy bear's neck. "I'm sorry, but I need to borrow this ribbon. I'll get you another parasol next time we go to Hunan Garden." The bear gave her his lopsided smile. By this time the faerie was up and moving about the tiny room. She watched Fiona gently talking to the large stuffed creature.

"What is that ye're talking to?" she asked.

Fiona looked over at the faerie and laughed softly. "Oh, that's Mr. Ruggly, my teddy bear." She saw the look of confusion on the faerie's face. "Hmm, a teddy bear is... well, here, look for yourself," and she started bringing the old brown bear over to the dollhouse.

"Nay, thank ye, I'd prefer not to."

"Oh, it isn't real. It's not alive. Look." She threw the bear up and caught it.

"Then why do ye have the thing?"

"Children love these kind of things. I used to sleep with him when I was little. They're very comforting. Don't you have stuffed animals where you come from?"

"Nay, we live with real creatures from nature's earth. We have no need of false ones."

"Then how do you comfort yourself when you're going to sleep?" Fiona asked.

The faerie thought about this for a moment and said gently, "We feel the earth's quiet movements, the sounds of the wind through the leaves of the trees, the music the stars make, like a lullaby, really. There's no need for anything else."

Fiona was quiet. Was life in her world ever that simple? Her mother had tried to teach her to care about the earth and to live simply, but it was difficult to do, especially when the whole world was into computers, cell phones and every other high tech thing. Her mother had resisted getting a computer for years. She had finally gotten one for work, which Fiona could use, only with permission. She was probably the only kid in school who didn't have her own computer, let alone cell phone or I-Pod. Fiona thought about Native American culture and how they used to live in harmony with the earth, taking only what was needed, living outdoors with just a portable shelter between them and the sky. In those days it must have been easy to be lulled to sleep as the faerie was. But not anymore. Modern life was far too complicated. Their two hundred-year-old farmhouse and its hundred acres seemed enormous and removed, but the modern world still encroached, as much as her mother tried to keep it out. No TV in their house; too much violence and scary stuff on the news.

Fiona remembered her mother once taking thick blankets and arranging them on the soft grass so the two of them could sleep under the stars. She wondered if they'd ever do that again. Right! If Maggie'd ever close the store and take a day off for something other than a protest march or her yoga retreat, Fiona sniffed to herself.

"Don't you ever get scared?" Fiona asked, coming back to the present.

"Aye, that I do."

"What do you do when that happens?"

"That depends on what I'm frightened of. Sometimes I think good thoughts and my fear dissolves like the mist; sometimes I call for my faither, but mostly I call on my Source," said the faerie.

"Your *faither?* Fiona questioned.

"Ye ken, the man who sired me. Do ye no have one?"

"No, I don't, actually," Fiona said matter-of-factly.

"Och," she said, "but ye do have a Source, do ye no? I thought all creatures had a Source."

"Do you mean a soul?" Fiona guessed.

"Perhaps ye call it that. My inner wisdom that knows everything. The part of me that has no fear. I sing to that and I feel comfort," the faerie said and quietly closed her eyes as if to demonstrate. A small sound issued from her lips and permeated the room. It started small and low, like the note of a flute played softly. The faerie's breath seemed to go on forever and the sweet sound filled Fiona's being until she felt a peace she had not experienced before.

Fiona watched the lovely creature sit on the tiny bed with her beautiful eyes closed and could barely believe this was a waking experience and not some whimsical dream. The faerie's dark eyelashes fluttered open and she smiled broadly at Fiona.

"I'm glad you're not afraid of me," Fiona smiled back.

"Aye, I am that as weel."

"Who are you talking to?" Maggie called from outside Fiona's door.

"Oh, God!" she whispered. "No one, Mom, just myself. Goodnight!" Fiona tried to sound casual. It wasn't her way to lie and it felt like a rock in her throat.

The door opened, Maggie walked in and bounced on the bed.

"It's kind of early to say goodnight. Tell me about your day. School good?" Maggie tried to make conversation.

Fiona was standing between her bed and the dollhouse, arms crossed in front of her chest with no intention of moving. "Yeah, Mom, great, but I've got a lot of homework tonight, okay?"

Maggie sighed and got up to leave. "Okay then, goodnight," she said. She pecked Fiona on the cheek and walked out.

"That was yer mither then?"

Fiona hesitated for a moment. "Oh, my *mother*. Yes it was. I hate it when she barges in!"

"Och, I ken what yer feeling. My mither does the very same thing and I want to scream," said the faerie.

Fiona was a bit shocked that she and the faerie had anything in common.

"Yeah, my mother spends her whole life in her shop and then she expects me to be thrilled to see her when I've basically gotten used to her not being around." Fiona looked guiltily at the door, wondering if Maggie's feelings were hurt. That hadn't been her intention, but what else could she have done?

"She's lovely to look at, yer mither. Yet she seems so sad," the faerie said.

"She's always preoccupied with one thing or the other," Fiona said.

"I dinna think she was so preoccupied just then. She wanted to talk with ye," said the faerie.

"Yeah, well, I'm not introducing her to you any time soon. I had to get her out of here."

"I suppose I might not want ye to meet mine, either."

"Why? She's not a witch is she?" Fiona said, trying to make a joke.

"A witch? Nay, she's a faerie, like me, but a powerful one she is."

"Is she bad?" Fiona asked.

"Bad? Certainly not. She's the Queen of the Seelie Court," the faerie looked over to Fiona whose expression betrayed her lack of understanding.

"The Seelie Court is the highest court in Scot's Faerie. There are kings and queens and all the rest. They spend all their time making the rain or snow, coloring the trees, designing flowers or competing in Faerie Rades. All utterly boring."

"What's a faerie rade? It sounds exciting to me," Fiona said.

"Nay, it's verra impressive of course, but it's just when faeries ride in a solemn procession. My mither prides herself on her horses."

"Do you know how to ride?"

"Of course I do. Any princess of the Seelie Court had better ride and no mistake. But I'd rather ride like the wind than in her snobbish pageants. She loves to compete with the other lower queens. She always puts on the best rade. Her horses are the finest. My faither built stables for them in one of the great caves in the hills. She shoes them with silver and she gives them golden bridles. They are verra grand." The faerie looked wistful, reminiscing.

"Sounds kind of like the way my mother feels about her store. But I don't get it, if you're a princess, what are you doing *here*?" Fiona asked.

"I ran away."

"You ran into my grandmother's car! Why'd you do that anyway?" Fiona asked.

"Och, that was daft. Well, when I landed, being blown off course and all, I was fair exhausted. But then I saw ye dancing with those creatures. I'd never seen aught like them, but I recognized *yer* kind."

"You saw me dancing? I thought it was a daydream," Fiona said, almost to herself.

"Well, if ye were daydreaming then, what are ye doing now? I'm real enough!" the faerie retorted.

"Yeah, I guess you are."

"Thank ye kindly. Now, where was I? Where I come from ye never approach beings ye dinna recognize. They're bound to capture ye. How ever did ye escape them, I'd like to know?"

"I thought I was having a daydream. I do it all the time. One minute I'm looking out the window, the next, I'm somewhere else. I think mostly with those... uh... people... things you saw me with. I think. But it's just my imagination, right?"

"Ye're open to it. It's all real, ye ken. How do ye think ye're seeing me? Not everyone can. Only those with the blood or those with an open heart and mind. Ye've got one or the other." She paused, then added, "Or both."

"This is too weird. My mom is so into this stuff it makes my head spin. She told me the crows talk to her. She said she learned all about raising flowers from little people in her garden. People think she's nuts; eccentric, they call it, and of course they think I must be too, for being her kid."

"She's no daft. She remembers what the others have forgotten. It was never a matter of belief; it was only being open enough to see beyond yer ken. Now the line between our two worlds is growing fainter and fainter. That's the shame of it," the faerie said sadly.

"Are you telling me my dancing daydream wasn't a daydream at all?" Fiona asked.

"I'm telling ye only that I saw ye enjoying the company of some very lively beings, and then ye just disappeared," the faerie said.

Fiona was stunned by this discussion. She suddenly remembered those eyes that drew her to them from behind the rock. Her head was reeling but she didn't want this conversation to end.

"My daydreams never last too long," she said, thinking about it. "I'm usually interrupted, teachers mostly. I used to tell my mother about my experiences, but she'd get so excited, say I had some kind of gift. Maybe like ESP or something. She freaked me out, so now I don't tell her anymore. She thinks I outgrew it and I know she's disappointed, but too bad! And I'm definitely not telling her about you!" Fiona plopped herself down on the floor directly in front of the dollhouse. "You still didn't tell me why you flew into our car."

"Well, I was trying to tell ye. As I said, I recognized ye for a human and I had no idea where I was, so I waited until ye left that place."

"The school," Fiona supplied.

"The school, then. I followed ye, but ye didna see me, so

I flew into that thing ye call a car. The lights nearly blinded me. Ye ken the rest," the faerie said, taking a deep breath.

"But *why* did you run away from home in the first place?" Fiona asked.

"Och, escaping an arranged marriage, but that's a tale for another time. I'm feeling sleepy and a wee bit peckish."

Embarrassed, Fiona grabbed the tiny piece of pizza from her pocket.

"I'm really sorry, I forgot," she said as she handed the faerie the miniscule slice.

The faerie looked at the thing in her hand, confused. Fiona realized that she hadn't explained it. "It's pizza; you eat it. You do eat, don't you?"

"Aye, that we do. Honeysuckle's my favorite," the faerie said.

So that explained the smell coming from the room. Fiona had been so interested in talking to the faerie she had forgotten all about the mystery odor. "So you already ate. We smelled it when we got home."

"Nay, I merely conjured the fragrance to give myself the illusion I was satisfied. I hope I caused ye no trouble."

"That's okay. I should've been more thoughtful and fed you before we went out. Anyway, please try it, it's delicious." Fiona gestured to the piece of pizza in her tiny guest's hand.

The faerie eyed it suspiciously, and hesitatingly took a bite. An enraptured look came over her face. "They said everything on this side was dull, but I disagree," she said with her mouth full, polishing off the tiny slice in no time.

Fiona wished they could continue to talk all night, but she really did have homework to do. The last thing she needed was another detention. She went to her desk, opened her backpack, and took out an enormous binder.

"Excuse me!" she heard from the dollhouse. She went

back over and looked in.

"Yes?"

"I was wondering by what name to call ye. If I need to speak with ye, I must call ye something," the faerie said.

Fiona remembered something her mother had once told her and spoke hesitantly. "My mother said you're never to tell a faerie your true name or they can have power over you. Is that true?"

"Surely, but ye seem kind enough, why would I want to?" the faerie asked.

"How should I know? What kind of power are we talking about, anyway?"

"Och, I could whisk ye away to my world to do my bidding. Have ye never heard tell of changelings?"

"Sure. Mom read me zillions of faerie tales when I was a kid and there were always changelings in them," Fiona said.

"For some daft reason, faeries think it's a funny joke to take a human bairn, ye ken, a baby, and leave a faerie in its place. There are a good many humans with the faerie blood from just that type of thing." The faerie shook her head at the thought.

Fiona poked her head into the dollhouse and said in a low voice, "It's Fiona."

"What's that, then?" asked the faerie, confused.

"Fiona. It's my name. Fiona."

The faerie seemed to consider this and Fiona felt a brief moment of fear. "Fiona." She turned it over slowly in her mouth. "Fiona. That's a name from my land."

"Yeah, I know. My mom is really into Scottish stuff. She plays the Celtic harp really well. But I think it's kind of a weird name considering I don't have any Scottish blood. But at least my mother didn't name me Thistle or Morgan le Fey!" Fiona said, rolling her eyes.

"And what might be wrong with those names?" the faerie asked indignantly.

"Well, uh, nothing," Fiona said, as she felt the red rising to her cheeks. She knew had said something wrong. "It's just that they're kind of hard to grow up with."

"Hmmph, not if ye live in my world." The last word sounded like 'whirrrled,' but Fiona wasn't smiling anymore. She hoped she hadn't offended the creature, whom she would like to befriend.

"I'm sorry, I didn't mean any disrespect. Could you tell me *your* name?" Fiona asked as sweetly as possible.

At this question the faerie eyed Fiona with mock suspicion. "How do I ken I can trust ye? Ye look innocent enough, but...."

Fiona interrupted and said in a rush, "I, I don't want to have any power over you or anything, I'd like to be your friend. Anyway, I told you mine."

The faerie laughed, "Aye, that ye did. All right then." She gave Fiona a sly look, "Thistle!!"

"Really?" Fiona was flabbergasted. Boy had she ever put her foot in it!

"Nay! I'm joking with ye. But I do have a distant cousin with that name! You may call me Rionnag. It means 'star.'"

"It's a beautiful name," Fiona told her and Rionnag seemed to swell a little from the compliment. Rionnag. Amazing, thought Fiona. There is a faerie in my room and her name is Rionnag! Unreal.

"Nay, it's real enough," Rionnag said aloud.

"You can hear thoughts?" Fiona was astonished.

"Only verra loud ones," said Rionnag.

Fiona told herself to think only good and definitely quiet thoughts about the faerie. She looked at her desk and saw her homework sitting there, undone and beckoning. She cursed under her breath and hoped the faerie hadn't heard her.

Chapter 12

Fearghas and Ceallach reached the ring just as the last of the swirling leaves were settling. Something unusual was happening in there, and they threw themselves in hoping to follow whomever or whatever had gone through before them. The sweet smell of Seelie made them wrinkle their noses, but confirmed their assumption. The princess must have gone through here.

They crouched hopefully in their original forms, waiting for the ring to work its fey magic, but they were too late. The passage had closed. They would have to go through somewhere else or find the correct spell to take them through this one. Fearghas cursed and snarled and Ceallach spat a green mucousy gob onto a stone. The gob sparked, and then exploded, making them jump.

"Arrgh, noo how will we find the sorry wench?" Ceallach growled.

"We'll have tae wait until All Hallows when we can

pass through again."

"We dinna have the time tae waste; I want me reward noo!" he declared, slamming his hairy fist onto the sharpest stone with such force that it ripped open. Yellowish plasma oozed from the wound, sparking some kind of freakish reaction, and he disappeared from the ring, leaving Fearghas alone, mouth hanging open, grayish saliva dripping in viscous droplets from his dingy teeth.

"Ye'll have tae draw blood yerself if ye want tae follow yer friend." Fearghas spun around to see who had spoken. He saw no one.

"Up here," the voice squawked.

He squinted in the sun as he looked up in the tree that stood near the ring. There sitting on a high branch, was a goblin, munching on a potato. He spat a rotten eye in Fearghas' direction.

"Eh?" Fearghas grunted.

"That's right, ye've got tae draw blood if ye want tae go through. I've seen it all too many times," the goblin said, green cap half covering his spherical head, bent ears like milkweed pods sticking out jauntily on either side.

"What've ye seen?"

The goblin scrunched up his face, his squinty eyes like slits. "Weel, today has been fair excitin', with sae many going through and all." He flipped and stood on his head, the potato stuck in his mouth.

"What're ye talkin' aboot? Sae many? Who? What, Pooka?"

Twirling right side up, the goblin grabbed the potato with large hands, completely out of scale with the rest of his body, and aimed it at the bogie. "Call me Pooka, dare ye! Ye've lost yer chance. Now, it's for me tae ken and ye tae find oot!" He thought better of wasting his potato and stuck his long purple tongue out at Fearghas instead and then he disappeared.

Fearghas snarled and lunged for the tree. He slammed face first into the trunk and fell to the ground.

"Hee hee hee, haa haa!!" Fearghas heard from behind him. He swung around and saw the goblin jumping up and down by the Ash tree on the opposite side of the stone circle. The goblin continued to laugh hysterically, the sight of Fearghas rubbing his rear end providing the goblin fits of glee. With one, great jump, the goblin sprang to the top branch of the Ash and razzed the hideous bogie.

Fearghas was far too confused and irritated at the moment to do anything intelligent, so he threw a wild tantrum. He kicked the ground hard, mud flying in all directions, and then pounded his fists on the moss-covered earth, not realizing that there were sharp rocks hidden beneath the moss. Screaming in pain, he began hitting himself on the head and boxing his own ears.

The goblin couldn't believe his fine luck. What a comedy! He hadn't been entertained this well for several hundred years!

By this time, Fearghas was wailing from his self-inflicted wounds and rage at the goblin, whose mirth surrounded him. He got up and stumbled about, arms flailing, trying to hit the goblin, who no longer was anywhere to be seen. The bogie tripped headlong into the ring, his head smashing into one of the stones, creating a lump the size of a toad. Fearghas felt the wound for blood. His entire head was slimy so it was hard to tell blood from the muck, so he licked his hand. No blood. He practically went mad and began more of his self-destructive behavior, flinging himself from rock to rock in an attempt to lacerate himself. He must be made of stronger stuff than Ceallach, he thought, for although his body now was covered with hundreds of welts, scratches and swellings, he simply could not draw blood.

The hilarity returned, this time at a volume that made him cover his ears. Goblins, coming out of the trees in droves, surrounded the ring, slapping their knees, hooting and guffawing. There must have been a hundred or more, all howling raucously at Fearghas as he tried vainly to find a way to follow his partner. One of the goblins threw a steel blade into the circle, and Fearghas shrieked like a banshee. Bogies could only touch gold, any other metal burned like fire.

The goblins were thrilled by his reaction and began throwing all manner of metal into the ring. Pewter coins, steel and silver knives were hurled in, and Fearghas did a maniacal dance to avoid the slightest contact with any of them. This got the goblins even more hysterical and by the time they had depleted their supply of metal objects, they were so exhausted they lay down in a heap, holding their bellies, laughing quietly until they fell asleep.

The original goblin, thinking he had bested the bogie looked at his brethren all asleep and continued to laugh hysterically, unaware of the bogie's true nature. It seemed the goblin didn't appreciate or have any awareness of the newly mounting power of the bogies and their kind, for if he had, he would have disappeared completely. And unfortunately for him, he had no more brass.

In the past, Fearghas might have simply spat a gob at the creature or crawled miserably home. In the past. But today, the bogie would have the last laugh. With eyes full of malice, the bogie caught the goblin in a stare that the poor helpless being was unable to break. Now it was Fearghas who was laughing.

"Me thinks yer mirth is displaced, Goblin! Pooka!" Fearghas growled, his laugh ugly to hear. The goblin's hilarity turned to abject fear, the knowledge that the bogie held him fast with no escape becoming obvious. He tried to look peripherally to his snoring friends, but Fearghas' eyes bore into the hobgoblin who was unable to scream or look away. Without warning, the goblin felt the meanness enter his body. Somehow, the bogie was twisting the goblin's insides, simply from a stare, the pain searing. Fearghas was enjoying inflicting such torture on the creature who was powerless to stop it.

"Ye laugh at me, do ye!"

"I meant nae harm, sir! Ooowww!" the goblin screamed as pain ripped through him.

"Tell me how tae go through and I may spare ye." He thought for a moment, and added, "Or no."

"I...I...I'll tell ye. Let me go!"

"What will ye tell me?"

"How...tae follow... yer friend, sir," the goblin said haltingly, through his misery.

"Dinna try tae trick me! I can burn ye up!"

"I willna, sir, I willna!"

"Tell me what ye ken! NOO!"

The goblin's suffering was too great and he faltered in his speech. He'd never known any bogie to be this strong and he regretted his dealings with this one, for sure. Knowing he was dying, he knew that his only chance of escape was to get the bogie to release his vice grip on him. "Just have tae trick him," the goblin thought to himself. As soon as he could convince the vicious horror that he'd actually tell him what he needed to know, and to do that, the bogie must release him, he'd use his magic to disappear before the bogie could finish him off.

"I...I...release me..." he said, chokingly.

"Ye tell me first!"

"I...I... ye..." and he gurgled these words, eyes rolling back in his head.

Fearghas knew he'd better release his hold on the

goblin for a moment, if he wanted the knowledge to follow Ceallach through the ring. Sure the creature would give him the information required, he let up. The goblin might have been in agony, but he still had his wits about him and within a moment of release, he was gone, leaving the bogie alone, and defeated.

Fearghas realized he'd been duped again and smashed his fist down on the rock with such force that he ripped his hand open, spurting ooze. A wisp of smoke and within seconds Fearghas was gone, following his friend into the unknown.

The coyote circled the house, then stopped, looking up at the window. The curtain shifted but on this night he did not see her peering out, catching his yellow eyes in her blue-green stare, her long brown hair moving in the light breeze. He sensed a feeling of unrest in the house and thought to stand guard until all was safe.

He heard the faint howls of his companions but he ignored them, feeling only the need to protect. He bared his teeth at the rustling wind. One by one the lights went out above him. He waited for the familiar curtain to open, but nothing. He stood, hair bristling, for long moments. Stars had shifted by the time he left and no creature seemed aware of his movement as he made his way into the shadows.

Chapter 13

Maggie, hurt by Fiona's reception, went to her room down the hall. She went to her dresser, an old pine chest of drawers with an oval mirror attached. She looked into the mirror and shook her head sadly. You did this, she said to herself. She noticed a few new lines from all the frowning she'd been doing lately. She smoothed her face with both hands and looked at the Celtic pendant hanging around her neck. She rubbed the stone set in its swirling silver design. "She's shutting me out. I wish... I need you here," she whispered.

The stone seemed to change color like the sky before an approaching storm. Maggie thought she heard faint whisperings emanating from it. She shook her head but was sure she heard a voice say, "...Find her, ye ken what'll happen if we fail!"

She grabbed her pendant in her hand in an attempt to hush the voice coming from the thing. She rubbed the

Jana Laiz

stone again, and it seemed to return to its original shade. She was tempted to take the pendant off, but it had never been removed since it was placed lovingly over her head fourteen years earlier. She knew the thing was a powerful object, but never had it done anything so strange. She felt unnerved and unsure what to do. She sat on her bed and closed her eyes. Were the voices speaking about her? To her? Or if not, who were they looking for? What would happen if they failed to find whomever they sought?

She shook her head and got into bed. Within moments, she was asleep and dreaming. In her dream, she was walking through meadows of heather and purple thistle, white clouds overhead. She knew exactly where she was going; she'd been to this place many times before. The air smelled of sweet grass and wood smoke. In the distance she saw someone. It was the one she was to meet. He stood tall and handsome, waiting for her by the edge of the woods. Her heart skipped a beat and she felt her cheeks burn hot as she approached him. The heaviness of her life without him eased and she felt as though she could float away. She smiled at him and waved her hand. Before she could reach him the sky darkened and an eerie tendril from a tree branch swirled toward him. It grabbed him into the shadows, wrapping itself around him like a serpent, and though he struggled to free himself, he began to fade. She called out his name and awakened in a sweat, her heart pounding. She grabbed her pillow with tight fists and tried unsuccessfully to get back to her dream and to him.

Others within the Harris household were dreaming as well.

Gram dreamed she was a child again, playing in her mother's garden, looking under toadstools and rocks for something she would not be able to name when she awoke. In her dream she crafted tiny beds out of bark and soft moss,

80

and left them near a gnarled hole in a tree. There, she was content to sit and wait. She smiled in her sleep, loving the feeling of youth and anticipation.

Kat dreamed of the newly hired science teacher who had the classroom adjacent to hers. He stood at the board, writing out an assignment. He turned and saw Kat standing in the doorway of his classroom and he smiled warmly at her. She felt the blush rising on her cheeks and wanted to speak, but instead, she simply smiled back.

Although Fiona had been sure she'd never be able to sleep with all the day's excitement, she fell asleep immediately upon turning off the lights. She was instantly launched into a dream, full of vibrant colors and fragrant aromas. She was flying over fields of green, though whether she was flying of her own volition or aided, she had no idea. She loved the feel of the breeze on her face. Someone was flying next to her, but she couldn't see who it was. She landed on the branch of a tree with leaves the color of a Caribbean sea, bearing fruit that smelled sweeter than anything she had ever smelled. She was mindful of this fact, wondering at fragrances in a dream. On the branch of the tree she saw a bird with plumage that matched the leaves though swirling with lavender on the tips of its wings. She watched as it began to sing a tune that she would remember when she awoke. It was filled with yearning and made her heart ache in her chest. The bird lifted off and Fiona, remembering that she too could fly, followed it, but it soared too high and too fast, and she lost sight of it. She touched the earth again, and again, lifted off the solid ground as easily as any bird. The dream seemed to go on all night.

Rionnag, uncomfortable with her bandaged wing, tossed and turned in her diminutive bed. When she finally fell into a fitful slumber she dreamed of a wedding. Hers. She wore a gossamer gown of creamy white. Graceful lady slippers adorned her feet but instead of walking down the moss-covered aisle, she flew above it, too fearful to touch down and fulfill her destiny and her duty. She heard a cry from below and looked in that direction to see all manner of angry faeries, sprites, pixies and elves all pointing up at her, her parents at the forefront, their livid expressions mottling their faces. In the dream, Rionnag froze in midair, and before she could escape, forces of her father's knights were raining down upon her with a huge net. They threw it over her and caught her like an animal before bringing her before her irate parents who shackled her feet and cuffed her hands and physically dragged her to stand beside the groom at the altar. Before he could lift his own veil, which covered his face, but not his disdain, Rionnag wakened. In fact, all five in the household awoke at precisely the same moment, as if it were a timed event.

Gram was serving oatmeal as Kat and Fiona sat down at the worn farm table. Maggie walked in looking haggard, barely acknowledging anyone. The teapot was starting to heat up on the white gas stove that dated from the '50s (worth a small fortune according to all the latest home style magazines). Gram added another log to the cast iron wood stove that stood by the wall. She rubbed her hands together in front of it, waiting for it to take the chill out of the autumn morning and cast its warmth throughout the kitchen and dining area. The exposed chestnut ceiling beams displayed festive bunches of herbs and flowers tied with raffia, but Maggie's mood put a damper on anything resembling festivity.

"Morning Mag. Any dreams?" Kat asked as she did

every morning since she and Maggie were kids, not letting her sister's dour face end the ritual. The question interrupted Maggie's fixation on her bowl of oats.

"No and I'd rather not talk about it."

Fiona would have liked to talk about her wonderful night, but the look on her mother's face kept her quiet. She, Gram and Aunt Kat exchanged glances. This was the one part of the day where Fiona could count on her mother to be animated. Maggie was a firm believer in the power and wisdom of the dream world. Today though, she obviously had private thoughts, so they left her alone with her reflections. The teakettle sputtered and shrieked, water spilling over its edge. Gram got up and took it off the burner, poured a large pot of tea, and brought the teapot to the table.

"I heard the coyote again," Fiona said, trying to make conversation. No one responded.

As they sipped their tea in silence, Gram decided now was as good a time as any to broach the delicate subject she had tried to avoid. "Maggie, I wasn't going to tell you this, but..."

Maggie looked up from stirring her cup with a worried expression. "What?"

"Well," Gram said, "Yet another realtor came over here yesterday. I didn't want to tell you last night."

"Frank?"

Her mother nodded her head.

Sighing, Maggie said, "He is relentless! What did he want, as if I don't know?"

"What they all want. This place."

"Why can't they all just leave us alone!" Maggie said fiercely.

"You won't believe the offer he made!"

"I don't want to know," Maggie said, looking at

her mother through narrowed eyes. "Mom, you're not considering it?" It was more a statement than a question.

Gram looked at Kat who shook her head warningly. "Well, it would certainly solve all our financial problems."

Maggie gave Kat a look. "You're not in on this."

"No, of course not, Mag; neither is Mom, but the offer was pretty incredible. It would be impossible not to spend a moment or two considering it."

Maggie got up from the table, disgusted. "Not for me. Fiona, do you want a ride to school? I'm done here."

"Maggie, c'mon, I'm sorry. I just wanted to tell you, that's all," her mother said.

"Well, next time, if you don't mind, *don't*." Changing the subject, she said roughly, "Fiona, do you want a ride to school or not?"

Fiona, who had been slyly putting tiny bits of oatmeal into one of her dollhouse bowls, looked helplessly between her grandmother and her aunt and said quickly, "Sure, Mom, let me get my stuff." She put her bowl and spoon into the sink and from the seat of her chair she grabbed the tiny bowl filled with breakfast for Rionnag.

She ran upstairs and into her room, closing the door behind her. She wished she had a lock on the door, but Maggie's fear of fire would never allow that. She found Rionnag sitting up in her tiny sleigh bed, looking like a princess from a fairy tale, her hair somewhat disheveled, her eyes sparkling.

"I brought breakfast," Fiona said. She produced the bowl of oatmeal and found a miniature spoon from the dollhouse cutlery set. "How'd you sleep?"

"I had a night filled with strange dreams, but I feel rested and my wing feels a wee bit better."

"I have to go to school. Will you be all right here by yourself for a few hours?"

"Aye. Ye might want to empty the pot."

The horn blared from outside. "Huh? What? Oh! So faeries..."

"Aye, we do!"

"Can't now, I've got to go. See you later!" Fiona grabbed her things and ran out the door, without emptying anything.

"People seem to be in a great hurry," Rionnag said to no one in particular.

The ride to school started off unusually quiet. Maggie took a different route this morning and Fiona was starting to get anxious as she looked at the clock on the dashboard. "Mom, why'd you go this way? I'm gonna be late!"

"I can't stand driving on East Road anymore. I *cannot look* at the new development going up. There used to be nothing but trees and farmland and trails, and now, there's one house after the other. Those damn developers buy up land and destroy what little wilderness we have left. I swear Fiona, what this town needs, what this earth needs, is a moratorium on construction. A moratorium on developers and greed. Maybe a chance to regenerate itself.

"What do you think those people coming to our place will do if we sell to them? I don't even want to think about it! There are so many perfectly good houses for sale, but *no*, everyone needs a brand new house! It's becoming sprawl here! I used to be able to ride my horse to school!"

Fiona regretted asking her original question. She should have gone with her aunt like she usually did. They pulled into the parking lot of the high school, Fiona wishing she was sixteen already and could drive herself. Just a little over two years to go. Fiona said goodbye and quickly got out. She was totally annoyed that her mother had been such a downer in the car. She was still half-dazed about the fact that there was a faerie in her room, and there was no way her mother or even Mr. Fisher would spoil her day today.

Gram cleaned up the kitchen, putting everything in the dishwasher. She patted the machine and blew it a kiss. She had spent years washing her dishes by hand, never complaining, but wishing they had a little extra money to get a dishwasher. Two years ago for her birthday, her three girls bought her one. Maggie and Kat saved up for a year, Fiona adding a few dollars here and there, from allowance, babysitting or working in the shop. It looked a little out of place in the old fashioned kitchen, but nobody cared, least of all Gram.

She put away the remains of breakfast and started upstairs. Along the wall lining the stairs was an assortment of old photographs. There was her wedding picture, Maggie and Katherine as babies, then through the years, Fiona in all stages, and a lovely, old portrait of a woman with an expressive and open face. She wore her hair in a chignon, wisps of curls gently falling around her high cheeks. Her eyes were smiling, as if she knew the photographer well. She wore a lacy blouse with a high collar and a cameo at her neck. Gram went over, kissed her finger and touched it to the picture.

"Mama, I wish you were here. I miss you so. Maggie is right, of course. How can we sell this old place? There's so much history here. And you're here. I can feel it. Talk to Maggie, would you, Mama? She's so bitter and sad, I feel as distant from her now as I did when she was a teenager." She lovingly touched the cheek of the woman and continued on upstairs.

As she entered Fiona's room to make her bed, which she knew Fiona hadn't done, she was slightly shocked at its chaotic state. Clothes were strewn on the floor; there were bits of a broken paper parasol on the desk. Mr. Ruggly, who normally sat up on Fiona's bookshelf was half-lying on the chair. The dollhouse, which normally stayed up against the wall, was pulled out slightly. Pieces of tiny furniture were on the floor. Gram bent to pick them up and put them back inside the house. She noticed a small bowl with what looked like the remains of oatmeal or glue. "That girl. What's all this? She can't still be playing with dolls?" she wondered aloud as she collected the little bowl.

"That'd be mine," she heard a voice say and spun around to see the person accompanying the voice.

"She acts as if she heard me," the voice declared.

To the room, Gram said nervously, "I did hear you, whoever you are. Show yourself, please."

"Och, ye daft thing, now Fiona will kill ye."

"I've never known my granddaughter to kill anyone, but you're obviously the reason for her strange behavior," Gram said more boldly.

"I dinna think Fiona is strange. I rather like her."

"I like her too. Now could you please show yourself or I'll start believing I have early senility!"

"Look over here, in the wee dolly house. Here I am." Rionnag stood looking at Gram and when Gram finally saw her, the faerie gave a small curtsy.

Gram rubbed her eyes in disbelief. Her breath caught as she slowly bent to give closer examination. A moment later, quite unceremoniously, she dropped to the floor with a thud.

"Oh, my," she said, holding a hand to her heart. "I knew it! I knew you were real!" She peered into the house excitedly.

"Thank ye," said Rionnag, a whisper of gentle amusement.

"Since I was a child, I've believed. I used to look in my mother's gard...Ooh! I dreamed of you last night! This is amazing! What are you doing here? Where did you come from? How do you happen to be in Fiona's dollhouse?" Gram could hardly contain herself.

"Ye ken what I am right enough. I've come from Alba. Scotland, as ye call it. I was blown off course trying to escape an arranged marriage and Fiona found me. My question to ye is how are *ye* seeing *me*?"

"Why, I really don't know. Are you invisible to other mortals?"

Rionnag rolled her eyes. "Aye, at least I thought I was invisible. Perhaps ye are as open as Fiona."

"From what I've read on the subject, it must be because I believe," Gram said with authority.

"I wouldna ken, but I suppose so."

"Can't you make yourself invisible if you want to?"

"I thought I could, but this place is so verra strange, I canna understanding how things work here."

Gram sat on the floor with a wide-eyed smile. Ever since she was a small child she had believed in the faerie folk. As a child, she had been desperate to see one and often went into the woods looking. But until this day, she'd never seen anything like this. Her mother used to read her fairy tales from the book which pictures now lined the walls of Fiona's room and she would fantasize about the conversation she would have, should she ever meet a faerie face to face.

Her heart was tripping along thrillingly and she felt about twelve years old as she watched the delicate creature move about the little room.

Rionnag looked back at the woman with a bemused look. She was as excited as the human, but she couldn't understand how she was visible. Did these humans have the blood? Or were they simply open to her world? She looked at the older woman and decided she looked like Fiona. She had reddish-brown hair streaked with gray, worn in a ponytail, with wisps curling around her face. Her eyes were a startling green and although her face was beginning to show her age, it held a beauty that went deeper than mere appearance. Rionnag discovered she felt the same kinship with this human as she did with Fiona.

Gram noticed the splint on the faerie's wing. "What happened to you?"

"Och, this," Rionnag gestured to her wing. "I had a wee accident with yer car."

"Oh my!" Gram exclaimed, and then gasped quietly, "The moth!"

"Never mind, Fiona taped it up and it's feeling better. I'll soon be flying again."

"How did you get to my car?"

"Och, I entered a faerie ring that brought me to where I saw Fiona dancing. I waited for her, ye see."

Gram looked puzzled. Fiona dancing? She'd have to ask her about that later. Instead, she said, "I have so many questions. May I ask? Are you feeling up to them?"

"What would ye like to be asking?"

"Everything!" Gram looked at the clock. It was still early yet, no sub call this morning and only the house to clean, and that could wait. "Are the stories real? Are there really changelings?"

"Of course, and captured mortals, and elves, and red caps, and selkies."

"I've always wanted to know about the Stag King. Is he

the faerie king or merely a tale?"

"He's my faither," Rionnag said.

"Your...your *father*? Then your mother is..."

"That's right," she nodded affirmatively.

"Then *you* are a princess."

"Aye that I am. And ye, are ye the mither of Fiona's mither?"

Gram took a moment to decipher the faerie's accent and said, "Why, yes, I'm her grandmother. Emily Harris," and she gently put her hand in the dollhouse to shake the faerie's hand. Rionnag immediately understood though this was not a custom in her world. She placed her hand in the older woman's. They both felt the energy of connection at the same time; both opened their eyes wider. Rionnag, as was customary in her land, bowed, then held her hands palms out toward Gram. Gram understood instantly and placed her big hands palm to palm with the faerie's. Again the surge of energy.

They smiled at one another and continued their rapid-fire questions and answers with eager pleasure.

The Lone Swan was off the main street but everyone who came to the area heard of it because locals and tourists alike came in daily to buy unusual books, handmade jewelry, Scottish and Irish woolens, music from around the world, (especially Scotland and Ireland, indulging in Maggie's obsession) homemade herbal teas, oils, remedies for tired bones, colds, coughs and lost loves. Fresh lavender hung on the rafters to dry, dream catchers hung from the ceiling. Sage bundles and candles, even recycled greeting cards were for sale. Its cozy and welcoming feeling added to its popularity.

Comfy chairs were placed strategically and customers were free to spend the day browsing, reading, sampling Maggie's extensive Celtic and world music collection or just sitting with a cup of tea. Thursday nights were open late and there was always a live musician playing. Once in while Maggie pulled out her Celtic harp and gave a mini concert.

The expansive shop had become a hub for environmental activists, often having meetings until well into the night, with Maggie leading the pack. She was as passionate about the spiritual health of the planet as she was about its physical health.

Maggie opened the door, took a deep, calming breath and looked around the shop. It was like coming home every time she entered. She was very proud of her business. She had been manager when the shop was merely an out-of-print and used bookstore. Fiona had been a baby at the time, but when Fiona had started school, the owner retired and gave Maggie a chance at ownership, a chance she jumped on, changing the name from First Edition to its current name, originating from an experience Maggie had had one late winter afternoon. Driving past a snow covered cornfield filled with Canada geese, a lone swan stood, completely out of place amongst the myriad migratory birds. Maggie had pulled her truck over to get a closer look, and the swan's eyes seem to penetrate her own. She believed it was some kind of omen just for her.

She designed the sign herself, and had sat at the kitchen table when Fiona was about five years old and sketched swans in various scenes. She let Fiona choose her favorite and Maggie was pleased, as it was her favorite as well. A single swan lifting off a snow covered hill.

But Maggie was in a pensive mood when she arrived at the shop this morning. Her dream weighed heavily on her mind and the fact that those damn developers wouldn't let up just added to her bad temper. What she really wanted to do was go home, curl up in her bed, and dream again. She tried to put her attention on the day's business and began brewing tea for the shop. She chose a special blend from her stock that had qualities to calm the nerves and settle the mind. A strong cup would do her good. The water boiled and she added her infusion, watching it change color as the soothing properties of the herbs were released into the liquid. She put her face over the steam and felt its warmth envelop her. When she looked into the pot to see if it was steeped long enough, she was sure she saw images in the water.

She rubbed her eyes and looked again. There *were* images. She thought she could make out a cloaked figure, coming out of a grove of trees. The figure stood at the edge of the grove as if waiting for someone. The longer she stared the clearer the image became. Her eyes nearly lost focus. There was no mistaking who was under the cloak.

Her heart twisted in her chest with longing, a painful physical sensation matching her emotions. The warmth she'd been feeling from the scene changed abruptly to ice as she watched a swirl of smoke twist around him, carrying him away into the forest. Maggie didn't realize she was crying until a tear fell into the steaming liquid, dissolving the image. She stared hard at the water as if willing the vision to return. Another tear fell in and she wiped her sleeve across her face, with a shudder of repressed grief. The cowbell hanging from the shop's front door rang, bringing her out of her reverie. Before looking up to see who was there, she dumped the contents of the teapot into the sink. She wiped her eyes once more and turned to greet the first customer of the day.

Maggie felt her stomach heave as she saw the slick figure of Frank Costa entering the shop and coming toward her, a lascivious grin on his somehow too handsome face.

"Maggie, you look gorgeous, as usual. Must be all these herbs," he said, sauntering over to where Maggie stood braced behind the counter, everything about her body language conveying her distrust and dislike of the land developer.

"Flattery will get you nowhere Frank," she said coolly.

"Not even dinner tonight?" he asked, grabbing for her hand, which she deftly pulled away.

"Especially not dinner tonight. Look, Frank, my mother told me about your little visit. Why don't you find someone else's land to exploit?" Maggie suggested and started to put out merchandise, hoping he would leave.

He picked up a candle and sniffed it. "Maybe that's not why I'm here. Can't you give a guy the benefit of the doubt?"

"No, Frank. I'm really not interested," Maggie said shortly.

"C'mon Mag. We used to be so good together."

"Frank, that was ancient history, a mistake. Now I've really got to get back to work, so unless you'd like to buy something..." she gestured to the candle still in his hand.

"You'd never have to work again," he said.

"I like to work."

"You could take care of your mother and your kid forever, no worries."

"My mother is quite capable of taking care of herself and as for my kid, my kid is fine. You just don't get it, do you, Frank? "

"How long do you think three and a half women can keep this up?" He gestured to the shop. "An old woman, a flaky teacher, and a kid? And you; you look tired, Maggie."

"I'm tired of people like you who think they can buy anything. I'm not for sale and neither is my property."

The cowbell jingled and a young pregnant mother walked in, pushing a stroller.

"Can I help you?" Maggie asked.

The woman looked over at Frank, questioningly.

"We're all finished here," Maggie said giving Frank a defiant look.

"I'll pick you up at eight."

"What are you talking about? I'm not going anywhere with you!"

"Scared of a real man, Maggie? Is that your problem?"

"Scared, Frank? Of you? I think it's time you drive your gas guzzling SUV out of here." She left the counter to help the pregnant woman who had moved discreetly to the tea aisle, whether the woman needed help or not.

Frank followed her. "People are talking about you, Maggie. In fact, the whole town is talking about you and your fatherless kid. If you loved that daughter like you say you do, you'd think about her future," he said.

"How dare you! I'd like you to leave now, so either pay for that candle or put it down and stop fondling it."

With an angry glare, Frank took his silver money clip out of his pocket, pulled out a fifty-dollar bill, threw it down on the counter and said, "Keep the change, you need it more than I do."

As Frank strode out the door, Maggie's customer looked to where the doorbell still jingled. "What a sleeze!"

"You got that right!" Maggie agreed. Taking a deep breath with a renewed sense of determination she turned a smiling face at the woman. "Now how can I help you?"

Chapter 14

Mòr and Jinty came through the ring with less force than their princess. They had stayed together, gripping each other the entire ride through, and landed quite softly in the same spot Rionnag had landed some time before. They looked around them, assessing their situation and surroundings. Darkness was setting in and they knew they'd have to find shelter before long.

"I think we're on the other side, Jinty," Mòr whispered apprehensively, with a touch of curiosity. "Look at the way the light falls. Look at the leaves on the trees. Sae different from home, aye?"

Jinty nodded, unable to speak, lest she voice her true fears, which were many indeed.

"We must find her."

Mòr gestured to Jinty to focus internally and try to get a picture of where their lass might be. The two sat for a moment, eyes closed, breathing deeply as if in meditation.

At the same moment, their eyes opened.

"Ye felt her, did ye no? She's been here, I ken for certain."

"Aye," Jinty nodded. "I feel her essence, but it's no strong."

"She must be close. We must pray she's close!"

"Aye."

"I feel others near as weel."

"Och Mòr, that's no what I wanted tae hear!"

"Hush child. What were ye thinkin', we'd be alone?"

"I was hopeful," she said pathetically.

Mòr shook her head and lifted off the ground heavily, Jinty following quickly, not wanting to be left alone in this strange wood. They flew over trees and streams, growing tired after a time. It was getting almost too dark to see when Mòr landed high on the branch of an old Maple. Jinty, in an attempt to stay next to her, practically knocked her off the branch.

"Careful girl! What is sae vexing that ye crash into me like that?"

"I want tae stay close, Mòr, that's all." Jinty looked frightened as they sat on the branch catching their breath. "Mòr, do ye feel it?" She looked down at the branch they were sitting on. Mòr looked down as well, then closed her eyes.

"Aye. This tree is verra old, ancient. It's speakin'."

"Can ye understand what it's sayin'?"

"Shh, let me have a wee listen." Mòr closed her eyes again and placed her hands on the rough bark.

"Can ye understand Mòr? Can ye?" Jinty whispered.

"Girl, hush noo, will ye! I'm trying tae hear what it has tae say!"

Jinty put her head down and mumbled an apology. Mòr, lifted her head to the sky dramatically and with her eyes still closed, cocked her head to one side, listening. "This tree is home tae someone, but I canna understand who. The tree is asking us if we have permission tae be here," Mòr said.

"Och, we haven't, Mòr! Let us go, then!" Jinty said, her voice rising.

"Let me answer, child," Mòr, continuing to grip the trunk, spoke in an old language. Jinty, who was not yet educated in this branch of faerie academia, listened hard but could not understand a word Mòr said. The words had a melodious quality as though Mòr was singing. The branches swayed as the tree and Mòr communicated. Jinty was dying to know what they were saying, but held her tongue until Mòr finished.

"Thank ye," Mòr said to the tree. To Jinty she said, "The tree was kind enough tae allow us sleep here for the night. Its occupant will be away until the morrow. She tells me we're in a land called 'America.' That's verra far from home, Dearie. I canna imagine why Rionnag would come here, but here she must be. The ring brought us, and I am certain the same ring took oor lass. The tree tells me that there are none of oor kind left here. The wood is quite small and getting smaller. The fey folk left ages ago in search of old forests. There are some wood dwellers, but none we'd recognize."

"Mòr, will they try and hurt us? Will they have power over us?"

"Dearie, I dinna ken, but we'd best find Rionnag and go home directly. There's power here, ye can feel it as well as I."

"Aye, that's what I'm afeared of."

97

Mòr and Jinty slept fitfully in the old tree who had so much to say it hardly gave them any rest. It had been so long since anyone really listened, the tree rambled. Mòr was such a sweet and accommodating faerie that she couldn't say aught, but listened and responded where necessary. The tree did have some vital information that Mòr would have to share with the King upon her return, but she knew well that she couldn't return without her precious charge.

"They're cutting us down by the thousands, old ones mostly, the ones with the most knowledge. Who will be there to teach the young ones to look up and reach for the heavens? Most of the folk who lived here have fled to older forests; soon there will be no one left. Where will they go when the old forests are gone? I myself will be moving north, as the earth gets warmer and warmer. Soon all the Maples will leave this land that has been our home since time immemorial, moving north to colder climes until the earth becomes too hot for us, north or south. And without the precious atmospheric covering we're getting sunburned on our trunks. My bark has never felt so raw.

"The one who lives here comes and goes, always searching for a deeper wood, a wilder spot. He'll be home tomorrow I feel, but for how long? And then he's not very talkative. It's so good to be able to tell someone other than one of my own kind who already know what is happening. How long do you think you'll be staying? I could put in a good word for you with the one who lives here. How would you like that? And did I mention the tent caterpillars? They're eating leaves like there's no tomorrow..." The tree went on like this for a good part of the night, and although Mòr was exhausted when morning came and brought the sun, she felt safe for the first time since arriving in this strange place. Jinty had managed to get a little rest and when the sun rose fully, she was eager to get on their way and get done with their mission, for she was scared and homesick and wished to return home as soon as possible. She told as much to Mòr. "We'll go when I am quite ready!" Mòr said a little crossly. "I want tae thank this generous tree for her hospitality."

"Och, Mòr, she didna settle down the whole night. I couldna understand her, but she did go on and on!" Jinty yawned loudly.

"Weel, my fine lassie, she had quite the lot tae say to me and I'll be thinkin' as you might want tae thank her as well for keeping us oot of harm's way!" Mòr said indignantly.

Jinty blushed at the rebuke and curtsied before the tree. "Tell her I thank her kindly for her hospitality."

The tree acknowledged her gratitude by waving several high branches. Mòr smiled at Jinty and said, "They're not sae bad over here, see? We're just unfamiliar, is all."

"I'm sure yer right, Mòr."

The two flew to a nearby stream to bathe and drink. As Mòr looked at her own reflection, her own face faded before her eyes and was replaced with a woman, an old human woman talking to someone. The woman's mouth was moving, but Mòr could hear no sound. What a strange vision, she thought, rather like the Queen's crystal visionary orb. She continued looking in the water and the image remained. The woman had a kindly face but Mòr was slightly confused as to why this woman's face should be entering her vision. She relayed this information to her protégé.

"Ye say ye saw an old woman. Pray, what does it mean, Mòr?" Jinty asked with a fearful expression.

"I saw her clear as day, but not a sign of oor lass. But I believe she may be where the old woman is. Look for yerself," Mòr said with assurance.

"Was she a hu - human, this woman?" Jinty stuttered,

turning pale.

"Aye, tae be sure, but I dinna fear that one. She had a light in her eyes. They're no all bad, Jinty." Mòr smiled at the inexperienced faerie, shaking her head. "Och, yer sae young, a mere bairn. There's many a human that I'd be happy to call friend."

"Well, I've never met one and I'd rather no. They're sae big and cumbersome," Jinty interrupted, shivering.

"I tell ye I feel Rionnag is close and she's with this human. Take a wee look."

Jinty lowered her lime head until it nearly touched the water. She exclaimed when she saw what looked like a comfy room, but no activity within it.

"Weel, I think we're seein' the same place, now the question remains, where? I tell ye, we'd better find her before the others do, and no mistake."

"Aye."

Chapter 15

Today, first period was gym and Fiona was grateful. Sitting in Mr. Fisher's class would have been too much to bear. Gym class was held outside today even though it was getting chilly, but they were playing field hockey and Fiona knew she'd warm up soon enough. She wasn't a particularly fast runner, but she could hit, and today she made a few goals. Ms. Stanley, the gym teacher was clearly surprised and impressed. "Way to go, Fiona!"

Fiona smiled and sat on the bench next to some classmates to catch her breath.

"Only six weeks 'til the dance! I hope my dress comes in on time, it's being ordered," one of the girls was saying to another.

"I know, mine too. I can't wait! They got Jess' band to play. Have you heard them? They're amazing."

"Yeah. Is your dad gonna wear a tux? My dad wants to wear his, but I told him he didn't have to...."

Fiona turned away. She couldn't listen anymore. It was that stupid father-daughter dance they were talking about. She couldn't understand why it was such a big event. Why would a teenage girl want to dance with her father anyway? It seemed kind of bizarre and creepy. Of course there were other dances, teenage dances where they had a DJ who played hip-hop, rap, and R & B—music kids could actually dance to. Not that she'd been invited to one of those yet, she didn't even like that kind of music, but she was hopeful. But this father-daughter thing, no, she just couldn't listen to any more of the conversation. She walked over to the edge of the track where the woods abutted the athletic field. She sat down under a tree and wrapped her arms around her knees. She leaned against the trunk trying not to think about the dance she wouldn't be going to, would never go to. As she sat breathing deeply, her gaze became unfocused and once again, a vacant body sat against the maple.

Fiona's ethereal self was walking in a deeply wooded area, the smell of balsam pervasive, reminding her of Christmas trees. She heard the gurgle of water and walked in that direction. She was startled to see two figures leaning over a stream bank, looking into a deep, still pool. Fiona crept behind a tree and watched quietly.

"What do ye see?" the thinner of the two figures asked.

"I dinna see a thing. Och, wait, there, I see an old woman. Look for yerself. Do ye see?"

"Och, what a lovely room, sae warm and cozy."

"I care naught for the decorations! Do ye see *her*?"

Fiona wondered who these women were. And then it became clear these were not women at all.

"Nay, I dinna see her, but I can feel her. She's close," said the first speaker.

The fatter one turned in Fiona's direction, spread a pair of delicate wings and said, "Then we'd better find her before the others do." Without further discussion, they lifted off and flew out of sight.

Fiona gasped, ran over to the pool, and got on her knees to look in. She saw only pebbles and a few small fish. She didn't know why, but she was sure it was Rionnag they were after. As this thought entered her mind, she was brought immediately back to her body; her hands still wrapped around her knees, the girls still gossiping on the bleachers.

She blinked, rubbed her eyes and looked in the direction from which she thought she'd come. There were two dragonflies circling, one bright blue and larger than the other, which was a brilliant green. She slowly got up and began to cautiously walk in the direction of home, away from school. She glanced around several times to make sure no one was watching. As soon as she got to the corner, she swiftly turned it and jogged the mile and a half home, never once looking back. She arrived home some twenty minutes later, completely out of breath and gasping for air. Her strong legs practically buckled as she opened the door and stood momentarily trying to catch her breath when she heard voices from upstairs. Alarmed, she ran up the stairs two at a time and threw open her door, only to find her grandmother sitting on the floor in front of her dollhouse, deep in conversation with the faerie.

She stood by the door; sweat streaming down her face, gasping for air, holding her chest, shocked. Gram and Rionnag stopped talking and turned towards her.

"Fiona, you're home early. You're wearing shorts!" Gram said, stating the obvious.

"I, um, didn't... feel well," she gasped.

"You look apoplectic."

Fiona ignored this and said, coughing, "What... are... you doing in my... room?"

"I came in to make the bed. It doesn't get made by itself everyday. That's when I met your friend here. We were just talking," Gram said.

"I can see that. And....how...did this happen?" Fiona shot a glance at Rionnag.

"Weel I was just talking to myself and she heard me. That's the truth of it. After that there was nothing I could do. Anyway, she's all right, she'll tell no one."

"How can she see you?" Fiona asked the faerie.

"Excuse me, but I'm right here! Let's talk about me *to* me, shall we?" Gram smiled to take the sting from her words.

"Look, I'm all confused. Gram, how are you seeing her?"

"Probably the same way you are," Gram said.

Fiona rolled her eyes and sat on the edge of her bed. Without warning she burst out, "Oh, my God, an old woman! That's what they were talking about!"

"What?" Rionnag and Gram said in unison.

Fiona took a deep breath. "The reason I came home is because I saw two faeries looking for Rionnag."

"Oh, my," Gram said.

"Are ye truly certain?" Rionnag asked, concerned.

"I was having another of my *daydreams*," Fiona said directly to Rionnag. Gram's eyebrows went up questioningly.

"And how can ye be sure they were looking for me?" Rionnag asked.

"They were looking into a pool of water and said they saw an old woman and that '*she* must be near.' They had your accent, too. Who are they?" Fiona pressed.

"What did they look like?" Rionnag asked.

"They looked like faeries!" Fiona said.

"Do ye think *all* faeries look alike?"

"Well I, uh, no, but they had wings and stuff. And one was kind of chubby and the other was skinny with green hair. I don't remember much else."

"That's Mòr and Jinty, my maids. My mither no doubt sent them to look for me. I dinna understand how they came this far. I was sure none could trace me, I used such an old ring."

"I don't know what you're talking about, but they're coming. So what are we going to do?" Fiona asked.

"Ye say ye were daydreaming. That could mean ye entered Faerie. That being the case, they could be anywhere, and mayhap not be able to find this place, being on the other side and all."

"When I came out of it, I did see two dragonflies," Fiona added.

"That might have been them as ye see them on this side," considered Rionnag.

"Rionnag, could you please tell us exactly what you did when you ran away from home?" Gram asked, hoping to come to some kind of understanding.

"Aye, I will." The faerie took a breath and began her tale.

"I am to marry soon, a forced marriage. I never wanted that, ye see. And so, I decided to run away, rather than marry. I found an old ring." She stopped, looking at the two humans who were obviously bewildered.

"A faerie ring, that is. One that can take ye far away or like what happened to me, to the other side. There's much power in the old rings, and this ring had been unused, now I see for good reason. As soon as I entered it the wind started howling and I was thrown all about. I tried to catch hold of a nearby branch, but everything was too wild."

The two women, the old one and the young one, were rapt with attention while the princess told her tale.

Having an audience put her in a story-telling mood and she continued her story with feeling.

"I was afraid. Terrified. My mind raced. What had I said when I entered the ring? I'd taken the spell from my mither's spell book, but I have none of her powers yet, and I likely said it wrong. I cried out for my faither, but no one came. Then I fell, hard. I lay there trying to contain the pain. I had no idea where I was. Nothing looked familiar except the Birch, but even that looked strange, a livid scar across its middle."

"The Wounded Birch! You know the one Gram. In the front of the building."

"Oh, yes, some angry students many years ago tried to cut it down, but they were stopped."

"I felt sick, and just then I heard something and I peeked over the rock to look. There were beings, maybe fey, maybe animal, I was unsure. I heard them talking about teaching the humans to respect the planet."

"Sound advice if you ask me," Gram said in agreement.

"And then I saw Fiona dancing." She stopped as she watched the two humans exchange a look, which spoke volumes.

"Gram, I..."

"Fiona, you aren't obliged to tell me everything. Or anything for that matter."

"I know. I wanted to tell you, but if I told you, I'd have to tell mom. And you know how she'd get."

"Yes, I suppose I do. So, do you do this often?"

"Not at will, if that's what you mean."

"If you want to tell me, we'll talk about it later. Rionnag, please go on."

"As I was saying, I saw Fiona dancing with the beings and though I did not recognize their kind, I did recognize Fiona as a human. For no reason I can understand, I felt drawn to her." She smiled at Fiona, who smiled back. "Anyway, I was resolved to find out more about her. And then she was gone. Disappeared."

"That's when Mr. Fisher called on me," Fiona added, glaring momentarily. "I waited for ye to return, but ye did not come. Then I looked up and found yer eyes."

"I remember," Fiona said quietly.

"And so I waited for Fiona, knowing we were meant to meet. Ye ken the rest. I saw her and followed her to that thing ye call a car." She stopped, waiting for more questions, but Gram and Fiona only nodded as in understanding.

"These faeries, how long could it take them to find you? What'll happen when they do? Are they as powerful as your mother?" Fiona asked nervously.

"Nay. If they find me I'll tell them to return to my mither and tell her I shall not marry. If she wants me, she'll have to come get me herself."

"I'm not so sure I want to face the wrath of a faerie queen, thank you very much," Gram said, putting her two cents in.

"Never ye mind. Until I see them I willna fret about it. I like it here. I think I'll be staying, if ye'll have me."

"Of course. Wait! I forgot to tell you something else they said. I heard the chubby one say, 'We'd better find her before the others do.' What others might she mean?" Fiona asked.

"I dinna ken, but I'm sure they will not find me here," Rionnag said firmly.

Gram tried not to be an alarmist but said, "Rionnag, if others are coming for you, in addition to your maids, don't you think there might be reason for concern?"

"Weel, that is a possibility, of course."

"I mean harboring a Faerie Princess fugitive is no

laughing matter."

"Ye may be right. Perhaps I should go."

"No! Don't you dare leave!" Fiona said adamantly. Then more gently she added, "I mean, your wing isn't healed. You'd have no place to go."

Rionnag sighed, grateful for the girl's insistence. "Thank ye, Fiona. I'd like to stay." She looked at Gram questioningly who answered gently, "Of course you can stay. I'm sure everything will turn out just fine." Gram put her hand out to the faerie's. Rionnag took it. Fiona, in solidarity, took both hands in hers and held tightly.

Chapter 16

Ceallach came to, blood still oozing from his open wound. He licked it and spat on the ground. "Aaarghh. Where am I?" he said aloud. His head was spinning from his ride through the ring. Within moments of his coming round, a tremendous weight rammed Ceallach's face into the dirt. Fearghas had landed on his partner's backside.

"Ge' off, ye lout!" Ceallach screamed, choking on the dirt that had found its way into his mouth.

Fearghas, apparently unconscious, didn't move. His weight was crushing Ceallach, and the unfortunate bogie struggled to free himself.

Ceallach was too busy trying to remove Fearghas to notice the extraordinary creature watching from a nearby hollow. After a couple of minutes of grunting and heaving, Ceallach managed to roll Fearghas off, and he lay quietly in a stinking, sodden heap on the ground. Ceallach sat up rubbing his back, exposing the fungi growing from his armpit. Voices were heard in every direction, but as Ceallach looked around, he could find no accompanying bodies. He had no idea where they had landed, but everything looked different, wild. Two strange creatures emerged from a copse of trees and looked curiously at him. They were human on the bottom, some kind of dog on top, with vivid yellow eyes that seemed to burn into Ceallach.

"What're the likes o' ye lookin' at?" he snarled rudely. They made no reply and Ceallach would have liked to throw a rock at them, but Fearghas was coming to.

"Where am I? Ceallach, are ye there? Och, me haid!" he yowled, putting his ripped hand on his forehead. "Ceallach, what's happenin'? Where are we?"

"Why do ye ask me? I dinna ken where we are. All I ken is that we've got tae find that winged-wench. I want me brass."

The remembrance of brass sent Fearghas shuddering. "Naiver say that word tae me again. Gold is what we want, gold."

"Gold, brass, it all means payment tae me. Now, get up and find the lass, I want me brass. Lass, brass, brass, lass!" he began shrieking with laughter at his own joke.

There were more of the coyote creatures coming out of the woods, circling the two. There were cloven-hooved beasts with goblin ears, and human-faced entities with animal torsos. The one characteristic they all had in common was their animal appearance. Fearghas and Ceallach watched them cautiously; to them, the only good beast was a dead one. But as long as no metal was used against them, they could shape-shift at will and fly away. Ceallach spoke in an undertone to his partner, "These hairy things are goin' to tak us, I can feel it. If we change shape noo, we can get awa' and find the wench. I dinna like this place any."

"Aye, let's do it! Before they use those teeth they keep

showin' off. And call tae yer cousin Fearchar! He'll be here quick as a bodach tae help us oot!"

"Then he'll want part of oor pay!"

"I ken that, but naiver mind, we might be needin' some assistance!"

"Aye," Ceallach said and out of his mouth shot a gob of foul smelling liquid into the ether, designed as an s.o.s. hoping it would reach his cousin and inform him of the situation. The message formed a rank bubble and was floating upwards when a crow flying by, spied it and with a poke of his beak, popped the heinous boil, leaving the message a sodden stinking glob on the ground. Fearghas bellowed seeing it lie there like a rotten egg. Seeing the crow gave Ceallach an idea and the two bogies recited a shifting spell before the canine creatures could anticipate their trickery, and changed themselves into crows. They cawed stridently and circled above the group. How they wanted to peck the yellow eyes of those animals, but the menacing growls and bared teeth kept them at bay and they flew up and disappeared from sight. They did not realize that these woods were filled with the very same black birds and that their cawing only made the announcement that they had arrived.

They landed on the branches of a sycamore tree that deliberately bounced them around, disturbed by their presence. They sat there trying to get their bearings, when the tree began filling with crows of every shape and description, resembling a morose Christmas tree. Jackdaws perched on every available branch and limb. Even some larger ravens flew over to join in the ribaldry. They began cawing stridently, mercilessly, until the bogies nearly went mad.

Highly amused by the imposters' plight, the birds strengthened their cawing and jeering with vigor. The bogies tried to fly away from their tormenters, but were surrounded, the crows thoroughly enjoying this game.

Fearghas was becoming frantic. The strident cawing and shrill calls were too much.

Ceallach, on the other hand was furious. He tried to get a message to his partner, but the piercing screeches were too loud and he could barely hear himself think. The birds moved in closer until he could scarcely see as dodging ravens and crows pecked him mercilessly and filled his ears with their caws and scolding. One crow flew off to tell the other forest dwellers the situation, while the others remained guarding the two imposters, knowing these were too sinister to let loose in their wood.

Chapter 17

Fiona woke up on Saturday morning as the sun came streaming in her window, experiencing a feeling that she almost forgot was still tucked inside. She was happy. She had so much to do, so many questions to ask and so many things she wanted to show her new friend. She looked over to the dollhouse to make certain Rionnag was still there, saw a diminutive hand move from under the coverlet, and smiled.

She wanted to jump out of bed, run to the dollhouse, and awaken Rionnag, but she restrained herself and let the faerie sleep. She looked at the clock. It was only a little past seven, an unthinkable time for a teenager to be getting up on a Saturday morning, but Fiona could no longer sleep.

As if sensing she was being watched, Rionnag threw the covers off, stretched her arms, and opened her eyes. Her gaze went directly to Fiona, who smiled her happiness, making Rionnag smile in return. Fiona climbed out of bed and went over to the house, kneeled and said softly, "Good morning. How are you feeling this morning?"

"A bit better. I think I'd like to try my wings if we can be getting out and into the pure air."

"Sure. I'll get dressed and we can go right out. Are you hungry?"

"Not at the moment. I'd really like to wash and try my wings."

"Do you want me to get you some water?" Fiona said, realizing she hadn't so much as offered her guest a bath.

"Nay, the dewdrops are just fine, but we'd better get out there before they all dry up with the coming sun."

Fiona threw on her favorite multi-pocketed khaki pants, a hooded sweatshirt, some wool socks and her high-tops. Her recorder, which she brought everywhere, lay on the floor next to her bed. She picked it up, and placed it in one of the side pockets of her pants.

"Let's go," she whispered loudly and started for the door.

The faerie coughed to get Fiona's attention. Fiona stopped and turned around. Rionnag was standing with her arms folded across her chest.

"Oops, sorry," Fiona said, realizing the faerie could not get outside by herself due to her splinted wing. She emptied the contents of one pant's pocket onto her bed, Rionnag marveling at the accumulating pile. "How's this?" she asked, pulling the pocket wide for Rionnag to view.

"Looks roomy enough."

She gently placed Rionnag inside the pocket, very quietly opened her door and headed down the stairs. There was no sound from the three other bedrooms down the hall and Fiona prayed her mother would stay asleep until she got out. She walked down the old staircase avoiding all the well-known creaky places, as only someone who had done this many times could do, grabbed her windbreaker off the peg at the same time she opened the front door, and stepped out into the morning sun, closing the door gently behind her.

She walked quickly to the crabapple tree in the back yard, and, getting her footing, climbed its branches until she was sitting in a well-worn spot. Then she reached into her pocket and lifted Rionnag out.

"This is my favorite place in the whole world," Fiona said. Rionnag stood on Fiona's open palm gulping in deep breaths of the clean, morning air.

"It's beautiful, Fiona." From where they sat perched on the branch they could see the not too distant mountains ablaze with amber, farmlands with rolling hills and huge bales of hay. The sky was a crisp baby blue with airy pink clouds resembling chimney smoke. Their breath came out in little wisps, the October morning refreshingly chilly.

Rionnag brought them out of their musing. "I hope ye do not mind, but I'd like to be having my bath, please."

"Oh, right," Fiona said and placed Rionnag back in her pocket and climbed down. She stood the faerie on the wet grass and watched as Rionnag found some Lady's Mantle filled with diamond-like dewdrops. The faerie cupped her hands and took the sparkling water in them. She splashed first her face, then her body, through her gauze shift. She shivered deliciously, looking enraptured.

"Fiona, could ye please take the wrapping off my wing. I could use a good stretch." Fiona did so carefully and Rionnag took the water from another leaf, gently covering her wings with it. Fiona saw her wings extended for the first time as Rionnag carefully spread them wide, mindful of her injury. Fiona gasped audibly. They reminded her of opals, the kind sold at her mom's shop. They changed color depending on the way the faerie moved, from blue to turquoise, lavender to purple, mixed with shards of silver and gold. Rionnag stretched and began to flutter her wings ever so slightly. Fiona watched as she lifted off the ground, hovering in one spot for a moment, as if testing her strength, and then with a slight tilt of her head she took off, soaring high above Fiona.

The faerie flew circles around the tree, and Fiona, remembering her dream of the other night, wished she had the ability too. The pure happiness on Rionnag's face as she dipped and glided was proof that flying was as wonderful as Fiona knew it would be. When she was nine, she'd read a book about some British children who were taught to fly by a strange boy who had come to their village. She would ask Rionnag to teach her, she thought. Inspired, she climbed back up to her spot and took her recorder out of her pocket and began to play a tune for Rionnag, one she made up on the spot. It was a light and airy tune making the recorder sound like an Irish tin whistle, with trills and low breathy notes.

Rionnag was looking all around at the marvelous landscape, wondering why at home they said this side was not very nice. She heard the sweet music below and swooped near to find its source. She was amazed to discover her new friend playing something that reminded her of home. She noticed Fiona watching her fly as she played and they both stared at each other with eyes open in wonder. When Rionnag landed on Fiona's shoulder, surprising her, Fiona stopped playing and turned her head to smile at the faerie.

"Oh, I feel so much better!" the faerie said breathlessly. Fiona put out her open palm and Rionnag left her shoulder to fly onto it.

"I wish I could do that! It looks incredible," Fiona said enviously.

"It is. But sorry to say, I've never met a human before,

but really, I dinna think it possible."

Rionnag noticed her friend's disappointed expression and added, "I wish I could play like ye. Perhaps ye'll be kind enough to play for me again."

Fiona blushed and smiled. "Thank you. I'd like that."

"Fiona, this is a lovely place. I can understand why it's yer favorite."

Fiona looked proud before her face darkened. "People are always trying to get Gram and my mom to sell it. We keep getting offers for it."

Rionnag could not hide her shock. "So it's true then! And what would they do with the land if ye allowed them to have it? Destroy it?"

"Yeah and build a ton of houses. Don't they do that in your world?"

"Never! We live as part of the Earth, we do not own her. She provides for us, we depend on her. My faither told me this was happening here, but I dinna really believe him. Och, I feel as if I could cowk!" She held her hand over her mouth and bent over as if she were about to be sick.

"Are you okay?" Fiona asked, worried.

"I'm beginning to understand why they tell me this world is not a nice place." Rionnag put her head down and shook it sadly. "Generations ago a meeting like this, between ye and me, was commonplace. Humans and faeries met all the time. They respected one another. Now, my faither says the faerie world is fading because all our sacred spots are being seized for human concerns."

"But I thought when you went into your world it was totally different," Fiona protested.

"Different, aye, but still the earth." Rionnag's tone was earnest, serious, for she was eager to make Fiona understand the importance of this fact. "When changes take place here, they take place in my world as weel. That's why I'm to wed:

to strengthen the faerie world."

"Why would your marriage have anything to do with that?"

"My wedding is supposed to bring the faerie families of Scotland and Ireland together, uniting us. Our strength as one will strengthen us all, so we can try and stop the dark forces that are gaining power as you humans destroy the planet."

"Then why won't you do it?" Fiona asked, wide eyed.

"Because it wasna my choice! I was never allowed to meet him and I refuse to marry someone I do not know, let alone love. Can ye understand?"

"Of course, but it seems like you have a pretty big responsibility to your people. What'll happen if you don't marry him?"

"Och, our world will fade some more, until the wicked side takes over completely," the faerie said, a little too nonchalantly.

"Rionnag! How can you know that and do nothing about it?" Fiona was indignant. She frowned and continued, "It's all my mom and I talk about! It's the only thing we have in common anymore. Don't you know that the world is heating up, the ice caps melting! Polar bears are drowning. They might be gone in my lifetime! The rain forests are being slashed and burned! And we can't even eat fish anymore. Gram and I used to fish in the stream near here, but she now won't let me, says it's spoiled. Loons in the lake we canoed in once are full of mercury! Have you ever heard a loon? What an amazing sound. So beautiful. My God, even honeybees are disappearing! Rionnag, maybe *you can* do something!"

Rionnag began to be filled with a dread so terrible that she could not speak. Her father had told her all this, but she didn't pay much attention. And now a human child was telling her the same story. And she *could* do something about it! How selfish. Shamefacedly she said, "Aye, maybe I could."

A flood of memories came to her, conversations with her father that Rionnag had never really cared to hear. She now repeated his words, "My faither says if all humans thought about the consequences of their actions, our two worlds would be safe. Every time humans befoul a river or cut down a tree, the home of some creature of the earth is destroyed. What happens to it? Where does it go if it lives at all?" Saying these things aloud gave credence and she felt that she needed to apologize to her father for her childish, willful act. Suddenly Rionnag made a decision within herself. She was about to speak when Fiona spoke up.

"Hey, I just thought of something. Are there faeries here? I mean in America?" Fiona wondered if the same fate Rionnag spoke of was happening here.

"Perhaps. I dinna ken. Those folk ye were dancing with, do ye not think they come from somewhere?"

"I, um, I told you before, I didn't think they were real. I thought it was just my imagination," Fiona mumbled, somewhat embarrassed.

"Nay, they are real."

"Yeah, I guess it's all real," Fiona said.

"Aye, the good and the bad," Rionnag said, then flew off Fiona's hand and into the blue. Fiona watched with wonder and wished she could follow right behind.

The faerie landed on the branch above Fiona's head. "How did ye dance with those folk if you dinna even ken it was real?"

"I don't know," Fiona said, puzzled. "If it's real then why can't I do it when I want to? It seems I can only do it when I'm daydreaming."

"I ken a way. Would ye like to try?" Rionnag's eyes

glittered enthusiastically.

"You mean at will? On purpose?"

"Aye, but we'll need stones."

"We have plenty of stones," Fiona said, pointing to a long stone wall that had been standing for over two hundred years.

"Nay, the stones must be special. Stones of power. We need twelve to create a ring." The faerie was now talking to herself, "Och, Rionnag, ye have to go back, but why would ye want to go through the same way again? Are ye cracked?"

Fiona was wondering what the faerie was talking about when she heard a familiar whistle. They turned to see Gram coming up the path towards them.

"Morning, Gram."

Gram smiled up at her granddaughter and then turned her attention to Rionnag. "And how is our little patient this morning?"

"Much better I am, thank ye. I've had my bath and my wing and shoulder are healing nicely."

"Are you two hungry?" Gram asked, opening the paper bag she held.

"As a matter of fact, I'm starved. What's in the bag?" Fiona craned her neck eagerly.

"Guests first, Fiona, where are your manners?"

"Oh, right, sorry. Rionnag?"

"I am famished, truth to tell."

"I've got two kinds of muffins; pumpkin and carrot. I made them myself," Gram said, pulling them out of the bag. Gram broke off a tiny piece of each and handed them to Rionnag. Then she took the remainder of the pumpkin muffin and gave it to Fiona. The three ate their muffins in silence, enjoying each other's company.

Rionnag broke the silence. "I feel as if I could stay here

for a verra long time. I'm not wanting to marry, at least not yet, and I like ye both."

Gram bent toward the faerie and smiled brightly. "Thank you for the compliment. I don't know what to say." Gram paused and then said, "But you must go back, you told me so yourself."

"Aye that I must. But I shan't just yet. I ken my mither will be verra angry, but it's so unfair."

"I know it's unfair, but Rionnag, what about the planet?" Fiona interjected.

"What if he is horrid?" the faerie asked, knowing full well Fiona was right, but ignoring the question completely.

"Rionnag, if what we talked about the other day is true, then according to faerie legend, you're the next queen and your betrothed is the next Stag king. It's destined. Am I right?" Gram asked reasonably.

Rionnag spoke bitterly, "Aye, but it was never my choice."

Gram looked thoughtfully at the faerie. "My dear," she said, "we all make choices, many before we come into this life. You, too, made a choice to be exactly who you are, and with that choice comes a fulfillment of your destiny."

Rionnag shook her head and said sadly, "I wanted to marry for love."

"Perhaps your betrothed will be wonderful," Gram said hopefully.

"I've thought of that and all, but it's the principle of the thing! I do want to marry one day, but I dinna want to be forced."

"Well, I don't blame you one bit. When my mother was a girl, arranged marriages were quite common. And believe me, there were a lot of unhappy people living together. But yours is a different story."

"Och, why did ye humans have to wreak such havoc

in the first place!" Rionnag declared, indignant, yet feeling more and more in the wrong about running away.

"That's a good question!" Gram retorted. "I wish I had the answer."

"I ken I must return, I've known it all along, but I did so want to marry for love."

"But, my dear, you have a serious responsibility. A marriage of two powerful faeries isn't something to take lightly," Gram said wisely.

"Well, I'm never going to get married!" Fiona said indignantly.

"Not even if it could save the earth from destruction?" Rionnag asked.

"In that case, of course I would. If it was the only way. Other than that, not a chance."

"Why do you say that, Fi?" Gram asked, frowning.

"Look at Mom, will you? She's beautiful and never goes out with anyone. I know she's lonely and forget talking about my father! I mean, what kind of relationship did she have with him? It must have been pretty awful. We all know what everyone in town thinks! And she never talks about him, ever! So for me marriage isn't an option!"

"You never knew your grandfather, but he was a wonderful man and a terrific husband. I wouldn't have changed a thing," Gram said.

"Yeah, but that was a long time ago. Times have changed, Gram."

"Love never changes. When you meet the right person you'll know it and if you're lucky and work at it, marriage can be a wonderful thing."

"Then what about Mom and Aunt Kat for that matter?"

"Katherine is young, she's still playing the field. Your mother, on the other hand, well, she's always been a different story. Even I don't know."

"I think yer mither is holding a verra big secret," Rionnag spoke up.

"What do you mean?" Fiona questioned.

"There's such a sad, faraway look in her eyes. Like she's longing for something."

"I know exactly what you mean," Gram said.

Fiona looked at both of them, somewhat confused and slightly jealous of the knowledge they seemed to share about her mother. She jumped out of the tree and started to walk around it, confused. Gram and Rionnag looked at each other and were about to follow when they all heard Maggie calling for Fiona.

"Wait up, Fi, I want to talk to you!"

Fiona looked quickly to her grandmother and gestured her to hide the faerie. Then she walked directly to join her mother while Gram fumbled with her sweater, hiding Rionnag in her baggy sleeve. "I'll just go back and start the tea water, shall I?" Gram smiled, and without waiting for a reply, walked swiftly to the house.

"I know what you're going to tell me. It's okay Mom, I know you have to go."

"Let's walk." Maggie slipped her hand into Fiona's. "I hope you're not too disappointed that I won't be here for Halloween," Maggie began.

"Mom, I'm fourteen. What's the difference? You missed every other one and now I'm too old, so you're off the hook." Fiona's tone was accusatory.

"Fi, baby, this is something I have to do. One day you'll understand. I'll bring you back something special," her mom promised with a half smile.

"What, another rock?" Fiona said, her sarcasm barely masking her deep disappointment, and sat down on the old wall, gesturing to one of many tumbled stones.

"Okay, I guess I deserve that, but if you knew the

significance of those stones... What would you like?" Maggie asked quietly.

"Never mind. Look, Mom, I'll be perfectly fine here with Gram and Aunt Kat. Just go and do whatever you need to do. I'm a big girl now."

"Yes, I know." Maggie touched Fiona on the cheek. "Maybe that's why I feel so bad about leaving. You're growing up so fast and I feel like I'm missing it."

"Oh well!" Fiona said flippantly.

Maggie so hated that expression, like a dismissal, laced with anger and sarcasm.

"Fiona, I'm committed and I can't miss it. Maybe next year you'll go with me."

Fiona was plucking leaves off the nearest tree, something she knew her mother hated her to do, but Maggie didn't comment on it.

"That's okay, Mom, I'm really not into yoga anyway. Can we go back now? I'm getting cold and I'm sure the tea is ready."

"In a minute," Maggie paused, then took Fiona's face by the chin and turned it toward her. Fiona deftly avoided her eyes. "Look at me, Fiona. I love you, you know."

"I know," came the reply in barely a whisper. "I love you too."

"So you're okay with it, then?"

"I never said that. I just said that I loved you. Remember, you always told me you can be pissed at someone and still love them. Right?"

"Right," Maggie said.

"Good."

Chapter 18

Queen Barabel was ripping the wings off an unfortunate bug that happened to fly into her salon. When she had first tortured, then denuded it sufficiently, pulling off each wing, she crushed it between her slender fingers. Wiping its entrails on her gown, she put her fingers into her mouth, sucking them clean.

She had been waiting for news from the bogies. So far there had been nothing. She sent several of her more pernicious crew to track them down, without divulging any particulars. Patience was no virtue of Barabel's and it would be another unlucky insect if she had to wait much longer.

There was a loud scratch at the door.

"Enter," the queen commanded.

Opening it cautiously, a Ghillie Dhu entered, shedding leaves as he moved into the chamber. He was an ugly, solitary faerie who really didn't want any part of this, but as the only birch thicket for miles happened to be on Barabel's lands, and that was where his kind dwelt, he had to do her bidding. Shaking and rustling his leafy garments, he bowed low before the queen.

"Rise, rise, get on with it. Any news yet of those two?"

"M...M...Madam, we ken only that they went through. A goblin, very reliable source, told us they both went through, but Madam," he paused and swallowed hard, "they went through separately."

"Separately! They can't speak a coherent sentence one without the other! AARGH!" The Queen's rage was explosive, making the Ghillie Dhu tremble and shed leaves on her carpet. "How did this happen?" she demanded.

The poor terrified Ghille Dhu related the story the goblin had told, minus the cursing and language that had gone with the goblin's original tale.

"WHAT *ring did you say they used*?" The Queen was beginning to swell with her temper. The hair on her head began to rise, her face turned a poisonous shade of green, and her eyes reddened.

The Ghillie Dhu had seen this many times but cowered nonetheless.

"Get out! GET OUT!" Barabel shrieked, almost insane with frustration. The informant flew out through the door just as the queen began to whirl with fury, becoming a blur of confusing color. Nothing in the chamber remained intact, possessions breaking into bits as if a cyclone had entered the room, but Barabel was oblivious. She wanted only one thing and she hated to be thwarted. With the two mindless bogies gone separately, the job was as good as gone. After a long while, when her fit had subsided somewhat, she reacquired her shape and paced the floor, kicking debris out of her way as she thought about her options.

That ring, the one they'd gone through, she knew that ring. None used it; it held too many unknown dangers.

It led to places the fey folk didn't care to consider, much less name. Some of those places were so distant that the travelers never came back. She cared naught about the two foul bogies, except insofar as they could get her what she desired. They could stay wherever they were and rot for all she cared, but they were all she had to do the job, except...

No. That was too hair-raising even for the likes of Barabel. Just the thought of *that one* made her stomach churn and her wings arch in dread. But what choice did she have? She *had* to get the brat. Her future power and prestige depended on it.

Nodding to herself, she shivered with sudden decision, for she knew what she must do. With trembling fingers she dragged a heavy, low chest from beneath her throne and took a large key out of the long pocket of her gown. She put the key into the hole and as it turned, swirling colors of energy rose from it like wood smoke. With an effort she lifted the lid. Fierce wind blew from within the chest, whipping her hair into a frenzy. She reached into the depths of the mysterious trunk, far, far down until her arm was nearly lost in it, and pulled up a crystal rock that was as large as a man's head and twice as heavy. It seethed with malevolent color, like old blood. She placed it on the floor next to the chest, and then sitting back, stared at the baleful object that seemed almost to breathe with wickedness.

Gulping, she tried to prepare herself for the summoning of purest evil and diabolical power. She thought of her golden mother, a faerie queen of surpassing goodness, and felt an unwelcome pang of guilt, before throwing it aside. Nay, her mother had turned against her, as had the rest of them. But they'd accept her once she was allied with the Irish Queen and King.

A moment later, she placed both hands on the crystal and spoke the unutterable words that would bring forth the beast she feared above all things.

"*Tha sgothian dubha anns an adhar,*" she recited, her voice quivering. "*Clach mhin mheallain sin tobar ud thall!*"

The colors within the crystal began to pulse. It grew increasingly warm to the touch until it was scorching. The procedure required her hands to remain in place until she called forth the spell completely. Her eyes were tearing from pain when the rock began to shake with tremendous force. Though it took all her strength, she held firm. She squeezed her eyes shut in anticipation. She never knew what form *He* would take, and although *He* sometimes might appear fairer even than her menservants, this was only a cruel illusion he assumed to cause confusion and wield his terrifying power.

She heard him appear in her chamber as the crystal stopped its frenzied rocking. Opening her eyes, she stared in horror at her hands, which were blistered from the heat, not daring to look up. A deep voice spoke, as if coming from the very depths of the earth and echoed throughout the room.

"WHY HAVE YE SUMMONED ME, BARRRAABELLLL?"

She tried desperately to keep him from sensing her fear. He enjoyed it too much.

"I need yer assistance in a rather delicate matter," she said in her softest, most submissive tone, her gaze slowly rising to regard the body that housed so terrible a voice. Her breath caught when she saw the shape he had assumed this day.

He was stunningly handsome and she allowed herself to be lured, like some stupid mortal, into his lecherous gaze. The Stag king didn't hold a candle to him in this form. His hair, which she had only seen in various shades of grayish green was now silky black, thick piles of it on a ruddy chiseled face, his eyes sparkling in iridescent green, with shards of blue surrounding his impenetrable, black pupils. His broad shoulders looked strong, and he wore a dark green cloak and tight stockings under dark leather boots. She had never seen him in this form, but what a perfect form it was! She inadvertently licked her lips. She nearly forgot why she had called him. Oh, yes, to capture her niece. Just the thought of perfect Rionnag having him like this brought on a wave of jealousy. Don't be stupid she reminded herself with a shiver, this is only a fabrication.

Slowly and deliberately, he walked over to where Barabel still sat on the floor. When he extended a strong hand towards her, she took it, feeling a burst of fire, almost painful, as he drew her to her feet. He was tall and she stood only to his wide chest. She raised her head to meet his eyes, fearing that at any moment he would reinvent himself, but he took her chin in his hand and put his lips to hers. Giving way, she opened her mouth, but his mouth tasted rancid and as Barabel tried to pull away, he held her tighter, kissing her more fiercely. By the time he released her from his grasp, her lips and tongue were burning as if touched by acid.

"NOT TO YER LIKING, ME BANRIGH?" His sinister laughter was awful to hear.

Barabel took a step backwards and looked up at him. At once he began to change, his hair turning a fiery red, his eyes like matching flames. His face distorted grotesquely, the cloak transformed to fur and feathers. She shuddered, repulsed.

"COME AND KISS ME NOO, AYE!" he bellowed and began to laugh hard at her discomfiture.

Barabel tried to regain her swiftly diminishing composure. "May we get down to business, Creaghan?"

"WHY DO YE CALL ME BY THAT NAME?" demanded the beast.

"Because that is the name I have always called ye. Do ye have a new name?" She knew he enjoyed changing all aspects of himself, and thought it might soothe him if she humored his whims.

"AYE, YE MAY CALL ME *UILEBHEIST* BECAUSE THAT IS WHAT YE ARE THINKIN' I AM!" He laughed harshly again. Barabel *had* been thinking him a monster, but how could he know that? She had no idea he possessed thought-listening ability. This unnerved her.

"DINNA FEAR ME... YET, BANRIGH; GET DOWN TAE BUSINESS, LET'S."

"Very well. I sent some bogies on a mission but they seem to have fouled it."

"HA! WHY WOULD YE START WI' BOGIES? DO YE NO KEN HOW STUPID THEY ARE? BUT, THEN, YE ALWAYS WERE A CHEAP HARLOT, AYE, ME BANRIGH?"

This made Barabel angry, but she made no retort. "They were available. I had no thoughts to disturb ye. But I need ye now, if you're willing."

"TELL ME, THEN."

"I need ye to find my niece, the Lady Rionnag, bring her here, but do not harm her."

"THE LADY RIONNAG. THAT COULD BE VERRA DANGEROUS. I THINK THIS WILL COST YE SOMETHING QUITE DEAR."

Barabel pulled out a long string of pearls and jewels from around her neck, which she held up for her guest's appraisal.

He took it in his gnarled hand, turning it over, scrutinizing it, then threw it back at her.

"NAY BARABEL, THIS WILL NAE DO. I HAVE ME TITHE TAE PAY THIS BELTANE AND I WANT ONE OF YERS FOR ME VERRA OON. THAT WILL BE PAYMENT."

He licked his thick foul lips, and a shudder went through her as she remembered their kiss.

She thought for a moment about his demand. One of her captives. She did not relish the thought of Creaghan having any of her men. They were hers. She needed them for herself, her tithing was coming soon as well. How could she choose one to part with, especially for this monster? As she thought the thought, he was in her face, growling low, "NO NEED TO CHOOSE FOR ME, BANRIGH, I WILL CHOOSE FOR MESELF. BRING THEM TAE ME AT ONCE. AND," he paused, moving until his eyes burned into hers, "KEN THIS, ME LADY, I KEN HOW MANY, WHO AND ALL, SO DINNA TRY TAE TRICK ME."

She backed up and said, "I will allow ye to choose, but ye may not take him until I have my prize, my niece, here, unharmed. That bargain I will keep. What say ye?"

He thought for a moment, and as if in answer, he began to change form once more, only this time into a creature, a female, so lovely, that none of her consorts would be able to resist. "CALL THEM TAE ME." His voice was the only part of him that remained to reveal his true nature.

"I suggest you keep silent if you want to continue your charade. Wait here whilst I call them to me." She left the chamber holding a hand to her chest. He unnerved her, yet she needed him and if it meant sacrificing one of her men for this purpose, it would have to be done. Calling her chief servant to her, she told him to gather all her prisoners to her at once. One by one they were brought before their fey warden, where she lined them up, assessing them as they stood before her as straight as any army assemblage, hating to part with even one of them. But one was missing. Her oldest, and most trusted. She wished she could keep him out of this mix, but she knew Creaghan would find him no matter where she hid him. She commanded her servant to find him and quickly.

Ewan was sitting on a log playing his whistle. The tones were eerie and sweet. He was lost in thought imagining how she would receive this tune, this latest gift. How her eyes would shine as he played for her. The time was drawing nigh, the only sweetness in his wretched life. Every year he had told her not to return, though it broke his heart. He wanted her to find some measure of happiness, even though it would mean never seeing her again. He wanted her to make a life for herself, perhaps have a family, though the thought of her with anyone other than himself pained him to no end.

But she was always there on *Samhain*, All Hallow's Eve. Steadfastly waiting for him. Nothing, it seemed, would stop her coming. Their bond of love stronger each time they met. They both knew it was mad, but the force of their passion was overwhelming. And, Ewan selfishly admitted, it was what he lived for.

He had written the tune for her, would play it for her when they met. He hoped she would cherish it. As he cherished her. His heart lurched and he felt pangs of longing the way he always did as time drew near. He wiped the tears from his eyes. He would savor their time together; it would sustain him. As it had for all these years.

"Ewan! What are ye thinkin', man! I've been callin' ye o'er long! Queen Barabel wants ye tae her chamber, noo!"

Ewan put his instrument into its woven case, flung it over his shoulder and followed the elf to meet the witch he hated more than the devil himself. The elf pulled him by the sleeve but Ewan yanked his arm away, and drawing himself up to his full height, which towered over the elf, walked with dignity into his captor's chamber.

He bowed before Barabel. She looked gorgeous, today her hair was crimson, but that could change with her mood;

her eyes were swirling colors from some magic, but as always, looked seductively into Ewan's. She had been able to deceive him once, so long ago it was practically an ancient memory, but never again.

He pretended to be affected at the sight of her and took her hand in his. He put it to his lips, cursing her to himself all the while.

"My Queen, what do ye need of me?" he asked, looking around to see the rest of her captives lined up in front of a magnificent-looking woman, dressed in a rampantly seductive diaphanous gown.

"Get in line, Ewan." She gestured to where the others were standing. Her heart gave a little lurch. Ewan had been her first captive, and he had pleased her for many years. She had lured him over a century ago, using her beauty and promises of love and eternal youth. He hadn't been as young as most of her succeeding captives, but he'd been so vulnerable, so desirable and so masculine. She clutched her throat. In the years since, he had become her chief counselor on all matters human. She had long ago discarded him for more pleasurable pastimes, instead carrying on with her younger captives, but Ewan held a place in her wicked heart still. She had thought many times to tithe him to Hell, but kept finding reasons to put it off.

Ewan glanced at the other men, who looked confused but aroused by the sheer physical glory of the strange, new female among them. She was tall and shapely, with smooth skin the color of ginger; her indigo hair falling seductively down her scantily clad back. Her perfect breasts nearly escaped her gown and her eyes were almond-shaped and of the lightest blue Ewan had ever seen. She looked him directly in the eye. He held her gaze.

As Ewan looked at the beautiful woman, he was sure there was more here than was immediately apparent and guessed that this was no woman at all. The idea that Barabel might permit another female, especially one of this magnificence, to appraise her stable of men-slaves was preposterous, impossible. She was too possessive, too jealous ever to allow such a thing. The woman walked slowly and seductively past the line of men, reaching out to touch a lock of hair or caress a cheek. The men decided this was some sort of contest and put on their most handsome smiles.

Stupid fools, Ewan said to himself. Don't they realize this is some kind of trick?

"And what kind of trick is it, young laddie?" the woman said in a rampantly sensual voice, answering his thoughts.

"I dinna ken. Why do ye no tell us, then," Ewan said, forcing his eyes down, trying not to be aroused, seething inside from his own weakness.

Barabel interrupted and addressed the group. "Gentlemen, this is Una. She needs one of you to work for her, and she would like to choose for herself. Una, come, look at this handsome lad..." She brought Creaghan over to her newest captive, a young man of nineteen or so whom she had captured this century. He was tall, gangly, and not too interesting to Barabel. She was probably going to sacrifice him this *Samhain*, anyway.

"Una" ignored Barabel, lingering in front of Ewan, who glared at her.

"Barabel, I want this one," Una said, putting her hand on Ewan's broad chest.

"Una, he is my oldest one; why not take a new one, they're so much fresher." Ewan heard some of the other captives mumbling angrily, "Always Ewan. Always the favorite."

Barabel did not want the monster to have her Ewan. She felt her stomach lurch. Oh, why did I summon him? she berated herself. Again, Creaghan/Una answered, "*I would have found him anyway, dear Barabel. My mind is decided. He will come tae me on delivery.*" With those words he took on his most loathsome form yet. The men started screaming as the stunning female turned into a hunched monstrosity, horns sprouting from an albino head, eyes the color of calves' liver, and skin covered in ghastly boils and pustules. In a voice that seemed to come from Hell itself, he pronounced,

"I'LL BE BACK FOR YE, ME FINE LADDIE. AWAIT ME, FOR I WILL RETURN WITH YER QUEEN'S PRIZE AND THEN YE WILL BE MINE!!!!!"

Before Ewan could react, Creaghan returned to formless smoke and a second later, disappeared. Throughout all this, the other men had been frozen in terror, but this final fright was too much for them and they bolted like rabbits from a fox. Only Barabel and Ewan remained, eyes upon the throbbing crystal that lay on the floor near Barabel's throne.

Chapter 19

On the day of Maggie's departure a cold, dreary rain splashed relentlessly onto the Harris house, dampening the clapboard but not the spirit of the one who was leaving. Maggie was filled with quiet anticipation, packing everything into a small and very worn leather backpack, too small for a week's trip.

She paused to look at a picture of Fiona as a toddler, her reddish brown hair pulled into two short pigtails, a huge smile on her freckled face. The frame was old, probably some thrift shop purchase. Maggie studied it for a long moment, then impulsively, grabbed it and shoved it into her rucksack. That done, she pulled the drawstring tight, snapped the buckle, and put it against the door, making sure the door was shut firmly. She walked to her dresser, an antique pine chest of drawers, made at least a century before. Keeping her eyes on the bedroom door, she crouched down and pulled the bottom drawer open. She reached all the way back, her face scrunched up until she reached the spot she wanted and pressed an unseen button. The drawer opened fully to reveal a secret compartment. Maggie looked at it thoughtfully and took out a large leather-bound book that was the object of her search. She opened immediately to the page she wanted, although the book was at least six inches thick.

This particular page had been opened many times before and was creased and worn with use. Crouching beside the dresser, she studied the writing, her eyes glancing swiftly to the door and back again. Her lips moved, mouthing something that no one would have understood, even had they been interested. When she was satisfied she had it in her head, Maggie closed the cumbersome volume and was about to put it back in its hiding place when there was a brief knock and the door opened, Kat letting herself in.

"Could you knock?" Maggie called from her crouched position.

"I did. Lose something?" Kat asked and bent to help her sister.

Maggie quickly shoved the book under the wool socks. "No, I'm just getting ready," Maggie told her, rising, silently reminding herself to put the book away promptly when her sister left the room.

"Got your plane tickets?"

"Check."

"Passport?"

"Check."

"Bus tickets?"

"Check, check."

"Good, we should leave in ten minutes. You want to catch the 4:30 bus, right?"

"Yes. Is Fi coming?" Maggie asked.

"I don't know what she's doing. I haven't heard a

sound from her room," Kat said. She grabbed her sister's backpack. "Are you sure you have enough? I've never heard of a woman who can travel this light!" she joked.

"What a sexist remark!" Maggie teased back.

"Who's making sexist remarks?" Gram stood in the doorway of Maggie's room.

"Your daughter," Maggie said.

"I have two."

"That one." Maggie pointed at her younger sister.

"I'm not surprised," Gram said.

"Mother!" gasped Kat, pretending offense.

"I made you something to eat for the plane. I know how you hate airplane food," Gram said, smiling at her daughter, glad she was happy for once.

Maggie went over to her and kissed her on the cheek. "Thanks, Mom, really. I love you."

"There's nothing to thank me for. You just have a safe trip and come back healthy and happy," Gram said, emphasizing the last word.

"I will," she answered and squeezed her mother's hand. "I want to say goodbye to Fiona. I'll meet you downstairs."

They walked out, Gram and Kat heading downstairs, Maggie to her daughter's room. She stood outside the door for a moment, and then knocked.

Fiona was sitting on the floor in front of the dollhouse rearranging furniture to make things comfortable for Rionnag. She felt glad of the diversion, hating as always to say goodbye to her mother, her feelings always a mixture of sadness and anger. The faerie watched her, smiling. At the sound of the knock, Rionnag, who knew the routine by then, hid behind the dresser.

"Who is it?" Fiona called.

"It's me."

"Come in, Mom."

"I came to say goodbye. Do you want to come with me to the station?" Maggie asked hopefully.

"Nah, I've got lots of homework. Have a great time," Fiona said, not daring to look at her mother. She felt a solitary tear slide down her face. Not wanting her mother to see her cry, she turned away.

"Fi, sweet..." Maggie bent down to the floor where Fiona was still sitting. "It's all right, baby. I won't be gone long."

Fiona sniffed and said, "What if the plane...?" not wanting to say the thing she dreaded most of all.

"Sweetie, I've told you before, even though it's terrible for the environment, flying is very safe, and besides, when it's my time, it's my time."

"Well, even if it's your time, what about *me*?" Fiona said.

"My darling girl, in life we've got to do the things that make us happy and bring us joy, even if they might be dangerous. Otherwise we live in fear and that's no life. Right?" Maggie said, stroking her daughter's head.

Fiona faced her mother for the first time and nodded in agreement.

"I'll miss you, but the time will go so quickly, you won't even notice I'm gone." She realized after she said that, it was true. She'd been spending way too much time at the shop. She vowed to herself to be home more when she returned. Maggie glanced at her watch. It was time to go. She got up but Fiona pulled her back down. "Mom..." Maggie turned and Fiona put her arms out to her and Maggie hugged her so tightly Fiona thought she would break.

After a second, she moved away slightly. She looked appraisingly at Fiona who began to squirm. "Take good care of Gram," Maggie said.

"I will, Mom. Have a good time, and bring me back

something special, okay!" Fiona said, feeling somewhat recovered.

"Like what?" Maggie asked.

"Oh, like a man in a kilt!" Fiona said with a Scottish accent, smiling mischievously.

"Fiona! Where on earth did that come from?" Maggie said, somewhat taken aback.

"I was just hoping you'd meet somebody nice. So you'd be happy."

"What makes you think I'm unhappy?" her mother asked.

"C'mon Mom, I'm not blind!"

Her mother hesitated, then gave her another squeeze, saying, "I'll certainly keep it in mind. I'll bring you back a sweater."

"Great," Fiona said, sounding most unenthusiastic.

The two were interrupted by Gram yelling for Maggie to come on if she didn't want to miss her bus.

Maggie kissed Fiona on the lips and again on her head, then walked out.

"Yer mither loves ye well," the faerie said, startling Fiona who stared at the door.

She peered into the dollhouse where Rionnag had been hiding behind a high cupboard. "Yeah, I guess she does."

The faerie flew out of the dollhouse and around the room, landing on the windowsill. She looked out and saw Fiona's mother get into the car. Maggie looked up at Fiona's window, and Rionnag was caught in a blue-eyed stare as the car pulled away.

She turned around quickly and bumped into something under a pile of scattered and dusty papers; one of the many stones lined up on the sill. As soon as she touched it, there was a silver spark. Fiona was watching and saw the flicker. She ran over to the window and moved the papers out of the way. "What was that?" she asked Rionnag, breathlessly. Rionnag stood looking at the stones with a mixture of apprehension and interest. She didn't speak but fluttered to the next one and touched that. It sparked as well. Testing all the stones lined neatly on the windowsill produced the same reaction. She turned to look at Fiona who watched this experiment with awe and fear combined, though by now little associated with the faerie surprised her.

Finally Rionnag spoke. "These stones...where did ye get them?"

"My mom brings me back one each time she goes on her yoga trips," Fiona said, wondering what the faerie was getting at.

"Fiona, do ye not know the significance of these stones?"

Fiona's eyes opened wide. "That's exactly what my mother said! No, actually I don't. Care to enlighten me?"

"Aye, these are faerie stones, from a ring."

"But they're so small. What kind of significance could they have?"

Rionnag gave her a withering look that made Fiona back up a few feet. She looked at the tiny creature and flushed.

"So sorry. Okay, tell me about them. Please," Fiona entreated.

"Ye're thinking of the massive stone circles and it's true, those have power, but these are enchanted stones. Any size can have the power if they are part of a faerie ring," Rionnag told her.

"So what good are these sitting on my window sill?" Fiona asked.

"Remember I asked ye if ye cared to see the other side?"

Fiona nodded, her heart pumping a bit faster at the thought.

"We'll need twelve to make a proper ring. Count them

Fiona, see if ye have twelve."

Fiona counted eleven. Rionnag's face fell. "We must have twelve, else there will not be enough strength to be getting us in and back. Sorry."

Fiona looked a bit depressed too, and then said, "Wait!" Rionnag looked at her, startled.

"Come with me." Fiona went out of the room, Rionnag close behind. The door to Maggie's room was shut and supposed to stay that way, but she wouldn't mess up anything. There had to be another rock in there. No, not a rock, a stone from a faerie ring!

Aunt Kat was driving her mother to the bus station. Gram was downstairs. The coast was clear. She opened the door and the two went in. As usual, Maggie's room was neat; the bed made, pillows fluffed on the white metal frame. Fiona went straight over to the windowsill. Clean and empty except for a pink conch shell Maggie had found on the beach when she was a child. Rionnag fluttered around the room looking for any sign of a faerie stone and spotted the altar before Fiona got there.

The altar was a small, low, rectangular table with a cushion on the floor in front of it. The table was laid with a batik cloth on which objects significant to her mother were placed. There was a piece of bright blue sea glass, two beeswax candles that Fiona had dipped at a country fair and given to her mom as a gift, a picture of Fiona's grandfather smiling with a much younger Maggie on his shoulders, a ceramic heart, incense in a incense burner made by a Navajo potter, and a rock. It was larger than the ones on Fiona's windowsill with symbols that looked like runes. Fiona turned as she heard the sharp intake of Rionnag's gasp.

Chapter 20

"Ye betrayed me, my Queen," Ewan said directly to Barabel, who was still staring at the pulsing stone. She moved her eyes slowly over him, taking in the rugged, handsome face, the tall, muscular figure, the angry, betrayed eyes. Her heart pulsed in her throat. She had feelings for this human she could never permit herself to acknowledge. But she mustn't be weak. The only way to get what she wanted was by sheer ruthlessness.

Pretending indifference, she flicked the air with her fingers. "Nay, Ewan, it would have happened sooner or later. This way, I will not have to tithe ye, Creaghan will do that instead and I will get the prin..." she stopped herself realizing she had said too much.

"Ye are a coward," he said and stalked out of the chamber.

"Come back here! Do not walk from me until I have dismissed ye! Ewan!" she screamed after him. How she desired him as she watched him stride powerfully away into the forest. She thought about putting a spell on him for his insolence, but instead, let him go, knowing his anger was justified and hoping that in his rage he would not realize her slip of the tongue. *Never mind, Barabel, dinna soften. Creaghan will get ye what ye need, then all will be as planned. It must be worth the life of a captive mortal. Even that one.*

Ewan walked in a blind fury. He walked until he was at the edge of Barabel's lands, where he could go no further. He howled at the sky. He got to his knees and pounded the earth. He cried out her name. How would he tell his love when she came? It would destroy her. He knew she lived for their time together as he did. He called her name again, keening like an animal that had lost its mate. He rocked back and forth, pounding the earth, his anger and despair so great that he didn't even feel the bruises forming on his hands. Tears spilled freely that had never been spilled, not in all the years that he had been captive here. He could endure anything if he could spend even a moment with his one true love. But Barabel had taken that away. She'd sell her soul if she could get a high enough price. How he hated her, and himself for being lured by her more than a century before.

At the same time he hated Barabel, he also realized that had he not been her captive, he would have been long decayed in a kirkyard and never would have met his beautiful lass, who had called him by the simple act of plucking a wild rose on *Samhain*. Since that time his captivity had been bearable. But no more. This *Samhain* would be their last.

He pounded the ground again and prayed, something he had not done in a time longer than he could remember. "Oh, dear God!" he cried, "I've endured sae much, taken from my family, a prisoner for lifetimes, don't let this be the last time I see my love. Perhaps ye'll take my soul and forgive my vanity and stupidity, being lured by that witch, but let me live for my love. She's naught but goodness! Don't destroy two lives! Oh, God!!" He broke into sobs once more. He sat there, on his knees, head on the ground, for some time. He looked up once more to the heavens and called a powerful plea, hoping God would hear it. It was the same word he had carved into the stone he had given her. As his sobbing subsided into angry gasps he wondered if God even heard him, here in this Faerie land. He recalled the hushed rumors that his own mother had been one of the fey, and if true, then by everything holy, there was a God, because wherever his mother was or had ever been, God had to be as well. It had been a long time since he had thought of her, that memory being so painful. He knew by now that if she had been fey, living too long on the human side would have aged her like a human, and no doubt she was long dead. Living on this side kept one young, but it wasn't worth it. What good was perpetual life without love? His beloved was aging as well, while he remained virtually unchanged. Soon she'd be older than he in looks if not in age. Not that it mattered; he was going to be sacrificed to the Underworld. Was this his punishment for succumbing to Barabel's fey charms in the first place? Was there no escape?

He had thought about this countless times. The problem was, with all his blood kin dead on the other side, there was no one who could take him out of this place. Not even his love. She had asked him when they first had met if she could help him and he had explained that the spell cast upon him was not the same spell that had held the legendary Tamlin. No, he had told her, we must be grateful we at least can meet when *Samhain* comes. When the moon glows yellow and the leaves change their colors, I will wait for ye. He had composed a poem for her, one he repeated every time they met:

145

I will wait for ye in that place between
That world between blinks of an eye
That place spoken only in whispers
When the moon is a hare in the sky

Wait for me there, in that place between
That place between nighttime and day
That world where the light and the sound
  are as one
Where humans can dance with the fey

I will wait for ye in that place between
That place ye're not lookin' to see
That place where our hearts beat together in time
That's where I'll wait for thee

And so he had, every All Hallow's since. It sustained him. Now, soon, even that would be taken away. As he had that thought, he lifted his head and looked towards the forest, and there in a clearing, just beyond the border of Barabel's lands, a Stag stood drinking. Ewan watched as the stag changed form and became a handsome youth. Their eyes met, and Ewan stretched out his arms beseechingly, as if begging the youth to save him from his looming fate.

The youth stood watching for a moment longer, before Ewan turned away in despair.

Chapter 21

Prince Kieran paced his room. His wedding day was nearly upon him. The *Deena Shee* was already planning the festivities for the long awaited event. His parents' joy was evident. His mother hummed all the day long. His father patted him on the back and winked.

It wearied him.

He hadn't met the lass yet, and though he'd been told of her surpassing beauty, kindness, and charm, he wished he could know her first. He had fantasized about her since he was a youngster: dreams of flying together, riding their steeds along the mountains. Yet he was sure his betrothed could never meet his ideal. After all, who could? And anticipating what she would be like made him afraid.

The Prince was a strong believer in tradition and although he greatly wanted a mere glimpse of his bride-to-be, he knew it was expressly forbidden. His honesty and duty to the throne made him far less reckless than most fey lads of his age. His father, King Eamon, often commented on his own reckless youth before he became king, but Kieran had known his own mind since he was small. He would never think to upset custom or break a rule unless for very good reason. Always honest, always true, his good humor and fairness, combined with a pleasing appearance, made him the pride of the *Deena Shee*. Everyone in the kingdom commented on what a virtuous ruler he would be.

But lately there were the dreams. They were disturbing and always the same, and came with increasing frequency. He had two dreams most nights and though they varied in place and detail, their essence was the same.

In the first dream he waited at the altar under a canopy of lilac. His betrothed's father appeared in his Stag form, carrying a cloaked figure on his back. He could never see the face beneath the cloak, but could feel her fear and judgment. His smile would fade and he'd feel a growing panic swelling to a crescendo before he awakened, bathed in sweat, his heart pounding like a bohdran.

Falling asleep once more, he would launch into the second even more disturbing dream. In this one he was being escorted down the aisle to meet his cloaked bride. His escorts were dressed gaily at first, merry music playing from pipes, but then the music would become darker and more melancholic, the figures on either side of him changing as well. Their clothes would fall off in torn shreds and clumps. Their hands that were gently holding his began to get tighter and tighter in their grip until his hands grew numb. In the dream he always kept his eyes downcast until this point, before looking.

He would feel the bile rise in his throat as he saw the monsters that held him fast. And the smell! Putrid, stinking, foul. As always, he would look at the bride, who now removed her hood, revealing her face. He watched in horror as the lovely hands metamorphosed into scabrous claws as she drew the cloak away. He never actually got to see any detail, for at this point, he woke up screaming.

The dreams were affecting his waking life as well. His good humor and friendly ways were replaced with dread and withdrawal. He took to riding far out, letting the wild wind blow, scattering his troubled thoughts. He would stand for hours at the edge of the sea and look towards the place she was born, wondering if she shared his anxiety.

He had decided he had to at least go to her lands, to feel her essence, her aura. He would not set his eyes upon her, although he had lately been sorely tempted. He knew vaguely where the kingdom lay, so it should not be too difficult to go, get a sense, and return. No one would be the wiser, and then he would know. And with that knowledge, perhaps his tranquil dreams would return.

He rose before the sun and while the fey folk slept in their trees and rock dwellings, he went to the edge of the land and looked out toward the place she dwelt. Touching the crown he wore on his dark head, he touched the empty space that would soon be filled with the most powerful jewel in all the worlds. The jewel that was passed from one... He could hardly think on it. He felt a spark there, knowing it would soon hold a power too great to take lightly for even one beat of a wing and with that, he became that which was his birthright. His masculine arms and legs turned to four strong limbs, his body to the Stag shape, which pawed the ground, and he took flight. He crossed the churning, leaden ocean, between the isles, as the sun appeared weakly on the horizon. He was completely alone. No creature of the sea or sky crossed his path as he beat heavy hooves and pawed the clouds. When he finally touched lightly upon the earth once more, he was bathed in sweat. Of course, he could have spelled himself over, but he needed the movement, needed the raw wind rushing at him to clear his thoughts. And he just needed to touch the earth that was her homeland, nothing more. Then he would face whatever this marriage would mean to his and the rest of Fey's future.

He touched down hard upon the earth in a land he had envisioned, but had never seen and stood at the edge of a stream. Hot, he bent down to drink the cool water. It tasted sweet and he hoped this was a good omen. He drank deeply and dipped his sweaty head into the icy stream. Puffing out his nostrils, he shook the water from his head. Not such an unusual sight, he thought, just another buck. No one will give me a second glance. He was about to start off when he remembered the crown, still perched on his antlered head. "Ijit!" he thought to himself. "How could ye be so careless?" He couldn't very well leave it; he had neither hands, nor pockets in his present form. "'Tis stupid ye are!" he chided himself as he changed back into the attractive youth with the curly brown hair and wide eyes, as green as his island. He took off the crown and placed it in his cloak. As he did so, he realized he was being watched.

It was a human, a captive. He knew by the vines around his wrists. He was kneeling on the ground, his face streaked with dirt and tears, his eyes wild. They faced each other and as he looked at the wretched fellow, the man stretched out his arms, a gesture so pitiable and careworn that his heart caught in his throat and he gingerly approached the captive. Seeing the prisoner turn away in despair, he approached cautiously, getting as close as he could without crossing the stream. Once more the man looked at him, eyes full of pain. Kieran nodded reassuringly, his eyes resting on the vine-bound wrists. The human looked to his own wrists and once more held his arms up, palms toward the heavens in a gesture of mercy. Kieran, touched by this sight, hovered to where the man stood by the stream bank and reached out a hand and touched the poor creature on the shoulder.

Chapter 22

Ewan watched as the stag changed into a faerie-man, boy really, for his youth was apparent in his innocent eyes. Those eyes penetrated Ewan and as the man watched, the faerie ventured forward. Ewan, his arms reaching out toward the boy, felt an innate sense of trust. Then Ewan became aware of the power crown on the lad's head, which he took off and placed within the folds of his cloak. A prince, a Stag prince, Ewan thought, as the youth came just to the bank of the stream, which separated them. Neither spoke, but Ewan watched as the prince's eyes fell upon his vine-bound wrists.

The youth ventured to the middle of the stream and reached out to touch him on the shoulder. It was an obvious gesture of friendship. He then flew back to where he had landed and was the first to speak, his voice different, a sweet and lilting tone that Ewan recognized as from across the gray water and the land of Eirinn. "On whose land do I tread, sir, and why are ye so forlorn? Apart, of course from the chains which bind ye?"

Ewan bowed low and said, "Ye tread on the border of Queen Barabel's lands. Cross the stream and ye'll be trespassing. Barabel willna be taking kindly to strangers, that is, unless she can use ye to her advantage. As for me, I have been captive here for a verra lang time, and am about to be tithed."

"I'm sorry, friend. I, too, am about to be tithed, leastways in a matter of speakin'."

Ewan's surprise enabled him to forget his own suffering for the moment. "Sir, I'm not understanding ye. How can a prince be tithed?"

"As I said, only in a matter of speakin'," he paused, "I'm to be wed."

"Should that no be cause for celebration?"

"Tis causin' me attacks of the psyche that I know I cannot dispel until I have seen her with me own eyes."

"Ye mean to say that ye have not met the lass?" Ewan said, the shock apparent in his voice.

The prince shook his handsome head. "'Tis just so. 'Tis a long and complicated tale. Do you know the Princess Rionnag?"

"Only by name. She is Barabel's niece and the two families have been estranged for longer than I have been captive here. I do ken that ye have landed miles from the kingdom of King Niall, yer betrothed's home."

"Could ye escort me there...?" asked the prince kindly.

"I am Ewan, Sire, and would if I could, but I am held to this land and can no leave. But I will see you safely to the west border where ye will find yer way easily."

"When is your tithing, Ewan?"

"Barabel has gone and made a deal with a monster, a fachan, who will have me upon delivery of a certain item."

"And what item is worth the life of a captive servant?" Prince Kieran asked.

"I dinna ken, nor care, as long as it is after *Samhain*," Ewan said passionately.

"And may I ask what *Samhain* holds in store for ye?"

Ewan's gaze turned inward and he said in a whisper, "Love, Sire. Love waits for me on *Samhain*."

"Then I envy ye, sir, for it would be worth paying a tithe to the Underworld if I could be blessed with what ye have."

"Sire, I have heard tell of Princess Rionnag's beauty and intelligence. I have no seen her, being a captive of her enemy, but..." Ewan stopped suddenly, struck by a memory.

"Ye were sayin'?" The Prince then turned to see his new friend with an angry look on his rugged face. "Ewan, me friend, what is troublin' ye?"

Ewan was shaking his head slowly, and thinking aloud he said, "She said 'I will a get a prin..' and then she stopped so quickly. Was she about to say princess? I wouldna be doubting it." He looked up to see the Irish Prince staring at him.

Ewan explained, "I think ye'll no find what yer seekin' yonder. I think the lassie's gone and Barabel has sent her horrors to bring her back. I dinna ken what trick she has up her filthy sleeve, but I'll be thinkin' it has all to do with ye."

Taken aback, the prince sat on the bank of the river to contemplate this new information. Ewan sat on the opposite bank and looked the young lad squarely in the eye. The lad could see the intelligence in those mortal eyes and listened carefully as Ewan surmised what he could.

"Barabel has promised me to a monster in exchange for somethin' she wants. I've been here long enough to ken the queen needs my service and guidance and would only do such a thing for somethin' she wants desperately. Aye, she is a teerible one. All her life she's been wantin' what her sister, yer Queen Catriona has, and this pendin' marriage between ye and Princess Rionnag has caused her no end of torment."

"How do you know this?" the prince asked.

"I am her counsel, Sire, have been o'er long, and she has confided in me on occasion. My suspicion is that she wants to prevent this marriage from takin' place."

"But why? What will its prevention get her?"

"I dinna ken, but why else would she be so rash as to use a beast. She's used bogies in the past to do her biddin', but never to my knowledge, a fachan. Even *she* fears them. That much I ken."

"But if she's sent a fachan, a beast, to the Seelie Court, wouldn't King Niall realize it, on his own land and all?"

"Ye yerself ken that fachans are deceptive shape-shifters. The King might no ken if he was face-to-face with one. And I'm recallin' somethin' more; whispers throughout the forest. I dinna pay much attention to the whisperins, but noo I think on it, somethin' about a lassie running awa'. It could be the Princess Rionnag, with the same misgivins as yerself."

"If this is true, it would explain me dreams, or nightmares, rather."

"What dreams would these be, Sire?"

"Horrible ones where me bride becomes a monster and I wake up screamin'."

"Aye Laddie, some think on marriage in that way, but if I could be with my love, I'd stay with her 'til my dyin' day. I think yer afraid, never havin' seen her, and I'll not be blamin' ye. 'Tisn't just. Some of these fey rules and laws, I dinna understand," Ewan said, shaking his head.

"Ewan, would ye lead me to King Niall's lands? I want to find out what has happened to me bride."

154

"I will indeed, Sire."

The two walked along the river, one on one bank, the other across. When they reached the border of King Niall's kingdom, Ewan put up his hand in farewell.

"I canna escort ye farther, but I wish ye all the luck. If I can be of service to ye, ye can find me by beatin' three times on the stump over yonder. I will hear it and come."

"Thank ye, Ewan. I will try to learn what the truth is and perhaps ye shall not be tithed after all. Maybe we can foil yon queen in her treachery," Prince Kieran said, with a gracious bow.

"Sire, I will also try and find what information I can, for if my suspicions are true, it's possible we can put a stop to a great injustice." Ewan reached his arm across the river and Prince Kieran reached out to grab it. The two held fast for several moments and then the prince shifted to his stag form and cantered into the forest.

Ewan watched him go, realizing that he might yet be saved. *Samhain* was coming fast, and he couldn't help but hold on to a tiny sliver of hope in his heart as he made his way to his unhappy dwelling.

Chapter 23

One hour until the plane would touchdown on the soil that was Maggie's true home, though she'd never voice that thought. She closed her eyes and remembered the last time she had been in Scotland, one year before.

He had told her, as he had every time, not to return. To stay away. She knew he hadn't really meant it, that he only wanted her to get on with her life. But she couldn't. The pull was too strong. Lifetimes too strong.

As she thought about it this time, she knew what he had said held truth in it. She *was* pining for a ghost, wasting any chance of real happiness, each year of her life living for one moment in time that ended far too quickly. But the thought of never seeing him again was insupportable, impossible! She had known that the very moment she had met him. The memories of lifetimes together were too strong. She had been meant to find him again. And he had known her at once. No, she had to find a way to rescue him. Life was becoming unbearable. She could barely pretend anymore, and Fiona was feeling the effect of it.

She put that unhappy thought aside and thought about what the next day would bring; her journey would take all day, first the bus ride, then the walk through forests, sheep fields, up steep hills, until she got to Glen Etive in the shadow of Buachaille Etive Mor Mountain. Then she'd have to find the spot, the white spot on the worn rock, undoubtedly lichen covered since last year, in the middle of a sheep pasture. It had been well worn over time and usually took a few hours to find, especially at this time of year, with the leaves down and covering it, but Maggie knew what she sought. Finding it was the least of her worries. What concerned her was whom she'd be meeting there. Would he be there? Would he be waiting? After her disturbing dreams and visions, she was afraid something terrible had happened to him that would prevent their meeting. She didn't think she could stand that.

The landing was smooth. While everyone rushed to get out of the plane, frantically grabbing at the overhead storage, Maggie kept still. The old lady next to her who had slept the entire trip was as anxious to leave as everyone and although their row was past the wing and the line was long with people standing and shoving each other, she had to get into the thick of it. "Excuse me, dearie. They'll be waitin' for me at the gate. Is there no one waitin' for ye at the gate, dearie?" she asked pushing by Maggie, a touch of curiosity in her voice.

"No, I'm on my own. I'm meeting someone later." It was the first time Maggie had said that to anyone. It felt strange, yet comforting in its truth.

"Have a verra nice trip, then," the old woman said as she hurried down the aisle.

Maggie sat quietly until the throng emptied. There was

no need to hurry. Tomorrow would come soon enough. She took a deep breath and got up. Her small, leather pack was in the open storage unit over her head and she reached up to get it. She threw it over her shoulders and made her way out of the plane.

She knew the routine. The bus to Etiveside would leave in less than an hour. She was exhausted, but just being here would be enough to keep her awake. She went to the ladies' room and splashed water on her face, then stopped at a teashop in the airport for a cup and a sandwich. She purchased her bus ticket, changed money before calling home to let them know she'd arrived safely. They knew the drill; she'd call collect and ask for Amanda (her middle name) and they'd say Amanda wasn't home, but then they'd know she was safe. She knew how Fiona worried. She'd call for real when she got to Agnes'. She wanted to hear her daughter's voice once more before she went to where there were no telephones.

The bus arrived on schedule and she took a window seat near the back. An older man got on and sat up front. Several women with bulging shopping bags got on as well. The bus pulled out of the terminal and Maggie sat back and tried to relax. The ride would take about five hours. They wouldn't arrive until nearly dark. She hoped Agnes, the gracious proprietor of the bed and breakfast, would be waiting. She gazed out the window as cityscape turned to farmland, and hills became dotted with sheep. She fell asleep as the bus rumbled along, heading far north of Glasgow.

When she arrived in the village, she and two others were the only ones left on board. Dusk had fallen. Maggie picked up her bag and got off the bus. The two older ladies who had gotten off with her, scurried away into the fading twilight, leaving Maggie alone. She hoisted her pack onto her shoulders and began the mile walk to her favorite bed and breakfast in the world, The Gray Goose.

The road was getting dark, the moon hidden behind clouds. Though familiar with the road, she stopped and removed a flashlight from her pack before going on. The nearly full moon pulled in and out of the cloudy haze, spreading light and casting shadows, retreating again behind its gauzy cover. She felt an unusual stir of apprehension. Maggie had never felt nervous walking this road, but tonight she found herself hurrying, turning several times to see if anyone was behind her in the settling dark.

Happily the lights were on at the Gray Goose and Maggie heaved a great sigh of relief as she approached. The flowered curtains moved as someone peered out. Then the door opened, and the owner, a cheerful, older woman with lively blue eyes and flaming red hair greeted Maggie at the door.

"Maggie, it's grand tae see ye again! Sorry it's only the one night though. Why did ye no call me when ye arrived at the station?"

"I didn't want to trouble you. It's great to be back, Agnes. Seems like ages. I'm really glad you weren't full up."

"Never for ye, Maggie. Breakfast tomorrow bright and early?"

Maggie nodded. "As long as it's no trouble."

"Homemade scones with my special jam and that tea yer so fond of. I'll have oatmeal and kippers as well," she twinkled. "Come, I'll show ye tae yer room, although ye ken it well. Ye can get settled, then come have a cup o' tea wi' me." She grabbed Maggie's pack off her back, threw it over her own shoulder and marched up the stairs, Maggie smiling as she followed.

The room was as she remembered it: an antique four-poster bed, with a crocheted canopy hanging from the four sides and lovely landscapes on the walls. Agnes pulled down the bedspread, hit the pillows with a bit more force than fluff and walked out of the room. "I'll be in the kitchen, waitin'," she said.

"Thanks, Agnes, be down in a bit," Maggie said, shutting the door. She sat on the bed and faced the large gilt mirror, looking at herself for a few moments. She pulled a brush out of her pack, unwound her braids, and began to brush her hair. She watched as it became staticky and flew around her face. That was how she had looked when they first met. She had been wild that night, dancing in the moonlight to the whistles and drums. She had plucked a wild rose, one of the few remaining, and stuck it in her hair. It was then he had appeared from the shadows. She had been startled but not frightened. She had thought he was one of the local men who hid in the bushes to watch the women dance in the moonlight on *Samhain,* Halloween. But he wasn't that, definitely not. She rubbed the pendant absentmindedly. "Soon enough," she told herself. "You'll see him again soon enough."

Agnes was sitting in an old rocking chair by the fireplace in the kitchen, a merry blaze burning. She gestured for Maggie to sit on the big easy chair near the hearth. Maggie loved this kitchen almost as much as her own. It was large, and served as sitting room as well. Maggie sat with a grunt and leaned her head back.

"Tired, love?" Agnes asked.

"Exhausted actually, but mostly happy to be here." She smiled at her hostess who took off the tea cozy from the large, slightly chipped pot and began to pour. "Ye ken, I'd be more than happy tae drive ye tae yer retreat. I wouldna mind gettin' oot a bit."

"Thanks, Agnes, but you know me, the inveterate hiker. I'll be back at the end of the week, and actually, I was hoping to spend another night then," Maggie said, deftly changing the subject.

"Tae be sure, Maggie. This time of year we're a bit slow. Ye seem tae have Halloween all tae yerself. Funny, too, I often wonder where all the other people stay who go tae the retreat with ye," she said and surreptitiously winked at Maggie, who caught her breath slightly, the color rising on her cheeks.

"I couldn't tell you. They probably just start out camping. I like to freshen up a bit first. And, anyway, Agnes, I'd miss those breakfasts of yours!"

"Ah, Maggie, a girl after *ma oon* heart. Here, have a scone. I made the jam myself." She proffered the plate.

The two chatted amiably by the fire for a while longer, but Maggie kept yawning, and Agnes, who loved a cup and a chat, finally took the hint and said, "Ye look fair fashed, love, get ye off tae bed." She stood up, took Maggie by the arm, and ushered her from the room.

Maggie made her way upstairs, feeling pleasantly drowsy and relaxed. She got to her room, stripped off her clothes, got into the high cozy bed, and was asleep in moments.

She woke from a deep and dreamless slumber. The sun was peeking weakly through the curtains. She looked at the small clock on the bedside table. 5:00 a.m. Not quite time to get up, but at least she had slept. Sometimes her jet lag was so bad it took a few days to get straightened out. This time her flight and bus ride had been perfectly coordinated and she was able to adjust immediately. Not that any of it would matter soon, she told herself. Time being what it was where she was going.

She smiled and hugged herself.

Chapter 24

"What!" Fiona whispered loudly enough to bring the faerie out of her daze.

Slowly Rionnag turned to Fiona who was waiting for an explanation.

"Fiona, I told ye yer mither had a big secret."

"What are you talking about?" Fiona wanted to know, but she knew she had better let Rionnag tell whatever she needed to tell in her own time.

"Fiona, the words on this stone are ancient, not even words really. They say 'Release me.' Do ye understand?"

Fiona shook her head.

"Do ye no ken the tale of Tamlin and Janet?"

Fiona nodded her head quietly. Her mother used to tell her that story when she was little. She remembered curling up in her mother's lap as Maggie told her the famous legend, not bothering with any book. She heard her mother's voice in her head, "...*she picked the wild rose and Tamlin appeared.*

The Faerie Queen had captured him and only his true love could rescue him, but she was long since dead. So brave Janet offered to be his love and risked her life to save his...she donned a green cloak and filled her pockets with hypericum and faerie flowers and rescued poor Tamlin..."

Rionnag continued, "Then ye'll remember that Tamlin was a human captive of a great and teerible faerie queen. Before the Queen made him her sacrifice to Hell, he carved this symbol on the trunk of a great Rowan tree. He was released by Janet, a human girl, but the carving remains to this day. It has become a symbol of the captive, yearning to be free. *Now* do ye understand?"

No, she didn't understand. She didn't want to understand. She covered her eyes. What did this mean? Had her mother been lying to her all this time? Lying to everyone? No, she didn't want to understand. She turned away from Rionnag and walked quickly in the direction of the door, but stumbled into Maggie's partially open dresser drawer, bruising her shin. She grabbed her leg, cursed, and unceremoniously flung herself onto her mother's bed. Rionnag flew over to her. "Fiona, are ye hurt? Fiona?"

Fiona sat up, rubbing her shin. "I - I don't know what to think. What does it mean?" She looked down at the open drawer and climbed off the bed to close it before it did damage to someone else. She tried to push it closed, but something was in the way. She felt around until her fingers touched what Maggie had hidden under her socks.

Removing the large antique volume, she placed it on the bed. She heard another gasp from Rionnag and spun around to face the faerie whose face had gone ashen.

"What now?" Fiona said, and then looked more closely at the book.

It was leather bound and obviously very old. The embossed lettering on the cover was in a language Fiona did not recognize. She gently flipped through the pages and it opened readily to a well-worn page. Rionnag was standing lightly upon her shoulder, whispering in the old tongue. Fiona ran her hands over the page, as if it were Braille and she could make out its meaning by touch.

"What does it mean?" she whispered.

Rionnag fluttered down and stood at the foot of the impressive tome. Her head moved from side to side. Fiona realized she was shaking it.

"Rionnag, what is it? Please tell me."

"Och, Fiona, this is a spell. It brings one to the other side. How did yer mither get this book?"

"I don't know," Fiona said, staring at the page. "The store she owns sells books." Even as she spoke, she knew how feeble it sounded.

"Nay, this book is from the other side. In hands that have never touched that side, it would crumble to dust. "

"So, what does that mean? I've never been there and the book is still here," she said, picking it up, page still open.

"Ye are yer mither's child. Perhaps that's why ye see me. I dinna ken."

"This is too much. What does it all mean?"

"Fiona, I think ye ken."

"You think she's meeting someone. Like, on the 'other side'. That's what you think, isn't it?"

"Aye, that's what I think."

"Oh, my God," Fiona muttered, balling her hands into tight fists. Her respiration increased until she was almost hyperventilating.

Had her mother been lying to her forever? Was there any yoga retreat at all? Maybe it was just a front. But why? Who could her mother possibly be meeting? Fiona knew full well her mother believed in all these faerie things she herself had just discovered were true and not simple bedtime stories. Did Gram know, too? Aunt Kat? They always seemed to make excuses for her mother, defended her. "...Oh, your mom really needs these retreats..." "...She works so hard, she needs a bit of R and R..." Was this why her mother was always so distant?

Fiona began remembering things: the faraway look in her mother's eyes, the sadness. The music that could always bring on tears that her mother couldn't hide. The fierce telling of the old Scottish story. Maggie, never relaxing or playing, busy always. Was she trying to keep her mind off something or someone?

"Why?" she said aloud. Rionnag lifted, fluttered around to face her and looked her straight in the eyes.

"Fiona, perhaps yer mither hasna found the right time to tell ye her secret. Perhaps it's not hers to tell."

"Then whose is it? Tell me that! Why does she have to hide her life from me? I'm her daughter!" Fiona began to cry tears she'd kept bottled up for years, accumulating pain like her incomplete set of ring stones. They came from a place so dark and deep within her, she had to bury her face in her mother's pillow to keep from screaming. She smelled her mother's sweet floral scent in the pillows, and this made her wail even harder.

"I hate her! What could be more important than me, her own kid? Obviously something is! Or *someone*! I hate her! Oh God, I hate her...!" She flailed her legs on the bed and pounded her fists into the mattress.

At that moment, Gram hurried into the room, having heard the commotion from downstairs. She stood silently watching her teenage granddaughter having a full-blown tantrum, her condition clearly too tender to touch without stinging. Rionnag gave her a helpless look.

Together they waited for Fiona's storm of pressurized emotion to pass and when it did, Gram softly rubbed her back. She whispered words of comfort, until eventually Fiona's breath caught in small sobs and she wiped her eyes with her sleeve and looked at Gram. She gestured to the book with her head.

Gram looked over to it. "I don't understand," she said. "What is it?"

Rionnag answered softly, "It's a book from my world, and this page is open to a spell that brings one to the other side."

"Oh my," Gram whispered as comprehension set in.

"Y.. you d..didn't know?" Fiona said between frantic gulps of air.

"No, darling, of course not. Your mother keeps things from me, too. I know it hurts."

"B...but I'm her daughter. Why does she leave me and lie about it?"

"I can't answer that. We'll have to talk to her about it when she comes home," Gram suggested wisely.

"Aye, ye must do it, now that ye ken, it'd be best to ken the lot," Rionnag said.

"Rionnag, tell Gram about the stone," Fiona said with a sniffle.

Rionnag flitted to Maggie's altar where the stone sat like a fetish and quickly recounted the story of Tamlin and Janet, which Gram knew well. "I never knew the part about the carving in the Rowan though. I always thought it was just a fairy tale. I'd always hoped..."

"Nay, true it is. There are teerible faeries who take humans, lure them with beauty and promises of gold and eternal life, then use them to pay their tithe to Hell."

"What's a tithe, again?" Fiona asked, regaining her composure. She knew she'd heard the word in some faerie story or another, but she couldn't remember the meaning.

"It's a payment. Like a debt that you have to pay.

Actually, more like a sacrifice." Fiona grimaced. Gram turned back to Rionnag. "So you think whomever my daughter is visiting is a captive of a faerie queen?" Gram continued.

"It seems to be so. I canna think why else she would have the stone. It must have been given to her, unless she found it, but I dinna think that."

"So my mother is visiting a faerie captive? Is that what's happening here?" Fiona said slightly hysterically. "Are we all losing it?"

"Yoohoo! Where is everybody?" Aunt Kat's singing voice snapped them out of their discussion. Fiona looked to her grandmother who shrugged her shoulders and rolled her eyes.

"We're up here, dear. Be right down," Gram called. They could hear Kat's light step on the stairs before Gram had a chance to move.

Fiona looked panic-stricken while Rionnag flew behind the curtain. Before anyone could say a word Aunt Kat was in the doorway.

"What are you doing in here? What's wrong, Fi?" she asked, seeing Fiona's tear-streaked face.

Fiona shook her head and Gram took Kat's arm, casually turned her out of the room and escorted her back down the stairs. Rionnag reappeared from behind the curtains and rejoined Fiona.

"Fiona, I ken this has come as a shock to ye. Some secrets are to keep and some are to give away. Perhaps yer mither wasna ready to give hers away."

Fiona took one last sniff, composed herself and said quietly, "I guess not. I'm sorry I acted like such a baby."

"Nay, Fiona, there's no need for apologies. Secrets can be harmful. Keeping my future husband a secret until the day I wed has been no end of trouble for me and I ken there's more to come," Rionnag said, her tone becoming prophetic.

"Aye," she added more quietly, "there's definitely more trouble comin'... for us both."

The two exchanged glances meaningful with apprehension.

Chapter 25

King Niall and Queen Catriona were extremely vexed. Their beloved daughter could be anywhere in Feydom, and Mòr and her silly helper, Jinty were Oberon knew where! Holding tightly to his queen's hand, he touched the Tanzanite stone in the center of his crown and called a meeting of his knights. The mysterious stone had been passed down through the centuries, its power strong in the right hands. His message was heeded well, for immediately his knights flew or rode in from their posts throughout Faerie. Each was well armed and ready at a moment's notice to obey his king's every command. King Niall glanced at his wife who nodded in encouragement and he shifted into his Stag form, his most imposing and powerful form. He then swore his troops to secrecy with an oath so powerful that anyone who dared break it would disintegrate into the mist until he was not even a memory. In the main, his soldiers were loyal and good, but long life had taught him that treachery lurked behind every stump, and with their cherished Rionnag's life in the balance he would take no chances.

Now standing imperiously before his troops, he pawed the ground with one, sharp hoof. An impressive snort issued from his flaring Stag nostrils. "Find my daughter. Ye'll all be well rewarded for her safe return. Remember, this is no contest, but it is a race. Do not let Barabel's folk see wing nor tail of any of ye. Faerie is depending on all of ye and..." he paused to let them know the force of his feelings, "So am I!"

The soldiers bowed low before their king, readied their weapons and took off. Those with horses mounted their steeds, and with a single click of their tongues, departed. Those who flew climbed up into the air and away as the king reared up on his hind legs, pawing the air in a gesture of goodwill and Godspeed.

After they were gone the king returned to faerie form, jeweled crown glistening on his jet hair, the horns receding. He took the crown off his head and again touched a finger to the violet-blue stone that dominated the pattern. Tanzanite. The stone had called his troops to him that day, but he had not yet tried to call his daughter to him. He stood beside his beloved queen, placing her hands gently on the stone, his atop hers, and said the words of power that made the stone spark and glow fiercely. For the second time that day, he spoke into the stone. This time though, he uttered words of endearment for his sweet child, calling her to him, to come home. He'd see she was happy, see she remained near him. There'd be no mention of her responsibility to their world, no, not until she was safely in his arms once more.

"Rionnag ban, my daughter, my love, come home to us. Our hearts are fair breaking from ye being gone. We promise ye, no harm will come to ye. We stake our lives on that promise. Come home, child, we'll make it right." And then he spoke shakily, the way he had when she was a babe, "Yer in my bones, my darlin', dinna ye ken that?" He spoke with such honesty that tears sprang from his cobalt eyes. He turned from his wife, not wanting her to see him cry; she then took her free hand and placed it under his chin, turning his face towards her, and kissed his tears away. Placing the crown on his head once more, he whispered an ancient prayer to the gods and goddesses of Faerie, kissed his wife soundly on the mouth and went in search of his precious daughter.

Queen Catriona stood silently watching her husband go. The love she felt for him had not ebbed since the day they met. Nay, it had grown. She shook her head sadly knowing that their precious daughter had seen their love all her life, and the fact that the child would have to marry someone she had never met was, if not unfair, at least the justifiable reason for her defiance. How could the queen blame her daughter? Her own marriage had been a love match. In truth and custom, her sister, Barabel should have been the one to marry Niall. The thought turned her stomach.

Nay, the girl was not to blame, but the queen regretted not better preparing Rionnag for this monumental event that could very well be the turning point for all of Faerie. She had waited until the birthday of her marriageable year, not wanting to spoil the child's young life with such a burden. But this marriage was so important and more so even now than when it had been arranged so long before. Faerie had been in a better state of affairs then, but presently, since the humans started erecting their steel structures, poisoning the water and destroying the land, it seemed the fate of Faerie was doomed. So many faeries were becoming ill, some of them merely fading into the mist. And so many shadows, where no shadows should be.

"Oh, my headstrong daughter, come home to us!" She watched her husband as he fled off in search of their daughter and sent a silent prayer on the wind after him.

Chapter 26

"Ma, what's going on with Fiona?" Kat asked with concern as her mother steered her into the kitchen.

"It's a bit complicated. I need to talk with Fiona, before I discuss it with you."

Kat's eyebrows went up.

"Let me go up and talk with her. It looks like you've got things to do," Gram said noticing the shopping bags on the table.

"Yes, I do, actually. See this?" she said showing her mother the bags filled with what looked like junk food. "A whole week of Maggie-free menus!" she said, smiling broadly.

"Are you planning on eating all this candy or giving some of it out to the kids who trick-or-treat for it?" Gram asked, rummaging through the groceries and pulling out plastic bags filled with chocolate, caramels, and licorice.

"I'll save *a little* for them…"

"For who?" Fiona was standing in the kitchen door smiling slightly at what she had overheard. She had composed herself and come down to get a snack for herself and Rionnag.

"Whom," Gram corrected.

"Never mind that. What's up with you, Fi?" Kat asked, concerned.

She looked over at her grandmother who said, "If you want to share your secret with your aunt, that's entirely up to you. I think it would be a good idea, myself."

"Fi, you can trust me. I hope you know that!"

"I know I can, Aunt Kat. It's just that it's been kind of a weird morning. I need some time to think about it. Okay?"

"Of course. Anyway, do you want some candy?" she offered a bag of chocolate bars.

Fiona helped herself to a few candies and went back upstairs.

Kat looked at her mother. "She's such a good kid; I hope whatever's going on isn't too serious."

"Oh, it's serious, all right," Gram said.

"Rionnag, what's wrong? Has something happened?" Fiona asked, bearing chocolates and a snack for her wee friend. Rionnag was sitting on her tiny bed, hands covering her eyes. Her petite shoulders shook slightly and her head rocked back and forth. She looked up at her human friend crouched down to face her. Her eyes were brimming over with tears and their unusual violet color was laced with cobalt, making them even more beautiful, if that were possible.

"While ye were getting me food, I heard my faither's voice. It was so loud in my head. He's only called me that way once, when I was a wee bairn and lost in the wood. He talked to me until I found my way back. He's calling me home. I dinna want to go but I ken he's suffering for me. Oh..." She put her head down and cried some more.

Fiona sat on the floor, helpless, while the faerie wept. With her tears came the smell of lavender, permeating the air. Fiona looked carefully at the diminutive tears spilling down Rionnag's face and realized with awe that they were lavender in color as well. She felt a little guilty about her rather clinical interest in poor Rionnag's tears, but she couldn't help it. Everything about the faerie amazed her.

She drew herself up and, for the first time she could remember, felt a surge of determination and courage. She had no idea from where it had come, but she was beginning to realize that more was possible than she'd ever believed. The words were out of her mouth before she knew what she was going to say.

"Rionnag, listen to me. You said the faerie world depends on your marriage to this prince, right? And it seems ours does too, pretty much. You know your father loves you, right? Well, I don't believe he'd make you do something you'd hate. Let's make a ring like you said, and go through. We can talk to your father together." Fiona finished her speech, surprised at herself. Who was she to know how to deal with fathers? What made her think that anything she could say would do anything to help her tiny friend? Yet the words seemed to come from deep inside and they pushed themselves out.

The faerie straightened regally and said, "Ye may be right. I ken I must go back and I dinna want to hurt my parents...." she hesitated, then continued, "Fiona, before my faither called to me, I was thinking that I need to meet yer mither, especially since we've found the stone and spell book. I need to ken why she has these things, and if our suspicions are true and she's meeting a captive, then perhaps my faither can help her. We will wait to leave until I've met yer mither, if it's all the same to ye."

"I think you're right." She thought a moment and added, "Rionnag, do you think we can tell my aunt about all this? She's really great and she deserves to know about my mom. What do you think, would you like to meet her?"

"I think yer right about her having a right to ken about her own sister, and if she's anything like ye and yer gram, I'd be honored."

"Oh, thank you Ri!" said Fiona. The faerie looked surprised at the nickname, but not displeased.

Fiona ran down the stairs, her spirit feeling lighter than at any time since this incident had begun. The two were sitting at the worn kitchen table, engrossed in what appeared to be a serious conversation, wearing identical frowns.

"What's wrong?"

Aunt Kat looked up and forced a smile for her niece. "There was another offer on this place."

"When was that?"

"They just called with it. The nerve of those people!"

"How much this time?"

"You don't need to know that," Gram said emphatically.

"We can't sell this place! Don't they know what happens when people keep building and destroying the planet!" Fiona said passionately.

"Some people don't care, Fiona. That's just the way it is," Aunt Kat said sadly.

"Some people are idiots and should be ashamed of themselves. As if they don't know what they're doing. Give me a break," she retorted.

"I never said they didn't know; I said they didn't care. There's a big difference."

Gram patted a chair for Fiona to sit and said, "Fiona, don't worry, we're here to stay. Now, did you want to talk about something?"

Fiona sighed. Her grandmother could be so blunt.

Kat waited patiently, her face a question mark. Fiona turned to her, and said, "Aunt Kat, there's something I need to tell you about Mom."

"Oh?"

"Could you come upstairs, please?"

"Sure, sweetie," she said, throwing a glance at her mother.

"You too, Gram," Fiona added, noting the exchange.

Kat and Gram looked at each other. Gram shrugged. It was, after all, Fiona's decision.

Together they went upstairs and into Fiona's room. Kat sat on the bed and waited for Fiona to speak. Fiona went to the window and found something there. She nodded and smiled at whatever was there and then picked it up and held it gently.

She returned to her aunt who was watching intently. Kat moved over to let Fiona sit on the bed beside her, and watched as her niece slowly opened her fingers.

"Can you see it? Can you?" Fiona looked at her aunt, eyes wide.

"Fi, what's goin' on? You're acting strange," Kat said, thinking her niece might be going over the edge.

"Just look! Do you see anything?"

"Yes, of course. Where did you get a dragonfly at this time of year?"

"Is that what you're seeing?"

"It looks like a dragonfly to me."

Suddenly it seemed as though the dragonfly was singing.

"I don't think she's seeing you as you are," Fiona

seemed to be answering the singing.

"I agree," said Gram.

"Are you talking to it?" Kat asked them in astonishment. They nodded simultaneously.

"Aunt Kat. I'm gonna tell you something that may flip you out."

"I think I'm starting to already."

"I'm not sure how to explain this. I'm not sure exactly what you're seeing, but whatever it is, it isn't a dragonfly." She paused, trying to think how best to continue.

"I kind of figured that one out. So what exactly am I supposed to be seeing? It looks a lot like a dragonfly to me!" She bent closer to the creature in Fiona's hand. "It's weird, it keeps changing in front of my eyes. I'm not sure what it is! C'mon, Fiona, what's going on? Is this supposed to be a joke?"

The 'dragonfly' started 'singing' again, this time louder and more adamantly.

Gram shrugged her shoulders at the thing, and said, "I was sure she'd be able to see you; she was always such an open child."

"Mother! Would somebody please tell me what's going on!" Kat was practically screaming.

Gram sat down on the bed beside her and said calmly, "Katherine, this is hard to accept, I know; even I don't understand it for sure, but this creature you think is a common dragonfly is, in reality, a faerie. A real, honest to goodness faerie, the kind out of legends and faerie tales. I don't know why you see her as a dragonfly." Gram looked at the faerie for information. The singing started up again. Gram seemed to understand the sounds issuing from the thing and translated for her bewildered daughter. "You need to look with your inner eye, your third eye if you will." Kat looked at Gram oddly. Were her mother and her niece crazy?

"I think I know what to do!" Fiona said excitedly. "Aunt Kat, remember that book with the 3-D pictures I have, the one with the dolphins and the puppies hidden in all that scribble?"

"I gave it to you," Kat said slowly.

"Well, you know how the only way to see the pictures is to kind of un-focus your eyes, then you can see the hidden picture? We've found the hidden pictures loads of times!" Fiona was practically begging her to understand.

"Yeah, I know."

"Do the same thing when you look at the thing in my hand. Please!"

"I'll do it, Fiona, but you're scaring me. And what does this have to do with Maggie, anyway?" Kat asked in a worried tone that was very unlike her.

"You'll find out. Just try."

Kat took a step back and then took a good look at the 'dragonfly' on Fiona's outstretched hand, attempting to un-focus her gaze. It was very difficult to do. She kept seeing double, and shook her head.

"Relax," Gram said comfortingly to her.

Kat took a few deep breaths; aware Fiona was watching her intently as she tried to see what they wanted her to see. What everybody but she could see! The 'dragonfly' remained motionless on Fiona's palm. Kat had never seen anything like it. She'd caught dragonflies as a child, but they'd only lighted on her hand for a split second. She shook her head again, forcing herself to remember that what she was looking at wasn't an insect at all; it was a faerie.

Yeah, right, the sensible schoolteacher part of her argued.

But what if...the other part of her that still believed, seemed to argue back.

Once more she nudged her mind into that place of dreams where what ifs were real, and where her sister, who she knew wasn't crazy, dwelt most of the time. What would a faerie look like? Wings, curls, a daisy crown? She had seen pictures of faeries all her life in Maggie's room as well as in Fiona's. She looked at the creature again and tried to relax and look with a more discerning gaze. She stared so long she began to get sleepy. Her eyes half-closed; everything blurred, and that was when it happened. One moment there was a very strange dragonfly sitting on Fi's palm, the next there was a beautiful, tiny winged woman. She was afraid to look at it. Afraid to look away. She was even afraid to blink. Had to blink, wouldn't blink. Eventually she couldn't stop herself and for a split second the faerie disappeared entirely. It reappeared when she opened her eyes and this time, she let herself focus naturally. The faerie was still there.

Kat looked from her niece to her mother, who smiled as if to congratulate her for her accomplishment, for it was obvious to Kat that they fully realized what she had done. She smiled back and looked at the faerie again. The faerie looked at her and smiled, but her smile was sad. Kat could barely take in what she was seeing, and she found herself breathing hard.

Gram took her hand and rubbed it gently. "Take it easy, love. She's really quite wonderful, don't you think?" Kat nodded, unable to answer, continuing to stare at the exquisite being nestled into her niece's palm.

Fiona, wanting to put her aunt at ease, smiled and said with reverence, "Aunt Kat, this is Princess Rionnag, Rionnag, my Aunt Katherine."

"Uh, how uh d-do you do?" Kat stammered.

"Fair, truth to tell, but it's grand to meet ye," Rionnag said, her casual tone making Kat stare openmouthed.

"You, um, talk," she said in disbelief.

"Aye that I do. I'm glad ye can hear as well as see me," Rionnag said, giving a small curtsy.

"Fiona? Mom?" was all Kat could manage.

"Aunt Kat, I've been wanting to tell you, but it wasn't the right time 'til now. I mean, how could I tell you and not Mom?"

"So Maggie doesn't know?" she asked seriously.

"No!"

"Fiona, do ye no think ye need to tell yer auntie the whole tale?" Rionnag interrupted.

"Oh, yeah," Fiona said. "C'mon," she said, taking Kat's arms and wheeling her out of the room and down the hall to Maggie's room. Fiona turned to her and said, "You've seen this much. You may as well know it all."

Gram opened the door to Maggie's room, walked directly over to Maggie's altar and plucked the stone from its place. Turning back toward them, she said, "Let's go down to the kitchen. I could use a nice hot cup of tea."

"Aye, that I could as weel," Rionnag agreed, still perched on Fiona's palm.

Gram left Maggie's room and shut the door, leaving it to its privacy, if not its secrets, and the four went downstairs. Gram put the kettle on and stoked up the fire in the stove to get the chill out of the kitchen, and out of all of them. Fiona and Aunt Kat sat at the table; Rionnag sat cross-legged on a cloth placemat on the middle of the table facing them.

"This is unreal," Aunt Kat said, watching Rionnag.

"Yeah, but it's real, too," Fiona agreed.

"What does all this have to do with Maggie?"

Gram cleared her throat, put the tea on the table and poured everyone a cup, using one of her china thimbles for Rionnag. She was about to begin, but something about the way the faerie looked at her made her close her mouth

181

and wait for Fiona to tell it. It was *her* story after all. When each of them was settled down with her warm cup, Fiona dropped the bombshell.

"Aunt Kat, Mom isn't on a yoga retreat." She had been wondering if her mother had told her secret to her younger sister and watched her aunt carefully for any sign of knowledge. Her aunt looked at her in genuine disbelief, so Fiona was reassured she didn't know.

"Um, if Maggie isn't on any yoga retreat, then what exactly has she been doing for the past fifteen years?" Kat looked at her mother for answers, who nodded her head in Fiona's direction, keeping unusually quiet.

"Well, that's where Rionnag comes in. Gram..." Fiona nodded to her grandmother who unglued her hands from her chin and took something out of her pocket. She placed the stone on the kitchen table. The symbols looked strangely out of place in the cozy kitchen. Kat wanted to touch the rock but for some reason, didn't dare.

"What is it?" she whispered.

Rionnag answered, retelling the story of Tamlin and Janet, while Kat's eyes grew wider and her mouth crept open until she had an almost comical appearance. But no one was laughing.

"So Maggie..." She let her words slide to a halt, astounded at what she was thinking.

Gram decided she'd been quiet long enough and said, "That's right, we think she's visiting someone on the other side," emphasizing *other side* as if she'd been using it all her life. "We found a book of magic spells, hidden in her dresser drawer."

"Oh, my God," was Kat's only response.

By the time the tale was told, their tea was cold and Rionnag was flitting restlessly around the kitchen. Gram and Fi looked like bookends, each with her head propped on

182

bent elbows watching the young woman who barely could believe what she had heard. They stared at the stone for some time until Rionnag brought them out of their reverie.

"Fiona, I've just recalled something. This stone makes twelve."

Fiona looked at her friend in comprehension, absorbing the full impact of the faerie's words.

Chapter 27

Maggie was full of nervous excitement as she threw on a sweater and jeans, towel-dried her hair, stuffed everything back into her rucksack, and headed down the narrow stairs. She knew Agnes was up; she had heard her humming and could smell the oats cooking on the stove.

"Good morning, Agnes," she said as she entered the cozy kitchen.

"And a verra good mornin' tae ye, dearie," Agnes said from the stove.

"Mmn, those scones smell divine." She smiled affectionately at the older woman who bustled around the kitchen preparing much too much food for her one guest.

"Agnes, I hope you're joining me for breakfast. I cannot possibly eat all this myself!"

"Och, of course. Maggie, dear, I do so enjoy yer company, and I'd love for ye tae stay long enough so I can really show off my cookin'!"

Agnes poured the tea into the blue and white flowered teacups. Maggie felt the tea warm her, calming her nerves. As much as she wanted to be on her way, she knew a good breakfast was what she needed. Anyway, she'd arrive too early if she left now, and that would make the waiting unbearable.

Agnes brought the hot scones from the oven and placed them on a plate along with a steaming bowl of oats, clotted cream and brown sugar. She brought out a large jar with no label, winked at Maggie and said, "This is my special recipe; blackberry, raspberry, and cherry combined. Taste it and tell me what ye think."

Maggie spooned some of the thick preserve onto her scone and took a bite. The look of rapture on her face sent Agnes sailing around the room.

"It will take first prize at the fair, do ye no agree?"

"Oh, yes. It's delicious. Agnes, you're a wonder."

Maggie finished her breakfast under Agnes' watchful, twinkling eye. Maggie made all the appropriate sounds of delight, and though she exaggerated slightly for Agnes' benefit, the breakfast was wonderful, and so was her hostess. She pulled out her wallet, paid for the night, gave Agnes a tight squeeze and then putting her rucksack on her back, headed out the door.

Agnes' house was on the outskirts of a tiny village in the Western Highlands and the bus that took her here last night also made stops at the most remote spots in the area. She walked the mile to the village bus stop. She thought there was a bus at eight and it was only quarter past seven. She had time to spare. She strolled through the village slowly, admiring the stone and thatched cottages with their gardens now safely put to bed for winter. A collie ran out of a yard and sniffed her but didn't bother to bark. An old woman was hurrying in from her chicken coop, a wicker basket tucked neatly in the crook of her arm. She wondered if the villagers knew the secrets hidden within their land. They must; there were so many legends of the wee folk and faerie stories, but did anyone still believe? She wondered if Agnes suspected what was going on. She had given Maggie such an odd look when she talked about the yoga retreat, as if she didn't believe it existed. Maybe when Maggie returned she would broach the subject.

"So Agnes," Maggie imagined herself saying, "Do you believe in faeries? How about changelings or little elves? Mortal captives, perhaps?" She shook her head and smiled to herself.

It didn't take her long to walk around the village, not even a village really, just a pub, a post office doubling as the bank, and the bus stop. The small place looked a lot more welcoming in the early morning sun than it had last night. She went back to the bus stop, an awning with a bench, and sat down. No one was around, but she saw a curtain move in an upper window. Within moments an old gentleman emerged. He smiled at Maggie. "Do ye wish tae buy a bus ticket, young lassie?"

"Yes, but I thought I could buy one on the bus."

"American, aye?"

Maggie smiled and nodded.

"I'm that sorry tae tell ye, the bus north came yesterday and willna be back until tomorrow. It runs every other day noo," he smiled regretfully.

"Oh, dear. I've got to be somewhere tonight and I can't be late. How far a walk is it to the Glen Etive road?" She wondered why Agnes hadn't told her. Maybe she didn't know herself; she had a car, didn't she?

"I'd say it'd take ye the better part of the day, if ye start now. But Molly and I will be goin' that way this mornin', if ye'd care tae join us. I can take ye as far as Dalness."

"Would it be any trouble? I don't think I'll make my meeting if I have to walk all the way." Maggie was beginning to feel very much alarmed.

"No trouble at all. Come inside and keep warm while I get ready." He gestured to the door. Maggie followed him, relieved. As it was, the hike from the spot the old man would leave her would take a good while.

She sat at the kitchen table while the man went up a ladder-like staircase. She was surprised at his nimbleness. This country life, she thought, keeps people young. The kitchen was a sparse room without much adornment, but it did have a warm fire crackling away in the hearth. There was an old, yellowed picture on the wall of a woman with the saddest expression upon her face Maggie had ever seen. It was crudely drawn yet poignant somehow. The woman must have been in her forties at the time, long hair framing a delicate face, a faraway look in her eyes. As Maggie got closer to examine it, she was shocked by the startling resemblance to her daughter, Fiona. She gasped involuntarily, just as her host came down the stairs.

"A rare one, aye? She was my great-grandmither. There's quite the legend surroundin' her." His eyes sparkled.

"Um, yes, she was quite a beauty. You can see that even though the picture is so old."

"Drew it myself I did, when I was young. I copied it from an old portrait. The original was wearin' away with time, ye ken. Are ye ready, lassie?" he asked.

"Yes, thank you. My name is Maggie, by the way." Maggie extended her hand.

The old gentleman took it and with a firm grasp and said, "Ewan. Ewan MacDougall. Grand to meet ye."

Maggie's hand grew cold in his grasp and she lost her balance. The old man caught her with a strong arm.

"Lassie, ye look as if ye've seen a ghost, yer that pale.

Are ye certain ye want tae go sae far?" He looked at her with alarm, and she returned his look with astonishment. As she regained her composure, she smiled and said, "I'm sorry, it must have been that long flight yesterday, then the walk here. I'll be fine. Please don't let me keep you waiting, I'm ready."

"If yer sure, then. I'll get Molly. Sit back down here while I do," and he hurried out of the house.

"If Molly looks anything like this woman on the wall, I'm done for," Maggie said aloud. She took a deep breath and stared at the picture. She fumbled in her bag for the photo of Fiona. She held it up and the resemblance was undeniable. "It's all a coincidence, it's got to be," she said to herself. "So they look a bit alike, that's not unheard of and the old man's name, so what? There must be thousands of Ewan MacDougall's running all over this country." But despite her thoughts, Maggie didn't believe in coincidences. She knew that what she was looking at had significance, but what that was, she wasn't sure.

Unable to sit still any longer, she followed the old man outside, wondering if Molly was a neighbor or maybe his child. He obviously lived alone, so it didn't seem as though she could be his wife. She waited apprehensively until she heard a loud whinny, and walked around the corner. The old man stood by a dappled horse. He was lovingly feeding her an apple while fastening on a bridle and hooking her up to an antiquated wagon. He looked up, saw Maggie and smiled brightly. "May I introduce ye tae Molly. Miss Molly, say hello." The horse whinnied in response.

Maggie smiled, "Hello Molly, glad to meet you." The horse whinnied again.

"This old pony would talk if she could, she's that smart. With just me for her company and her for mine, we do communicate quite well, don't we, sweet?" He patted her on her flank as she nuzzled him. "I ken this will tak a rather longer time than the bus, but it will be a good deal quicker than walkin'."

"Yes, it will and it will be a pleasure to keep company with you and Molly," Maggie said. She picked up some grass and opened her palm to the horse who sniffed it and then took the sweet grass into her mouth.

"It seems Molly likes ye," remarked the old man, smiling.

"I like her too, she's lovely. I grew up with horses." But horses are not as fast as busses, she thought, and for a second she contemplated running back to Agnes' and taking her up on her offer to drive her, but upon reflection, sensed this meeting was more than chance.

"It was a lucky coincidence that today of all days ye showed up looking tae take the bus. I'd normally be oot by five, but last night I wasna able to sleep until almost mornin'. Had the strangest o' dreams. I thought I'd catch just a wink, but when I woke up again the sun was streamin' through my window. My customers will be worried, that's for certain. But will they be worried about their tea or me, that's the question." He chuckled aloud and Maggie laughed with him, understanding his joke at seeing the milk bottles in the back of the wagon.

"Hop in lassie, do." The old man gestured for Maggie to climb aboard.

The wagon jerked to a start as he coaxed Molly onto the road. The day was crisp and Maggie was sorry she hadn't worn her gloves. Her backpack was in the back of the wagon, along with the milk. She blew on her hands and tucked them into the sleeves of her jacket. She looked at the man's gnarled hands loosely grasping the reins. Weathered hands, old, but still strong. She wondered what his dream had been about. Normally she wouldn't have asked, for the Scots folk were as private a people as could be, but the compulsion to ask was so strong and there was something so open about him, she finally said, "You know, Mr. MacDougall...."

"Please call me Hugh, everyone does."

Maggie was glad she was sitting down, for had she been standing she surely would have fallen. "Hugh? Impossible!" she thought. She had heard of lots of Scottish men with the name Ewan, but how many used Hugh as a nickname? Beads of sweat formed on her forehead.

Hugh looked questioningly at her, the smile fading from his face as he registered her pale one. "Miss, are ye sick?"

Maggie shook her head, perhaps too vigorously. "Uh... Uh, no, it's just...nothing," she blurted out, feeling foolish.

"Och, I thought ye were havin' a fit."

Luckily they had come to his first delivery stop and he nimbly hopped out of the wagon and brought a glass bottle to the cottage. Maggie hoped he didn't think she was some sort of lunatic and when he got back in, began to ask him questions about the weather, the politics of the town and other mundane topics. He seemed relieved somewhat, but was certainly unwavering in his friendliness. They continued on this way for some time.

"Now where was I?" Hugh returned to the wagon, which stopped frequently to deliver the creamy white milk to cottages along the road. Maggie sat on the wooden bench next to the old man and watched his bright eyes wink at her in a smile so warm it dispelled her anxiety. "You were telling me about Mrs. Stewart's cow calving in the middle of the road to town," Maggie reminded him, her smile matching his.

"Och, right ye are. Weel, that cow bellowed something fierce. No one tae this day has any notion how she got from the field, what with the fence and all, but there she was ready tae pop in the middle of the road. What a sight!" He laughed, a sound so sweet and sincere that Maggie's heart lurched.

"Hugh, please tell me about the picture in your kitchen." Maggie had wanted to ask him the moment she saw it.

His expression darkened briefly, then he smiled again sadly, and said, "Ah, lass, it's a sorrowful tale, that is. Do ye really want tae hear such a tale?"

"Oh, yes, very much. I mean, the picture was so lovely and you said there was a legend surrounding it."

"Aye, there surely is. Settle back, lass, it's a lang one," he said, pulling a tiny pipe from the breast pocket of his vest. As he put it empty, to his lips, Maggie looked questioningly at him and he laughed again. "My wife, God rest her, made me quit the tobacco, but she let me keep the pipe so long as it stays empty. Canna tell a tale without it." He threw his head back, chuckling. "Noo," he started, getting serious again, "The picture ye saw was a copy of the original. It's my oon great-grandmither. Her name was Fiona, but everyone called her Fi," he said. Maggie had turned some shades paler, but he was watching the road and didn't notice.

"Aye, a bonnie lassie, she was. A mystery surrounded her, ye ken. No one actually kent where she came from, just showed up in the village one day. She took an old cottage near the moors and lived alone, which was verra strange, especially in those days. She was a wild thing, runnin' through the meadow, hair flying loose behind her. She had great love for all wild things. She rescued birds and mended broken wings, looked after orphaned creatures, feedin' them from her fingers. Her beauty made her the object of many a man's desire, but her secrets made her the object of rumors as well. Folk talked of her emerging from Faerie and starting a new life as a mortal. But that talk meant naught tae my great-grandfaither. They met one day while she was out piling lavender and heather into her apron, just for the smell and beauty of it. He was on a roan horse, just walkin' that fine day. He spied her reddish gold hair fallin' tae her back, loose and dancing on the breeze. His horse whinnied and she turned tae see who was there. When he saw her, the story goes, he jumped off his horse and boldly went over to her and with a finger under her chin, pulled her face up tae meet his gaze and kissed her. And as I heard it told many a time, she kissed him back, dropping flowers at their feet as her arms went 'round him. He threw her onto his horse, rode tae the kirk and married her that verra day." Hugh looked at Maggie, whose eyes were filled with tears. She laughed and wiped her eyes.

"Aye, 'tis that romantic! But sorry tae say, it doesna end that way." He stopped to make a delivery, while Maggie sat silently, having a feeling she knew how it ended.

He hopped spryly back into the wagon, clicked to Molly and with a little jerk they started down the road. "Noo where was I?" he said. "Och, of course, they wed, and he took her tae his home, but she would have none of it. She told him that if he wanted her tae be happy, they should live in her moor cottage, where it was wild and free. His agreein' tae that made the village folk believe she'd spelled him, but he cared naught aboot that and told the folk that if spell him she did, he was the happier man for it. She lived as a wife did in those days, but her husband, seeing her for what she was, gave her the freedom she needed. He never minded her long rambles into the hills or the injured creatures that often sat in his oon kitchen. He loved Fi as none other and she loved him that well, too.

"Before their first year was oot, she gave birth tae a son, a strapping boy, dark of hair and eye. He was his mither's darlin' and his faither's pride, learning tae ride before he could walk, knowin' the names of the flowers his mither so loved. Two more sons came, one bein' my oon grandfaither. Excuse me lass, next stop." He hopped out of the wagon again. Maggie was so caught up in the story she was wondering who the lass was, until she realized he had interrupted the story to make another delivery. She sat watching him say a friendly good morning to the woman who came out when she saw him with his bottles. She handed him something and he tipped his hat and made his way back to his passenger.

"Hot scones, lass," he said, handing her one wrapped in a cloth napkin. He waved to the woman who had given him the treat, while she stood leaning by the doorway, a bright smile on her handsome face. There was something about the way she looked at him that made Maggie think this was something more than a bit of food for the milkman. She smiled and waved also, but held her tongue. Hugh reached under the seat and pulled out a bottle of his fresh milk and handed it to Maggie. "Open it, would ye, dearie. There's two cups under the seat as weel. Ye pour, I'll keep driving, that way I'll get ye tae where ye need tae be."

Maggie obliged and before long the two were drinking fresh milk and eating hot scones, Hugh handling the reins with one hand, eating and drinking with his free one. "That Mrs. Burns, she bakes quite the scone!"

"Yes," Maggie agreed, "they are delicious." Then she slyly added, "I'm sure her husband loves them in the morning."

Bait taken, Hugh said, "Nay, lass, she's a widow. Has been these fifteen years." He turned and gave Maggie a bold wink.

"Please Hugh, could you finish the story?" Maggie sounded like a child eager for the conclusion of her favorite bedtime story.

"I've told ye the happy part. Are you sure ye want tae

hear the rest of it?" he asked, knowing full well she would have it no other way, and neither would he, for that matter.

"Of course. Please, go on."

"Aye, then. The three boys grew into fine men and were good brothers tae one another. They stayed near their parents, working the land, raising sheep, writing a bit of poetry. I've seen some of it myself. The younger brothers were homebodies, but the older one, weel... he was like his mither in his wild spirit. Untamed, it was. After his work was done, he'd be seen climbin' about the heather or riding in the hills. And what a handsome youth he was! Many a lass fancied him, but he loved only one, true and all, a lassie from the village. She was a flower, they say, delicate and rare. The villagers loved her well, with her sweet ways and healing hands. She kent all the plants and herbs and it came naturally tae her how tae use them. She often was called tae cure folk of this ailment or that. They courted for over a year, and before they were tae wed a sickness took hold of the village and in her effort to help, she caught the disease herself. She got it right bad she did, and never recovered. The lad pleaded with God tae save her, as she'd helped sae many others, but she died there in his arms. His grief was sae strong not even his dear mither could touch it. She worried as her precious son became reckless and wild. He went tae the city, drank too much, mayhap gambled as weel, feeding his misery. Stayed away for some time. His mither let him be, knowing that the only way for him tae heal was time, and that he would return. And return he did, a bit rougher, but still her lad. He tried tae go on as he had before, but he had become a sad young man. Nothing his mither did could make him smile. No amount of ribbin' from his faither or brothers touched him.

"Then, the story goes, one fine October day, much like this one, a tinker band came to the village, selling their wares. They stayed on the outskirts though, not bein' too well liked, their kind and all. But there was a woman among them who was a rare beauty. My grand-uncle saw her and it was as if he was mesmerized," he paused to take a swig of milk and Maggie felt her face growing red. She felt a flush of jealousy, unable to imagine why. It was just a story from the past, wasn't it?

"Weel," he continued, "the young man spent a fair amount of time at the tinkers' stand that day, examining not the wares, but the maiden. She teased him and acted coy, not understanding nor caring about the sensitive nature of the lad. When night approached, she boldly went up tae him and taking his hand, ran off into the meadow. There, the story goes, for no one really kens, she lured him into a faerie ring and took him captive, for she was believed tae be a faerie in disguise, set oot tae make a capture."

Maggie almost felt the seat give way beneath her. Her breath came fast and she had to put her head between her legs, for fear of passing out.

"My dear, are you all right? Let me stop," Hugh said, worried.

"No, no, go on, finish the story. I'm all right," she said, getting up and wiping the cold sweat from her brow. She knew this was true, didn't she? She'd known all along. But this brought it all too close. Perhaps she had been pretending it was all a wonderful fantasy, like Brigadoon. It wasn't. It was real.

"Lass, you dinna look well. Is it the rough road?"

"I'm not sure, I just feel a bit sick. I'll be all right. Please, go on."

"Weel, if you're sure."

Maggie nodded affirmatively.

"His mither had been restless that day, as if somethin' was in the air that she couldna quite place. Afterwards in the village, some said she'd smelled her oon kind nearby. Anyway, the lad had been oot all night before so she didna worry until the next mornin' when he hadn't arrived tae take breakfast before work. The work needed tae be done and so she went looking for her son. A neighbor told her she had seen the lad goin' off with the tinker woman. Well, Fi, the strong woman she was, went boldly to the tinkers' wagon and demanded tae ken where the woman and her son were. They said that the woman wasna part of their band, had just arrived there that yester morn. They weren't sure who she was, but they were afraid of her, fearing something about the way she spoke and in her movements. A very superstitious group, they said nothing to her, but were only too glad when she went away with the man. Now, Lass, some say that my great-grandmither's hair began tae rise on her head and that she changed color from the anger, others tell it that she angrily demanded them to tell her where they went. The tinkers only pointed tae the hills and said they knew nothing more, but that neither the woman nor the lad had come back. Fi, her husband, and their two sons searched and searched, but tae no avail. The story tells it that Fi could have saved her son if she had gone back tae her fey home, but that she wouldna leave her husband and other sons, because according tae legend, she would never be able tae return." Hugh rolled his eyes and said, "That part of the story is how we keep up the superstitions round here, but it serves us well, I suppose. Brings the tourists."

Maggie, who by now was staring wide-eyed, said slowly, "They say there's always a grain of truth to legends."

Hugh smiled at her and winked, "That'd make me have the faerie blood, wouldn't it just? Anyway, a few days later, my great-grandmither was looking into the woods nearby and found an embroidered handkerchief, the initials E.M. there in the corner, a tiny heart below, and she knew it belonged tae her son. His oon love had made it for him."

"E.M.?" Maggie whispered.

"Ewan MacDougall, lass, my great-uncle. They called him Hugh as weel, like me. Dearie, are ye all right?"

Tears sprang to Maggie's eyes and unable to control herself, unable to keep her feelings wrapped up any longer, she began to weep freely. The old man awkwardly patted her on the back and tried to comfort her as she shook. She looked the old man in the eye, her tears making her eyes even more startling in their color, and she whispered, "I love him."

"Dearie, it's just an old tale, aye, 'tis that romantic in its tragedy, but nay, ye can't love a ghost..." and he patted her again. This time Maggie sat up straight, wiped her eyes with her sleeve and said in a stronger voice, "I love him because I know him. I'm on my way to him now, thanks to you."

"I dinna understand," Hugh said, starting to feel very uncomfortable.

"He *was* captured by a faerie. The story is *true*," Maggie said, looking imploringly at the old man who was shaking his head.

"Mr. Mac...um, Hugh, please, listen to me," she continued. "My story is possibly more incredible than the one you just told, but it's true."

He looked up at her. "Impossible. Just an old faerie tale, the kind we're famous for over here," he said with finality.

"No, Hugh, it's not impossible. Please, let me tell you my tale. Then you'll understand." Maggie put her arm on the old man's shoulder. He slowly sat up and looked into her eyes. He saw sadness, but also sincerity in her gaze, and nodded. He pulled the wagon off the road and let Molly have her head, the two of them sitting on the wagon's bench. While the mare grazed quietly, Maggie told her story.

"When I was twenty-four years old, I was finishing my Master's degree in anthropology and folklore, focusing on folk medicine. It was my last semester and even though I haven't a Scottish bone in my body, I'd always been interested in Scottish history and folklore, so I applied for an exchange program and was accepted. I also wanted to study the Celtic harp, traditional music, and I was thrilled to be here. I fell in love with Scotland the moment I arrived. It was as if I were home. I got a tiny flat near the university and I was having the time of my life listening to traditional music, meeting all kinds of interesting people. There was even this guy.... Anyway, I had a break from classes and decided to come to the Highlands to go camping on my own, check out the herbs that grew wild. I found a lovely place to pitch my tent, on a sheepherder's land. I never met the farmer, but there was a welcome sign to travelers, giving permission to camp. It was late October and it was getting chilly, especially at night, so I'd build tiny fires and curl up in my tent in my warm sleeping bag. One evening, two nights before I was going back to the city, I was outside my tent, sitting by my little fire and reading by the dimming light, when I heard bells and the sounds of laughter. I got up and walked over to where I heard the sounds. There were a bunch of people playing music, candle lanterns glowing in a circle, and women were dancing around the lights. It was a lovely sight and I was intrigued. They didn't look like druids or hippies or anything, just regular folk. Then I realized it was October 31, *Samhain*. I had been so busy collecting plants that I had lost track of time and forgot it was Halloween. I guess I had stumbled across a celebration of some kind."

"Aye, people still do it up here, tonight will be the night, dinna ye ken?"

"Oh, I ken, all right." She paused, and then continued.

"I watched, fascinated as they danced. The music was wonderful, a fellow on a fiddle and a woman on a whistle. One of the people saw me standing there and took me by the hand and into the circle. I danced with them until late. At one point they stopped dancing and made a bonfire. I was so dizzy and exhilarated that I went over to a grassy mound and lay down on it. I was lying there on my stomach, head on folded hands, watching the people as they held hands around the bonfire that was now burning high. I looked down for a moment, noticed something dark curled near me. I thought it was a snake at first and it scared me, but then I saw it was only a vine. I'm still not sure why, but I followed it. It twisted around an old tree and there I saw a wild rose, only one. Probably the last of the season. I picked it and..." Hugh interrupted, "There's an old legend about pickin' a wild rose. They say it opens doors to the other side."

"You're right, Hugh, it did just that, although I didn't realize it at the time. A man stepped out from the shadows like mist. I caught my breath at the sight of him, so handsome... I thought he was one of the dancers, but I hadn't recalled seeing him. I would have remembered him. There was an ethereal look about him. He didn't seem to see me, though I was right there. It was kind of weird. Not scary, though. I felt no fear at all. He began to look around, looking at everything, smelling the earth, as if he'd never seen those things before. I watched him, couldn't take my eyes off him. I was drawn to him in some inexplicable way. I was bold that night; I went right up to him and touched his arm. It was the strangest feeling when I touched him, it was like touching smoke, but not really because I felt something alive and real, too. It was then that he turned and saw me for the first time. Our eyes met and there was instant recognition. That's the only way to describe it. We stood there, staring at each other, transfixed. I knew him from the very depths of my soul, though of course I'd never seen him before. He didn't say a word for the longest time. I wasn't even sure that he could speak, but when he did, it was as if he hadn't used his voice for a long time. It was almost a whisper, creaky and low, and he said, 'How?'

"I don't know how I knew, but I knew exactly what he meant. I couldn't answer, because I didn't know myself. '*I thought you were...*' he said, gingerly touching my face with his hands. He looked searchingly into my eyes and again said, '*How?*'

"I told him I didn't know. I asked him who he was and why he was as familiar to me as my own self. He shook his head and said a bit more firmly this time, '*How did you call me here?*' As he said it, he looked at the rose I still held in my hand. '*Ahh,*' was all he said. He took the rose from my hand and placed it tenderly in my hair. '*Thank ye,*' he said with such a look of gratitude that tears formed in my eyes. What was he thanking me for?" Maggie looked over to Hugh, who was fully engrossed in her story. She went on. "I said there was no need to thank me, I had done nothing. '*No lass,*' he said, '*Ye have let me remember what it is like. Ye have called me oot of a dream from which I thought I should never wake.*'

"I was confused by the tumultuous emotions inside me. I looked over to the bonfire to see if the other people were aware of us, of what was happening, but there was no bonfire, not even a trace. There were no people at all. Just this man and me. Alone. I thought I should be afraid, but I wasn't. Something about the gesture of placing the flower into my hair so lovingly had evoked memories I didn't even know I had. I knew there was nothing to fear from him. And then, I don't know what impelled me to do it, but I held out my hand to him. He took it and there was... it was like a charge, yes, an electric charge. We both felt it because he turned to me with a look of wonder. *'Let's walk a ways,'* he said, not letting go of my hand.

"I walked beside him and for the first time in my life, I felt I knew exactly where I was supposed to be. Then he started to speak. He started telling me about himself and what had happened to him, and it was almost as if I knew everything he was going to say about a split second before he said it. You know the story, because, Hugh, it's the one you just told. The man I'm going to meet is...." Hugh held up a hand to stop her and wiping fresh tears from his eyes, said, "My dear, if yer wantin' to get to young Ewan, we'd better be gettin' on. Any longer and ye'll no get there in time."

He clicked Maggie to walk, and the wagon jostled down the road to its clandestine destination.

Chapter 28

Kumsah had been prowling around the area, looking for anymore of those fiendish horrors that had changed themselves into crows. He was relieved to find the woods clear of any destructive force, and as he was about to head back to the others, padding quietly through the forest to return to his dwelling, he heard voices.

"Mòr, Mòr, I dinna like it here. Let us go back."

"Nay, we must go on. Quiet noo, I'm listening to these woods."

"All I hear is my oon heart."

The coyote-boy stopped to listen and hadn't moved from the spot as Mòr and Jinty emerged from a copse of trees. The two faeries stopped short as they saw the wolfish creature. Jinty stifled a scream. Mòr took a deep breath and said a faerie spell of protection to herself. Jinty heard it and did the same. They hovered frozen while the boy circled. "What is it going tae do?" Jinty whispered on the verge of hysteria.

"How should I ken?" Mòr whispered back. "I'll talk wi' it."

"Nay, Mòr, dinna! Dinna tell it anything."

Ignoring her, Mòr ventured, "Ehm, please, excuse me, could ye tell us where we are?"

"First I'd like to know what you are and what business you have here," the boy said, authoritatively.

Mòr thought about keeping quiet until she knew his intentions, but she was tired and knew they'd never find Rionnag without help. "We are faeries from a far off land and we are in search of our charge. The old tree from yonder wood thought we might get some assistance from some of the folk who reside here."

He relaxed visibly at the mention of the tree. "Ah, so Saska told you, did she?"

"I dinna understand. Saska?"

He looked at her strangely, trying to decipher her odd way of speaking. "Saska is the name of the tree you spoke to. We know the name of every tree, rock, and flower in this wood, as they know ours."

"The tree told us yer forests are getting smaller."

He paused, took a deep breath, and continued. "Yes, our world has been shrinking for a long time now. It used to be that we were connected with those on the other side, but as more of them came from across the great water and began cutting down the trees, we lost contact. We can't even tell them to stop. They no longer hear our cries. They don't believe we exist, and those who do are not strong enough to defy the destructive ones." He shook his angular head sadly.

"It's the same with us. We used tae play wi' the humans; we'd leave gifts for one another. I havna received a gift in a verra long while. I think we've been forgotten as weel," Mòr commiserated.

"Tonight is one of our most important celebrations. We will invoke the remaining spirits of this world to give us strength to survive." The coyote-boy continued, "We need to strengthen our side and penetrate the veil that once was like gossamer and thistledown, and now is like the concrete and steel with which they so love to replace our brother trees. We will attempt to remind them."

Mòr listened to this boy, marveling at his wisdom, wondering at his age. He led them to a circle of beings so strange that both faeries cried out in surprise. The beings, so different from the fey folk at home, were engrossed in their ceremony and were unaware of the new arrivals. A female creature, reminiscent of a sleek otter but with human-like hands, was beating a drum. The other animal-like creatures were swaying and chanting low. The coyote-boy gestured them to sit and they thankfully did. Jinty began to sway with the rest, and to Mòr's utter surprise, she began to sing in a most beautifully high, clear voice, a song in the old tongue, one that could invoke the fey. Her song held longing for the natural world to remain, for faerie and human worlds to mesh, with the understanding that without one, the other could not survive. For all Jinty's fear of the other side, she knew well that the destruction of one side was surely the destruction of it all.

The human-like animals looked up for the first time, though they expressed little surprise at the sight of the two faeries and listened to this new song approvingly, tears coming to some of their old eyes. Jinty's song was so sweet and clear and so very melancholy that they seemed to understand, though the language was not their own. Mòr was astonished and began to feel somewhat embarrassed by all her scolding and harsh treatment of the poor lass. But she put her guilt aside and listened to the words. Softly she began to translate them into the tongue the boy understood, which she assumed the rest would as well,

> "Oh fey world, world of love and of joy,
> Open your heart and your eyes.
> Oh spirit world, world of light and of sound,
> Help us to break down our ties,
> The darkness of night and the brightness of day,
> Let us merge into one and rejoice.
> Sing us your song, the song that remains,
> We'll sing it in one sacred voice.
> Earth of above and Earth of below,
> Let us rejoice together.
> On this sacred night, pervious night,
> Close the gap between flesh and fey feather.
> Oh, earth world, world of beauty and strife,
> There's never a reason to fear us
> Oh temporal world, world of black and of white,
> Forget your closed hearts and hear us.
> Together as one, on this sacred night
> We will dance in the fey light between.
> Joining spirits and hands
> We will strengthen the bond
> 'Tis with true eyes we each can be seen."

When Jinty finished singing, she looked sheepishly around at the beings, and then at Mòr, who smiled approvingly, much to Jinty's astonishment.

The female drummer spoke. Her voice had a singsong quality to it, quite pleasing, "Your song seemed to hearten the folk. Maybe this night will make a difference. Unless the humans understand their decisions affect all of us, there's no hope left."

"That is why we are here," Mòr said.

"I don't understand," the drummer said.

"We are here to find a princess gone from our world. She has an obligation tae marry a prince from another fey family. Their union will rekindle and strengthen the faerie folk and our world. It is our last hope," she said.

This time the coyote-boy spoke. "Might there be others who want to find your princess?"

"What are ye suggesting?" Mòr asked, worried.

"There were two who arrived on these shores, with similar, though, cruder accents, than those with which you speak. They were quite likely the most hideous creatures we have ever encountered." There was a murmur of agreement from the group.

"What did they look like, if ye please?"

The boy described in detail the appearance of the two bogies and Jinty gasped, as Mòr became obviously agitated.

"So you know of these things," the otter-woman said.

"Yes, I'm sorry tae say. They are evil ones, from where we dwell. And who sent them, I think I ken." The group looked at her strangely. "I think I *know*," she adjusted her speech for their benefit. "Where are they now?"

"They changed their appearance to those of crows and flew off, but sources inform us that they are trapped, and will make sure they remain so until we can figure out what to do with them."

"Thank you for your kindness. If we ever get home, I'll make sure you are informed how to take care of the likes of them."

"Rest now, then we will help you with your task."

The steady drumbeat was lulling the two exhausted faeries into a hypnotic state and the otter-woman smiled indulgently with a strange grin that likely would have petrified Jinty had her eyes not been closed.

She got up and joined the others who were now moving

in a slow circle, a dance of invitation to the humans, whom they hoped, even in their dozing dream-state, might gain some understanding that their actions were destroying what the fey folk held dear. And just maybe, this time, they would pay attention.

Creaghan was barreling across the churning waters when he felt the drum beat and headed fast for the spot. He knew he would find what he needed when he arrived at his destination and approached at blurring speed. The air was energy charged when he touched down and he grinned to himself, knowing *he* would charge the place up in more ways than anyone would ever imagine.

He saw them first, sitting in a pleasant circle, a band of wood dwellers, survivors, swaying to the rhythm they thought would bring friends over. But not tonight. Creaghan is here instead. He laughed aloud at this, remaining disguised in one of his many shape-shifting personas. For now he had chosen an eerie mist, swirling restlessly with malevolent intent.

The humanimal folk felt the negative invader as Mòr and Jinty felt their skin prickle, knowing with certainty that whatever horrible thing was coming, was coming for their lass.

The leader stood up, and with a firm gesture, commanded all to remain seated. She began to chant again louder than before. This time she used a word of power and protection, an ageless expression that once uttered, would bring any evil to a standstill.

As Creaghan felt the power of that sound, he halted in midair as if flying into a wall. He flew away as fast as he could, realizing that the sound was too strong even for him to overcome. He would have to approach from a different angle.

He was vexed with himself for his arrogance. "Ye stupid fool, ye think they on this side remember naught? Noo they're on tae thee." He cursed himself over and again, aware his surprise charge had backfired unforgivably.

Taking the shape of a small animal, he sat down to think things through. He had been so bent on getting the wench and returning to claim his prize, he hadn't been thinking clearly. Now he had revealed his presence.

But all was not lost. He still had many different energies he could command. He was the master shape-shifter, the unparalleled energy deceiver, was he not?

With that thought, he assumed his most tender guise yet. That of a tiny fawn, a blonde and spotted babe of the woods that could never evoke fear, just disgusting adoration and compassion. Satisfied he looked the part, he shifted the energies inside himself to match his new exterior, so that none would suspect the truly horrific force that lurked hidden within the creature's innocent appearance.

Mòr and Jinty felt the malevolence dissipate with the chanting, as did the animal folk. The female spoke, "We seem to have invited the wrong kind into our circle. For now we have succeeded in stopping it, but we must be on guard. Everyone not known by name must be suspect. Be reserved in judgment to any who might cross to this place."

Another creature spoke up. "But we have invited them! This may be our only chance to fulfill our mission!"

"Yes, we have called them and should they come

through we will be cautious, guarded, until we know their true intent. Is that clear?"

Everyone nodded. Mòr was wringing her hands. "Please, I feel responsible for this, for I have the distinct feeling that whatever it was is searching for our lass and he may have recognized our presence," she said, gesturing to herself and Jinty.

"You may be right, but this is not your doing. You are looking to do good. Evil intent is no cousin to you. We feel more determined than ever to help you find your princess."

Mòr breathed a sigh of relief, knowing that without these kind folk, she and Jinty might never be able to fulfill their mission. As it was, she despaired, but at least she had the support of folk who knew this strange place and who might guide them to Rionnag.

Chapter 29

For the first time in years, Maggie felt as though a great burden had been taken from her and she settled in comfortably for the long ride ahead, helping Hugh with his deliveries whenever he stopped at a farmhouse or crofter's cottage. She felt as if she were in another century, one where things happened in their own good time and there wasn't the mad rush to meet deadlines or accumulate wealth. She felt at peace here with the old man. Hugh practically sparkled in his skin with a sense of happiness and well being she rarely had seen in anyone. He was robust and full of life, with a spring in his step, and as he jumped out of the wagon to tip his hat and deliver his milk, Maggie smiled broadly, thinking of what was ahead. Life was good. She had something to look forward to once a year, to bring happiness. And back home she had a beautiful daughter and a loving family. And now she had *this* Hugh. The old man had recognized the family connection without disbelief. He didn't even seem surprised when Maggie told him her daughter's name was Fiona. He was her daughter's distant cousin, and her lover's grand-nephew, the young man who in all reality should long since have been dust in the ground, but who, due to the magic of Faerie, in only a few hours would be holding her in his arms.

"Maggie, when yer back, please come and visit with yer family. I mean, *my* family. I want tae meet little Fiona and tell her all aboot this side of her family."

Maggie's happiness was overtaken by guilt. "Oh, Hugh, I would love to, but Fiona doesn't know about her father. She doesn't know about any of this. God, I've been lying for years, to everyone," she said, her good mood suddenly taking a downward turn.

"Lass, I think the time has come for ye tae free yerself from lies."

Maggie raised her head slowly. "You know, when I told you, it felt like the weight of a mountain had been taken from me. But after all these years, how can I just tell Fiona?"

"Maggie, dearie, ye tell her the same way ye told me. She'll understand."

"You don't know my stubborn daughter. She's a teenager and ready to make me her worst enemy."

"Stubborn, aye? It must be the MacDougall blood in her. Nay, lass, she has a right tae know."

"You're right. The worst part is, *my* Hugh doesn't know he has a daughter. I've never told him either."

"Weel, I think this is the time tae tell all. I dinna think ye can hold it in any longer. Do ye?" He smiled and patted her hand.

She looked up at him, her blue eyes shining. "No, I don't think I can. You know something funny, this time, for the first time, I took Fiona's picture with me. I've never brought one before, but I had an urge to take it; I even fantasized about showing it to him. I think I will this time."

"Wise lass, verra wise. He has a right tae know as weel."

Maggie reached into her rucksack and pulled out the picture and handed it to the old man. His eyes opened wide and he said quietly, "Aye, I can see the resemblance. She's lovely."

"Thank you."

The two rode on in companionable silence, Maggie looking at the scenery, Hugh humming to himself. As the sun went high and began its retreat, Maggie felt the old flutter in the pit of her stomach.

Her fears always rose up at this time. What if she forgot the words? What if she couldn't find the spot? What if he wasn't there to meet her?

She shook her head, hair flying. Startled, Hugh turned to her, "He'll be there, lass, he will that."

Maggie stared at her companion. "How...?"

Hugh laughed. "I reckon I do have a wee bit of the blood in me. Look there, lassie," Hugh went on, pointing to a worn and weathered sign. An arrow pointed in the direction of Maggie's destination. She clutched her chest in a reflexive gesture. "We're almost there," he said.

"Yes," whispered Maggie.

The old man took her hand. She squeezed it gently. They sat this way for the next few miles as the wagon jostled through the path of the Royal Forest. Maggie always smiled to herself when she thought how fitting the name was, as she was about to enter the land of a faerie queen.

When they emerged from the forest, Hugh pulled Molly to a halt. They looked up to see the great mountain passes of the highlands ahead and the fourteen-mile Glen Etive road, locally known as the "road to nowhere." Hugh looked worriedly at Maggie. "Weel, lass, I wish I could take ye farther."

"This is wonderful, Hugh, and don't worry, I'm not going all the way to the end, just a few miles." Maggie didn't dare tell him how far she had yet to travel.

"Weel, that's a relief. I'll be back this way in a week's time and if ye happen tae be here, I'd be happy tae take ye back tae the village."

Maggie knew this place was miles out of his way. He had no reason to come this far, and she smiled, aware that he was being a gentleman, that he was letting her be independent, and that without him, it would be a day's hike back to the village.

"Thank you, Hugh, I'll be back in a week. Time's a bit different where I'm going but a week is all I have. We've worked out the time differences. It's a bit of a challenge, because it hardly seems any time passes before the week is up. I look forward to seeing you, and I'm going to tell Hugh about his nephew!"

"Tell him I look forward tae the day we meet, whenever that may be."

"I will." She hesitated, then said tentatively, "Hugh, may I give you a hug?"

"That ye can, lass, and gladly." The two embraced. Hugh looked at her, his eyes serious. "Godspeed, Maggie, and God bless." She hoisted her pack over her shoulders, and with a wave and a smile, started down the path lit by the late afternoon sun. Hugh turned the wagon and clucked Molly to hurry home before the faerie hour.

Maggie walked down the meandering road, in the shadow of the great mountains, recalling particular trees and landmarks. The road she followed was well marked and she kept on at a steady pace, watching the sun retreating through the canopy, her heart quickening. She walked this way for almost two hours and then made her way into a rocky field she recognized. Here a footpath was barely trodden, but still perceptible to Maggie's keen eye. Hardy sheep dotted the hillside and Maggie hoped that she wouldn't meet up with their shepherd.

The sun was getting lower, still a good hour or so from setting, and Maggie, though tired, knew she didn't have the luxury of a rest if she wanted to find the place while there was still daylight. She allowed herself to pause briefly for a drink, pulling her water bottle from the outer pocket of her pack. She drank deeply, her sweat chilling her as she cooled down. As she was putting her bottle back in her pack she noticed something glinting at the bottom of the outer pocket. She reached in and pulled out a little package tied with gold ribbon. Completely baffled, she opened it. It was a tiny silver pendant, a Celtic cross, on a slim black thread. Maggie turned the thing over in her hands, wondering. Then she noticed the writing on the wrapping paper.

"To keep you safe, my friend. Agnes." Maggie smiled and fastened the necklace around her slender neck. She looked up to see the sun sinking below the crest of the hill, spreading out in color like a palette of watercolors splashed with rain. Hoisting her pack, she picked up speed. The air was intoxicatingly sweet and crisp, and Maggie was glad for her heavy sweater. The temperature dipped as soon as the sun slipped beneath the rugged horizon.

She reached the bottom of the rocky hill. This was where she had to be very sure she was going the right way. She searched the piles of rocks for the one with the splotch of whitewash someone had put there years ago, a landmark that would send her counting her steps to the tiny overgrown circle where she would wait until moonrise. Moss had grown on the cairns and they looked deceivingly alike. She looked up at the sky darkening in the twilight and her heartbeat sped up. No need to panic yet, she told herself. Just calm down and try to remember. It was on a somewhat steep angle, wasn't it? You should know this by heart. But a year in the open air and weather changed things, even those that looked as if they hadn't changed in two hundred years. She looked up higher than she thought the rock should be, but peeking out from behind newly grown moss, she saw a tiny shimmer of white. She ran up the hill, her pack swinging sideways. So steep was the way, she had to drag herself on all fours. She got to the cairn, and picked the moss off the top rock, and there was her landmark. Her relief was so profound she began to cry. Tears streamed down her face as she thought how unfair it was that she had to do this, that she couldn't just be normal. No, not Maggie, never Maggie! *She* had to come miles through forests and hillocks and count steps in the dusk just so she could see the man she loved once a year, only to always come home alone. She let out a cry and pounded the ground. Some sheep grazing nearby lifted their heads. One bleated and she looked over. The sheep seemed so concerned Maggie had to laugh. It broke the tension and she was able to think more clearly.

Seven steps to the right, seven more straight up. She bent down and brushed aside an accumulation of dead bracken and found the small, barely distinguishable circle of stones. She stepped inside, bringing her belongings with her. She brushed off a spot on the ground and sat down to wait for the *Samhain* moon to ascend.

It was getting chillier, and pulling her knees up to her chest she stretched her big sweater over them and wrapped her arms around herself. Not much longer. She remembered the words she would soon have to repeat and said them over and over inside her head. The sky darkened until the dusk was lost to the past. One by one, stars came out, filling up the sky. An owl hooted in the distance as Maggie waited. Eventually weariness overtook her and she dozed.

She woke with a start as a light touched her sleeping

eyelids. At first she thought someone was shining a flashlight at her, but it was only the waxing moon. She sat up, and quietly, with studied reverence, said the words she had committed to memory. With impatience almost impossible to bear, she waited for her lover to appear.

Behind her, a cloaked figure emerged from the mist. He stood, watching quietly, eyeing the dark head still gazing at the moon, waiting for him. His heart was full as he tenderly approached. A twig snapped under foot.

Maggie gripped herself ever tighter, afraid to turn lest it was only some creature of the woods and not him. A warm cloak was draped over her shoulders and she felt him lifting her into his strong arms. Warm lips touched her neck, and her name was spoken again and again in ragged whispers. She felt warm tears on her cheek, his mixed with her own. Turning to face him, she tilted her face to meet his, and before she could speak his name, his mouth was on hers, and it seemed they would be swallowed up by their passion. When their frantic greeting waned, he quietly spoke, the same words he said every time they met. Her eyes were luminous as she repeated his Gaelic words in English. "Aye love, it seems a thousand years since I've seen you."

With that, he bent down, more gently this time, to kiss the lips of the sole person who brought hope to his otherwise miserable existence. She kissed him back as he led her into the mist and to the place between worlds where for a brief time they could forget everything but each other.

Chapter 30

King Niall had searched every spot high and low within his own kingdom and outside it before returning to his queen, who under normal circumstances would have gone with him, but who had waited behind in the hopes that their daughter might return. Queen Catriona was wringing her hands when he arrived. The sight of her made his heart lurch in his chest and he opened his arms to allow her entrance. She hugged him tightly and then pulled away, shaking her head, a letter in her outstretched hand. He took it and frowned deeply. It read:

Greetings King Niall and Queen Catriona,
This most glorious year brings our two 'babes' to the age that will unite our two kingdoms. We await with pleasure and prospect the nuptials, which will take place this Bealltainn. Time is of the quintessence for this marriage, and our son eagerly anticipates fulfilling his

obligation to your charming daughter. We expect she is looking forward to her matrimony with as much zeal as is our son. We plan on bringing upwards of seven hundred of our closest relations, friends and allies from throughout the Daoine Sidhe and beyond. We joyfully await seeing you in the near future for what has been envisaged to be the most significant wedding of our era.

Blessings on your Court and family,
Sincerely,
Queen Deirdre and King Eamon

The King handed the letter back to his wife and began pacing the room. "My dear, this comes at a bad time. All their talk of obligation and duty makes me uneasy in the face of our daughter's defiance coupled with her disappearance. There has been no sign of the child and I like it not at all. Besides the fact that we know not where she is, which is worry enough, should these two hear of her headstrong behavior, I shudder to think."

"Och Niall, I do not like it either, and though I trust Rionnag is a resourceful, albeit willful lassie, I am filled with dread that this may be more than merely an act of rebelliousness. My intuition tells me something is wrong."

"I hope yer intuition for once *is* wrong. My knights are scouring every square inch of this kingdom as well as those of our allies. I have to believe they will find her," he said.

"I'm afraid that the one kingdom ye can not search is where our lass will be."

"Yer sister's?"

"Aye, that is what I am most afraid of. Barabel is wicked and this is just the opportunity she craves. A chance to ally herself with our Queen Deirdre."

"We can not allow that to happen. Perhaps Rionnag received my message and she is on her way back to us at this very moment. Let us hope for that outcome." It was the only outcome he would accept.

Queen Catriona gave voice to his thought, "Aye, it is the only acceptable outcome."

The King turned to his wife and took her hands into his. "Love, reply to the Irish king and queen and tell them our daughter will make a beautiful bride. Now, though I am loath to part from ye, I must leave again. I will not stop searching until the lass is safe home."

"Go my love, go and find our intractable daughter."

Chapter 31

How could anything be wrong with the world when Maggie is in my arms, thought Ewan as he held her to him, his cloak draped around her, breathing in the fragrance of her hair. He had been so anxious the whole of *Samhain*, wondering if finally this year, she would have listened to him and remained home. The waiting for the moment when he could cross over was terrible. For a change, Barabel had been unusually quiet, with none of her usual demands made on his time and person. He was grateful for that. As he did every time the occasion approached, he stayed as far from Barabel as he could. This time was easy, for she had wanted naught to do with him since her betrayal. She had left him alone, which suited him fine, but he had kept an ear open for the goings on inside the castle. All had been quiet, save for the rumblings about some stray bogies. He realized now that she had tried to use them for some ill will, perhaps concerning his suspicion about the princess, but they had apparently failed in their attempt, causing her to call up the odious fachan. But for now, there was only one thing on Ewan's mind, and that was Maggie.

Thinking of her brought a sweet smile to his lips; his faithful Maggie, sacrificing a world of real and every day love for this perennial romance. The day she had called him with the wild rose had been the happiest in his life, a day that had called him out of eternal bondage, if only for a short time.

He hoped she would like the gift he brought her this feast night. He had brought her one every time they met, though mostly, his gifts were intangible. Usually they were those she could carry in memory only, like the tune he would play for her this time. The book of spells had been no gift. He had given her that book only as a means for allowing her to return and meet him. Stealing it had cost the life of an innocent sprite. Ewan knew he could never permit Barabel to find out, for that might endanger Maggie as well as his chances of seeing her again. As for the stone, Maggie had found it long ago in the pocket of his cloak. It was his very own reminder of Tamlin and his brave Janet. Maggie had turned that stone over and over in her hands and asked if she could keep it. How could he refuse? And surprisingly, it had remained intact when she returned to her own side. The pendant had been his, a gift from his mother, and had remained on him through his crossing and capture. Maggie had never removed it from her neck since he had placed it there these many years ago.

Nay, the gift he would give her tonight was from love, and a dream, not from desperation or grief. When he was with her, he was in bliss, and his joy lived longer each time, for her unceasing faithfulness sustained him until the next *Samhain* and the next. He had decided the last time they parted that a tune would be the thing. Sweet and clear, like

Maggie's voice.

He heard it first from a wildly plumed bird in a recurring dream, and he tried to recreate the tune, composing it on the low whistle, the other possession from his human life that hadn't been appropriated by his cruel mistress. It was a curiously affecting tune, with moments of joyous revelry dispersed throughout, expressing his mixed feelings of joy and sorrow for Maggie and their situation.

He kissed her head, breathing in her scent.

"I've missed you so much, I can hardly believe we're together. It always seems like a dream," Maggie spoke in his ear, bringing him back to the moment.

He kissed her again sweetly and put her gently down on the soft ground. "Aye, my love, I feel the same, though my dream is one from which I would as soon never wake."

His heart hurt from the strength of his love and tears came into his eyes until they escaped and slid down his cheek. Maggie stood on her toes and kissed them away.

He would wait until the last moment to tell her his news. Let this time, this last time be filled with sweet memories for his beloved.

They walked hand in hand, the flush of their night's passion still warm on their skin. The morning was clear and bright as they walked the fields and meadows of the place between his world and hers. And they talked.

"I had a wonderful breakfast before I came to you. Agnes, the woman who owns the bed and breakfast, you remember I told you about her, well, she makes the most marvelous jam and scones," she smiled.

"Aye, I remember, but Maggie, please dinna tell me aboot scones and jam. It's been a century since I've tasted the likes." He hesitated, thinking, "Och, never mind, describe it tae me, Maggie, and tell me, were there kippers as weel?"

"Kippers and clotted cream and lovely tea."

"Maggie, yer killin' me, love. Stop!" He laughed and she laughed with him.

"Look there, Maggie, can ye see the woodpecker, just there?" he pointed to a large tree and a busy bird with the red, black and white markings.

"Beautiful."

"Aye. The birds go in and oot of Faerie, so sometimes I can see them. Some strange and different birds live inside. Strange and sorrowful songs, they have. I dreamed of one the other night with feathers the color of the sea, which sang a tune sae sweetly. I dreamed of it before."

"Can you play it for me on your whistle?"

"Of course. This is for you, my love. I wanted to wait, but listen." He pulled the long silver whistle from the pocket of his cloak and played the sweet melody, remembering his dream and the strange bird's song. Maggie watched his strong fingers move quickly over the instrument, and watched his face, so handsome, eyes closed as he concentrated on the tune. It was worth it, she thought. Every minute. She reached up and touched his cheek and he opened his eyes and smiled as he played. His eyes were Fiona's eyes, Maggie thought, and wondered how she would tell him about his child. The tune over, he put his whistle back into his pocket and put his arm around her. She snuggled into his warmth.

He stroked her hair lovingly, lamenting with the knowledge that soon his time with her would be over. For good and all. He tried to get his thoughts on to other subjects but it was no use. His hands clutched her arm protectively, instinctively.

"Ouch!" Maggie said, raising her head. One look told her something was wrong. Usually the anger and the tears began towards the end of their time together, not the beginning.

"Ewan, my love, what is it? You have that look, and I'm not ready to see that look yet."

He cupped both his hands around her face and bent down to kiss her mouth. It was a kiss filled with such sweetness that Maggie felt her own tears forming.

"Och, Maggie, my oon, I didna want tae tell ye sae soon, but it seems as though I canna hide my feelings from ye."

At these words Maggie felt her heart fall to her stomach. "What could be so bad, love? I don't want to think about parting yet. We've only just come together."

"How can I tell ye?" Ewan said, shaking his roan head back and forth like a restless horse.

"Tell me what?"

"That witch, Barabel, has made a deal with a fachan for something she covets, with myself as payment. When he delivers tae her what she craves, he'll tithe me this Bealltainn."

Maggie grabbed his hand and held it tightly. "What's a fachan?"

"The worst kind of faerie, pure evil. A shape-shifter sae disgusting yer blood could curdle. His tithing day is Bealltainn, only a short time awa'."

"Bealltainn is in May, isn't it?"

"Aye."

"So we've got six months to get you out of this," Maggie said trying to sound optimistic, though her heart was sinking to the soles of her feet.

"Lass, ye dinna understand. There's no escaping a fachan. Their power is great, and they seem to be gaining in it," Ewan said, his tone hopeless. "This is oor last time together, and the sooner we face that, the better we'll be for it."

"I can't. No, I won't. I won't let some fachan, or whatever you call it, have you. Take me to Barabel, let me have a few words with her."

"Are ye daft, lass? She'd kill ye right there on the spot, wouldna she just, and revel in it! Nay, there's no hope." Maggie refused to accept defeat. She began to pace, wearing a track in the soft earth beneath her feet.

Stopping short, she said, "What if this thing doesn't get what he's looking for? Didn't you say she traded you for something?"

"Aye, but it's rare that a fachan doesna get what he's after." He hesitated mentioning his meeting with the prince. It would do no good to get Maggie's hopes up.

"Isn't there a chance?" Maggie asked full of determination.

"A rare one."

"Oh, my love, there must be another way! I must get you out of here! Can't I?" Maggie pleaded, losing hope in the face of her lover's resignation.

"Maggie, we've been through this before. Tamlin's spell was different from mine. His lover was able to set him free. Barabel cast such a spell as to make me hers for eternity. Until noo."

"I'm sure I'm strong enough to withstand anything Barabel can throw at me! I've read the stories. I can get the holy water, the green cloak! I can do it, Hugh! I can. I can't let you go. No, I won't let you go!" Maggie was becoming increasingly hysterical, almost talking to herself.

Ewan grabbed her and held her fast. "Maggie, ye must listen! Ye canna release me. No one can! Barabel saw to that! Ye must let me go. Ye must have a life wi' out me."

"No!" Maggie shouted, beating his chest, sobbing. Ewan held her until her sobs subsided and her breath came in ragged gasps. He kissed her face, wet with salty tears. "Love, let us make the most of the time we have."

Hardly able to bring herself to speak, Maggie whispered,

"I can't."

"Ye must, lass."

Maggie sniffed. "You never told me exactly what her spell was. Tell me now."

"What good would it do? I've no one left and Barabel saw to it that there'd never be one born to help me, or if there was, I'd be no more than a legend by the time."

"Love, I don't understand a thing you're saying. Start from the beginning and tell me," Maggie said, still gripping his strong hand. He sat down on a grassy patch and gestured for her to sit beside him.

"Maggie, my darlin', as well ye ken, Tamlin's only escape was to be rescued by his true love. Aye, Barabel kent that and transformed her spell so only one of my oon blood could take me awa' from here. I've got no one left, of that I'm sure. They're all lying in the kirkyard; bones, they are, by noo."

Maggie felt her stomach heave at his words. Why hadn't they talked about this before? Was it because this was her secret romance, her timeless lover, her fairytale? In the past when she had talked about taking him away he had made it clear how impossible it was, and she had resigned herself to the fact that this would be their existence until she was old. He, though, more than elderly in years, would remain youthful long after she was dead and gone. She had let any thoughts of rescue fade, believing it to be hopeless. Learning that there might be a way after all, made her sick with remorse.

"Ewan, why didn't you tell me this before?" Maggie cried, a trace of hysteria in her tone.

"Och, Maggie, what's the good in it? I've none left on this earth tae help me, and even if I did, would any believe it?" He shook his head sadly.

"My love, you do! You do! I met him on my way here.

I was going to tell you. His name is Ewan MacDougall. Can you believe it? He's your grandnephew! He lives here! In Scotland, I mean."

"That's all well and good lass, but the only one that can save me must be a lassie of my oon blood. A man will no do and Barabel saw to it that none in my family should bear a lass after me. Did yer good man no tell ye that there are only lads in his family?"

"Actually he did tell me that, but..."

"Maggie, it's of no use tae dwell on this. We must make the best of this time together and ken that we'll see each other in heaven, if the good Lord will allow me entrance."

Maggie, at a loss for words reached into her bag and pulled out the old black and white photograph of Fiona she had so impulsively brought along. She handed it to Ewan, who took it with a puzzled look. He glanced at it, then handed it back to her with a confused half smile.

"Lovely, Maggie, ye were lovely as a lassie. Ye still are."

"That's not me," Maggie spoke quietly, looking at him searchingly, hoping he could accept the truth and forgive her for keeping so important a secret.

Ewan took it back and looked at it again, comprehension dawning on his face. His words were barely a whisper, "She's got my mither's brow, yer chin." He sat down on a rock and scrutinized the photo. He looked from the photo to Maggie, shaking his head. "Och, Maggie, how could ye keep this a secret from me!" He gripped her hand, his other still gripping the photo.

"I'm sorry. I didn't want you to be sad, knowing you'd never see her."

"Maggie, it was my right!" He turned away, letting go of her hand.

"Please, don't turn away from me! I'm sorry, Hugh, you can't know how sorry, but I thought I was protecting you from any more pain! Ewan! Please believe me! I never wanted to hurt you." Now Maggie was crying hot tears of shame, guilt and too many secrets. "I love you," she whispered, desperate for him to hear.

He slowly turned to her, a careworn look on his handsome face. "Maggie, my love, my oon, I understand why ye never told me, but it's a shock, ye ken."

"Of course it is."

"Does she ken aboot her faither?" he asked in a whisper.

Maggie shook her head, eyes cast down.

"Och, Maggie, who does she think her faither is, then? Do ye have another man back there? Do ye, Maggie?"

"No, of course not. There's no one else, there never has been anyone but you. She...nobody knows about you. She thinks, oh, I don't know what she thinks." Maggie put her face in her hands.

"What is her name?"

"Fiona. Her name is Fiona." Maggie watched through her hands as the strong man beside her dissolved into tears.

She let him cry until he was done, appreciating the depth of his emotion. When at last his ragged breath became steady again she sat beside him, her knees barely touching his. When his hand finally touched her, she let out a long sigh.

"Tell me about oor daughter. Is she a wee thing? Can she speak yet? Has she taken her first step?"

"Hugh, she was already three years old in the picture."

"Aye, Maggie, how daft of me, of course. So she can walk and talk."

"Yes, love, she can walk and talk. Hugh..." Oh God, how am I going to tell him that she's fourteen?

"Can she say her letters?"

"Darling, she can read and write and play the whistle and ride a horse. Oh, Hugh, she's fourteen years old!"

Ewan was silent for a moment. "When is her birthday?"

"August 11 is her birthday. She was a few days late."

"Maggie, it was the first time then. Ye've kept it tae yourself all this time," he said slowly. Maggie thought he would be angry but instead he took her hand and kissed the palm. "Oh, my sweet Maggie, what a burden on ye tae harbor this secret for sae many years."

"You, you're not angry with me?"

"How can I be angry? I see noo that ye were trying tae protect me from hurt. But Maggie, please tell my child aboot her faither, please Maggie, tell her so she kens who I was and that she *had* a faither."

The meaning was clear and the knowledge that there *was* a chance of escape, but that neither would risk the life of their child, remained unspoken.

"Tell me about my child, Maggie," he said, resigned.

Maggie thought his expression so heart wrenching, she grabbed his face in her hands. "Oh, Ewan, my dearest love, I wish..." she said, looking at the portrait of their smiling child.

"Nay, never even wish that. Just tell me about her and when ye return, tell her aboot me. I can die happy."

Maggie was at a loss for words, for so resignedly did he speak that there was nothing more to say.

"She's beautiful and willful and stubborn and talented and oh, I don't know where to begin."

"So, ye'd say she's like yer oon self, then?" Ewan said, trying to lighten the terrible tension.

"Well, she definitely has a few drops of you in her too. She loves nature above all else, rides like a champion; she's a musician and a dreamer. She's not very tall, though. Her hair is long and her eyes are an amazing blue-green with a crazy orange ring around the pupil, like yours. Exactly like yours."

"Och, Maggie. What must she think, not having a faither? Doesna she question ye about her parentage?"

"Oh, Hugh, of course. She's been wanting a father for so long. So many times I fantasized about telling her, her reaction, even bringing her here to meet you, but in the end I couldn't. I guess I'm a coward."

"Nay, love, no a coward. Just a mither trying tae protect her child from suffering."

"Yes, but in the course of all my secrets I've created a chasm between us that I'm afraid will never close."

"Then ye must go home and close it. Find love, Maggie. Not only for yerself but for oor child as weel." He put his head down; unable to look at her, for though he tried to be sincere his own words were torture to him.

She pulled him next to her and placed the cloak over them both like a shroud of despair. She encircled his broad body with her arms, never wanting to let go. All happy thoughts were gone. Their moment was over. Taking comfort from one another, Maggie lay still, trying to imagine a life without him. Once a year was hardly bearable, but never again! She searched her mind for any possibility, any way to override this heinous spell of her nemesis. She would do her research. There must be a way, she thought. I won't accept this. And then a thought occurred to her. She sat bolt upright, startling Ewan, who had been drifting to sleep. "Old Hugh said that his great-grandmother, your mother, had faerie blood, but I thought he was only teasing me. Is it true?"

"If my mither did have a wee touch of the blood in her, then it's still coursing through me, but certainly not enough tae fight Barabel on my oon, if that's what yer wanting tae know."

"No, that's not it. I was thinking that if you have the blood..."

"Then my daughter, oor Fiona, does as weel."

The two gazed at one another, imagining the possibilities this information might hold.

Chapter 32

The time is too short, Maggie said to herself. Their time together was always too short for her, yet there had always been the next year to look forward to and the one after that. This time though, would be their last. She could barely contain her despair.

Ewan took her in his arms, hugging her tightly, and then he sat her down upon his knee and began kissing her in earnest. She never wanted him to stop.

"I can't leave you," she whispered into his ear. "I'd rather die than never see you again."

"Dinna say such. I dinna want tae hear that," he said, shaking his head. "Ye must be strong for Fiona," he said with finality.

"I won't be any good to her or anyone else." She put her head down and cried.

He put his arms around her once more and held her close. He buried his face in her hair. They stayed this way for some time until Maggie felt him shaking. She pulled herself slightly away so she could see him. Tears were streaming down his face and he shook his head.

His words sounded choked as he finally spoke, "Maggie, it's just that I love ye so much. The thought of never seein' ye again is more than I can bear." Then he released a sob so deep that Maggie could no longer contain herself and the two held each other and let their sorrow and a myriad of feelings overtake them.

Together they thought of life without the other: Ewan destined to some heinous end at the hands of the fachan, leaving his Maggie alone; Maggie, trying to go on, knowing that their child could have saved her father, but for Maggie's secrecy, and now, even if they told their daughter and she agreed, it was too late. *Samhain* was over and by the time the worlds could be crossed again, Ewan would have been tithed.

When their tears were spent, the sky was steely gray, and the wind rose, stirring the trees like emotion.

"I can't say goodbye. Oh, God."

"We must part and ye must live, Maggie. We will see each other again."

"I have to see you again. I will!" she said, vehemently

"Ye canna know how good that sounds tae my ears, my *mnathan*."

Something about the way he said that word told Maggie that its meaning was vital to him. "Hugh, what you just called me, what does it mean?"

"It means wife, Maggie. Wife. Would you... that is, if we could have been together, would ye marry me, Maggie?"

Maggie stood before him, tears streaming down her freckled face into her mouth. "Of course," she whispered, overcome.

"Och, Maggie! I should ha' done it properly," he said

getting on to one knee, guiding Maggie by the hand to his knee. Eye to eye, they locked into each other's gaze. Ewan spoke in low tones. "Maggie, my *beannachd*, my blessed love, in oor next lifetime when we step upon mortal soil together again, into the world of men... and women, would ye give me the greatest gift and become my wedded wife?"

Without hesitation Maggie said simply, "Yes."

At that moment the full moon rose from out of a copse of trees, shining light upon the lovers. They looked desolately up at it. "There's the hare, Maggie, do ye see it?" Ewan pointed to a shadow on the face of the earth's satellite.

"Where? I've often tried."

"There are two things tae notice about Lady Moon: her beautiful face and the hare. Ye must put aside the vision of her face in order tae see the hare. See the outline of the hare's tall ear? Just there..." he said, outlining it with his finger.

"Yes, Hugh, now I see it. Seeing the hare is good luck, isn't it?"

"My mither always said as much."

"Then we'll take it as such," she said. She added under her breath, "We've got to."

As they sat together, Ewan wrapped his big cloak around them both and he again played the tune he had written for Maggie, letting his love pour into the sound until it filled them both. On the last note, Ewan broke down, throwing his whistle on the ground. He let out a keening sound so pitiful that Maggie had to grab him and hold him tightly. "No, love, don't. The fachan still may not find what he's searching for. You've got to have hope. Please. I love you, Ewan MacDougall. I won't give up," she said, mustering more hope than she actually had.

Ewan looked up at her, his eyes hard. "Neither will I."

They remained entwined in each other's arms until the

light found them again. They made their way back to the "spot" where after reversing the spell that brought her here, Maggie should find herself standing in a sheep pasture by the whitewashed pile of rocks.

"*Gus an till thu*, Maggie! Until ye return, my love," Ewan whispered. The familiar words sounded hopeless and with one last look, Maggie left their place between with a cold heart, unable to turn away until she saw Ewan fade from her vision like a specter.

As he faded into the gloom, Maggie crumpled to the ground, any semblance of dignity discarded. She knew she should be getting back, the small window of time for a safe return was *now*, but at this moment, her despair was overwhelming and though she had been a veritable emotional wreck with Ewan beside her, seeing him go for what might be the last time was too much. She allowed herself to wallow in misery, her mind trying to wrap around the possibility of how much emptier her life might soon become, should she find no way to help him escape.

Looking at the mist beginning to lift as *Samhain's* magic faded made her realize that she'd better get out of this place and fast. Her mind was so filled with every imaginable scenario of rescue, escape, sorrow, that though she fumbled around in her mind for the right words, she found she could not remember what to say.

"Oh, dear God!" Try to get it right, try to get it right! Gaelic phrases danced through her thoughts and she tried to arrange them in the correct order to produce the right magic, but now she was panicking and panicking made her forget. Her thoughts were no longer coherent and the words that finally escaped her lips in an attempt to find her way back, came out completely erroneously and before the last word was out of her mouth, she felt herself being flung into the air as if a twister had her in its grip. She had nothing to hold on to, and as she tried to protectively pull her arms about herself she seemed to have lost all control of her muscles, some force flinging her arms until she was afraid they would be wrenched from their sockets. Her neck twisted painfully and she hoped she would not end up paralyzed.

When she returned to earth, hard, Maggie was in no place she recognized. She was completely disheveled and disoriented landing alone in a green darkness unlike anything she had ever seen before. The green engulfed her senses and for the moment, she allowed it. The setting sun sent diffused light through the leaves, making shadows flicker with movement. She was too confused to even question the fact that the sun had just risen from where she had come and it was setting now. She heard muffled sounds, high pitched and musical, and she looked around to try to locate their source. Quick movements from within the green caused her pulse to quicken, and she hoped that whatever entities were watching her, for there was no doubt she was being watched, were benign.

Holding on to a nearby tree, she tried to stand, assessing any damage her botched spell might have caused. Though sore, there seemed no permanent damage and she steadied herself. She began to walk away from this place, though where she was going, she had no idea. She knew she would have to be on her guard. Caution was paramount in these enchanted woods. Under more happy circumstances, the trees would have fascinated her, with their strangely shaped leaves and colors. She stood under what resembled a willow, its hanging limbs covered in leaves, the sweet pastels of a nursery room. She heard giggles and looked up to see sparkles of light winking on the tree, flitting from hanging limb to hanging limb. One of the lights flew off the tree, hovering directly in front of her. A minuscule face with slanted, jade eyes and ears that came to a sharp point, stayed there in mid-flight, like a hummingbird at a feeder, and then buzzed off and another took its place. Maggie stood, unable to move, spellbound by what was happening as the faeries inspected her.

She shook her head in disbelief. She thought she knew where she was, and it wasn't anywhere she wanted to be alone. She knew all of this was real, of course she did. Her lover was a captive of one such, but being in these woods, in this space, made her feel completely helpless. She had never truly been inside before, only in that place between this world and her own.

The tiny faeries followed her as her head cleared and she walked lightly and quietly over what seemed a trail. The sun was fading and the dusk spread like quicksilver. As the sun sank in whatever direction it did in Faerie and the shadows became more penetrating, she began to hear unpleasant sounds, whisperings and creaky mutterings. And there was increased movement from every direction. Within moments, the sparkling faeries were gone, likely fleeing to another part of the forest. They were afraid and Maggie felt her own heart close with fear. She tried to stave it off, knowing that her fear would only bring whatever lurked in these woods closer. Too late. They must have felt it at once because they were already moving in on her, whatever *they* were. She began to run, wildly swinging her hands in an attempt to protect herself from an onslaught of flying entities or debris, she wasn't sure which.

She was being battered by the attack, as if bats were flying in every direction, blindly crashing into her. These though, were no bats, she well knew. She could hear angry exclamations as they assaulted her, though she couldn't make out what was being said. She kept running, falling once over an exposed root and scraping her knee. She covered her head with her hands, trying to get up before they killed her or caused her real harm. She rose to her feet as quickly as she could and jumped over a small stream. At once, the assail ceased. She turned to look behind and saw a line of deranged bantam creatures, dark shapes, eyes glaring, shaking their runty fists at her, but obviously unwilling to cross the stream, though it wasn't the stream that stopped them in mid-flight.

Maggie walked slowly backwards, keeping her eyes on the sprites or hobgoblins or whatever those things were that had suddenly stopped chasing her, wary that they would begin the chase again. But as she backed off, they seemed to lose interest and flew off in the direction from which they had come. She was about to turn forward when she stumbled into someone or something. She shrieked, putting a hand over her mouth.

Chapter 33

Fiona and her friend were waiting in the kitchen for Aunt Kat to return from the airport with Maggie. Fiona would just spring Rionnag on her, the way she herself had found out about her mother's secret. Let it be a shock to Maggie; let her mother know that she wasn't the only one who could kept a secret. Plus, a Faerie Princess could get information out of her close-lipped mother, and it was high time to get things out in the open. Fiona was nervously harrumphing when the car pulled in. She breathed an inward sigh of relief. As angry as she was, she was glad her mother was home. She hated Maggie going away, flying across the ocean, and even though every time she left, Fiona was furious with her, she liked it when Maggie called upon arrival and was especially glad when her mother returned safely. She left Rionnag sitting on the kitchen counter while she ran out to meet her mother. Gram followed her out.

They saw Aunt Kat sitting alone in the car, her head

Jana Laiz

down on the steering wheel. Fiona bent over to look for her mother on the passenger side, and not seeing her, ran around the car to double check, and then stopped short as she took in the scene; the empty passenger seat, no luggage in the car, her aunt looking miserable. Maggie hadn't come home.

Kat looked up, her face stricken, and it became worse as she saw her niece and her mother standing before her in disbelief. They looked at each other in dreadful understanding before Fiona ran into the house, slamming the door the behind her. She was upstairs and on her bed before Aunt Kat had opened the car door and climbed wearily out.

Gram came into the kitchen and saw Rionnag sitting on the counter looking somewhat confused.

"Gram, I thought I saw Fiona run by. Has something happened?"

"Yes, it seems" she said, voice cracking.

"What is it? Gram?"

"Katherine went to get Maggie and she apparently wasn't there."

At that moment, Kat walked into the kitchen. "Ma, I checked with the airline, and she was booked for that flight, but never checked in or boarded. And God forbid Maggie should have a cell phone! We'd better call the B & B in Scotland, where she stays. I know Maggie's been full of secrets, but this just isn't like her. I'm scared."

"I am too," her mother agreed.

"I think something may be wrong," Rionnag said ominously.

"I'm sure you're right. Oh dear!" Gram put her head in her hands. Sniffling she said, "We'd better tell Fiona."

"Ma, before you panic her, call Maggie's hotel, what's it called?"

"The Grey Goose. I'll do it right now!"

Although it was late in Scotland, Gram put a call in to the bed and breakfast and found, not surprisingly, that there had been no word from Maggie. Agnes told her that Maggie said she'd be back, but had never showed. More alarming, but again, not surprising, was the fact that Agnes knew of no yoga retreat anywhere in the area. Kat was standing next to her, ear to the phone, listening to the conversation. They looked at each other in disturbing understanding as Gram hung up. Neither one of them was barely able to take a breath; their anxiety was so high.

They went upstairs, dreading the conversation. Gram knew full well that Fiona would feel abandoned and betrayed by her mother. She remembered the conversation she and Maggie had had only the week before.

"Mom, I don't know what to do to make it right with Fiona," Maggie had said.

"Well, Maggie, I can't tell you what to do, but what I can tell you is that Fiona needs your attention, and it's never too late to start giving it. I hate to say this, but you really haven't been there for her in quite some time."

"I know, I know," Maggie said, her hands over her face. "I'm a terrible mother! Are you sure it's not too late, Ma? I mean she's already a teenager. I really blew it, didn't I?"

"Look, my love, I don't know what happened to you to make you so sad. So... distant. I thought you had a happy childhood..."

"Oh, Mom, I did. Very."

"Nevertheless, you need to start paying more attention to her. You know, take her to the movies, out to dinner. To one of your marches! Without your sister or me. You know she's in the throes of that charming adolescent rebellion/ separation stage. It's perfectly normal. You and your sister certainly did it, and I know I did. The only thing is, when she tells you she hates you, don't believe her. And don't get so hurt that you ignore her. Yes, give her space, but *be* there when she wants to come to you. Don't shut yourself away from her. From any of us. Can you do that?"

Maggie had looked out the window for a moment before she replied. "Yes. I can do that. In fact, I will do it. As soon as I come home from this trip, you'll see a difference. I promise."

"Maggie, be careful of making such promises. Small changes are good."

Gram opened the door and entered Fiona's room, Kat and Rionnag following behind. She sat down on the bed, the faerie alighting on the headboard. Gram rubbed Fiona's shoulders and whispered, "Fi, sit up and let's talk." Her face deep in the pillows, Fiona's response was muffled, "Go away, Gram. I knew she would do this." As she continued, she sat up, her eyes fiery with anger.

"She's probably still with her *boyfriend*. She was having so much fun, she forgot to come home."

Before Gram could reply, Rionnag flew down and landed on Fiona's pillow, looking the child in the eye. "Fiona, I dinna think that. I think she might have gotten caught, perhaps she overstayed, through *Samhain*, and couldna get back through."

"Fiona, your mother may be secretive, but she isn't irresponsible. You know this isn't like her."

"We think she must be in some kind of trouble," her aunt said depressingly.

Fiona could feel the blood rush from her body and her heart start to pound.

"Gram!" she said, her eyes wild. Her grandmother grabbed her fiercely.

"Gram, Ri, what do we do?" she cried.

"We find her," Rionnag said gravely.

Emily Harris watched her granddaughter's face as Rionnag said those three words and at that moment, she knew that Fiona was going to enter Faerie with Rionnag and there would be no way to stop her. She realized that this was something Fiona had to do, and try as she might, she could think of nothing to tell the child that would dissuade her. She also knew that she must stay behind to take care of the shop and the house and to wait in case there was a call from Maggie, which she knew there would not be. The thought of letting her granddaughter enter that realm, filled with magic and danger and uncertainty seemed incredibly irresponsible, but in her heart of hearts, she knew that there was no other solution. This was Fiona's rite of passage, her journey to the east, her taking the sword from the stone. She knew she had to let her go.

"Fiona, go and find your mother. Bring her home."

Fiona looked at her grandmother in disbelief. It was exactly what she had been thinking. As angry as she was at her mother, if she were in danger, Fiona had to help her. And if she weren't in danger, then Fiona would find her and tell her off. Either way, she was going in and she could hardly believe Gram was going to let her go, let alone, encourage her. Her aunt was uncharacteristically silent.

Rionnag looked at the three humans and saw the determination in Fiona's eyes. Standing her full six-inch height, she said with authority, "We'll go at midnight, when the moon is high."

Fiona and Gram nodded in agreement. Kat stared at her mother and niece in disbelief. When she finally spoke, she was shocked at her own words.

"Are you insane? Are you both insane? No offense Princess, but this is ridiculous! Mom, how are you going to explain to Maggie when she comes home that you let her daughter go into faerieland? No way. No way, I'm sorry. I'm not letting you go!"

"Aunt Kat! What if Mom is really lost? Do you think I can know that and do nothing? Think about it? We're just going to sit around here waiting for her NOT to come home? C'mon, you know you'd do the same thing if it were Gram."

Her aunt looked at her niece as she spoke, noting the fire in her eyes. She did not want to acknowledge that Fiona was right, but she knew she was. Fiona had to rescue her mother, and Kat was going to have to let her.

"Fiona, fetch the stones if ye please. Bring them here; place them on the floor by the bed in a circle. I need to make certain if together they have power. We can leave tonight at moonrise, and if ye are still willing, together we will go through."

Fiona ran to the window ledge and one by one took all eleven stones and lay them on the floor with Maggie's special one. The curtain shifted and she saw the coyote again, as she had so many nights before, eyes glowing yellow in the twilight. Rionnag fluttered over to the window and peered out into the dusk. The coyote caught her eye and they stared at each other for a long moment. Suddenly, he howled. It was a high-pitched howl that carried warning. He howled again, ran back into the darkness of the woods, and was gone.

"Fiona, that was no ordinary animal. He is one of the fey folk. I ken by his eyes. I fear he was warning ye of something."

"I've seen that coyote here before. He's stood there lots of times. Watching. He kind of reminds me of the coyote-boy I danced with." She looked over to her grandmother who gave her a wide-eyed look.

"I recall the beings ye danced with, I was watching ye. Listening too. They were a right lively bunch. Maybe it is the same one. Shape-shifters take many guises. We must be careful."

"I don't think he means me harm. I think he's watching over me. Mom's seen him too. She says he's my spirit guide."

"She may be right, but I'm thinking now ye shouldna come through with me. It could be dangerous for ye."

"You see! Even the Princess thinks so!" Kat argued.

"No way, I'm going. If my mother can go gallivanting all over faerieland, then so can I. And if she's in trouble, I'm getting her out of it. Besides, you can't go alone," Fiona said adamantly to Rionnag.

Fiona arranged the stones in a circle on the floor. She could feel the energy dancing about the room. Rionnag could feel it too and fluttered around in a rather frenzied way.

"Do ye feel them working their magic, Fiona, Kat, Gram?" she asked, landing on the floor beside them. She stood without touching them, standing as high as the largest one. Maggie's.

"Yes," Fiona said, the single syllable leaving her mouth as if in slow motion. Gram and Kat simply nodded.

Rionnag was muttering some words in what Fiona now knew was the "old tongue," and with each click of her tongue a stone sparked, sending streams of blue light into the air. "Fiona, these are verra powerful, and with or without a spell, we'll be able to enter. But I must warn ye, I dinna ken what we might find there since it isna my world, at least, not my part of the world. Do ye want to change yer mind? I'll understand if ye do."

Fiona sank to the floor, crouched down, face to face with her friend. "Rionnag," she said softly, "I have to do this as much as you do. Whatever happens, I feel ready." She smiled with courage and determination. Rionnag saw the emotion shining out of her friend's eyes, and Fiona saw it reflecting back in the faerie's amethyst ones. Gram and Kat, watching this moving scene, felt like intruders and moved to the door.

"We will take the stones and bring them out into the air. We must do this in the elements, with the living Mither Earth beneath our feet. First, I'll try to get a feel for the spot we are to create with the stones. It must be a place of strength, where the energy from the earth pulses with power. Then, if all goes as planned, at moonrise, we leave. Let me out the window, I'll be back as soon as I find the spot."

Fiona went to the partially opened window, pulled back the curtains and looked out into the soft evening. She pushed the glass up higher and lifted the screen. Putting her head out, she looked for the lone creature, the coyote that she had felt such a kinship with, but the moon was not yet risen and he hadn't returned. She gestured to Rionnag who landed on the sill and breathed deeply the fragrant air that stirred the curtains.

"I'll be back for ye," she whispered, and flew out into the twilight.

Fiona watched her until the faerie was a mere speck, but she sensed where she was heading. Fiona guessed Rionnag would find her secret place and that would be where the magic would happen. It was a spot in the small orchard where Fiona liked to play her recorder, open enough so she could feel the sun on her face yet hidden among the apple trees. It was a place that Gram had let her wander into as a toddler because she could watch her from the kitchen window. It always made Fiona feel safe knowing her grandmother was watching over her, but it was secluded enough to feel private.

She left the screen and turned to her grandmother who stood by the door, her face an open book of pride mixed with apprehension. Without a word, Fiona ran into her arms. The two embraced, hugging each other fiercely.

"I cannot believe I'm letting you do this!" Gram whispered loudly, her face next to Fiona's.

"Gram, you couldn't stop me, so it's better this way. You know I'd hate to have to lie to you." She could feel her grandmother nodding her head.

She turned to her aunt who could barely look her in the eye. She grabbed Fiona's arm in a fierce grip.

"I'm scared for you Fi. I don't know what I'll do if I lose my sister and my niece. How am I supposed to be okay with this!"

"You don't have to be."

"I'm going to go to Scotland and wait for you and Maggie at Agnes'. Yes, that's what I'm going to do!" she said determinedly, putting particular emphasis on the word "you."

"Okay, Aunt Kat. That's a good idea."

Fiona gently pulled away then went to the stones. She tentatively touched one. Nothing. She tried to see if she could pull sparks from any of them. She touched all the small ones lightly, somewhat afraid. No sparks issued from any of them. She laughed at herself. You don't have "the blood," she told herself. Still crouching on the floor, she crawled over to Maggie's stone, the one with the word on it. She reached part way, then withdrew her hand. She had felt a buzzing run through her body as her hand had neared the stone. Again she reached toward it. Again, she felt as if an electrical current were running through her. She *had* to touch it, but she wondered if, because of the power of it together with the others, she would explode. Its pull was magnetic and she reached out a third time, the electrical feeling intensifying the closer she got to it. As if by force, her hand opened wide and was flung upon the stone. She gripped it, feeling only the current, and with her hand still upon it, the stone gave up a sound. It was a low keening, musical sound, haunting in its melody. Out of the keening came a name, one Fiona knew well. Two long syllables drawn out in a cry of despair so great it brought tears to her eyes. She listened until the sound was gone and the familiar sounds of the house returned. Only then did she let go of the stone, and, looking down at her open palm, thought she could make out the imprint of the word that graced the stone. She blinked once and it was gone. She looked at her aunt and grandmother who were crying softly, such a great feeling of loneliness having come over them.

Rionnag heard the sound just as she reached her chosen spot, and this confirmed her choice. She marked the spot with a little spell and sent some sparks flying out of her fingers, causing the spot to glow faintly. She stood for a moment looking past the orchard to the edge of the forest and felt the slightest of forebodings.

Fiona placed the stones into the leather bag she had found in her mother's closet. She put the strap over her shoulder, then over her head, like an army duffle, and stood by the window waiting for Rionnag to return. She saw a tiny light speeding through the sky and in a moment her friend alighted on the windowsill, breathless and exhilarated.

"I've found the right spot, Fiona. We wait for the Lady Moon."

"Yes," Fiona agreed.

While they waited, again Rionnag searched Maggie's book for a spell that would bring them to the other side, once they entered *here*. Soon she found one that she hoped would work. She had Fiona carefully copy the Gaelic words from the page onto a sheet of paper so that they could say the right words once they were ready. Fiona put it carefully in her pocket, safely next to her recorder.

They were yawning as they sat waiting. Both Gram and Fiona dozed several times before it was finally time to go.

"Are ye ready?" Rionnag asked Fiona.

"Yes, I'm ready."

"Do ye have the spell?"

"Yes, I've got it. "

"All the stones in the sack?"

"Yes. Let's go," Fiona whispered to her friend.

"I'm coming," Gram said loudly. They both looked at her, startled. Her daughter grabbed her arm. "To say goodbye," she explained.

"I'm staying. I cannot bear to watch you leave," Kat said and grabbed her niece in an embrace and went into the kitchen to make arrangements to go to Scotland where she would wait for them. Her mother could substitute for her, she decided.

Rionnag perched on Fiona's shoulder as they stole quietly out the back door and into the darkness. The moon was hidden behind some clouds and neither Fiona nor Gram had thought to bring a flashlight. Rionnag softly muttered some words and began to glow like a tiny light, illuminating the gloom.

"Follow me!" Rionnag flew off and started toward the orchard, just as Fiona had guessed she would. To Fiona's surprise and delight, a circle glowed in blue light as they approached.

"Rionnag, how did you do that?"

"Fiona, it's not polite to ask a magician her secrets," Rionnag said with a smile. "Now, place the stones around that circle, the large one here," she pointed. Fiona did as she was told, the blue light glowing brighter as each stone was placed carefully on the soft ground. When all twelve stones were placed the light abruptly went out.

"Now we wait for the moon's entrance," Rionnag told her friend. The faerie flew to Gram and landed on her shoulder. "Hold me in yer hand, if ye please," she whispered. Gram put her hand up to where the faerie stood and held it out. Rionnag climbed on and Gram brought her hand in front of her. Rionnag looked deeply into the old woman's eyes and said seriously, "We will find her. I make this a solemn promise to ye. I willna falter. I will never waver in finding yer daughter," she said. "And I will keep Fiona safe." She put her tiny palm up and Gram touched her free hand to Rionnag's. "Ken this, a faerie promise is binding. Fiona and Maggie will come home to ye. I want to say…" she choked with emotion. "I want to say that ye have made me more welcome than I ever would have believed. I will never forget ye or yer kindness." Gram was wiping tears from her eyes as the faerie spoke. The faerie kissed her own palm and flew to Gram's shoulder and alighted. She took her kissed palm and pressed it gently onto Gram's cheek. "Remember, a faerie promise is binding." As she said those words, the moon appeared brightly in the dark sky. The faerie looked up at it and whispered, "Now, we must leave."

Fiona grabbed her grandmother once more and said, "I love you, Gram."

"And I love you. Be safe and Godspeed."

Rionnag flew to Fiona and sat upon her shoulder, the girl reaching to hold the faerie's petite hand. She felt Rionnag's hand curl around her index finger. One by one the stones began to spark. Fiona turned towards each one, drawn by the light. As the eleventh stone sparked, Fiona knew the last one, the twelfth one, Maggie's stone, would be the one to send them. When that large stone began to spark, a sound issued from it, but unlike the first time, this one was a beautiful sound, a low whistle filled with gentle longing. Abruptly, the wind rose and Fiona felt the faerie grip her finger tighter. Fiona realized that Rionnag was frightened and was astonished to find herself growing protective. Wasn't she the child who needed protecting? Yet she was not afraid. She lifted Rionnag to the palm of her hand, the little hand still gripping her finger. The wind blew stronger until Fiona had to sit or be blown away. Her hair whipped around her face as the wind blew more intensely. The moon cast an eerie light and as a cloud passed in front of the brilliant orb, Fiona and Rionnag dissipated like mist burned by sunlight.

Standing at the kitchen window, transfixed and unable to move or call out, Kat watched as her niece disappeared into the night. She stood there at the sink, her mouth open wide, her eyes wider.

Gram stared after her precious granddaughter, the moonlight revealing a determined look on Fiona's tense face, and a moment later both she and her bantam friend vanished.

She stood in front of the circle of stones and watched the stones fade in color and become dark. "Fiona..." she called weakly. A moment later, Kat was standing next to her mother, a strong arm around her. They stood there for a long time. Gram was as cold as the stones that now lay still and empty as Kat helped her make her way back to the house. She walked slowly back inside, feeling totally helpless. She would be there when Fiona and Maggie returned, because that was the only outcome that was possible in her mind. She refused to let any other enter her consciousness.

Nighttime was gone and the day was dazzling as the two entered the fey realm.

Fiona, forgetting momentarily the ominous reason they were there, cried out, "Look!" She was marveling at the profusion of flowers she had landed in, each a color unlike anything she had ever seen before. "They're so beautiful. So different, but familiar at the same time."

"Aye, different and familiar. It is different in its color and feeling from Scotland. More mystery here; it feels more, ehm, wilder." Rionnag was standing behind Fiona, who was still looking intently at the flowers. Something about the way Rionnag's voice sounded in her ear made her turn and look at her friend for the first time since they crossed over. What she saw made her fall back into the cluster of bright purple flowers.

Rionnag reached to help Fiona rise from of the patch of blooms, and as Fiona stood up, she found herself blue-green eye to amethyst eye with one who had been her tiny friend only a moment before. Seeing Rionnag this way made Fiona catch her breath. The faerie was so beautiful and so... well, big!

"How are you so ...? I mean... am I tiny?"

Rionnag laughed, amused. It was a rich, warm sound that filled Fiona's ears. Hearing it come out of a life size faerie made her stare in wonder. For effect, Rionnag spread her wings wide, their colors swirling deliciously. Fiona gasped audibly and Rionnag laughed again, delighted by her friend's wonderment.

"Whether you are small or I am big is no consequence; we are equals on this side, friends and all."

"We're the same size!" Fiona sputtered.

"Aye, it seems to be so; we could be mistaken for sisters but for the color of our hair. But I've no sister."

"I don't either. I wish we could..."

"...be sisters?" Rionnag finished.

"Well, I know we can't be real sisters, but you know, maybe..."

"Faerie sisters!"

"Yes, faerie sisters. Is it possible?"

"Have ye no realized it yet, my wee friend, anything is possible." Rionnag smiled. "Everything is possible," she said softly. "Come, take my hand, I ken what to do to make ye my sister. Mind ye, ye willna become a princess for it, but then, it's no great title anyway."

"I'm not sure what being a princess means in this world, probably not much, but I know it means something where you come from, Rionnag. Don't belittle it. You are very important. Probably the most important faerie of all!"

Rionnag blushed. "Thank ye for saying it. Now, let's get on with this sisterhood ceremony."

Fiona could barely contain herself. A sister! Who cared if she wasn't a real sister? Fiona had always wanted one, asked her mother for one, not fully understanding why it was impossible for her mother to give her one. When she got older, she longed for someone to share secrets with at night, in the same room. Someone to fight with when she was in a bad mood.

It wasn't the same with adults. She could talk to her mother and grandmother about many things, but still she wanted someone to gripe with about personal stuff that she couldn't tell them. Friends could dump you, but a sister couldn't stop being a sister like a friend could. A sister was always there for you. Didn't they have to be? Wasn't it the rule? Even one who lived in another world would be better than none at all.

She never understood why people envied her for being an only child. She thought it should be called a "lonely child" instead. "But you have your own room," they would say jealously. "You don't have any competition." No, the fact was, being an only child stunk. But now she was going to have a sister, an older, beautiful, magical sister.

Rionnag took her hand and led her to a small mound of grass and flowers. She sat Fiona down and then sat down herself, facing Fiona. Taking Fiona's hands in hers, she faced the human child, linked to her by hands and eyes. They sat that way for a long moment, and then Rionnag spoke. "*Cairdean*, my friend, I invite ye into my heart, as a true sister, not of blood, but of spirit. Do ye accept?"

Without hesitation, Fiona answered, "I do."

Rionnag whispered back, "Now repeat it to me."

"Rionnag, my friend, I invite you into my heart, as a true sister, not of blood, but of spirit. Do you accept?"

"I do." Rionnag then opened her wing and under the large, magnificent ones, new ones were forming, like feathers of a bird, but made of the same gossamer fabric as the large one. She pulled two out of herself, kissed them, and gave them to Fiona. Fiona took the tiny wings in her fingers, turning them this way and that to catch the light.

Rionnag took them back and said, "Quickly, while they still live, I'll place them here," Rionnag said touching the spots on Fiona's back that her mom always called her wings whenever she wanted a back scratch. Fiona lifted her shirt and as they touched her skin, they stuck! Fiona felt a tremendous surge of energy, as if she were being filled with an inexpressible joy.

Rionnag gasped as she watched Fiona's being change and fill with light. "Fiona, ye must really have the blood; they've taken to ye as if ye were one of us!"

Fiona felt tears of joy spring to her eyes. She smiled and nodded, unable to speak. When she could manage it, she tried to think of what gift she could give in return. From her head, she plucked out three strong strands of chestnut hair, kissed them and handed them to Rionnag. Rionnag looked at them and held them to the light, smiling. Fiona took them back again and placed them on the faerie's head. As they adhered, Rionnag felt a wave of love sweep over her and tears sprang to her eyes as well. The two sat together, joyous tears falling, laughing gently. Finally Rionnag stood up, bringing Fiona with her. Rionnag kissed Fiona on each cheek then gave her a powerful hug. Fiona hugged her back as tightly.

Rionnag then handed Fiona a tiny bouquet of such exquisite flowers that at first glance Fiona thought they were porcelain. As a child she had always wondered how flowers could be so beautiful with such exquisite detail and was slightly flabbergasted when Rionnag told her that their designs and intricate patterns were created by faeries.

"Aye Fiona, we are responsible for the flower designs, did ye no ken?" Rionnag was laughing a little.

"Wow. No, I can't believe it. No wait. I take that back. In fact, I don't think I'll ever say that again!" She shook her head at her own confusion.

She looked down at the bouquet in her hand and then unbelievingly at her friend and whispered, "Are we really sisters now?"

"We are, for all time."

Fiona smiled and said, "I'm so glad."

"Aye," Rionnag said, "I am as weel. I've been wanting a sister o'er long." And she touched the three dark strands that for some strange reason, stood out quite clearly in contrast to her golden hair. Fiona, without touching, could feel the tiny faerie's wings stuck fast to her own back.

The new sisters were both smiling as they made their way through the meadow, Fiona gasping often at the unfamiliar colors and shapes of everything around her. There were no dwellings; no roads or any structures at all, no outward signs of human activity, just wildness. But there were places where there were dark shadows. Dark, dismal patches where there ought to be life. The closer she looked, the more she realized that some of the flowers showed signs of decay. She wondered about them. How could there be shadows when the sun was shining? They weren't like shadows cast from trees, but places devoid of light. Rionnag noticed Fiona's consternation and looked to where her young friend looked.

"Sister, dearie, are ye wondering about the shadows?"

"Yes, what are they? They're creepy."

"I am saddened to say this, but Faerie is fading here as weel, perhaps faster than on my own side. Soon, unless the humans who are destroying the earth change their ways, all will be in darkness. These shadows are the places on yer side of the earth that have been desecrated. My faither told me of your streams and rivers poisoned, so many creatures in peril. I see now he was right. Sacred lands they were, but on yer side, the human side, they have been befouled in some way. The same is happening in my world across the sea. We fear that if these shadows overpower the light, then the UnSeelies will take over. They're gaining in power as is it."

"What are the UnSeelies?"

"They are the opposing clan of faeries, evil ones through and through. Some folk call them 'the host' and they are night fliers, capturing whatever gets in their way. They love humans."

"Love meaning…?" Fiona asked.

"Meaning they love to capture and torture them."

Fiona swallowed hard. "Oh."

"Dinna ye fear, now we're sisters and my wings are there," she said touching Fiona's back lightly. "Ye are one of us, so here ye'll have the essence of faerie, rather than human."

"What do the UnSeelies do to faeries?"

"They dinna bother with us, *yet*... The Seelies are far too powerful, but as I said, the more the darkness takes over the light, the more they will come to power. And believe me, that will effect yer kind as well as mine."

"Let's change the subject, okay?" Fiona said quickly.

"Okay," Rionnag said, trying out the word for the first time and rather liking the way it sounded. "Okay," she repeated. "Now, I've got to find my bearings and figure a way to get us home. I believe yer mither is still in Scotland," Rionnag said and flew up, circling around Fiona's head and higher. Fiona took the spell from her pocket, ready for Rionnag's instructions.

"I wish Gram could have come. She would love it here," Fiona said and bent down to examine a brilliantly colored wildflower in shades of cherry pink and lime green.

"Let's try to find a spot where we can go through. I'll ken it when we come to it and I hope it's close. This place feels so wild to me, I'd like to get back to familiar surroundings."

"Aren't we through? Wasn't that what the ring was for?"

"The ring brought us through to the other side. Now we've got to find the spot to get us across the sea, to my home."

Fiona was confused, but didn't bother to question further.

They walked through a meadow, Rionnag stopping every now and then to get her bearings. Ahead in the tall grass Fiona noticed some movement. Walking over to see what it was, she spotted a tiny fawn lying helplessly twisted in some undergrowth. Ever the rescuer, she ran over and bent down to help the poor thing. She reached over to try to get it unstuck and the little thing wrapped its spindly legs around her. How adorable, she thought, until the grip around her grew first tight, then crushing. Try as she might, she could not free herself and she realized something was dreadfully wrong. She struggled against this thing she now understood was no fawn, but something dark, fey. She was indeed on the other side, not in some children's tale.

"Hey! What the..." the words died in her mouth as the fawn became larger, the grasp even more stifling, and the thing raised up on two long, strong legs, and broke into a shambling run, still gripping Fiona. "Rionnag!!" she screamed. Only the first syllable was heard by the owner of that name as she flew down only to see her friend being carried away by what appeared to be a large animal, a piece of white paper dropped and flying out of reach with the wind.

"Fionnnaaaaa!!!" she screamed, helplessly.

The harder Fiona struggled, the tighter the creature's grip became, until the fawn swelled in size and, still holding her in its grasp, began to run with increasing speed. Fiona watched in horror as spindly legs exploded into skin, shattering bone and transforming soft brown deer fur into ghastly white derma dotted with red. Wiry hairs stuck out everywhere. Fiona's eyes stayed frozen on the limbs that coiled restlessly around her torso. She knew if she dared look at the face of the horror, she would pass out, or go mad.

The thing was running fast and breathing hard. It was difficult to take in air and when she tried, the stench was so disgusting Fiona's stomach heaved and she vomited all over the monster's arm. He stopped short and bellowed in rage. And then he grew larger still, until Fiona was merely a toy in his knobby hand. She tried to wriggle out of his grasp but he held her fast. She felt something sharp by her leg and with effort, pulled her instrument out of her pocket. She tried to hit him with it, but her attempt was futile. He merely laughed, a splitting, shrieking sound. She put her hands to her ears.

"DINNA THINK OF ESCAPE! YE CANNA ESCAPE, BAWD! I'LL SOON FIND THE WAY BACK TAE BARABEL, YE VILE CREATURE OF THE WOOD! AND THEN I'LL GET ME MORTAL!"

Creaghan opened his hand and looked at Fiona for the first time. She forced herself to look and what she saw was more abhorrent than even her vivid imagination could have depicted. The face returning her scrutiny bespoke volumes of enmity and loathing, its demonic eyes smoldering crimson in stark contrast to the bloodless face.

"YE ARE A FOUL TERMAGANT. SHE CAN HAVE THE LIKES O' YE. IF I HAD ME WAY..." and he put his face close to hers and stuck out a violet tongue, forked at the tip, and thrust it over her face, testing her. She flinched as revulsion rose up in her throat, threatening to overflow once more. There was a dull ache in the place her new wings were hidden.

She closed her eyes and tried to clear her mind. What was that word Rionnag had taught her, that protection word? She was grasping at her memories when the creature seemed to make some kind of decision and then they were traveling at nauseating speed. Her thoughts became confused and she fought to keep from heaving again as they hurtled by landscapes blurred by velocity. She felt wetness on her face, spray, and she realized they were crossing the ocean at too dizzying a speed to venture a look.

After many moments they slowed and Fiona realized she was gripping a bristly growth on the creature's hand. Quickly, she let it go but lost her balance and grabbed it again. She looked around her through hoary fingers like prison bars and to her amazement, she was in a place of unparalleled beauty. Verdant green hills and brilliantly adorned trees, colors and shades of light that bore no comparison to any of her world greeted her astonished eyes.

As she marveled at her surroundings, momentarily distracted from her captive state, the hand that held her changed from a gross appendage to swirling, wet smoke. Frantically, she grabbed at nothing, feeling as if she was going to fall, but found herself mysteriously supported. She heard the bellow of laughter at her fumbling. And then once more the foul extremity held her fast. Her heart beat frantically and tears fell down her face. They were passing faerie trees with leaves the color of glacial lakes. Her thoughts tumbled about incoherently and she tried once more to beat the monster with the only thing she had, her recorder. She pounded his hand with it, over and over, like some wild thing, until she saw it oozing with what might be blood. He stopped abruptly and they dropped to the ground. He shook her off him like something disgusting and again shifted his shape. He shrunk to a fraction taller than Fiona, only this time his color was ochre, the color of muddy clay, his eyes were the color of eggplant, their whites shot with specks of blood as he glared directly into her own.

"DINNA TRY THAT AGAIN, HARRIDAN!"

Wha...what do you want of me?" she stuttered.

"DINNA QUESTION ME, SLATTERN! YOU WILL COME WITH ME, NOO!" he shoved her with his knee and she stumbled to the ground. He laughed viciously as she lay there, trying to think of some escape.

"ESCAPE WILL NAE DO, MINX. DINNA THINK ON IT OR I KNOW WHAT! I WILL HAVE ME PRIZE OR YE WILL DIE!"

Fiona trembled, shivering. She'd never been this terrified before. She felt his hand on her belt loop and then she was standing again. This time, she stood by what seemed a gentleman from the 1800's, tight pants, a blue coat and white cravat. Handsome. He smiled savagely at her, his hot breath too near her face. His tongue darted out, touched her cheek. He pulled one manicured finger from her thigh to her neck. Her muscles clenched and she turned away in terror. "HA, HA, DO NOT LIKE ME ATTENTIONS, ME PRETTY?"

"N...No, I don't."

"MAYHAP YE LIKE THIS!" And again he changed, this time to his original self, his visage gruesome. "BETTER!" He laughed as she cringed in terror, watching his clay colored face come closer and closer to her own. She squeezed her eyes tightly waiting for the worst. But the monster only laughed at her fear; that fear amusing him greatly.

And again he changed, this time to what appeared to be a small child. Fiona knew not to be tricked again, as she was with the fawn, but it was hard. The child looked up at her with large blue eyes that were brimming with tears. Her natural instinct was to lend comfort, but she knew this was another of the monster's disguises. The little child put his hand up to Fiona in a pathetic gesture and she almost reached for it, when the fingernails began to grow sharp. One swiped her face, slicing it.

Fiona screeched in pain as droplets of blood dripped down her cheek. She put a hand to her face in an effort to stop the bleeding, watching through tears as the child changed again. An old woman with large glasses appeared now, clucking comforting sounds. "Come here, Dearie. Did that bad boy hurt ye? I'll fix ye up right, eh?"

"Get away from me!"

"Is tha' any way to speak tae yer granny?"

"You're not my granny. You're... you're..."

"AND WHAT AM I?" the old woman bellowed with the voice of Fiona's captor. The bespectacled eyes turned a gruesome glowing red, and as the old woman began to shift her shape, Fiona began to run. She ran fast, stumbling over fallen logs and bracken, her senses blurred from the pounding of her heart and the fear lodged there. From everywhere she heard the roar of her subjugator. The forest reverberated with his voice, mocking her.

"DO YE THINK YE CAN ESCAPE ME, PRINCESS? I CAN SEE IN ALL DIRECTIONS. I'M WATCHIN' YE NOO."

Fiona stopped, her breath ragged. He had said "princess." He thought she was Rionnag. Fiona looked all around her and saw nothing. His voice continued, this time more controlled, trying to be gentle through suppressed rage.

"COME OOT, COME OOT WHEREVER YE ARE. I CAN SEE YE, I KEN WHERE YE ARE. DINNA MAKE ME REACH MY CLAWED HAND TAE TAKE YE."

Realizing that he could *not* see her, that he did not know where she was, Fiona made herself very small, and crouched down by the roots of an overturned tree hoping he'd search in another direction. Suddenly, all around her she heard the sound of leaves rustling, slithering. She knew without needing to see that her jailer had turned into a serpent. That thought nearly sent her mad, her fear and aversion to snakes, palpable. As she crouched by the tree, something grabbed her and pulled her down, under the tree itself.

Chapter 34

Prince Kieran walked over the burgeoning green hills of his homeland. He had gotten on to Rionnag's land undetected and though he noticed a lack of guards, nothing seemed amiss. Perhaps his mortal friend's suspicions might be correct and the guards were out searching for the princess. Or perhaps nothing was wrong, and he was in a place he should not be until Bealltainn. The Spring Feast Day. His wedding day. He had listened for anything questionable, but things were quiet and as much as he wanted to go right to the door of the castle, he knew he had to restrain himself. Should Princess Rionnag be there, should they meet prematurely, there could be dire consequences from the court and, he reflected, who knew what magics would be unleashed should the two meet.

He traveled home, stopping several miles short of his own dwelling. He needed to think about his future. He walked slowly, mist settling in his path. So typical of this land, he mused, where the mist rose up like a phantom trying to make travelers lose their way. He stopped for a moment, waiting for it to settle so he could see his path clearly, when he realized it was no fog or mist at all, but something alive and tangible. As he stood watching it, the mist changed to what appeared to be a fachan, an UnSeelie. He knew it the moment he saw it. Nannies and parents often told their youngsters about the odious creature, using the monster to threaten children into doing their chores or settling down to sleep. He backed up and stood behind a tree, watching and wondering why it had touched down in his part of the world, and not across the channel, where it lived.

He watched in horror as it released a young lass from its grasp, then shoved her until she fell. The girl was visibly terrified, and rightly so. His skin crawled as he listened to the evil laugh. He remembered once hearing his own nanny speak of the fachan, so easily recognizable in its present, heinous form. "Never approach one, they're bound to eat ye as soon as look at ye! And if yer a human, well, there's no escape. Death to humans, that's the fachan's decree! I've not seen too many on this isle, but across the sea, well, don't they like to cause mayhem! I saw one once…" She held a hand to her heart, dramatically. "There's only one way of escapin' them." She lowered her voice and made the faerie sign, and into the young prince's ear, whispered, "The drink, strong drink, distilled under the full moon. Give that to a fachan and he'll forget ye for a time. That's when ye run!"

The beast shape-shifted into a handsome gentleman and was looking too lasciviously at the girl. Touching her. Kieran knew she needed help. But he knew that if he came out of hiding and demanded the fachan release his captive, the fachan might kill the girl before Kieran had a chance to rescue her. Kieran's own powers were possibly strong enough to fight the fachan himself, but what of the lass? He waited and watched. It was obvious that if the fachan had wanted to eat or kill his captive, he would have done so already.

He watched as the monster changed shape over and over again, confusing and terrifying his captive. And then, unexpectedly, as the beast left the guise of an old woman, the lass ran. Brave thing! Kieran applauded her to himself. Kieran followed her, and saw her crouched by the exposed roots of an overturned tree. Making himself invisible to the fachan, he went down into the tree's underbelly and pulled the girl down into it from where she hunched. She was about to scream when she saw Kieran, but he put a strong hand over her mouth. She fought him like a wildcat. Kieran spelled her into frozen silence and she could only stare, wild-eyed at him as he disappeared, leaving her alone and unable to move or call out. From above, he shifted his own shape to that of a toothless witch. He could hear the sound of rustling getting close. The Prince looked around and saw a huge serpent slithering toward the tree where his hostage was hiding. Kieran, as the old crone, moved to a far off rock, holding a keg and pretending to drink from a huge cask of such powerful ale the fachan's head would swim. With the voice of a drunkard, Kieran began to sing bawdy drinking songs. The fachan/serpent heard the singing and smelled the moonshine before he saw it and slithered in the direction of the drink. Kieran disappeared, leaving the cask propped against a rock. He returned to his hiding place behind the tree and watched the serpent shift back to form. The fachan drained the keg and then stumbled and fell. Seeing this, Kieran spelled himself back to where the lassie was frozen. He reversed the spell and realizing she could move, she scrambled as fast as she could out of the root system, but Kieran grabbed her leg, pulling her back down.

"Don't come near me!" she told him, terrified, grabbing a loose piece of root, aiming to throw it.

"Please put that down, miss. I've no intent to harm ye. Now is not the time to leave here, I can assure ye."

"How...why should I believe that? You'll just change again. Go ahead, just get it over with, kill me."

"I've no intention to kill ye or do any such thing. Allow me to introduce meself. I'm Kier," he said giving her his pet name and bowing majestically before her. She seemed very young but resourceful, he thought, as he looked into her eyes.

"That doesn't reassure me a bit."

"Ye've no reason to fear me, I can assure ye of that. Perfectly harmless I am. I've told ye who I am, might I have the pleasure of makin' yer acquaintance?"

"You're not... that thing?"

"The fachan? Of course not. But how would ye know that? I had ye bound down here, did I not? Ye were makin' a dreadful fuss! No need to fear, he's ehm...indisposed, momentarily, that is. So, now would ye tell me who and what ye are?"

"I'm not sure I should."

"Well, suit yerself, but as I said, ye've no need to fear me and that's the Rowan's truth," he said smiling at her.

"All I know is that I've got to get out of here. I've got a monster after me, and who knows when he'll be coming back!"

"I suppose yer right about him coming back soon. And this isn't the most pleasant place," he said as he removed a large centipede from his shoulder. "Come, let's go," he said, offering her his hand.

"How about we run?"

"I tell ye, there's no need of it, but all right. He'll be indisposed for some time. Mark me words." They climbed out of the ground, brushed themselves off and hurried down the path until they found a small grove of tall trees. Stopping, Kieran gestured for Fiona to sit down upon a fallen log.

"And how would you know he won't come back?" Fiona asked, suspiciously, as she slowly took a seat.

Before she could blink, the crone stood before her, smiling toothlessly, holding a keg. "Fachans like the drink. It's their weakness," the crone said.

A moment later, Kieran reappeared.

"You! You did that? You tricked it?"

"Yes, to tell the truth. I know what that fellow is capable of, and it didn't look like ye and he were bosom companions."

"No, we definitely were not! Thank you!"

"More than welcome ye are. And why do ye think the creature would want to bring ye here?" Kieran asked.

"Could you tell me where *here* is?"

"Why, ye are in Erinn, me green and beautiful land."

"So, I'm in Ireland," she said almost to herself.

"'Tis and all. And where might ye be from?"

"West of here," she said cryptically.

"So I'm to be understandin' that yer west is west beyond mine? Perhaps beyond the great waters?"

"Yes, that's right and all," she said with the trace of a smile.

"'Tis a far way to come. What brings ye here?"

"That *thing* brought me here," she shuddered. "And I know he'll be back. Can you help me?" she looked pleadingly into his eyes. There was something very kind in those eyes, Kieran thought, not doubting her sincerity.

"Well, I don't know if I can. Not knowing why he wanted ye, I'm not sure what should be done. Can ye shape-shift?" he asked, hoping she could, thinking that might buy some time until he could decide what to do.

"Shape-shift? No way. Oh my God, you don't think... Oh, I'm not what you think!" she said, her eyes flashing in alarm.

"And what would I be thinkin' ye are, then?" he asked.

"A faerie, of course."

"If not, then what might ye be?" he asked her gently.

"I'm a human girl," she said folding her arms tightly around her. "That's what."

"Is that right? I've never had the pleasure of meeting a human girl. Grand meetin' ye."

"Nice meeting you too. I'm Fi, by the way," she said, deciding not to give her full name.

"So, Fi by the way, me question to ye is, why would a human girl be in the grasp of a fachan? Ye should have been a meal by now. So, what would it want of ye?"

"I really don't know. It started out as a fawn. Or so I thought. It looked hurt so I went to help it, and then it grabbed me with a vice grip and turned into the most disgusting thing I've ever seen. And then it turned into mist or smoke and back into whatever you saw. I need to get out of here. He's definitely going to be back for me. I know it," she winced.

"And how can ye be so sure?"

"He said something like 'she can have the likes of you' and getting something in exchange for me."

"I suppose the true question to be askin' ye should be, where did ye start out from? Where did ye find the creature lyin' in wait for ye?"

"That's kind of hard to say. We went through a magic ring, right in my backyard, and then we were in a kind of faerie land, I guess." She wasn't making a lot of sense to Kieran, but he was patient and tried to ease her anxiety.

"'We' ye say? So ye weren't alone then?"

"No, I was with my... my uhm, sister." He noted the hesitation.

"Yer, ehm, sister. And did she not see the thing take ye?"

"She did and she screamed, but it was too late." The girl's eyes were welling up with tears.

"'Tis all right, now." Kieran touched her shoulder. "Well, me beauty, do ye think yer, ah, sister, is in any danger?

"I'm sure of it. She's the one he was after, not me."

"So ye think yer sister is the one he wants. Why do ye think that would be?" he asked gently, looking directly into her eyes, trying to make her see that she could trust him, but thinking her story sounded feeble.

"Because he called me 'princess.' I'm not a princess, but she is. She ran away and her family wants her back. Maybe they sent him to get her. Oh, I don't know!"

Kieran watched the girl dissolve into tears. He sat down on the soft ground by the log, whistled softly, patted her shoulder in a comforting gesture, but his mind was now elsewhere. The fachan had called the human girl "princess." Why? He had a foreboding feeling he knew.

Fiona stopped her tears and half smiled at the man. Had he not shown her his magic, she never would have guessed him anything but a young man. He was wearing comfortable trousers of a natural fabric and a light green tunic that matched his eyes. These were clear and held a merry twinkle. He was taller than Fiona by many inches, and she wondered if he would be palm-sized if he visited her on her own side. She liked the way his long hair fell in shiny, dark curls over his shoulders. She especially liked the way he called her "me beauty."

"Ye say *her* family? I was thinkin' she was *yer* sister. 'Tis what ye told me. If she's yer sister, are ye not also a princess as well?"

"Okay, she's only my *spirit* sister, not my *real* sister. She's a faerie."

"A faerie, aye? And how might ye be connected, if ye don't mind me askin'?"

"We exchanged something precious to each of us." She refused to say more.

"Ah, the truth reveals itself. So yer sister is not really a sister at all but a true fey lassie, a princess. But, Fi, me beauty, if this sister ran away, do ye really think her family would send so vile a creature to bring her back?"

Fiona hesitated for a moment. "I guess not. Then who would have sent it?"

"Now that's a question." Again, he had an inkling he knew the answer. "But me question to ye is why did she run away from her family in the first place?"

Fiona hesitated, wondering whether she should tell this stranger, but decided he could be trusted. "To escape an arranged marriage."

Kieran stood still, his attention completely focused on the girl's answer. He hoped the answer to his next question was not the answer he had the suspicion it was.

"And what might the lassie's name be, if ye don't mind me askin'?"

Something about him made Fiona want to confide in him. "Rionnag," she said in a whisper. "Princess Rionnag."

She watched the young man's face change, as she said Rionnag's name, the sparkle in his eye giving way to a glint of anger. She felt a stab of fear and wondered if she had done wrong in telling him. Why was she always so trusting? What if *he, too,* was out to get Rionnag?

"Are you all right? I mean, you look pretty fierce," she said cautiously.

"Eh? What?" Kieran looked into her eyes and his own

softened. "I was thinkin', I know of the Princess and I'm a good friend to the one she is to marry. It seems a bit self-indulgent for her to run away when both kingdoms are dependin' on this marriage to take place. The Prince would never allow *his* apprehension to get in the way of his duty."

"Isn't your friend nervous about marrying someone he's never seen or met?" Fiona asked.

"Of course he's nervous. More so than a normal bridegroom, but that's not the point. Responsibility still has meaning here and I'm surprised yer friend, ehm, sister was so cavalier in hers." He was becoming indignant, almost too indignant. What business was it of his anyway? Fiona wondered.

"You can tell your friend that she's the kindest, most beautiful faerie I've ever seen," she retorted.

He didn't want to take his umbrage out on the girl. She wasn't to blame for Princess Rionnag's lack of maturity. He smiled and said more gently, "Yes, and how many would that be?"

"That's beside the point. She's beautiful and funny and sweet and I love her. She ran away because of your friend."

"Because of him? That's ridiculous. He's a fine fellow! And what of her responsibility? Her promise?"

"She *is* coming back! We were coming back. She realized she made a mistake running away. Anyway, we've got to find my mother!" she said with more vehemence than she intended.

Kieran looked at her in confusion.

"My mother didn't come home from her trip to Scotland and we think she might be here. Scotland, I mean, in Faerie," Fiona said matter-of-factly.

"And why would ye think that yer human mother would be somewhere in Faerie? She *is* human, is she not?"

"Of course. Because we think she's been meeting

271

someone here every Halloween."

"Every Halloween, ye say. *Samhain*. Ye know that's when the veil between the two worlds..."

"...opens. I know. We found this rock. And a book... We just think so, so of course Ri's coming back. She made a promise and you know a faerie promise..."

"...is binding. I know. Ye must understand, being born royal has its responsibilities...not that I would know anything about it," he added quickly. "'Tis a good thing yer friend, ehm, sister, had a change of heart and decided to return and fulfill her responsibility."

"She just wanted to marry for love. But she felt badly and we were on our way back to speak to her father, when that thing took me."

"We'd better find her father and tell him what's happened, but before we do, would ye tell me about her?" Kier asked. His request held such longing that Fiona's suspicions became tangible and she couldn't help smiling to herself.

"Well... okay. I already told you her name. It means 'star.' She's very smart. She's got lots of opinions, speaks her own mind. She's got the loveliest, long blonde hair and the most incredible eyes. They look like... what's that stone, the purple one?"

"Amethyst."

"Yes, amethyst. She has a beautiful voice and she's funny and witty and very wise. And she can ride a horse."

"I should hope so. Did she say anything about me... ehm, me friend, to ye?"

"How could she? She doesn't know *him*. She was just angry that they weren't allowed to meet first. I think it's a stupid rule."

"Do ye now?" His look changed. "Perhaps ye are right, but it is the decree, and it must be abided. Did she tell you what's been happening to our world?" he said.

"Yes. She told me Faerie was fading. She said her marriage might help to save it." Fiona gestured to their surroundings.

"She's right. Too many evil creatures like the one that took ye are gaining power here. I'm sorry to say, we blame ye humans for that. All the fey folk need to band together to fight this evil. Princess Rionnag will help do that, if she comes back and fulfills her obligation, that is."

"She *was* coming back to talk to her father, I told you that." She hesitated, then added, "I do understand why you blame us. I'm sorry."

"For meself, I've naught against ye or yer kind, it's just that we fey folk, well, we leave the earth alone. And though there's always been fightin' amongst us and there are depraved ones in our midst, until now they've been manageable. But their power grows as each tree comes down on yer side, as each human loses sight of what is good and true. Do ye understand?"

"Yes. What we do on our side affects what's happening here. It makes perfect sense," Fiona said, remembering what Rionnag had told her.

"Exactly. Fightin' over land, destroyin' that which is natural, lack of respect for the earth we all share, all that creates darkness here. The greater the darkness, the more we, the light beings, are forgotten, and if we are forgotten, we'll simply fade from existence. And the opposite is true as well. The darkness will go on, like in the shape of that thing. His kind will become stronger and stronger. And that, me beauty, will affect yer kind, make no mistake."

She thought of the creature, so evil and disgusting, then she thought about the people who wanted her land, and those who clear cut the rain forests, the polluters and destroyers her mother was always fighting against at all her

Jana Laiz

rallies. Was the darkness already taking over the earth? It was a frightening thought.

"If that's true, then why don't you let humans see you? Why don't you come over and show us you're real?"

"It's not so simple, Fi. Times past, we used to get along well. We respected each other, knew of the existence of the other and honored it. Every *Samhain*, Halloween, we'd invite the humans to come over, to dance with us, make merry. Some folk still do, but the fact is, the ways through are disappearin', and again we blame the humans for that. 'Tis hard to get through steel." He looked at Fiona pointedly and said, "I'm sorry."

He continued, "We must find the princess' father, King Niall, to tell him what's become of his daughter, but before that, there's someone I must speak to. One of yers."

"One of mine what?"

"A human."

"You mean there's another human here, wherever we are?" Fiona asked incredulously.

"Nay, not here exactly. We'll have to travel across a wee sea, if you don't mind me for a companion. I think this one can help ye, but unlike ye, he is not free, but a captive, captured by one of those nasty folk I mentioned."

"What do you mean captive?"

"As I told ye, there are evil fey folk, and some like to take mortals, humans, for their own. This poor soul was taken and he's not seen his home for a very long time. I doubt he shall ever see it again for that matter, as he's about to be tithed. 'Tis a pity. He seemed a good man to me."

"Tithed? You mean sold to the devil?"

"In a matter of speakin', yes. 'Tis a terrible shame. But he might know somethin' about yer faerie sister. I think he'll be glad for the knowledge ye have to share."

"Well, then, let's go. I'm sure that monster's going to

274

come back and I don't want to be here when it does!" Fiona said taking Kieran's arm.

Fiona decided she very much liked this faerie-man. Was there another word for a guy faerie? she wondered, giggling inwardly. And if she was right about him, she hoped he wouldn't hold it against Rionnag.

They walked through a blossoming meadow where tiny blue hollyhocks lined a path and the small flowers seemed to bow as they passed. Fiona glanced at her companion who made small bows of his head as they walked, and she realized that he was returning the flowers' greetings. This made her like him even more. When they came to a ridge overlooking the sea, Fiona stood transfixed by the rugged beauty of the land. She watched the terns swooping over the cliffs, saw the bright green hills behind them, velvety moss lining the great rocks, the crashing surf hundreds of feet below. She looked toward Scotland to the east, where her mother was, right this very second, probably still with whomever she was meeting, forgetting all about Fiona. The thought gave her heart a little twinge. While the child was musing, Kieran took his crown and placed it out of sight, on a moss-covered rock. He protected it with a spell, making it visible only to him, then gently touched the girl's arm to bring her attention back. She smiled and he returned the smile.

"I've got to change meself now for the crossin'. Ye'll get on me back when I've done. Hold on and close yer eyes if you like. It may be a bit breezy."

With those words, before Fiona's astonished eyes, he transformed to his stag form, that which was his birthright. His masculine arms and legs turned to four strong limbs, which pawed the ground. He knelt to make it easier for her, and, hesitating for only a moment, she climbed onto his back. He was the size of a small horse, and she pretended to be riding bareback as he moved toward the edge of the cliff. As he stepped off, she let out a startled cry, but quieted when he moved as assuredly through the air as on solid ground. Fiona tightened her arms around his muscular neck and closed her eyes against his flank as the salty spray touched her face.

From the cliff they heard the macabre, inebriated bellow of the fachan, who had stumbled back to claim his captive, only to find her flying away towards Scotland on the back of a stag.

Chapter 35

"What do ye want on the Queen's land?"

Maggie turned to face a hideous creature wearing what appeared to be a uniform. She didn't know whether to thank him for stopping the onslaught or wish it was back. His face was carroty in color, with egg-shaped eyes the color of paste, the pupils slits, vertical and red. His spiky ears pushed out from under a helmet, sticking out sharply to either side. He was much taller than Maggie and carried a weapon of some kind. She guessed he was a soldier or guard. She tried not to faint.

"I'm sorry, I didn't mean to trespass. I lost my way. Perhaps you can help..."

Before she finished her plea, the guard grabbed both her hands by their wrists and with a flick of his weapon, she was bound with strong green vines.

"We'll see if the queen will take kindly tae ye on her land."

He shoved Maggie ahead of him, the butt of his weapon pushing into her back. She felt sick with fear and something else. Guilt. Guilt that she had gone and left her only child for her own selfish reasons and now she would never see her again, never be able to explain, to make it right. Of that she felt certain. Wherever she was, she had landed in unfriendly territory, and she had a horrible feeling she knew exactly whose land she was on. She hoped she was wrong, but where else would she have landed? It seemed horribly obvious. Ironic in the worst sense of the word. Well, she would know shortly, she imagined. The soldier was in a hurry. Maybe he'd be rewarded. She wanted to throw up.

She was taken to some kind of cave carved into the side of a mountain and shoved in brutally. She fell to the hard ground, both knees bloodied from scraping the sharp cave floor. The guard made a frightening face that Maggie thought was actually a mocking smile as he looked down at her, his eyes lustily taking in the blood that showed through her pant legs. He edged closer, nostrils flaring as they neared her bloody knees. His slick yellow tongue came shooting out of his mouth and Maggie squeezed her eyes shut, but never felt a thing, for at that moment she heard a hiss that sent chills through her.

"Do ye dare!" the voice screeched. Maggie peered through eyes that were still slits, not really wanting to see what caused the guard to stop what he was about to do.

"Ppp..please yer Majesty, Queen Barabel, I meant no harm, it's just that human blood..."

"Never mind that! Tell me what it is!"

"It is human and it was trespassin' on yer land." He stood taller, sticking his chest out. "I was bringin' her tae ye."

"Not before ye'd taken some for yerself," the queen remarked caustically.

"I didna mean…" Before the words were out of his mouth, with one swift movement, Barabel turned her own hand into a blade and swiped it across his neck, his head propelled from his body. Maggie watched in horror as the guard's headless body began to twitch in a maniacal dance until it burst into flame and turned to ash.

Ewan was walking back, head down in despair, when he was almost hit by a head catapulting from inside one of Barabel's prison caves. He stopped, watching the head slam to the ground, the guard's eyes rolling around, still animate. Ewan watched, repulsed until the eyes finally closed and the head shrunk until it disappeared leaving behind an empty helmet. Then peering inside the entrance to the cave, his heart froze in his chest as he saw Barabel standing before Maggie, a lascivious smile on her malevolently beautiful face. He watched as Barabel's long, be-ringed finger touched his Maggie's face under her chin. Ewan stood there, paralyzed with a fear unlike any he had known before, and watched his beloved try not to flinch. She did not see him standing there, dumbstruck. Without taking her eyes off the human woman, Barabel said softly, with the voice of a serpent, "Look, Ewan, it seems we have a human caller." Her voice venomous, she continued, "But an uninvited one. She should have known never tae come onto Barabel's land without an invitation. Tsk, tsk, puir lass. What do ye think, Ewan? She'll make a fine tithe. Dinna ye agree?"

Chapter 36

Rionnag was chasing after whatever it was that had her friend. She was nearly hysterical when she saw the thing change from some kind of animal into what she recognized as a fachan. She had never seen one, so protected had she always been within the kingdom, but Mòr had described them well enough in her gruesome stories, and now Rionnag knew that was what it had to be. She flew faster and faster, tears blinding her as she tried to imagine what she'd do when she caught them. She had just told Fiona that an UnSeelie would not dare touch a faerie; their power was far less than those of the Seelie Court. But Fiona *wasn't* a faerie. And though she herself was a faerie of the Seelie Court, still, her fear and revulsion at the sight of the fachan was almost uncontrollable. "Oh, puir, wee Fiona! She must be mad with fright! I promised I'd keep her safe!" she said aloud as she flew. "Fionnaaahhh!" she cried again.

The sound of the name lingered on the wind, which

held it tightly, blowing it in the four directions. When the wind found what it was searching for, it let a gust down where the folk were sitting in discussion about what to do next to dispel the terrible energy that had entered their land. The gust held the long drawn out name "Fiona" and two of the circle recognized the accent and tone of the voice that called it.

"Och, that's our oon dear Princess calling oot that name!" Mòr said as soon as the last syllable disappeared on the breeze again.

"Aye, right ye are. Unmistakable it was. But who is 'Fiona'?" Jinty asked in confusion.

"I dinna ken," Mòr said,

Those around the circle began to chant, softly at first, but more loudly as the seconds passed until there was a strange buzz in the air. Every object seemed charged and electric.

Rionnag flew through the thick woods, not really knowing where she was going or how she would know when she found whatever she was looking for. She looked up as she heard the sound of drumming, and some kind of singing or chanting. It held an oddly peaceful quality that slightly eased her anxious mind. She landed on a tree branch and stood listening for several long moments assessing any danger and decided there was none.

She followed the sound to a large clearing surrounded by towering trees. There, in a circle, were beings unlike any from her world. As she stared, they began to change; animal faces blending with human ones until she was unsure exactly what she was seeing. Suddenly Rionnag remembered the animal-like dancers at Fiona's school. One of the beings spotted her, although she had approached silently and remained perfectly still. They locked eyes and he nodded in recognition. She tore her gaze away and looked at the other members of the circle still sitting solemnly, heads erect, eyes closed, bodies straight and strong. She gasped when she saw something familiar, yet entirely out of context in this scene. She wondered if she was beginning to see things, but Mòr and Jinty turned with the rest as they heard her gasp, and nearly fell over each other as they realized who was standing before them.

Rionnag stood staring, her eyes taking in the familiar loving presences, tears coming to her eyes, then ran over to the two who were stumbling over one another to get to her. There was a jumble of hugs and kisses, a babbling of some dialect incomprehensible to any of the onlookers.

Rionnag disentangled herself from the grip of her nurse as the obvious leader of this bizarre assortment of entities came forward. Rionnag came toward her with all the grace and presence she was raised with and extended her hand. "I am Princess Rionnag. I heard your chanting and followed the sound. As you are undoubtedly aware, these two are my ladies," she said, her speech clear and formal for these folk to understand, gesturing to Mòr and Jinty, who were standing close on either side of her, "...who have certainly told you of their search for me. I must find my friend!"

"Know that we will assist you in any way we can. We know of your situation," the leader said graciously.

"Please tell me what you know," Rionnag said anxiously.

"Our brethren, the crows, hold two captive. What did you call those *things*?" the leader asked Mòr.

"Bogies," Mòr answered. "These fine folk," she said, gesturing to the animal-like creatures, "captured two of them. I can only assume the bogies are here tae capture ye. And ye well know who likely sent them."

"Bogies? After me? Why?" Rionnag was genuinely confused.

"We're sure Barabel sent them," Jinty blurted out. Mòr nudged her hard with her elbow. Rionnag looked at them askance. "Why would my aunt send bogies after me?"

"To prevent ye from marryin' the prince."

"Take me to the bogies," she said, comprehension dawning.

Mòr looked to the leader of the animal folk, who nodded. The coyote-boy stepped forward and quietly presented himself to Rionnag. "I am Kumsah, friend of your friend."

"Aye, from the window."

"Yes. I sensed danger, and I am sorry to say I was right. Please follow me," he gestured. Rionnag followed, her two maids gripping either arm.

They walked through the woods, and heard the racket before they saw anything. There, sitting amidst hundreds of blackbirds, sat two bogies. Still in their crow form, but recognizable by their eyes, burning red with rage and enmity.

Rionnag flew up to them and said imperiously, "Tell me who sent ye here!"

The bogies cawed stridently, but their guards pecked at them until they quieted.

"If ye canna speak in that form, change to one ye can!" Rionnag demanded.

Ceallach was the first to change back to his grotesque visage, Fearghas followed suit, very nearly losing his balance on the branch.

"Wha' do yer want tae know!" he spat. Rionnag was unmoved by his rage or his appearance.

"Again, who sent ye here? Answer quickly or deal with the consequences!"

Fearghas was jabbing Ceallach on his side. "Ceallach! Ceallach! It's her! The wench! Can ye no smell her?"

"Shut yer gob!" To Rionnag, he growled, "Dinna think ye can frighten me, Princess!"

"Aha! Ye ken who I am, right enough! Who sent ye?" Rionnag demanded, her eyes glaring at the creature. She saw him back up slightly, unwilling to answer and so she continued, "Crows collect shiny objects, do they not?" The coyote-boy nodded vigorously. "Good," she said. "Please ask them to show me all their shiny toys."

Suddenly, Fearghas' moronic expression changed to one of comprehension as he took in the princess' words. He screamed at the top of his voice, "Nay! 'Twas Barabel!"

Ceallach struck his partner on the head. "Ye fool! Shut yer gob, I tell ye!"

"Jinty, Mòr, ye were right," she said to her companions. To the bogies, she said, "Tell us why she sent ye."

"Bugger off! We'll say naught!"

Rionnag smiled sardonically and said to the crows, "Show these two your treasures. Your shiny treasures." From all directions, crows, ravens and jackdaws flew, bringing back in their beaks bits of broken tin, copper coins, shiny brass keys, and all assortments of metal, until Fearghas was screaming in terror. "Ceallach! Tell her what she wants tae ken! I canna stand it!"

Ceallach eyed Rionnag venomously. She didn't flinch, but merely smiled. "Give one of yer treasures to our friends here!" she said to the crows, her voice calm, her anger controlled.

"*She* sent us tae find ye!" Ceallach conceded.

"I ken that, but tell us why and what for!"

"Tae keep ye from marryin' the prince. There, that's all we'll tell."

Rionnag flew back to the ground, where the coyote-boy waited. "Please tell your friends to guard these two well. You now know their weakness. Metal. They will not move if they are surrounded by it."

Kumsah, the coyote-boy nodded, agreeing. They made their way back to the circle and sat down, Rionnag thinking aloud, "It becomes clear. She wants to prevent my marriage. Perhaps she thinks this will put her in the good graces of his Irish family. Well, that makes sense in her way of thinking. Barabel must have gotten impatient waiting for the bogies and sent the fachan for me. It must have mistook Fiona for me." Rionnag's face became despairing.

"D...d...did you s...s...say fachan?" Jinty asked, turning shades of gray.

"Aye! It captured Fiona."

"So that was what we felt! Who is Fiona?" Mòr asked.

"She's my friend, a human girl. We've become sisters." A thought struck her and as understanding dawned on her, she felt sick. "Oh, dear Oberon! When the fachan finds that he has Fiona instead of me, there's no telling what he'll do!"

The coyote-boy rose from his place, troubled. "I will go after her and I will find her," he said to the elders.

"Kumsah, you've never been out of our territory," one of the beings, a fox-man, spoke in raspy tones.

"I want to help and I've got the keenest nose here, you know that. If they're still in these woods, I'll track them down. And," he added more quietly, "she is my friend." The elders said nothing, but their furry eyebrows twitched.

"I'll go along with ye, Kumsah, of course," Rionnag said.

"We'll all go. Ye'll not leave my eyes for a moment again, do ye hear?" Mòr declared, firmly taking Rionnag's hand.

"Aye, we'll go tae find yer friend," Jinty said, courage coming upon her like a wave, and to the astonishment of Mòr, and herself, took Kumsah's hand in hers.

"Kumsah, you may leave the confines of these woods

if you must, but do not go far into unknown territory. Remember the *word* and use it if necessary. It certainly had an effect on our unpleasant guest," the otter-woman said, her gurgling words giving everyone the feeling of cleansing water. "Good luck to you all, but remember, Kumsah, stay close. The dangers beyond these woods are many and great and if you venture too far, returning might prove impossible. Your place is here among your kind."

It was a peculiar group traveling to find Fiona. Kumsah took the position of leader, which was fine with Rionnag. They walked through this feral land, the three faeries commenting on how different it was from home. The trees were taller and much younger, and the strange colors! Shades that had long since departed their own land. Mòr always wondered where they had gone. They all noted that the dark shadows were the same though, and there were far more of them here. Rionnag in particular noticed the grim darkness that seemed to whisper malevolently from the recesses of the forest. Kumsah noticed them looking toward these gloomy places and said, "Do not look to the shadows nor pay them any heed. The more energy you put on them, the stronger they become. Forget them, ignore and spurn them. The only way to find the girl is only to be open to the light."

Suddenly, Rionnag stopped, stood, head cocked to one side, listening. The group continued ahead, but all froze, when she called, "Stop, do you hear it? Listen!"

"I dinna hear anything. What are ye hearin'?" Mòr asked.

"I think I heard my own name in the wind. Shhh. Let me have another listen." She closed her eyes this time, paying inward attention to something no one else seemed to hear. The group watched her intently. Her eyes opened wildly like a sleeper who senses she is being watched. Her voice was a low whisper, "It's Fiona calling to me. Smart lass. She's not here, she's already crossed."

"What do you mean 'crossed'?" Kumsah asked.

"I mean she's crossed from this continent. She's likely across the sea by now."

"I think we'd better go to the place of power," the coyote-boy said, knowing if the girl left the continent, that might be the only way to get to her.

"Where is that place?" Rionnag asked.

"I'll take you there."

They followed Kumsah through the forest. His footsteps made no sound, even on the dry fallen leaves. They made their way to a white birch standing alone, its middle deeply scarred. Rionnag looked around her, turning this way and that. She was shaking her head, standing near this sacred spot. "This place looks so familiar to me, this tree. But of course there are no landmarks I can recognize. I wonder...Wait! This is where I first saw Fiona! And ye!" Comprehension dawned on the princess. "When I first saw her, she was dancing a lively jig with ye and many of yer kind." Kumsah nodded affirmation. Rionnag recognized it as the same place from which she had entered. There was the white birch, though this time she couldn't see any part of the human side, though the tree still held its scar. Mòr and Jinty recognized it, too. "This is where we came through, isna that right, Jinty?"

"Aye, right here. From that old ring we found whilst we were looking for the princess," Jinty said, giving Rionnag a reproachful look. Rionnag in turn cast her eyes downward, ashamed of all the trouble she had caused so many.

"As I said, this is a place of power. Humans have entered here before. This is where we have often met your human friend. She comes in dreams, both day and night."

She looked at the tree again and then at the place where

the building would be on the other side. In its place was a very dim shadow.

"This is where we should enter to find the girl," Kumsah said, interrupting her thoughts.

Rionnag remembered that getting to this place had been a frightening ride and one she didn't care to repeat. She also knew that this might be their only way of getting home and rescuing Fiona. But how? She now had no spell to use. It was lost along with her friend and she could not recall the words she said when she had ventured into this unknown land in the first place. She looked at Kumsah and shook her head.

"I did come through here, but I do not know how to return. Mòr? Jinty?"

"Sorry, lass, we merely followed ye through and came oot here. And let me tell ye, the ride wasna pleasant in the least."

"Aye, I can swear to that!" Jinty said vehemently.

Rionnag thought for a moment, trying to assess the situation. It was all so confusing. When she went through the ring at home, she had picked a dreadfully powerful ring. That coupled with the spell from her mother's book was enough to send her clear across an ocean. When she arrived she had seen both sides at the same time. Well, there was no going back. She'd have to try to use her own magic. Her parents and tutors had taught her, and she would use what she had.

"Are ye ready? We have no time to waste."

"We've been ready to return home o'er long!" Jinty said, emphatically.

"I am ready," Kumsah said, having the feeling his work might be done, and not liking it.

Rionnag looked long at the coyote-boy. "Thank ye, Kumsah, for rendering such grand assistance. Without yer help, we would not have been able to find our way, but ye must stay here, in yer own land. Ye must stay. What trials ye may meet in my world are untold, and that ye might not be able to return is a true possibility. Ye must keep working here to save this land."

"But, I promised to help you find the girl! Coming this far, what help is that?" he said, dismayed.

"Enough so that we might return to our home and from there, we will find friends who will help us with the situation. Yer place is here, among yer kind. Under other circumstances, ye'd be most welcome to visit my land, but for now, please stay. Watch over Fiona's family."

Recognizing this as more of a command than a suggestion he acquiesced, reluctantly admitting to himself the princess was right. His place was here amidst the ones who remained in these disappearing and sacred places, trying to keep them alive and to call out to those across the veil who still had the ears to hear with. Like Fiona and her family. He would watch over the girl's loved ones like a sentry, until her return. And he would act as her spirit guide. That he could do. And then they would meet again, and he would tell her the old stories and teach her the old ways, so that perhaps, she could bring back the knowledge and teach others.

He nodded his canine head and said sadly, "Yes, I will see you off and I will return. I will make sure to keep those foul fellows guarded well. Perhaps when you return you could send word of what we should do with them. And tell Fiona..." he hesitated, looking down.

"Tell Fiona?"

"Tell her I will look forward to dancing with her again."

"I certainly will."

Rionnag took hold of Mòr and Jinty's hands creating a circle of protection, or so they hoped. As they stood at this entry way, this portal of power, a brilliant arch of light appeared as Rionnag recited her own hopeful spell, and they felt a surge of energy and saw a dazzling flash. Kumsah seemed to shine like a beacon, lighting their way, and howled such a howl as to cause their collective skin to prickle. One last flash and they were hurtling through space and time, on their way to Fiona and home.

The coyote stood watch from a distance guarding the women who were standing at the window, looking out into the garden, eyes searching. He knew what they were looking for and he vowed to stand guard every night until her family safely returned. The older one caught his eye and nodded in recognition, the faintest of smiles appearing on her pained face. He howled softly in return. They stood this way for a long moment, until a cloud covered the moon and he disappeared from whence he had come. He could feel her watching him as he became one with the night and returned to his place.

Chapter 37

"My Queen, wherever did ye get *that*?" Ewan said with false contempt, his heart ready to burst forth from his chest as he saw his love in the clutches of his own enemy. He saw Maggie's face twitch when she heard his voice, but she never moved her eyes in his direction and for this he was grateful.

"She was trespassing, Ewan. And that is something I dinna take lightly to. What do ye think I should do with her while I wait for my tithing day?"

"Och, yer majesty, I dinna ken. Ye could fatten her up a bit. She's a skinny thing. Dress her up; make her do yer biddin'. Perhaps ye could use her as a maid or better yet, a plaything."

"Ooh, I like that notion. My mither stopped letting me play with dolls when I was wee. I'd crush them. Perhaps that's the cause of all my suffering." She threw her head back and laughed wickedly.

"Then, Majesty, it's time tae have a dolly of yer oon, dinna ye agree?"

"Aye, Ewan." To Maggie, "Get up! Ye are my game now and until I tithe ye to the underworld, ye will do my bidding! One look at any of my men, just one, and I'll do to ye what I did to him," she said, indicating with a finger the spot that once held her guard.

Maggie, not daring to look up, nodded her head and slowly rose to her feet. She stood taller than Barabel and she tried to will herself to shrink, hunching her shoulders and keeping her head down. Barabel seemed not to notice the difference and was at once absorbed in deciding where to place her new toy.

"Ewan, where should I put her? Do ye no think she smells too human? Maybe she should stay here."

"My Queen, aye, she does stink some, but no enough tae bother ye comin' all the way oot here tae play wi' her. This is no place for ye. Bring her inside the hill tae one of the servant's rooms. Clean her up and then ye can play wi' her anytime ye like and order her around at yer will." Ewan hoped his voice was not shaking as he spoke, and hoped Maggie knew he was trying to trick Barabel into letting her live.

"Ewan, what would I do without yer coun...?" Ewan knew why she stopped. She would soon do very well without his counsel, seeing as she'd traded him to a fachan for a bounty.

"I dinna ken, Majesty. Ye'll soon have tae find another tae help ye in such matters. Fachans rarely fail and I'll soon be his." As soon as the words were out of his mouth, Ewan regretted them.

Barabel stood stock still, and stared at him, then at Maggie. She walked around the woman, appraising her as if now for a new purpose. She flipped the woman's hair, pinched her arm, held her face and looked into it. Maggie kept her eyes cast down, never once recognizing Ewan and certainly never looking Barabel in the eye.

"I wonder if Creaghan wouldna rather care for a female. I could bargain to take ye back, Ewan, and give him this *thing* in yer place. Perhaps I'll call him."

Ewan felt faint at these words, but tried to steady himself and sound coherent. He took a quiet breath. "M'lady, my Queen, ye canna trust a fachan, ye ken that! If ye bargain *it* for me, he'll tak her and he'll still find some way tae get me. I think ye will be deceived."

"Do ye think me stupid, is that what ye think?" Barabel said menacingly.

"Of course not, Majesty, but …"

"Do ye think I do not ken the nature of a fachan? Do not tell me what to do! I will make all decisions! Do ye hear!! If I choose to trade this loathsome creature to keep ye, I will. If I choose not to, that will be MY decision alone! DO YE HEAR!"

"Aye, my *Banrigh*." He knew Barabel liked it when he called her this, the Gaelic word for queen. It seemed to take on more meaning for her. At that moment, Ewan did a bold thing. He took Barabel's hand in his in an attempt to calm her. But instead, it served to infuriate her.

"Perhaps ye'd like the thing for yerself Ewan, is that it! Ye feel sorry for it, being the same species! Well, my fine fellow, this thing will never be yers, or Creaghan's. It's mine! Mine!" Barabel began to scream, the word echoing throughout the cave. "And ye are still mine! Do ye hear!" she shrieked.

Ewan bowed before the queen, eyes downcast. A tiny smile formed on his lips, as he realized that now she would never give up this captive, and thus, his Maggie would be safe. For the time being.

Chapter 38

The ride on the stag's back was so exhilarating that Fiona almost enjoyed it. The faerie-stag-man spoke not a word and Fiona wondered whether he was capable of speech in his present form or was just being quiet. She liked the way he spoke, the lilt, and his gentle humor. If her suspicions were correct, she doubted her sister would be too disappointed. He was nice and funny and handsome. And he *really* seemed to want to get married! Thinking of Rionnag, she remembered her friend's ability to hear her thoughts, if they were loud enough, so she sent out a call from her mind into the atmosphere, calling Rionnag's name over and over again. She recognized that she was calling in rhythm to the beat of the stag's movements and it became a game for her as they made their way across the sea.

Fiona was almost sorry when they finally touched the earth again. The stag was wet from salt water and Fiona was soaked as well. He bent his forelegs so she could get down easily. She slid off his slippery flank and he shook himself like a dog in the rain. The next moment, he was himself again, the winsome faerie-man with the twinkle in his eye. He ruffled his curly russet hair with his hands and shook his head, droplets of water and sweat spraying them both. Fiona did the same to her own and they both laughed as they sprayed one another.

"Well, did ye enjoy the ride, me beauty?" he asked charmingly.

"Actually I did, until I remembered why I was sitting on your back crossing the Irish Sea."

"Ah, that, yes. Let's go sit upon those rocks and let the sun dry us and rest a bit before I bring ye to the Seelie lands. 'Tis quite a big place, is Faerie."

"That's a good idea, I'm soaked and I am kind of tired."

They made their way to a rocky cliff facing the sea they had just crossed, and sat down on the sun-warmed rocks.

"Can ye tell me about yer side? I've never been across and I'm curious now that I've met so lovely a human lassie," Kieran winked, sparkling with good humor.

"Where I live it's nice, though not beautiful like this." She gestured to the view, both magnificent and rugged. "I guess it's pretty cool, except for lousy teachers like Mr. Fisher. We have pizza and great music, ice cream and my grandmother's angel food cake. There are buildings and roads, mini malls and parking lots, and woods. What else do you want to know?"

"I want to know about humans. What are they like?"

"They're harder to describe." She thought for a moment. "People are very different from one another and they come in all kinds of shapes, sizes, colors, and beliefs. Some are nice and good, and others are mean and horrible. We have emotions like yours, I guess: happiness, anger, sadness, and joy. And we need food to eat, water to drink, air to breathe, a house to live in. And love. We need that, too, a lot."

"Ye sound very like us. Not too different, only ye don't have powers, do ye?"

"Not like yours."

They sat quietly for a time, the warm breeze lulling Fiona to sleep. Kieran watched her eyes begin to close, and realizing that their safety was likely only temporary, rose and extended his hand, "Now I think we're dry enough to get on with our journey. Are ye ready?"

She wasn't really ready to face whatever it was they were about to do, she would rather sit here on this rocky perch with this handsome young, could she say, man? But she knew procrastination was pointless.

"I'm ready," she lied, taking his hand. Fiona walked beside Kieran, taking in the incredible beauty of her surroundings, trying not to look behind her at every sound and movement. They walked on the fringe of a deep, primeval forest, trees thick on one side, a meadow of the brightest green she had ever seen, on the other, so profuse with wild flowers in hues that even her crayon box of 64 colors seemed bland compared to them. Out of the corner of her eye, she saw beings flittering here and there, wispy creatures, who appeared and disappeared at will. At one point she saw a group of tiny children, or at least they looked like children, pointing at her, their tiny mouths open in disbelief; the next moment they were gone, leaves swirling on the ground in their wake.

"What were those?" she asked Kieran who was walking determinedly beside her.

"What, lass? I didn't see a thing? What did they look like?"

"Like little children."

"Well, they might have been human captives, or just faeries in disguise. We're a very mischievous bunch, ye know. Always playing tricks and practical jokes. The good faeries that is. Although the Fir Darrig is known to be a practical joker of rather gruesome nature. The ones ye have to be careful of are the bogles and the bogies and especially the fachans, but I needn't tell ye that. And then there's Wicked Annis. Ooh, ye wouldn't like her. She likes to lure children to her cave and then devour them. And of course the Nuckelavee, mind, we're not near water so ye needn't fret," he said, watching Fiona's face turn pale. "Here in this land, ye'll stay close by me and I'll let no harm come to ye."

"I don't think I want to know anymore."

"As ye wish," he said, giving her hand a friendly squeeze. She kept a firm grip on it as they entered the dark woods.

Kieran was watching the face of the human girl and he thought how lucky it was he should have stumbled upon such a one as she. Not only was she a sweet and loyal youth, he could tell that by her passionate defense of her "sister," but she had also given him pertinent information regarding his betrothed. What he would do with that information, he was still unsure, but he wanted to help this human.

Kieran knew the way, recalling his previous journey. His friend, Ewan's suspicions were exactly right and he wanted to tell him so, perhaps saving him from a terrible tithing. He knew there was no time to waste.

He sped up his step, practically pulling Fiona along with him. She looked at him questioningly but didn't say a thing. He saw her unrest and slowed slightly. "Don't worry, lass, I just want to find me friend before night falls. I want ye to have shelter before that time as well."

Fiona breathed a sigh of relief. "Oh, that's good. Are we close?"

"Aye. Let's stop here and have a wee drink." They stopped by a tiny creek that Fiona hadn't noticed; it had blended with their surroundings as if deliberately camouflaging itself. The water changed color before her eyes. First it was green, like the surrounding woods, with which she was familiar, then it shifted to a misty purple, and from there to a silvery lavender. Eventually it returned to the clear look of water. Fiona could see tiny fish swimming around and on a lily pad, sat not a frog, but a fairy the size of a seed, perfectly proportioned and exquisitely beautiful. She pointed and it disappeared.

"They are very shy, those tiny sprites. They don't like to be noticed," explained Kieran.

"Oh, I feel terrible. Did I scare it?"

"Nay, it's over there...Slowly, slowly...," he said quietly indicating a rock a few feet downstream. Fiona turned her head and saw the creature sitting on it and facing the other way.

"Wow. It's beautiful," she whispered.

"Lovely. Now come and drink. The water is giving itself to us for that purpose."

"Is that why it changed all those colors?"

"Aye, it's clear and pure for drinkin' now. Hurry before it changes again."

Fiona bent down and rather than using her hands, copied Kieran and took the water out of the stream with her mouth. She felt like a cat and tried to be delicate and not slurp it up. It tasted sweet and very pure, like maple sap before it becomes syrup, and it was so cold her teeth fairly rattled. They drank until their stomachs could hold no more and just in time too, for the stream began to change the moment they lifted up their heads. Kieran bowed and swept his hand into the water, nodding at Fiona to do the same. She did, feeling a little silly but realizing it must be a way of expressing gratitude to the stream for giving them the water.

Full of sweet, clear water, Kieran reached over to a bush and pulled off some very odd-looking berries. They were larger than cherries and dark blue, almost black, with a glossy sheen to them and tiny yellow spots on one side, orange spots on the other. He gave Fiona a handful and she stared in amazement as the spots began to change color and switch sides right before her eyes. The yellows turned to green and pink, the orange spots to pastel blue and lavender. Kieran smiled at her expression and popped a few into his mouth, gesturing for her to do the same.

"Are you sure they're safe for humans?" she asked uneasily.

"Safe as yer own food."

She wanted to tell him that that wasn't exactly reassuring, but instead popped one in her mouth. She rolled the berry around for a moment then squeezed down on it letting the juice explode. The taste made her gasp. It was delicious, exquisite in flavor, something part way between a cherry, a lemon and the sweetest mango. Kieran laughed as he saw her face change from apprehension to rapture. "They have no pits!" she said delightedly and popped two more into her mouth, reveling in the incredible sweetness and zest.

"What are they called?" she said with her mouth full.

"I don't know how to say it in yer language, but the meaning in mine is 'charmed fruit'.

"Charmed fruit," she repeated. "I love that name! Do they grow only in Faerie?"

"Since I've not spent any significant amount of time anywhere else, nor am I an expert on fruit or berries, I cannot say, but I think so, sorry to tell ye. But they're plentiful here and ye can pick as many as ye like," he said smiling, then added, "as long as ye thank the thicket for its generosity. In Faerie we know all living things are conscious, so we always thank those that give us their bounty."

"Of course," Fiona said, liking this way of interacting with everything around her and she bowed before the plant, thanking it.

She pulled several more handfuls off the bushes, trying hard not to look piggish as she shoved them into her mouth, but she was very hungry. Her lips were stained blue when Kieran finally laughed and asked, "Are ye full now? Good. Let's move on. Night falls quickly here and we don't want to get caught in it. Fachans thrive in darkness, but they wouldn't dare set foot upon Seelie lands." He took Fiona's empty hand and they walked on.

The woods were alive with the sounds of the day, birds calling raucously to one another, the gentle hum of bees, and sounds very different from those Fiona heard at home. There was the sound of singing; small voices that sounded like tinkling bells, rendering melodies that though were unfamiliar to Fiona, were sweet and clear. The sinking sun was warm and dappled through the canopy of green, and as the two walked, Fiona felt as if her whole life had been leading up to this moment. Everything her mother had taught her, every experience she'd ever had, all of it, led her to these green, green woods with Kier, who was taking her to find Rionnag and hopefully her mother. She couldn't have explained why she felt this way, only that the feeling was very strong and grew stronger as they walked. She basked in the sensation, refusing to let anything negative come between it and her. Kieran seemed to sense she was having an epiphany and didn't interrupt. Feeling her recorder in her pocket, she pulled it out. To her amazement, she saw that it wasn't a recorder at all, but a whistle, made of tin. She hadn't noticed it when she was hitting the creature with it, but she examined it now. Instead of the seven holes, there were only six and only on the front. She put it to her lips and began to play. Kieran looked over in surprise to hear the sounds issuing from the girl. She played a tune filled with joy and sorrow, longing and hope, melodious and discordant at the same time. When she finished the piece, Kieran was standing, clapping. She curtsied and smiled at him.

"Ye must be one of us to play like that, me beauty!"

"I have no idea where that tune came from, but it was just there inside and needed to come out," she said, suddenly remembering her dream of the brightly plumed bird that had sung the same song.

Their pleasant repast was disrupted by a sound so heinous in its malevolence that they immediately froze, crouching on the ground. It was a cry, a scream of such anger and malice that Fiona felt her toes curl while the hair on her neck stood on end. Kieran, keeping his wits, grabbed her and carried her quickly to a rocky outcrop, large boulders creating a hiding place of sorts. He quickly guided her into a cave-like nook, scrambling in fast behind her. They sat silently; their hearts beating in unison, listening to the screams that made them want to squeeze their eyes shut and cover their ears. The woods became still, as if all sentient creatures had fled.

"I KEN YE ARE NEARBY, DECEIVER! COME TAE ME NOO AND THERE'LL BE NO BLOOD SPILLED. HIDE AND I WILL FIND YE. I WILL SMELL YE OUT, DIG YE OUT, BUT YE WILL COME TAE ME IN THE END...WHY DO YE HESITATE? DO YE NO BELIEVE ME WORDS? COMMMMMEEE OUUUT NOOOOW!!"

They waited, huddled together until they heard the fachan moving in the opposite direction, moving away, at least for the time being. Kieran shifted back to his stag shape and Fiona climbed on. He ran to the river that bordered the Seelie Courts' lands, and with a great leap, crossed onto safe territory. He cursed himself for breaking tradition again, but chivalry was more important than tradition at the moment, and he hoped he wouldn't regret his decision.

He ran to the spot by the river, let her down gently, assumed his fey form once more and knocked hard on the stump, three times.

Chapter 39

Ewan left Maggie while she was being dressed and commanded by Barabel, who seemed to have regressed considerably by the mere experience of having what she considered a dolly to play with. Well, he thought, for the time being, it was better than having her killed or traded with the fachan. He must come up with a rescue plan. But of course rescue now was unlikely. With Maggie a captive here, ironically by his own jailer, she would never be able to return home and tell their child, who was their only hope.

He walked blindly along the edge of the river bordering Barabel's lands to that of the Seelie Court, lost in thought. He fantasized about the meeting between father and child. In his mind, she welcomed him with loving arms, forgiving his absence these fourteen years. They would ride together and play the whistle together. Maggie had told him that she could play. In his fantasy, they were playing together, tunes made up on the spot to the delight of their Maggie.

As he imagined the scene, he was suddenly struck by a tune that seemed to come from nowhere and everywhere at once. He was shocked to recognize it as his own tune, the one he had played for Maggie. Not the one full of romance and longing, but the other, the one his dream had given. He remembered the songbird that had taught it to him.

And how well it was played! He was wondering what magic had brought this about, his own song coming to him. He wanted to find out. Perhaps it had something to do with his dream, or maybe it had to do with Maggie. His mind raced with possibility. But suddenly it stopped. All was still, all except for his own hammering heart in his breast. He whirled around this way and that, waiting for the tune to begin again, trying to hear the last wisps of it on the wind. But there was no more. Without the tune to follow, there would be no way to find its source in these deep and enchanted woods. He sat down, putting his head on his knees and stayed this way for a long time. Hours may have gone by for all he knew or cared.

His head came up as he heard a new sound. Three loud whacks on what he knew was the stump by the river. Yes, he heard it as clearly as he had heard the tune. It had to be his friend the Irish Prince. He remembered telling him to knock on the stump three times and he would come. And good to his promise, he brushed himself off, rose to his feet and made his way to the spot where they had parted not too long ago. He bumped into a urisk sitting alone by a pool of water and Ewan's heart nearly jumped out his chest at the figure's hideous countenance. A urisk wasn't a particularly dangerous faerie, only so peculiar and strange in appearance that even when it approached in peace, it tended to frighten away any possible friend. Ewan, regaining his composure, nodded to the urisk who gave him a sad and lonely look, accompanied by a pathetic, outstretched arm.

He knew where he was going, but these woods never ceased to make him uneasy. He knew no one would dare touch a mortal captive of Queen Barabel, but still and all, his heart beat uncomfortably in his chest as he made his way through the winding path trodden by centuries of faerie folk. He startled a tiny sprite who nearly flew into him and his heart lurched again. He realized he was edgier than usual here in this bewitched thicket, and wondered why. Of course, there was the fact that the tune he had heard had stopped so suddenly. Perhaps it had been a dream. Had he really heard it at all? He'd heard about people in prison for so long that their minds grew unreliable. He shook his head firmly. "Stop these thoughts, ye daft fool. Find yer Irish friend and think on naught else," he said aloud.

"THINK ONLY OF ME, FOR I AM GETTING NEARER ME PREY. AND THEN YE WILL BE MIIIIINE!"

Ewan heard the sound all around him. Running now, and turning in every direction to find the source of the voice, he tripped over an exposed root and fell headlong to the ground. He lay there sprawled on the leaves, his face in the dirt. Blackness engulfed him, but not the sweet blackness of the unconscious. No, in this blackness he saw the face of the monster, the fachan, who would be his new master if he couldn't get out of this menacing situation. The face was leering at him, laughing with malevolence and bloodlust. A moment later he returned to normal consciousness and lay still, listening to the erratic hammering of his heart. He lay there until the fitful pounding slowed to a steady pulse. Slowly he sat up, wiping dirt and leaves from his face and hair, feeling wetness on his cheeks and aware it had not come from the ground.

Angry now, but filled with more determination than he had in a century, he threw back his broad and powerful shoulders and spoke loudly with all the authority he could muster, "I will naiver be yers, Fachan, naiver. Ye will die before ye tak me, or I will. And tha' is a promise!" He didn't know if the creature had heard him, and he didn't care. Somehow, he would get out of this place. He would do everything within his power to free Maggie and himself and escape from this enchanted and dangerous world so they could return to the world he had lost so long ago.

Chapter 40

"AAARRRGHHH!!!" Creaghan was swirling with rage. Rage at the wench and rage at himself for letting her out of his grasp. He had watched her fly away on the back of that stag, but he'd been so drunk, he couldn't follow, could barely see straight. By the time he had come to his senses, they were out of sight. Now he would have to rely on his keen instincts. He had found her once; he would find her again. And his prize was near. He had heard him clearly, threatening him. How he would revel in his victory, when he delivered the brat to Barabel.

Barabel. Did she realize she was the object of his loathing? He thought not. How he wanted to take her, make her scream and beg for mercy before he devoured her. He imagined the first taste of flesh and bone upon his tongue. She had used him to do her bidding before, and her arrogant air made his blood burn. But she paid too well for him to destroy her. But he'd take her slave, that mortal she so coveted. The one he knew she wanted to keep secret. That was why he had chosen the wretch. He didn't give a rat's dropping which one he picked, but knowing Barabel's preference made him choose as he did. And there'd be time before his tithing day, he thought, licking his lips, just imagining what he'd do with his treasure when he brought him to his lair.

He would go back there now, to do his planning. That was better. There were too many tasty distractions in these woods. He had to be focused.

He swept quickly across the moors where his den lay hidden between two rocks, just accessible enough for some unsuspecting prey to burrow in or stumble upon. He'd had no end of meals from just that type of thing.

He made his way down, down into the depths of his dwelling. His nose quivered with excitement. A rabbit was standing frozen, paralyzed in fear, hoping to blend in with the surroundings.

"SURELY YE WON'T TRY TAE ESCAPE, VARMINT. I'LL BE QUICK. NOO COME TAE ME!"

The poor creature shook convulsively as Creaghan came closer, closing in until he was upon the thing. "HOW DID YE GUESS I WAS RAVENOUS, *COINEANAICH*, RABBIT, MY FAVORITE MEAL! HA!" The monster grabbed it by the throat and slowly, delightedly, squeezed the life out it, and with one bite, devoured it whole.

Barely satiated, Creaghan paced across the grimy floor of his dwelling, reeking of his own scent in combination with the animal skins, many still fleshy and rotting that lined the walls.

First and foremost he must recapture the little horror. Had there not been the deal with the witch, oh, what he would do to her when he found her! Seelie Court or no! He could almost hear the soft bones cracking, the taste of her.

He licked his lips, visualizing her screams as he sunk his teeth into her flesh. He shook his head like a wet dog, trying to regain focus. She was with that stag, probably of filthy royal blood. That was no problem; stags were vulnerable in the right places. And in battle, Creaghan always wins, he sneered to himself. He would wait for the cover of nightfall and then in his most insidious guise, he would root her out until he found her. And find her he would!

Chapter 41

Rionnag and her ladies came through the old ring from which they earlier had left. The correct spell held none of the nauseating terror that their previous journey had. Although they were jostled and bumped by unseen forces, it was nothing like before. And for that, they were grateful. They brushed themselves off and climbed out of the stone circle, taking care to be quiet lest any spies were hovering.

Rionnag got her bearings and immediately set a tracking spell in motion to find Fiona. As she recited the words in their strange sequence, a wisp of blue smoke escaped from her lips as the last of the magic was spoken, whirling off in search of her dear friend. The thought of waiting until the spell returned was impossible, but wait they must. Rionnag had no idea where Fiona might be, and to roam hither and yon around Faerie with no direction made no sense. When the smoke completed its task, it would return to Rionnag and furnish Fiona's whereabouts. As long as her captor did

311

not see the smoke first and intercept it, that is.

Mór was the first to speak, "I ken we must find the child, but what of the fachan? Shouldna we go and get yer faither? I dinna think we should search alone!"

"Mòr, if I return home now, there'll be no end of explaining, and by then, Fiona might be a fachan's dinner. Perhaps ye and Jinty ought to return and tell my faither what's happened," she said.

"Princess, do ye think us daft? Yer faither would have my head if I returned wi' out ye. Nay, we'll help ye find yer friend, but then we must return immediately!" Mòr gave her charge a stern look.

Rionnag nodded and said, "As soon as we find her, we'll go directly home. I promise!"

Making themselves blend in completely with their surroundings, the three waited, not speaking a single word between them. At last the blue wisp returned, swirling around Rionnag's ear, whispering the whereabouts of her spirit sister, locating her essence not too far from their present position.

Kieran gestured to Fiona to sit down on a stump at the river's edge, noticing how tired she suddenly seemed. Fiona was happy to comply and sat down hard; looking first to make sure there was nothing sentient she might sit upon. She pulled her legs up, crossing them under her and put her head on her knees. Kieran patted her on the back and said, "Ye'll be safe here and ye look as though ye need to rest. That foul fellow wouldn't dare enter these woods."

Fiona replied, "I hope not. Are we on Rionnag's land?"

"Aye, rest now while we wait for me friend. I do believe he'll come directly." His voice was soothing.

"I hope so. What if that thing comes…?"

"Shh, now. He cannot set foot upon this land. Ye must believe that. Rest now."

The forest was still active, the sounds of the day clear and sweet, but Kieran looked to where the sun shone and knew day would be coming to a close shortly. He grimaced at that thought. A fachan's time of day. He hoped his friend would come before too long.

Kieran watched the child try to stay awake when he saw a wisp of blue smoke circling above their heads, as if searching for something. It swooped down and swirled about Fiona, then left as quickly as it had come. Fiona was mumbling in her half sleep, but did not stir as the smoke swirled and left.

"I'm thinkin' yer sister is close by," he whispered mostly to himself, hopeful that the blue smoke he had just seen was sent by Rionnag to find her friend. If his suspicions were correct, he also knew he had better get out of there before his fiancé arrived. He had no idea what kind of spell had been placed on their betrothal should they see one another, and he did not want to find out. He quickly got up and crossed the stream until he was no longer on Seelie land. Feeling responsible for the child, he decided to stay until she was safely with her friend. But at least he had not disobeyed the decree. He hid behind a tree and watched the girl sleep, shifting to his stag form to blend into the landscape, camouflaged. From out of a copse of trees three figures emerged. He recognized them as his own kind. There was a stout one who looked as old as his own mother and a lean one, younger, but older than himself. They were both wearing the colors and designs of ladies in waiting, the same fashion he had seen every day of his life in his own castle. The third faerie had her back towards him, seemingly looking for something. He watched as she turned and a breath escaped from his nostrils. She turned, hearing it. He stood motionless so she couldn't make out his flesh-colored fur hidden behind the Rowan. He watched as she peered around, her brilliant eyes sparking, her flaxen hair charmingly disheveled around her face. Seeing no one, she turned back to her companions.

He shifted back to his fey form and watched enraptured, mesmerized, her beauty dazzling him, and for a moment he forgot who he was, and where he was, and why. His heart wanted to leap from his chest as he watched her movements and expressions. Her hair was soft around her face, like wheat fields in the sun. He blinked once and she was gone. He felt a strange and sudden emptiness arise within him. "Get hold of yerself, ye ijit," he said reproachfully to himself.

"So ye were hiding there, like some kind of spy." The voice came from the other side of the tree.

He turned and saw the face that he would like to see everyday from this moment forward. She glared at him, but her ire turned to amusement as she watched his face change between all the colors of the ruby spectrum. The others were still out of sight.

"Weel? Do ye no have an answer, man?"

"Uh, I, uh..." was all he could muster.

"What kind of answer is that? Were ye spying or no?"

Kieran barely heard what she was saying, only that whatever it was, it was coming out of the most exquisite lips he had ever seen, the color of peonies, and her eyes; oh her eyes. He watched them spark as she accused him. They were a color neither from nature nor the most precious gem.

"...listening? Are ye daft? Maybe deaf? One or the other, to be sure."

From behind the tree, the stout faerie burst upon the scene. "Princess Rionnag, I dinna see the girl. Please let us leave and go find yer faither. I'm sure by noo he's worried sick!"

Kieran snapped to attention as he heard these words, realizing whom he was watching as if some daft ijit! As if with the force of a blow, he came to his senses and he screwed his eyes shut and waited for the lightning bolts of thunderclouds or whatever force was going to come down upon him from breaking this faerie law, but nothing came. He opened his eyes slightly, hearing a familiar voice calling.

"Kier? Where are you?" Fiona's sleepy voice called. "Where are you? Oh, there you are, I thought you were gone....Oh, my God! Oh, my God...Ri!!"

Rionnag, hearing that voice practically knocked Kieran down in an effort to get to her friend. Fiona scrambled off the stump and flung herself into the arms of her beloved sister. The two hugged and grasped each other, the maids standing open-mouthed at this happy reunion. After they pulled themselves apart long enough to take a breath, the questions came fast and furious in a jumble of Gaelic, Faerie and English.

"Och, Fi, I'm so sorry I let the thing take ye. Are ye hurt?"

"No, I got away, but what happened to you after it took me?"

"I came upon Mòr and Jinty and some friends."

"Friends?"

"Aye, I'll tell ye about them in a minute."

"I'm afraid that thing is closer than you think. We just heard it a little while ago. He wants me."

"Nay, Fiona, it's me he wants. My aunt sent him to kidnap me to prevent my marriage from taking place. Two more creatures, bogies they were, were sent after me first."

"But why does she want to prevent your marriage?" Fiona asked.

"She wants my prince's parents to declare war on our

court. I think she wants my mither's power."

Kieran, who was duty bound to return to his hiding place was startled to hear her say "my prince." Fiona, also hearing the reference to which she was sure was the prince in question, saw him lurking behind the tree and was unsure what to do. Had they met? Should they? She knew they were not supposed to. Before she could decide what to do, Rionnag spied him too.

"So there ye are, spying again!" she declared.

"Ri, that's my friend, uhm…"

"Paddy," Kieran said, coming forward and bowing, and hoping against hope there would be no consequences.

"Weel, Paddy, I dinna ken how ye met up with Fiona, but I'm mighty glad ye did. Thank ye."

"At yer service," he said and bowed, his eyes never leaving her face.

"Ahem!" Rionnag turned to Mòr who had stepped forward to meet this 'sister' of Rionnag's.

"Sorry. Mòr, this is Fiona. Fiona, this is Mòr, my nanny."

The older faerie grasped Fiona's hand in hers and kissed it. "Thank ye for keeping oor lass safe."

"I..I saw you…" she said wonderingly and turned and looked at Jinty. "I saw you both that day at school." Mòr smiled and nodded, unsure what the child was talking about. She turned to Jinty and said, "Come here, girl, she'll no bite ye. Fiona, this is Jinty, my helper." Jinty bowed to Fiona, who bowed back.

Mòr, full of motherly authority, said, "Noo that we've found yer wee friend, we'd better return tae the castle. The king and queen will be most anxious."

"Ri, how did you find me?"

"I used a tracking spell and it worked. Now that I've found ye, which was my priority, of course, I shall use the same spell on yer mither."

"Princess, really, stop all this! We must return tae yer parents. I ken they are frantic!" Mór said, wringing her hands.

"First I'll send the tracking spell and then we'll leave. Ye worry too much, Mór!"

"Worry too much! What ye've put us all through!"

"We're safe on our land. I'll be quick."

"I dinna like it. We're still far from home. Why can ye no wait until we're safe within the confines of the castle?"

Ignoring her, Rionnag sat down on the stump and Fiona sat next to her. Once more Rionnag uttered the strange words and again, a wisp of blue smoke came from her mouth and away. Fiona watched the blue smoke curl, and rather than dissolve into mist, this smoke, like a long tendril, stayed as a unit, moving towards the river, then across it in the direction of the setting sun. Fiona sent a prayer with it.

They sat waiting; Rionnag and Fiona, for the tracking spell to help them find Maggie. Kieran, though, didn't have to wait long, for at that very moment, Ewan came out of the woods and stood on the other side of the stream, Barabel's lands separating him from the others. He stood observing the group for several moments before making his presence known. He recognized his friend, the stag prince, but the rest were strangers. He saw a lass, perhaps fey, perhaps not, the age of a child, yet almost a woman. She was talking with a faerie who seemed to know her. He watched her face, its seriousness as she spoke. He saw the whisper of a smile light her features, softening them. Her hair, the dark color of autumn leaves fell to her waist, and the sight of it stirred memories. His mind went back to the past and he remembered such a face, older for certain, but oddly similar, looking lovingly down at him as he played in the garden. He felt confused. Memories of childhood rumors came back to him. "Yer mither's a witch..." "No one kens where she comes from..." "Some say she was from the fey world...." "She goes back when your da's away..."

He almost turned and ran, not wanting to be seen this way, disoriented and disheveled from his fall, face streaked with tears and dirt. He looked harder at the child and tried to shake off whatever it was that made him feel this way. There was no likeness now that he looked closer. Just his mind playing tricks. Anything could happen in these woods. He straightened up, took a breath, walked forward, and raised his hand, calling out a Highland greeting.

The strangers looked up. Kieran smiled hugely and came forward, walking halfway into the river, palms raised in faerie greeting.

"Me knuckles did the trick, for here ye are, just as ye said ye'd be," Kieran said, happily.

"Aye, Sire."

Kieran leaned closer and whispered, "Don't call me that! Call me Paddy, would ye. I don't want anyone to know who I am."

Ewan raised his eyebrows slightly and nodded, then spoke normally, "Aye, Paddy, I heard yer call and came directly."

"Well, me friend, I have some information that may prove helpful to ye. Ye remember when last we met? Ewan? Ewan?"

The man was looking again at the girl who had stepped closer to the riverbank. Kieran saw Fiona watching the man, an expression of curiosity in her eyes as she took in the vines entwined around the captive's wrists.

Then he noticed something extraordinarily similar in the two human expressions. They wore the same furrowed brow, the same squint of the eyes. Their mouths were set in the same line. He knew humans were like faeries in that each one was different, but this similarity could be no accident and he could not shake off the odd feeling that this was more than mere happenstance. The two were locked in a stare that revealed nothing and yet everything, and Rionnag came forward boldly to look the stranger directly in the eyes. She was about to speak when a horrible scraping sound like the screech of metal against metal drove all thoughts away. Everyone looked frantically to see where it was coming from and then from the borderland, like a colossus, the fachan appeared, taller than the Rowan tree and just as wide. He was at his most hideous and frightening, his chalky skin seething with open sores, his mouth open showing barbed teeth dripping with slime, his eyes slits that seemed to smolder with wickedness. But what made him even more terrifying was the malicious smile on his death-white face and the luridness of his expression. He licked his purple lips viciously, a forked crimson tongue darting as he glanced at his man-prize. His crimson eyes, full of malevolence, flicked to where Fiona and Rionnag were standing together. Although Creaghan could not set foot upon Seelie lands without being reduced to dust, he reached a long, thick arm across the border and with one smooth movement, he picked them both up until they were higher than the top-most branches of the Rowan.

"THE SAME STENCH COMES FROM YE TWO TERMAGANTS SO I'LL TAKE YE BOTH. BARABEL WILL HAVE TWO PRIZES AND THEN I'LL BE BACK FOR YE, ME PRETTY," he growled, his last words for Ewan alone.

The beast felt their fear growing as he lifted them higher, separating them, squeezing them tighter in each hand. He began to laugh insidiously as his mind first went into Fiona's and he spoke loudly her deepest fears, "YER MOTHER WILL DIE A HEINOUS DEATH AS WILL YER RELATIONS AND YE WILL BE ALONE! YER FAITHER

KENS ABOUT YE BUT CARES NAUGHT FOR YE!"

Fiona began to cry helplessly. Rionnag picked up bits of Creaghan's lies and managed to say, "Dinna listen to him, he's a deceiver!"

Aloud, the monster shrieked, "DECEIVER! HAH! YE HARRIDAN, YE SHALL NAIVER MARRY NEITHER FOR LOVE NOR FOR ANY REASON AND YER WORLD WILL PERISH BECAUSE OF YE! AND KEN THIS; I SHALL RULE!" Rionnag wanted to claw at his face, but he had reached down into the recesses of her deepest dread and the menacing lies paralyzed her.

Fiona, who had almost given in to the monster, had desperately called on her Source, as Rionnag had taught her, and to her surprise, the clear image of her coyote, her spirit protector had appeared on her inner screen. She felt renewed strength and yelled, "Ri! Don't listen, you're right, he's a liar! Fight, Ri, we've got to fight!"

The two began clawing and kicking at the beast. Mòr and Jinty were hysterical, flying in all directions, charging into the brute. Mòr lunged and the fachan hit her hard, and she fell to the ground, unconscious.

Ewan tried to jump across the river to rescue them, but the vines held fast and he could do nothing but watch helplessly as the monster took the faerie and the child for whom he felt such an odd connection. He screamed a bloodcurdling cry full of torment and frustration as he tore at his bound wrists, knowing that his tithing would come now. And the thought of what would come before the tithing was too frightening to endure.

Kieran watched as the fachan's bloodless body began to writhe and twist in an attempt to shift his hideous shape, and at the same moment Kieran shifted once again to his stag form, only this time, the anger in him allowing his antlers to reach their ten point sharpness. As the creature sprouted bat-like wings, rising from the ground and carrying the two screaming friends high into the air, Kieran pawed the ground hard, charged forward, lifted off, kicking the air at furious speed, and flung himself at the beast. The fachan dodged, the antlers missing by fractions, and he laughed with megalomaniacal glee, enjoying the contest. Tendrils of vapor emanated off the creature in another shift attempt, but before Creaghan had time to become smoke, Kieran spun around and charged furiously, this time taking him on his side. The antler plunged deep into the monster, who bellowed hideously. Kieran pulled free from the ogre, black ooze dripping off his antler, backed up once more and rushed at it, this time plunging the sharpest of his points into the stomach of the beast who dropped Fiona on impact, howling in agony.

Jinty who was trying in vain to revive Mòr, saw this last attack and without a second thought, flew and caught Fiona before she crashed to the ground. Fiona felt the faerie's arms around her, holding her, then hovering in the air before laying her gently on the ground. Ewan watched the battle helplessly, cursing Barabel mightily.

They looked up at the same moment hearing a thud and a grunt of pain. Holding Rionnag tightly in one hand, his other now free of Fiona, Creaghan was able to jab at Kieran as he made another attack. Kieran, still in midair was doubled over, the pain obvious. But unwavering in his determination, he clumsily flew around behind the fachan, grimacing in agony and drove his antlers deeply into the fachan's back.

"AAAAAAGHHH!!!! I'LL GET ME PRIZE NOO AND THEN I'LL COME BACK AND DESTROY THE LIKES OF YE!" Creaghan screamed, squeezing Rionnag around the neck.

"Nooooooo!!!!" Fiona screamed.

"Noooooo!!" came a voice behind them, the deep angry cry of Rionnag's father who had been searching with his troops for days. He was at that moment riding out with them to alert his other men to guard every faerie ring or portal, when he had heard the fachan's roar. He pulled a spelled arrow from his quiver and pointing it at the creature's heart, or whatever it was that kept the beast incarnate, readied, aimed, but never let his arrow fly; for once more, the young stag lunged at the beast. He knocked the monster on his side and Rionnag was thrust from his grasp. The fachan, realizing he might be caught, disappeared into the dusk. Before Rionnag came crashing to the ground, released from the fachan's clutches, Kieran, though bent over in pain, shifted back his fey shape, swept forward, caught her in his arms and gently flew to the ground where Jinty and Fiona watched in horror, wringing their hands and biting their lips. Mòr, who still had not come to, lay on the ground.

Fiona, seeing Rionnag was fine, ran to Kieran, threw her arms around him somewhat less than gingerly, and cried, "Thank you, Kier! Thank you for saving us! You were so brave!"

"Ouch, that hurts!" Kieran said, rubbing his side.

"Sorry, but I am so grateful to you. Thank you."

"I'd save ye fifty times over if I have to, but stop gettin' yerself into trouble, will ye!"

"I'll try."

The king who had been focused on his wild daughter, looked up when he heard the name the human girl had called the lad. Irish name? Stag? He looked closely at the youth and thought he saw a familiar face, one he had seen through his crystal globe many times throughout the years, as he watched him grow. He nodded to himself and turned back to his child. She too had been staring at the youth and blushed deeply when she finally took her eyes off him and turned to look at her father. She gave him a loving gaze. "Faither," she said hoarsely, her throat aching, "I'm so sorry for troublin' ye... Where is Mór?" she asked anxiously, suddenly remembering.

"Mór will be fine. We're going home."

The King placed his daughter on a horse, then walked over to Kieran and said, "Sir, I dinna ken who ye are, but I thank ye for the life of my daughter."

Kieran knelt before the king and said, "'Twas me honor and privilege to save the princess," he said, blushing.

"Child," the king said to Fiona, acknowledging her for the first time, "I ken not who ye are, but ye will come home with Rionnag and me..."

"Faither, this is Fiona, my dear, dear friend."

As the King took her by the hand, Fiona looked searchingly at Kieran, wanting him to know how much she cared about him, how grateful she was and said, "Thank you, uhm, Paddy, thank you. I hope I will see you again."

"Ye certainly will, make no mistake. One thing, me beauty, if yer ever needin' me, just call me with that whistle of yers. Ye know the tune. And call me name loudly in yer head and I'll find ye." He started to leave, but Jinty blocked his way.

"Sir, ye are a fine fellow and I... we... oh!" The faerie began to cry. "If Mór could tell ye herself, I ken she would say the same! We are more than grateful tae ye. Ye'll never want for anything if we can help it. Anything we can do for ye, just ask." Jinty grabbed Kieran's hand and kissed it.

"Ye are more than welcome," Kieran said, embarrassed.

King Niall commanded two of his troops to conjure a stretcher, which Mór was gently placed upon and then he himself placed Fiona upon Rionnag's horse. She quickly put her arms around Rionnag's waist as the horse began to move. The princess turned once more to gaze at her rescuer, before urging on her horse. The king flew at their side, Jinty fluttering closely behind. Mòr lay pale and listless on the stretcher.

Fiona's mind filled with anxiety for her mother, knowing the fachan was on the loose and her mother might be anywhere in these magical woods.

They traveled quickly. As night descended, they arrived at a hill covered with the most incredible assortment of wild flowers Fiona had ever seen. There were bluebells and daffodils, primroses and hollyhocks, flowers the color of the sky after a storm, and flowers with designs Fiona thought looked like art. Rionnag turned around, and said croakily, "This is home."

An elegant woman dressed in flowing silks appeared out of nowhere, running towards them. Rionnag flew off the horse and hurried to meet her, replete with apologies, hugs and tears.

"Och, my willful child, never do that to me again! I've had no end of worry," said her mother, hugging her fiercely. Her face softened as she looked at her daughter as she said, "Ye mustn't give yer old mither such trouble, do ye hear?"

"Aye, Mither, I do hear and I willna again." To her father, she said, "Faither, please take care of Mór!"

"Of course, child, she's being taken directly to the infirmary."

"Thank Titania! Do ye think she'll be all right?"

"We can only pray."

"Then I will pray day and night!" She turned to her mother, "Mither, please, I want ye to meet my dearest friend in all the worlds. Mither, this is Fiona," she gestured gracefully to Fiona who climbed nervously off the horse. Fiona knelt before the Queen who unexpectedly grabbed her by the arm, and pulled her to her bosom and held her tightly. Fiona was surprised and honored. When the Queen let go, Rionnag took Fiona's hand as they made their way inside the hill. To Fiona's astonishment, the interior was lavishly furnished in polished rose wood and soft fabrics. The floor was moss, richly green, and soft. Flowers grew from the walls and the heady fragrance that wafted through the air made Fiona a little dizzy. She held more tightly to Rionnag, who gripped her reassuringly. They entered a large dining room, urged by the king.

"Mither, could we eat later? I want to sit with Mór."

"I think ye should let the healers do their work. I'm sure yer wee friend is famished. We will eat a little something now, and wait until we ken the situation with Mór."

Everyone was somber, waiting for news of Mór and until they knew she would be fine, no one had much appetite.

Rionnag glanced at Fiona who was fading fast, took her arm and said goodnight. Fiona managed to mumble her thanks and followed her friend, who escorted her to her room. And although Fiona was concerned about her missing mother and more exhausted than she could remember, she couldn't help but express her delight at the room's natural beauty.

"Ye like it, then?" Rionnag said, pleased.

"Oh, Ri, it's lovely. I'd give anything to have a room like this."

"Ye ken, Sister, my home is yer home. Forever."

Fiona put her arms around Rionnag, Rionnag's going around Fiona's back and squealed delightedly when she felt the tiny wings there. "Ye are my sister, true, dear friend."

Fiona looked at Rionnag's golden hair and saw her three dark strands standing out like a beacon and said, "Yes, we are truly sisters." She smothered a yawn and said in a nervous tone, "Ri, what about my mom?"

"Fiona, tonight, ye must sleep. Tomorrow we will find

yer mither. The tracking spell should find her, so we must wait. My faither has already sent his soldiers after her and if by morning there's no news, we'll go ourselves. We *will* find her!"

Fiona nodded, smiling slightly and then Rionnag handed her a nightgown made of the softest material Fiona ever felt. The softness practically melted into her hand and she wondered what fabric it could be. She changed into it and climbed into bed. Her blanket, like Rionnag's, was of spun silk and felt warm and luxurious. Fiona closed her eyes, but Rionnag was too excited to sleep, tired as she was.

"Fi, that Paddy! Tell me about him! How did ye come to meet him? Did ye see the way he charged the fachan?" she said, eyes glazing as she stared at the ceiling, her expression rapturous. Fiona smiled and said, "He's very nice. Goodnight, Ri."

"Nay, Fi, dinna say goodnight yet. Tell me, how did ye come to be with him?"

"He saved me from the fachan the first time."

"Ye dinna like him, do ye? I mean..."

"No, Rionnag, I don't like him that way. But he is cute."

"Cute? I dinna ken that word."

"You know, handsome, sweet..."

"Aye, he is that. Cute. Och, I'd better stop. I'm to marry soon," she sighed deeply and whispered, "Goodnight, dearest sister. Tomorrow we must speak more." She looked over at Fiona who already was breathing quietly, fast asleep. She whispered a faerie prayer for Mór and one for Maggie and fell asleep as well.

Chapter 42

Kieran watched the party disappear behind the riverbed and sat down on the ground, holding his side. "Is she not the most beautiful creature on earth?" he grunted through his pain. He looked over to his friend, whose face was grim.

"What is it Ewan?"

"I'm sorry that I couldna help ye. I stood here like a tiny bairn, helpless, because of these!" He spat angrily as he looked down at his bound wrists.

"Never mind, friend," Kieran called across the river. "I know ye would have helped if it weren't for the chains on ye."

"Ye ken it *was* Barabel who sent the fachan." Ewan angrily threw a rock into the river. It splashed hard creating ripples that seemed endless.

"Ah, so ye are the fachan's reward."

"Aye, I am the prize," he said shortly. More gently he said, "Kieran, could ye tell me aboot the child? She's human,

327

isna she?"

"Ye mean, Fi?" He didn't notice Ewan jump slightly at the name. "Aye, ye guessed. Charmin' girl. Funny and smart and she can play the whistle like nothin' I've ever heard."

"So it was *her* playin'," Ewan said mostly to himself.

"Ye heard it too?"

"Aye."

"Well, I helped her escape the fachan the first time he had her. I was bringin' her here to find her sister and mother when the fachan came again and, well, ye know the rest of it," he said modestly.

"A human girl lookin' for her mither? Why would that be?" Ewan's heart raced slightly. If his suspicions were correct, how would she know where her mother was? "And sister?" he said more loudly than necessary.

"The Princess, that's her sister, in a matter of speakin'. They had a ceremony of some sort, and well, now they're sisters. As for the mother, she said something about her mother meetin' someone here and not comin' home when she was supposed to."

"Aye, that's so," he concurred. Almost inaudibly he added, "How did she ken?"

Kieran looked at him oddly, but Ewan continued, "But why did the fachan have her? She's human and he didna kill her!"

Kieran shook his head. "As I told ye, 'tis because Fi and the Princess Rionnag made a pact, each givin' somethin' precious to the other and so they are linked now by bonds of love. Because of the pact they made, the child somehow resembles Princess Rionnag, at least to a fachan, and that's why the fachan mistakenly took her."

"I dinna want tae think what Barabel would have done tae her had she found her first. And let's hope the fachan was wounded badly enough tae stay away," Ewan said, shuddering. "Thank ye for saving them."

Kieran nodded wondering why the man seemed so grateful. He was watching Ewan and suddenly remembered something he noticed before, but hadn't registered in his head until just now. The expression on Ewan's face was the same as he had seen on Fi's. He looked into his friend's eyes and saw the same startling blue-green surrounded with starbursts around dark pupils.

Kieran decided now was as good a time as any to bring up this startling resemblance. "I notice, Ewan, that ye and me beauty, Fi, have a similar look. I'm not sayin' mind ye, that all humans look alike. I would never presume, but there is such a look..."

"Aye, my friend, I believe ye are correct. I think I can tell all tae ye, in fact, what a great relief it would be if ye'd allow me the privilege."

"Of course." Kieran was about to cross the river to sit with the man, but Ewan stopped him. "Please dinna. Ye ken, I stand on an evil one's land and any trespasser is in danger, fey or human." Kieran nodded, but edged closer, sitting upon a slick rock in the middle of the river, his feet dangling. Darkness was spreading over the forest, but neither man moved as Ewan told his story to Kieran who listened intensely. "...so ye see, my Maggie is noo here wi' Barabel. And I believe that child is my oon daughter. It seems rather an impossible situation."

Kieran nodded and said, "Well, Ewan, it seems we are connected. I, the bridegroom of yer daughter's sister, ye, the prize if my bride jilts me at the altar! And yer love, the object of my bride's search. It seems we will both be responsible for foiling Barabel's wicked scheme if all goes as planned."

To himself he said, "Although I'm not sure that capricious princess is the right one for me, beauty or no!"

"Sire!"

"Nay, man, no titles, if ye please. We are friends now. My name will always be Kieran to ye, unless ye like Paddy," he winked. "Now, not a word to anyone about Barabel's plan. Let her think her niece is still fair game. The less she knows the better, aye? Perhaps we can catch her in her own sport. I will have me manservant contact King Niall and tell all to him. He's a good king and he'll tell the child about ye and her mother. The girl has pluck. And I think she'll know what to do."

The two parted with plans to come together again soon. Ewan gave his friend instructions to tell the child, should she be willing to rescue both Maggie and him. Kieran promised to relate all to the king, then shook his friend's hand and disappeared, leaving Ewan shaking his head in wonder (even after all these years) at faerie magic. He walked slowly back to Barabel's castle, thinking about Maggie, hoping she was not being ill-treated by her evil wardeness and wondering if there might be a sliver of hope. His thoughts then turned to a human child, who had two sides of faerie royalty for her friend. He had much to think on.

He suddenly felt weary and very old. For all his youthful appearance, he had lived on this earth for over a century, most of it loveless and alone, excepting those precious occasions where he could bask in the warmth of the one person whose smile lit the darkness inside him like a flame. He wanted to go home, wherever that might be, home to love and laughter, to hearth and family, to Maggie and Fiona.

He knew he would never sleep this night; his anxiety for the safety of his Maggie was so high. Instead of returning to his own mean dwelling, he made his way to Barabel's castle where he would stand vigil outside and listen to the sounds of the night, hoping all would remain quiet while he waited for the morrow and whatever fate had in store for him.

Chapter 43

The day dawned darkly, the sky a deep gray, fine mists swirling like spirits on the many mounds dotting the kingdom. From behind a low cloud, a single shaft of light appeared, coming directly into Rionnag's window illuminating Fiona's sleeping face, rousing her from sleep. As she opened her eyes she looked to the window where the ray was still focused, dazzling her. She blinked twice as a face appeared on the beam, an old woman's face, smiling and crinkled, her mouth moving though Fiona could hear no words. She sat up, leaning on her elbow, eyes riveted on the face, which oddly caused her no fear, only curiosity. The woman's lips continued to move, and as the light shifted and her mouth came under the ray directly, the silence was broken. Her words began to have a tangible quality to them and Fiona was able to make out what she was saying.

"...like him, I can see it in yer eyes. Rescue him, as I wasna able tae do..." The sun burst forth and the room

brightened like a flame. Fiona looked at the window but all she could see now was its curved frame with the view of the Rowan tree and the brightening blue sky beyond. She lay back against the pillows, wondering what to make of this, wondering if it had been part of a dream. She let the thought drift over her until she fell back to sleep.

Rionnag had been up long before Fiona, the familiar smells and sounds of the morning bringing her out of her own dreams. She had quietly left her chamber, not wanting to disturb her sleeping friend, and had gone directly to the infirmary where she found Jinty sitting at her mentor's side, quietly weeping.

"Och, Miss! She hasna wakened! She stirred some time ago, but nothin' since. I dinna ken what tae do!"

Rionnag said nothing, but sat beside her nanny, whom she loved possibly more than she loved her own mother. She took the plump hand in her own, felt its clammy coolness. Closing her eyes, she squeezed the faerie's hand and said a prayer, sparks flying around the bed as she spoke. "Mór, ye must wake. Please!" She was crying along with Jinty, as she looked at the familiar face covered in bruises. Rionnag, who had never commanded anyone to do anything cried, "Mór, I command ye to wake! Obey me!"

"It's no use, Miss. That thing, that horrible monster has taken her from us."

"I refuse to believe that! Mór! Mór! Wake up! Oh!"

The two sobbed, heads in hands, until they heard a groan from the bed. Sniffling, they both stood and watched their beloved Mór struggle into consciousness. She moaned softly again and raised her hand to her head. The two faeries watching grabbed each other, straining to hear the older faerie. "Och, my haid. Where…"

"Mór, ye are right here where ye should be, with us. Mór!" Jinty whispered through her tears, as Mór opened one eye. Rionnag was on her knees now, her head resting near her nanny's breast, one hand on Mór's head. Mór's other eye opened and looked at Rionnag. She closed them again, a relieved sigh escaping from her lips.

Rionnag slowly stood up and noticed a group of nurses hovering, waiting to do their job, but not willing to interrupt the scene. "Please," said Rionnag, indicating her nanny, and she took Jinty by the arm and led her away.

"Let her rest, Jinty dear. Ye did well. Now, go and rest yerself."

"Yes, Princess, thank ye. Thank ye! Ye brought her back!" The maid prostrated herself at Rionnag's feet.

"Please dinna. We all love her. We both brought her back. Come, get up. Go and rest, Mór would want ye to."

"Yes, thank ye."

"Nay, thank *ye*! My parents willna forget all ye've done!"

"That is true. Never will we forget the service ye both rendered," Queen Catriona spoke from just outside the room. Jinty and Rionnag turned to see the king and queen enter the infirmary.

Jinty blushed and bowed deeply. Mór seemed to have awakened at the sound of her queen's voice. She struggled to sit up, but the queen laid a hand on the faerie's shoulder and gently pushed her back down.

The king spoke first. "Mòr, Jinty, ye have done well by us. Ye risked life and limb for our daughter and yer services will not go unrewarded." He smiled at them. Jinty blushed furiously. The queen tenderly placed a pendant hung on a thin braided leather cord over Mòr's head, then kissed her lightly on both cheeks. Mòr lifted her head, but was too weak to see that the pendant was made of highly polished Rowan wood and carved with the ancient symbol of bravery. Normally such favor was bestowed only upon the most courageous knights. Rionnag gasped when she saw what it was and knew that when Mór was well enough to see what was hanging around her neck, she would be impossible to contend with. But happily so.

Next, the queen placed a smaller pendant on Jinty's neck, the ancient symbol of loyalty and truth. The younger faerie could barely breathe, the honor bestowed upon her so great.

"Now, Jinty, yer work is done. Go and rest, child," the king said patting her on the back.

She was about to leave, when she turned round, facing the royal couple. "Yer...yer Majesties, I...I... I only did what any loyal subject would have done."

"Nay, my dear, ye went above and beyond any duty assigned ye," Queen Catriona smiled. "My husband told me how ye charged the fachan! The fachan, we realize, my own sister sent!" These last words were uttered with contempt. She calmed herself down, smiled once more at the maid and said, "Ye are a brave, brave lass. Now off with ye to eat, then sleep. Mór will be up soon enough barking her orders at ye. Take advantage while ye can!"

"Oh, yes, yer Majesty!"

The royal family smiled as the faerie hurried out of the infirmary. They left Mór to the good care of the healers and went back to the hall where the king and queen had news for their daughter.

"Rionnag, we have something of the utmost importance to tell ye. Besides yer own aunt sending that horror after ye to prevent yer marriage; a deed for which she will pay, have no doubt; that fine fellow, the friend of Fiona's, sent his elfservant to see me. He told me the most extraordinary tale. He says that..."

"...the human with the vine bindings by the riverbank... is Fiona's faither."

Her father looked astonished. "How did ye ken?"

"The look. By the look, Faither. Aye," she swallowed, "Fiona and I knew her mither was meeting someone here. We found the Tamlin stone in her mither's room. We guessed he was a captured mortal." Her father shook his head, hearing the same tale he had just been told now unfold from his daughter's lips.

Rionnag's eyes became wistful as she narrated what she guessed was the truth. "They met one *Samhain* and continue to meet every *Samhain*. Fiona doesna ken that the man is her faither." She took a deep breath, hoping her father would have something to say, some advice to give her.

He nodded in agreement. "Did ye know that his captor is yer own aunt, Barabel and the same wicked one has hold of Fiona's mither as weel?"

"What!"

"Aye. The captive, Fiona's faither told the whole story to that Paddy fellow." The King ignored the blush he saw creeping over his daughter's face.

"I sent my own tracking spell after Fi's mither, Maggie, but it hasna yet returned. My aunt must have intercepted it!"

"That would no be good."

"Advise me, Faither. I dinna ken what to do next."

"Child, the bad news is this; the only one who can rescue Fiona's faither and now mither from Barabel's enslavement is Fiona herself."

"What! Why? How can *she* rescue them? She's just a lass!"

He explained about the spell Barabel put on Ewan and assumed it would be the same with her mother.

"Ye've got to tell her," he said gently.

"That's what I thought ye'd say."

"I'm thinking it will come as a shock to the lassie."

"Aye, I'm thinking it will as weel. Faither, did ye ken my aunt sent her bogies after me first?"

"Ye say she sent *bogies* after ye?"

Rionnag nodded. "Aye, they were captured across the sea and when I came upon them, they told all to me, most unwillingly, I might add."

This was new information. King Niall knew Barabel used bogies occasionally to do her nastier deeds. They could be a threat, and though generally they were more stupid than dangerous, they were gaining strength. Was the lady crazed, trying to seize power from the Seelie Court? Bogies and a fachan! Nay, enough was enough! She had to be stopped.

"I'll have her arrested immediately!"

"Nay, Faither, no yet! Let her think she can win. Barabel doesna ken I am safe home. Let Fiona have time to rescue her faither! And her mither!"

"Mayhap a visit to yer auntie will be enough to make her think twice."

"Dinna Faither! Dinna do anything that could jeopardize Fi's rescue. Let Barabel think she still has a chance."

King Niall looked admiringly at his child. "Ye are right, child. We will wait. For now, ye are safe and sound. But when the time is right, Barabel will get hers and no mistake."

Fiona awoke this time, to find herself alone in Rionnag's room. The walls were birch bark, the floors were moss, the bed: a quilt of softness made from velvety flower petals, the frame, gnarled branches in intricate patterns. The small window was round, mimicking the hill. She stretched, rubbed her eyes and lay back on the bed knowing that she wouldn't have much time here. She must leave the deliciously cozy room and find her mother.

The door opened and Rionnag bounced in, full of vigor, with a bright smile for Fiona that was as brightly returned.

"Good mornin'! Did ye sleep well?"

"I'm feeling kind of guilty at how well I slept. How's Mór?"

"She's better, thank Oberon!"

"Thank goodness. Ri, we've got to go find my mother!"

"Aye, that we do, but first, are ye hungry? There's a good breakfast waiting for ye in the dining room. All the others have eaten."

"Oh," she said embarrassed.

"Ye needed yer sleep. I've only been up a short while myself. Come now, I'll take ye to breakfast," she said pulling her out of the room. "I'll even have some more myself! We'll need our strength today."

"Ri, I'm in a nightgown!" Fiona exclaimed, uncertain of castle etiquette.

"Och, I forgot. My mither had the house maid wash yer clothing so ye'll have to put on something of mine." She moved her hand in a flourish and produced a periwinkle blue silk gown, two slits in the back to accommodate her wings, and handed it to Fiona who held it up and turned it around. It was almost see through and she was about to protest, but Rionnag just laughed. "It willna be so when ye put it on. Just try it. There. Lovely. Would ye like to look in the glass?"

"Yes," Fiona said shyly, completely unaccustomed to wearing so feminine a garment. From a wall, Rionnag opened a door that Fiona hadn't noticed before, to reveal a mirror. Fiona stepped up to it hesitatingly and gasped as she saw herself in its reflection. She had never thought of herself as beautiful before, but by some magic or faerie spell she seemed to have transformed into someone more lovely than she had ever imagined she could be. She was almost embarrassed, but decided to let herself enjoy this feeling, reasoning that it must be part of being here in this enchanted place. Rionnag eyed her approvingly, aware that her friend was growing into a beautiful young woman. "Ye can keep the dress. I never wear it," Rionnag told her, not entirely truthfully, but glad to see Fiona's pleasure and surprise.

"Wow, thanks," Fiona whispered, awestruck.

"Now, let's go and eat."

"Yes, but let's hurry." They entered the dining room to find the queen and king waiting for them. Fiona felt glad to be dressed so well meeting the royal couple. The queen snapped her fingers and the table filled with foods of all kinds. Fruits of every color and description, dark breads and creamy butter spreads, vegetables a spectrum of green, roasted meats, glazes dripping with mouth-watering flavor. There were chocolates in the shapes of flowers, shells, animals and insects, ices the colors of the rainbow that didn't seem to melt. Fiona stared in amazement until her stomach spoke up.

The queen chuckled, "It's there for the eating child, not for the looking!"

Fiona piled her plate full and Rionnag did the same. She popped a Charmed fruit in her mouth and said, "When Paddy and I were traveling back here he gave me these to try. Mmmn, incredible."

"Yes, he is," Rionnag replied dreamily.

"I meant the fruit."

"Oh. What?"

"Never mind," Fiona said smiling indulgently. She ate her breakfast, thinking what the day would bring and hoping her mother was safe. Her face became serious.

"Rionnag, has there been any word about my mother?"

Rionnag who was busy recreating yesterday's rescue in her mind snapped to attention at the question. "Fiona, I have something to tell ye. Fi....och Fi, I dinna ken where to start."

"Start what?"

"I've got something to tell ye. I want to tell ye gently."

"Ri, you're getting me nervous. Besides the fact that my mother is lost and that fachan is still on the loose, what else do you need to tell me?"

The faerie looked over at her parents who nodded in unison. She put her head down and lowered her voice dramatically, "It's a long and tragic tale, one of enchantment and love, romance and magic." She hesitated for a moment, then went on. "It seems as though we were right about yer ma meeting someone on the other side. She's been doing it these fifteen years."

"Fifteen years," Fiona said slowly, registering this information.

"Aye. Fifteen of yer years ago, Maggie went to Scotland, and one strange and glorious *Samhain*, All Hallows eve, ye ken, she met a man in that place between yer world and mine. There was a bond of love between them. Ye are the result of that meeting," Rionnag said, getting dreamy again.

Fiona, mesmerized, said only, "Go on."

"Aye. They fell in love, but the man, who was no faerie, but human, like yerself, was a captive of a great and teerible enchantress. She had lured him into her world more than a century ago, through cunning and deception, but once a prisoner, there was no escape." After a pause, she went on, "Until now."

Fiona looked at her strangely but said nothing, so the faerie continued, "Every year at *Samhain*, yer mither returns to meet the man she loves and while she grows older, he remains essentially the same. She has never told him about ye, nor ye about him, so as not to cause suffering to either of ye, until this year."

"What do you mean? How do you know this?"

The king finally spoke up, "Yer friend Paddy's servant told all to me, the captive himself having told the story to him."

"The captive?" Fiona said, suddenly remembering the man by the river, vines around his wrists.

"Fiona, I think ye ken," Rionnag voiced the truth.

"Does he know about me? She told him about me?"

The faerie nodded solemnly.

"He knows about me? Why *this* year? Why now? How did he react? Did he want to meet me?"

"I'm sure he did. Does."

"Was he angry at my mother for keeping this secret?"

"He was sad maybe, but nay, not angry, for her heart was in the right place and she was just trying to protect him. And ye, too. They had talked about her rescuing him in the past, but it seemed naught could be done, until he found out about *ye*."

"What about *me*?"

"The faerie that spelled him made it her curse that no females be born to his kin, for only a female of his own blood could free him."

"If the faerie put a spell on him that no female be born into his family, what am I then? I am definitely a girl," she said, gesturing to her developing bosom.

"Yes ye are, but the curse went to his family in Scotland. He was never meant to meet anyone. And yer parents were never married, no oath was taken, so they're not family and the curse wouldna apply to their...ehm...unique situation."

"Excuse me, did you say a century ago?"

"Give or take, aye."

"You're telling me that not only do I have a father, but

341

he's over a hundred years old?"

"Fi, time is verra different here in Faerie. Our cycle of birth and death is so unlike that of ye humans. That is why I told ye before, faeries die, but not for what would seem centuries when counted in yer time. Of course more of them are dying earlier these days, what with all the destruction... Anyway, when yer faither became captive here, his time slowed as weel. So ye see, had that witch not captured yer da, ye wouldna be here. Ye wouldna have been born at all, for the man that Maggie loves would have been long dead by the time she came to Scotland all those years ago. Do ye understand what I'm telling ye? Ye look pale."

Fiona felt the blood leaving her face, could feel her heart racing and tiny beads of sweat forming on her upper lip. She wiped them away unceremoniously. "So I'm the daughter of a captive, a mortal captive who has been living in Faerie for about a hundred years? My mother has been meeting him every Halloween when the door between the worlds open. Oh, my God, this is like a faerie tale."

"Exactly."

Fiona took a sip of her tea and leaned back in her chair. "This explains so much. My poor mother, no wonder she's always so sad and faraway. I wish she could've told me, but how could she? I would've thought she was psycho! God, I feel guilty. I was so mean to her, always telling her to go out on a date and stuff like that, telling her how miserable she always is." Tears slid down her face as she recalled her mother's sadness, always trying to cover it up with work. Fiona remembered that the only time her mom was ever happy was when she was leaving to go to Scotland. This had always made Fiona feel angry and terrible, thinking how her mother wanted to get away from her. Now she understood. "That man by the river didn't just tell Paddy the story, it's him, isn't it...."she trailed off.

"Aye, Fiona, he is yer faither. Even had he not revealed all to Paddy, I would have kent it; he looks just like ye."

"You think he looks like me?"

"Aye."

"What's his name? Do you know?"

"Ewan. Ewan MacDougall"

"Ewan MacDougall. MacDougall. Fiona MacDougall," she said trying it on.

"Aye, Fiona, I kent ye had Scots blood in ye."

"And the evil faerie?"

"Ye ken that as weel."

"It's Barabel, isn't it?"

She nodded. "It was her land he was standing on. And ye are the only one who can release him."

Fiona suddenly recalled hearing that word before. A stone sitting on a shrine in her mother's room, carved with Celtic symbols meaning 'release me.'

Her father had given that stone to his dear Maggie. He had been waiting to be rescued and no one could do it, except her. She could rescue her father from his prison. Her poor father captured by the same evil faerie who sent the fachan after Rionnag. She felt her a hot fire rise inside her. Her eyes flashed and Rionnag thrilled to see it.

"What do I need to do?"

Rionnag threw her arms around Fiona who returned the hug tightly. "There's something else I must tell ye. This is even harder."

Fiona looked alarmed, knowing that what would come next might be even worse. "Fiona, Barabel has captured yer mither and taken her prisoner."

"Oh, my God!"

"Yer faither tells Paddy that she is in no certain danger yet, but will be as soon as Barabel gets bored with her."

"What do I have to do?"

"Ye are to bring yer parents home."

"I'll bring my parents home," she stated firmly. "I will."

"It could be dangerous for ye, ye ken. A rescue of a fey captive let alone two will be fraught with peril. Ye must perform rituals around yer parents and then hold tight on to them, never letting go, no matter what form they take, ye must never let go, for if ye do... Well, dinna is all."

"What do you mean 'no matter what form they take?"

"I mean to say, when Barabel finds out ye have a hold on them, she'll work her wizardry and change them to all forms of beasties, horrible ones, ye can be sure."

"Like Tamlin."

"Aye."

"Will they try to hurt me if they're in these horrible forms?"

"There is that chance, but I dinna think it likely. Whatever happens, ye must hold fast. Close yer eyes if ye must, but once ye get through the worst, ye'll be able to pull them through, though the coming through might be hard."

"Hard?" Fiona swallowed.

"Frenzied? Dizzying? I truly dinna ken. I just want to prepare ye for the worst of it. I will come with ye, but I canna lend a hand. Ye'll be on yer own. Today, ye'll need rest and good food in yer stomach. Ye must be strong. The sooner we leave the better, but oh, Fi..." she stopped and threw her arms around her again.

"I'll miss you too, Ri! Will I ever be able to come back?"

"Aye," she said sniffling. "Ye've got the magic now." She touched Fiona's back and felt the tiny wings there hidden under her gown.

"I want to go to your wedding!"

"And I want ye there! Fiona, I was thinking. Since ye *will* be able to return, do ye think ye'd be my maid of honor?"

"You have them here, too? Oh, yes, Ri, I'd love to!"

Rionnag's parents smiled at one another, proud of the way she had handled this very sensitive situation. They knew she would make a fine leader and knew too that she was ready to meet her responsibility with regal maturity.

Chapter 44

"Come, dolly! Do a dance for me! NOO!" Barabel shrieked.

Maggie had been dressed in about sixty different gowns, the queen pulling tightly corset after corset, yanking on her hair in an attempt to put it up, covering her face in heavy makeup, making her bow down. Maggie's cut, which had closed slightly, kept re-opening as the queen painted her face. The queen seemed to delight in using Maggie's own blood as hideous makeup.

Barabel had cast a spell that had Maggie moving like a marionette, feeling unseen strings attached to her back. Bored with that, the queen was now making her dance on her own. But Maggie didn't care. She was thankful. She knew this idea of Ewan's, to have her be a plaything for the queen was the only way she could be safe. She would allow the queen to seize every bit of dignity from her as long as she remained alive. She had to stay alive. As she danced a ridiculous jig, she thought of her daughter. What must Fiona be thinking now? She would think her mother had abandoned her, and she'd never know what had happened. And I'll never be able to tell her I'm sorry, she thought sadly.

"Stop looking like that! Smile!"

Maggie forced her face into a hideous grin, but it did not seem to satisfy.

"I do not like yer dancing! Change it!"

Maggie was no dancer and she knew it, but she could do yoga. That she could do. She bowed to the queen and began doing asanas on the floor. Downward Dog, the Cat, the Crow; mimicking the posture of a cawing crow, the Cobra; arching her head back, her feet practically touching the back of her head. She peered at Barabel who watched in seeming fascination. She breathed and continued. Triangle pose, Sage Twist, the Locust. As she began to twist into the fish posture, the queen flew into a rage and pushed her down hard. "IS THAT DANCING? THOSE MOVEMENTS! NEVER TRY TO TRICK ME, OBSCENE *HUMAN*!" The last word was spat out with such rancor Maggie began to be really afraid. She cowered on the floor, uncertain whether the queen would have her killed right there on the spot. Instead, the queen flung her hand up in a sweeping gesture and Maggie's gown was replaced with metal chains allowing her no movement. They dug into her skin. She tried to speak, to apologize for not doing as she was told, but no words were able to leave her lips, which seemed closed with an unseen gag.

"DO NOT TRY TO TRICK ME! DO YE THINK ME STUPID? I COULD TURN YE INTO A GHOST RIGHT NOW! OR A BLOODY HEAP! DO YE HEAR? DO YE? DO YE?"

Maggie tried to nod her head, but her chains halted all possible movement. She was sure she was going to pass out.

Her body was shaking, chains rattling. Maybe she would become a ghost.

"ANSWER ME!"

Maggie wanted to scream that the only way for her to answer was to be released from the chains, but she was dumb, her tongue frozen. Barabel stood before Maggie, looking ready to strike and with a flick of her wrist, began to unwind the chains, never laying a hand on her captive. As the chains began to unravel, Maggie spun faster and faster. Barabel's wrist continued flicking as she roared with laughter. Maggie's body was gyrating out of control, and as her terrified thoughts spun around her brain, the queen continued her screaming. "DO YE NO KEN THE STORY OF THE RED SHOES?? WEEL, I CAN MAKE YE SPIN FOREVER IF IT BE MY WILL! SPIN HARLOT, SPIN!" The insane laughter flew in all directions around Maggie's poor head. With eyes closed, she tried to drop to the ground, but some unseen force was keeping her upright.

"My Queen!" Ewan had come to spy the situation and hearing Barabel's shrieking, he ran to the room and saw his beloved becoming a human twister with no end in sight.

Barabel's head spun around and her wrist stopped in mid spin. Maggie fell to the ground, unconscious. Barabel began pulling on invisible stings, lifting one of Maggie's flaccid limbs after another. In a childlike voice unlike any he had ever heard from her she pouted, "Ewan! See what my dolly can do! She was bad so I had to punish her!"

Oh dear God, she's mad, Ewan thought, regretting ever suggesting this doll business to her. He had never seen this side of her: evil, angry, wild even, but fanatical, never. Then again, he'd never seen her with another female. As this thought struck him another entered his mind. In all the years he'd been held here, there had *never* been a female within her borders. Och, why had I no realized that before!!

At that moment a strange wisp of bright blue smoke entered the chamber. Ewan, remembering the scene from the river realized that this must be some spell from the princess and wheeled the queen around before she saw it. Grabbing her by the arm he whispered in her ear, "Yer Majesty, why no leave the dolly be and come ridin' oot wi' me?"

"Ridin'? Oot wi' ye?"

Was she now stupid as well? Her head snapped and her eyes focused on him. She smiled and licked her lips. "Aye, man, I'll ride out with ye." He placed his hand over hers, and though his eyes were inviting, his heart was sick with deception. He watched as the smoke swirled around Maggie and leave as it had come. Barabel thankfully saw naught. He took the queen's hand and put it to his lips. He saw Maggie had come to her senses and was looking at them. He hoped she knew what he was doing and why. He looked away, not wanting Barabel to note any communication between them. The queen looked at him with a look that made his skin crawl. Tilting her head to one side, she ogled him. Sultry voiced, she crooned, "Ewan, it's been lang and lang since ye've been my, ehm, *counselor*. I suppose *this*," she flicked her chin at Maggie, "can wait." Ewan smiled back, though sickened, he felt better knowing he had bought Maggie some time.

Chapter 45

"Fiona, I'd like ye to contact yer Irish friend." The king watched his daughter's face turn a deep red at this command. Fiona saw it too, but ignored it.

"Yes, Your Majesty."

"Do it now if ye please. I must meet with him. Please tell him to meet me by the river's edge, where we met the first time."

Fiona bowed her head and pulled out her whistle. She hesitantly put it to her lips, the king nodding in approval and she played the same melody that Paddy had heard when he first met her; the one he told her would call him to her. She concentrated as hard as she could on Kier and the meeting place and only hoped she did it well enough. This done, King Niall kissed his wife, daughter and to Fiona's surprise, her as well and set out to meet her Irish friend at the designated spot.

Queen Catriona spoke next and Fiona, sensing the

queen's goodness, pushed her nervousness aside. "Fiona, my husband has gone to inform yer friend what is to take place, and will instruct him to contact yer faither and have him ready. I wish ye all the luck and I want to give ye a piece of advice about my sister, who, I am ashamed to tell ye, is Barabel."

"Thank you, Your Majesty. Any help from you would be most appreciated," Fiona said, hoping her most formal vocabulary would please the queen.

"My sister is very strong and does not like to lose a battle. First, ye must declare yerself to her. Tell her who ye are and what ye've come for. Then ye must take hold of yer faither and yer mither, however ye can, for once ye have them in yer grasp, they're yers. As ye are holding yer parents she'll try to offer ye riches in return. She'll try to lure you with greed. Do not listen to her. And as Barabel shifts them into whatever she will, and do not doubt they will be heinous, ye must hold tight. Do not lose yerself to the fear, child, for ye *will* be afraid, no mistake. Once ye've got hold of them, there'll be naught she can do to keep them, except make their appearance so frightening that ye let go. And if ye let go, ye've lost them. But as ye hold on, they are yers. "

Fiona nodded quietly. The queen looked at Fiona, assessing her. Making some internal decision, she said gently, "Fiona, there is a spell that will protect ye from any curse Barabel might throw at ye and one that will make the crossing over easier. Without the words, ye and yer parents may no be able to leave, not easily at least, as this is no a feast day. I will teach them to ye. Ye must only repeat them aloud in the presence of Rionnag, my husband, King Niall and myself. And of course at any moment of peril and at the time ye and yer parents are ready to step through. Ye must keep these words secret. Once ye are clear through, ye may never repeat them again, is that clear?" Her tone was kind but authoritative.

"Yes, Your Majesty. May I repeat them in my head to remember?"

She smiled affectionately, put her hand on the girl's hair and tousled it. "Of course ye may."

"Please, Rionnag, make sure the halls are free of listening ears." Her daughter did as she was told and closed the door.

"Now, Fiona, these words are neither Gaelic nor English, but are older than Time itself, from before the first stirrings of our world, which is older than ye can put a number on. Now come close so I can tell ye." Fiona leaned next to the queen and into her ear she spoke three words, which sounded like music, deep and dissonant, but clear. She said them over and over again, and then asked Fiona to repeat them softly so that only those in the room could hear. She did so cautiously, afraid of the power in them.

"Do not be afeared of the words, Fiona, for though words have power, if spoken with righteous intent, they will never bring harm to ye. And this thing ye will do is as honorable as anything I have heard. Now say them again, with intent."

She repeated them until they became like a mantra inside her mind. She recited them perfectly, as if she'd been speaking this language forever. The queen clapped her hands, delighted that the human girl should be such a quick study.

"Fiona, be sure, we will come with ye as ye enter Barabel's kingdom. That we can do for ye. Unfortunately, we can do naught about her spells, but perhaps our presence will cause her to acquiesce. I truly have no idea what she will do."

"What will *I* have to do? How am I going to get them both? What if my mother is in another place, like a dungeon?

Will I have to pull my father off a horse, like Janet did with Tamlin?" She was beginning to get frantic as the time to leave drew closer.

"That I do not know. Fiona, there's no telling what the circumstances will be when ye get there. That is why King Niall is talking with yer friend Paddy. He'll hopefully tell yer faither to ready both himself and yer mither for when ye come. What I *do* know is that ye'll need all yer strength to pull them out. That whistle of yers might come in useful. Do not forget it."

Fiona and Rionnag followed Queen Catriona to the garden room, where she instructed her flower maidens to fill Fiona's pockets with Hypericum flowers to protect her against evil. She also had a branch cut from the Rowan tree outside Rionnag's window as protection from Barabel's magic, and placed it in Fiona's pocket as well.

"Now, go and get some rest before my husband returns, for when he does, I do believe it will be time for us to leave."

The two friends went back to Rionnag's chamber and instead of resting, Fiona frantically began to pace the room. Rionnag watched her friend in the midst of such anxiety and she felt her tension. She knew the child needed help and after a moment's hesitation, decided to share this precious and very private exercise.

"Fiona, ye must calm down. Ye'll be no good to either of yer parents if ye are this frantic. Sit down, I've something to teach ye."

Fiona tried to take a deep breath, but she barely inhaled a full one, so fraught with apprehension was she. But she sat down, crossing her legs under herself.

"Now, focus on the place between your eyes and just above and see if ye can find the blue star there. Can ye see it, Fi? Can ye?"

"I can see it," she said, wondering how Rionnag knew

the star would be there, or if perhaps the faerie put it there magically. Fiona saw the spark of light within her mind's eye and followed it as it danced across her inner screen.

"Now that ye see it, sing this with me." She began to chant a word older than time itself. The word sounded like a sigh, like a melody from her most inner reaches, like the low note of a flute. Together they sang it until Fiona had to take another breath and she let it out again. With her next intake of breath, the blue star disappeared and the image on her inner screen became a familiar one. Her coyote. He was there again, her spirit guide, his amber eyes penetrating hers. She felt suddenly as if cloaked in protection. The sounds reverberated against the natural walls like some great concert hall. Fiona felt buoyed and strong and not alone at all. As if reading a sheet of music and coming to the last note, she and Rionnag simultaneously ended their chant on the same long breath.

Quietly Rionnag said, "Ye are ready now to face this moment and whatever it brings. Yer spirit is strong as yer heart. My love will be with ye as ye step over the border of my land into that of yer captured faither and mither and then back to yer home. Never forget that!"

"I won't," she said quietly, her eyes filling.

Mòr, who was considerably improved, entered the chamber with Jinty in tow, who was practically hanging on to her mentor, and together they fussed over Fiona, fixing her hair into braids intertwined with potent faerie flowers, cowslips and pansies. "Och, such a lovely child. Ye'll make yer faither proud," Mòr cheered, the bruises on her face fading.

"Aye, ye will." Jinty bent low and whispered into Fiona's ear, "I'll miss ye, dearie." Fiona reached and gave Jinty's hand a loving squeeze.

Fiona paced about the room reciting, in her head, the words the queen had taught her, over and over until they were adhered to her mind when King Niall entered the room.

"The plan is set. Paddy will contact yer faither and tell him all. Hopefully he'll be able to lure yer mither out with Barabel. If not, we'll find another way. For now, we'll surprise Barabel and when she is at her most vulnerable, that is, after she loses her captives," he said, looking at Fiona, his eyes full of encouragement, "which I have no doubt she will, I will arrest her for attempted kidnapping," he added seriously,

Fiona's eyes widened at the compliment. She stood a little straighter, her resolve a little stronger.

"Ready the horses," he commanded one of his men-at-arms. "We leave at once."

Fiona and Rionnag went outside to the stables where the grooms were making the horses ready. Queen Catriona stood by her husband with Mòr and Jinty next to them.

Fiona went to say goodbye to the maids. Mòr and Jinty fussed about with her clothes, straightening her shirt, smoothing her hair, wanting to express their affection through service.

"I'll see you both at Bealltainn for the wedding," Fiona said, putting her palms out in the faerie way for them to touch.

"Aye, and we'll have a dress ready for ye tae wear for the occasion," Mòr said. "Godspeed, child." Ignoring Fiona's outstretched hands she threw her arms around her, Jinty awkwardly grabbing on with her.

"We leave!" the King commanded.

King Niall and Queen Catriona rode side by side on what looked like twin horses, each turquoise with sparkling crimson manes. Fiona saw that Rionnag had told the truth what seemed so long ago, that the horses were shod in silver and had golden bridles. They were an impressive sight.

Chapter 46

Ewan was readying the horses when he heard Kieran's call. Quickly and stealthily he ran to the riverside where Kieran was waiting. The prince told him what was to come and Ewan had to think of some way to get Maggie to come riding with them. He strode back to where Barabel was awaiting him and made a bold suggestion, "Ehm, my *Banrigh*, Queen Barabel, it seems that many of yer subjects have heard of yer new captive. They're sae proud that ye caught a human, and a female at that! They've been requesting ye do a rade and show her off."

"I wonder how they heard. Proud ye say?"

"Aye. Frankly, some are disputing the truth of it. Sayin' ye've never been able tae catch a woman... ye ken how the gossip flies."

"How dare they! I'll show them. Who said it? Do ye ken?"

"Nay, majesty, just rumor and innuendo. Pay no attention." Ewan hoped that she wouldn't take her anger out

357

on any innocent sprite, but he needed to save his Maggie's life as well as his own.

"A rade, hmn? I thought that we…but never mind, later. *I'll show them.* Tell my manservant to ready the woman-doll. I want her in the finest. Tell him Ewan, now!"

"Yes, yer majesty. Then I will ready a steed for her, shall I?"

"Of course. She will ride behind us. Is that clear?"

"Certainly, my *Banrigh*." He took her hand and put it to his lips, groaning inwardly.

"And Ewan, I do not like the way she looks at ye. I think she'll be tithed today, after we rade."

This was unexpected and Ewan felt his stomach lurch. He knew her tithing was *Samhain*, and *Samhain* had just passed, and this was not her tithing year.

"My Queen, isna *Samhain* past and gone?"

"Aye, but no matter, a tithing before my seventh year will put me in good graces with the lords of the Underworld! And believe me, they'll greedily accept one, *Samhain* or no! Were ye worried they might not like it? Were ye worried for me?" she said, her voice became unnaturally high and childish.

"Of course, yer Majesty," Ewan lied wretchedly. Try as he might to think of a way to get to Maggie and help her escape, Ewan knew that it was futile. Barabel's spies were everywhere and should she hear of their meeting, he knew the result would be Maggie's immediate death. He prayed that his child would be strong enough to rescue both Maggie and himself and get them out of this prison forever. The only thing he could do was to do as he was told and try to convince Barabel not to sacrifice Maggie to the bowels of Hell before the others arrived.

Maggie, dressed in satin splendor, sat upon a horse, resigning herself to the fact that there would be no rescue, knowing she would never see her daughter again, nor would she know any happiness. She knew where they were riding; Barabel had told her when she had come out, dressed in a diaphanous gown. "Ye dolly, nay, *woman*, ye will be tithed to Hell. Today. Ye'll be no plaything for me anymore. I'm bored with ye." Barabel had laughed sardonically, no modicum of compassion living in her wicked frame.

As she sat upon the pale green pony, Maggie tried to come to terms with it. This, her end. She was afraid for herself, but mostly, she wished she could say goodbye to her mother and her sister, and apologize to her daughter. Tell them how sorry she was. Tell Fiona how much she loved her. They must be frantic now with worry. And Fiona must be feeling so abandoned.

You did this, you selfish woman! she berated herself. You'll die here in this otherworldly place and no one will find your body, and Fiona will never know what happened to you. She clenched her fists together and tried to keep from becoming hysterical. She wanted to run to Ewan and throw her arms around him. She wanted to weep for their suffering. She was feeling very much a victim, something she had always tried never to do. She knew this kind of thinking was only going to send her deeper into despair, and then Barabel would not only win, but win grandly. She shook off these thoughts and sat upright in the saddle.

Ewan tried to talk to the queen as in the past, in role of counselor. Trying to sound casual, he said, "My dear Queen, why would ye want tae sacrifice such a homely creature? It might be an insult tae the devil himself. Why no put the lass tae work for ye? That's all human women are guid for anyway." He feigned a laugh.

"Nay, the woman goes. I want no distractions here for my captives. I've decided. The tithing will be done today."

Ewan's heart sank.

Chapter 47

Fiona and Rionnag were mounted on the King's fastest steeds, a dozen knights armed with magical swords behind them. Fiona couldn't help but be in awe of her pale lavender mount, with violet mane. They rode along the King's private hunting trail, practically flying, as they galloped together over the well-trodden path. Rionnag's horse was a dusky blue stallion with a pure white mane, and Fiona could see that Rionnag had not exaggerated her equestrian abilities. What a horsewoman she was! She barely touched the horse's flanks and the animal responded perfectly. They rode swiftly and Fiona, though a good rider herself, had to use all her concentration to remain seated. She scanned the countryside commenting to Rionnag on the beauty of the place, the purple heather reflecting onto the distant hills, the forests thick with trees in every shade of green.

"Och, Fi, it used to be far more beautiful here. The flowers are dying. See there, the empty spot," she pointed. "The lovely Bell of Rowan flower that I loved to pick as a lass is gone forever."

At any other time Fiona would truly be interested, but she was trying to concentrate on the task at hand. Even that wasn't working for all she could think about was her father; picturing him as he stood on the riverbank, wrists bound in vines. She couldn't visualize his features clearly, since she had only seen him from afar. He was handsome, though. Tall and rugged, she recalled. Of course he would be. It was a fairy tale, after all. Did she really look like him? Were his eyes really the same as hers, unlike anyone else's in her family? She was nervous about meeting him. What would she say to him? What would *he* say? Was he happy to have a daughter, or did he think she'd be a burden, someone to take his time away from Maggie? If she *could* rescue her mother, that is. If she could rescue *any* of them.

Rionnag reined her horse in and Fiona pulled to a halt. "Fiona, I hate to eavesdrop, but yer thoughts are just spilling out of ye like a stream after a rain. Yer da is rejoicing at having a child of his own. Of course he wished yer mither had told him before, but the time wasna right, as ye well know."

"I'm so confused. Wouldn't you be? I mean, my God. Suddenly I have a father, a hundred and fifty year old Scotsman who's been imprisoned by a terrible faerie queen and I'm the only one who can rescue him!" she said, somewhat hysterically.

"Of course, dear sister. But ye are ready, Fiona. I have every confidence in ye. Ye must have it in yerself."

Fiona took a deep breath. "I don't know if I can do this. What if I'm not strong enough? What if I mess up? Besides, I'm scared to meet him, Ri. All my life I've tried to imagine who my father was. He was a sea captain lost at sea, a spy from a foreign country who couldn't meet me because it would put me in danger, the math teacher from the high school who kept asking my mother out when I was in fourth grade, an astronaut lost on a space mission; but never, *never* did I imagine this. A faerie captive? No way!"

"But Fi, that's what he is. Ye must accept this and find the strength to help him. Then ye'll have the family ye've longed for these many years. And a real faither, not one of yer invention."

"Ri, I don't know the first thing about having a father. Will I have to obey this guy?" She paused and added quietly, "Will he love me?"

Rionnag regarded her for a moment. "Fiona, I ken it'll be difficult for ye to accustom yerself to having a faither, but they're not so bad. In fact, mine is so much easier than my mither. And I do believe yer's will be wanting to get to know ye and there'll be much for ye to teach him. Remember, when he comes out, he'll be coming into a time he'll no recognize."

"I know."

Rionnag indeed hoped that Fiona would be strong enough to take both her mother and father out of Barabel's captivity, as she was the only one who could. It was a daunting prospect, but she kept her worries to herself.

Many of King Niall's knights had gone on ahead to assure safe passage; several hundred were accompanying the group as they made their way to Barabel's territory. In a short time, Fiona would be face to face with her fate and she knew it. It terrified her but she knew it was what she needed to do and she was ready. She clicked her tongue and rode up next to Rionnag.

As the party approached the border of Barabel's lands, King Niall was the first to spot Kieran as he sat with eyes closed on an overturned log. The king called out a greeting and the prince awoke instantly, getting to his feet, hand shading his eyes from the glaring sun. Fiona, seeing her friend, reined her horse, dismounted and ran to meet him. Rionnag watched as her friend was lifted off the ground and twirled around in a fierce hug. She felt a twinge of jealousy and longed at that moment to be in Fiona's place.

"Oh, Ki...Paddy, I'm so glad you're here!" Fiona said, somewhat breathlessly.

The king marched over to them. Rionnag followed. "Well, sir," the king said, "I'm glad ye're here. Everything set? Good. We'll be crossing the border to Barabel's lands, and the lass could use all the support she can get. As ye helped with the fachan, it'll be good to know ye are near, in case we need yer services again." The king was tempted to say, my daughter will be glad to see ye, but said nothing. As he watched his daughter and the Irishman exchanging blushing glances, he decided that the whole tradition of secrecy was quite silly and caused no end of harm.

Fiona broke into the king's thoughts, saying, "Okay, now, tell me what I need to do. I'm scared." Before anyone could answer, Fiona's head snapped upright as she heard a tune wafting over the treetops.

Kieran grabbed Fiona by the arm and said, "That's yer father." Though she knew she should have been surprised to hear her tune, she wasn't.

Rionnag took Fiona's hand and gripped it as tightly as she could. Kieran let go of her arm and took Fiona's free hand in his, gripping it with fierce emotion. She turned to him. "It's time," she said resolutely. He nodded. Rionnag put her head on Fiona's shoulder and let it rest there.

"We must go. I think, Fiona, that ye are needed," King Niall said. He nodded to his daughter and Kieran, who helped Fiona to her mount.

They were quiet as they crossed the border, knowing that they had all better be prepared to face whatever would come. With determination, they made their way to the heart of Barabel's kingdom.

As they came to a knoll, Fiona reined her horse and whispered loudly, "Wait! I need to do something." She pulled her whistle out of her pocket and put it to her lips. She played the same tune that they had heard only moments ago.

They rode on.

Chapter 48

Ewan felt ill. If he continued trying to convince Barabel not to tithe Maggie, she'd become suspicious. Then Maggie would be killed for sure. He was at a loss, grasping at anything that might save his Maggie. He pulled his whistle from his plaid, turned his head jauntily, half-smiled and lied, "This is for ye, my *banrigh*, my Barabel." It was a bold act and he knew he had taken a risk, using her name in such an informal way, but the stunned way she looked at him, and the way she half-closed her eyes, confirmed her pleasure. Whistle to his lips, he played for her the tune he had written for Maggie, slow and full of feeling.

When Ewan had finished his melancholy air, his horse began pawing the ground nervously. He tried to rein it in, but it turned circles and pawed again.

"What is wrong with yer horse, man? Or is he just as anxious as ye to get back to the castle?" She threw her head back and laughed.

He laughed with her; hopeful he was correct about

why his horse was so agitated. And then the sound came. Lightly at first, the notes drifting over the treetops and down again like a soft wind. The same notes he had played only moments before. He was unsure how his child would contact him and his heart nearly stopped as he heard the tune come back to him, not understanding how she knew it, or how she played it so well. He glanced over to Maggie, whose eyes were opened wide with amazement, knowing intuitively that it was Fiona coming for her. She looked at him and he nodded imperceptibly. Coming for both of them.

"Yer tune for me is coming back again, Ewan. How sentimental. However did ye think of it? Learning magic are ye?"

He smiled, but said nothing. He hoped the child had the strength.

"Let us back to the castle, my Ewan." She gestured for him to ride up closer to her.

"Why no finish the rade, Yer Majesty. Yer folk in the south are waiting for the procession and tae see yer captive woman. Why no gi' them a show, eh?"

She squinted at him and smiled conceitedly. "I do have the finest horses. Perhaps ye are right. We can tithe the wench in front of one and all. And then we will have time, after, to get, ehm, reacquainted."

They looked up as they heard the beating of hooves along the trail. Ewan was the first to notice a group of riders standing in the woods. He knew the group. One dismounted, a girl with long reddish brown hair, who walked purposefully out of the woods and into the clearing. He watched the child take in the scene playing out before her. Watched her locate her mother among the riders, watched as her eyes swept the procession until they came upon him. They stared at each other for a long moment and then she spoke in a clear, unwavering voice.

"Queen Barabel!"

The queen turned sharply, inhaling the scent of human, as if it were dung. From her steed, she looked down at Fiona. "What do ye want on my land, *human* child?" she said with such animosity, Fiona cringed.

Fiona stood frozen, hesitating for a moment. Barabel urged her horse forward, but Ewan put his horse between the two. Before the queen could utter another word, Fiona lunged at her father, pulling him off his horse.

"I'm here to rescue my father!" she said clearly, full of feeling, looking directly at her father, powerful emotion sparking between them. Fiona wasn't sure what to do about her mother who was blocked by the queen. She glanced meaningfully at Maggie who was bug-eyed over this new turn of events.

"Ewan, what is the meaning of this!!" Barabel screamed, her hair turning stark white and rising, sparks of energy flying off her like fireworks.

"My daughter is here to tak me oot of this prison forever!" Ewan called back, gripping tight to Fiona's small hand.

"NEVER!!!!" Barabel screeched, her horse rising up on hind legs. She wheeled as if to attack the child, but seeing her grip on Ewan, could only stare furiously at them. She took a deep breath, trying to master her rage. Then the queen smiled caustically and hissed, taking in the child's hair, sprinkled with magic flowers, "Ye have no need of the cowslips and hypericum, child. Just give Ewan back to me and you will have as much gold as a train of my finest horses can carry." Fiona remembered Queen Catriona's words, "She'll try to lure ye with greed, dinna listen."

"What need have I for gold without a father to share it with? Keep your gold," was Fiona's retort.

The queen's white face turned a dark purple, her eyes glaring and sparking crimson with the weight of her anger and she said again, "Give him back and you shall have my finest horses."

"I ride the horses of the Seelie Court, what would I want with your nags? Keep your horses. I shall keep my father," Fiona replied, looking challengingly at the queen.

Maggie wasn't sure what to do. She knew what Barabel was capable of and if she tried to get to Fiona and missed, that would be it. That Barabel would kill her was certain and she did not want Fiona to see that happen. The child had been through enough. She watched for an opportunity to get past Barabel who was mounted between her and Fiona, because there was no way Fiona could get to *her*. The child was holding on to Ewan and Maggie could see Barabel losing her patience. It was only a matter of time before she *did* something and Maggie had read enough legends to guess what the queen might do. She knew that the time was now. She looked around and saw all eyes upon her daughter, Ewan and the queen. No one was paying attention to her, neither Barabel nor any guard. Maggie took her chance, jumped off her horse and ran to Fiona, throwing her arms around her daughter, gripping her fiercely. Fiona grabbed her back and then took her hand, squeezing it to the point of pain.

"Actually, I'm keeping BOTH my parents!" she screamed to the queen.

At this the Queen turned true green with rage and betrayal, for as she glared at the three humans, she knew she had been duped. She wailed once, a scream so deep it seemed to come from the very depths of Hades and suddenly

Barabel was invoking the spirits of the dead, the wicked, the devil himself. Arms raised, her gown began to swirl around her as she turned three circles. The riders could see sparks flying from her fingers, her face contorting in a twist of rage, passion and power. "LORD OF THE UNDERWORLD, SHOW THE CHILD HER PARENTS' TRUE FORMS AND TAKE THEM ALL TO HELL! I GIVE YE THREE INSTEAD OF ONE!"

Barabel pointed at Ewan and without warning, he took the form of a hideous serpent, the upper half of his body writhing and twisting, sharp claws where his hands should be. His pointed face with its lidless eyes were rolling, forked tongue darting. Fiona's grip was precarious as he slithered and squirmed, but she dug her fingernails into his slimy hide. Nauseated but determined, she held fast. Her mother's hand still felt human in hers and Fiona felt Maggie's nails digging into her palm. She looked briefly, afraid of what she might see there, but it was her mother, face twisted in horror. A forked tongue lashed in the air by her ear. Fiona winced, but held fast. As Fiona's hands tightened, a shadow passed over the sun.

Creaghan watched from a lofty perch as Barabel paraded his prize around, the captive's hand on hers. He seethed with a fury stronger than any he had ever known. She would pay for her deception and he would take his prize. And the torture would be sweet, for both the queen and her captive. My captive, he corrected himself. He dripped saliva as he thought about what he would do to the deceivers. He would fly in as a wind, whipping their horses into a frenzy of fear. He would grab first Barabel and tear her limb from scheming limb, savoring every bite, as she screamed in anguish and pleaded for her worthless life.

And then, he would take his prize and bring him back to his den where he would make the man wish he had never been born. Such torment would he bring to him, and he would take his time, aye, relishing every moment as the man begged for his life or better yet, for a quick death. He began imagining the cruelties he would bring upon his treasure, when he saw another human enter the display. It was the same wench who had escaped him. Ah, could it get any sweeter! He would have them all!

He thundered down to them all standing there, looming over them like a goliath, dripping sores and saliva, taloned claws reaching and the sound that issued from his corrupt mouth was intentionally agonizing.

"I AM HERE, VILE *BANRIGH*! GIVE ME MY PRIZES AND YE MIGHT LIVE. DEFY ME AND DIE!"

Barabel cringed slightly, her power intoxicating her. "*I WILL NEVER RELINQUISH ANYTHING TO ANYONE! I AM BARABEL, ALL POWERFUL!*"

He readied himself for his victory when he saw the wench grab hold of *his* prize! His prize! He stopped dead and roared. He burned in desperate outrage as he watched Barabel dare to turn his prize into some overgrown basilisk. Creaghan twisted and formed himself into such a creature to bring nightmares to even the cruelest savages, but even he knew that as his prize was held, he was helpless to do a thing about it.

Barabel pointed her finger at Ewan's serpent form and it changed to a bear, so fierce that Fiona had to turn away in terror. He roared, showing a full set of barbed teeth. The sound of his roar was deafening, as she grabbed a hold of his fur, digging her hand into it.

Barabel pointed at Maggie in an attempt to transform her. Maggie shuddered and tried to shield her body as

Barabel screeched her frightening words. Suddenly Maggie had a wild thought and pulled something hanging on a slim cord from around her neck. How it had remained unharmed through her captivity was a mystery, but there it was, Agnes' gift, the Celtic cross she'd found in her backpack. She thrust it before Barabel's distorted face, who bellowed when she saw it. Maggie had known the Scots viewed it as a powerful talisman, but she had had no idea how powerful it was. She shielded herself with it and from her core, such a burning outrage radiated forth, it nearly stopped the queen in her tracks. No one, not even Creaghan, interfered as the words escaped in an enraged whisper.

"Don't you dare, you, you... you greedy, loathsome, despicable excuse for a queen. Taking *my* love captive all these years and destroying our happiness is one thing, but you will *never* destroy *our* daughter's. She's stronger than you! You've destroyed enough happiness. I'll kill you myself!" Maggie lunged, but Fiona held her back.

Fiona, still holding on to her father as he writhed in her grip, watched as Barabel's twisted face contorted in frustration and rage. The queen screamed and again let loose her magic, but Fiona had remembered the words Queen Catriona had taught her and she said them aloud. The witchcraft stopped dead in its tracks, the power of the words protecting them.

"AARRGH!!" screamed Barabel.

The fachan laughed hideously and said, "YE WEAK, FOOL! YE SHALL NAIVER DEFEAT ME, HARRIDAN! GIVE ME WHAT YE PROMISED OR I WILL TAK HIM AND YE WITH HIM," Creaghan bellowed, his voice reverberating. He bluffed, knowing as well as the queen, that as long as the child held tightly to his prize, he could never obtain what he sought, nor touch them through the powerful words. It enraged him and he moved to stand before the child, his countenance so horrific, she would have to let go. His face directly in front of hers, he seethed and whispered things into Fiona's ear that no child should hear. Maggie shuddered, shielding her eyes from the fachan, but was awed by her daughter's courage. Fiona stood unwavering, repeating the Queen's words over and over, gripping her parents with all her strength. She didn't know if they would protect her against this new threat, but she had to try. The monster backed up a step as he heard the words again. His face twisted, livid. Fiona's arms were burning in pain and exhaustion and she was afraid she might let go.

From the woods, Kieran was beside himself. "Let me take him on! I'll tear him apart!"

King Niall restrained him. "The child is holding her own."

"Faither, Paddy is right. DO something! I canna just stand here and watch!"

"Neither the fachan nor Barabel can do a thing if Fiona continues to hold on. If I interfere now, there's no telling what the fachan will do! He could take Fiona's mither. Did ye no think of that? I think this will play itself out."

"But Faither, Fiona must be getting tired. How lang can she hold on? And when will it end?" Rionnag wailed, feeling utterly helpless and terrified for her friend.

"Fiona has more resolve than ye give her credit for. I will poise my arrow to strike, but that is all I will do at this time. I do not think I will need it. Have faith, child." He patted his daughter on the back, and pulled a deadly arrow out of his quiver and took aim.

Barabel was beside herself with fury, "SHALL YE KEEP

YER FAITHER NOW?!" her voice reverberating until Fiona thought she would go deaf, still gripping tightly.

"I'll never let go, Barabel! You'll *never* get him back!" Fiona wished it would end. It felt as though her arms were being pulled from their sockets.

Barabel's anger at the insolence of so wee a girl was vented on Ewan, "IS THIS THE FAITHER YOU DESIRE?!"

"I will keep him in any form!"

"WILL THIS DO?!" she exploded as Ewan's upper half took the shape of an enormous lion, his lower half that of an eagle, sharp talons digging into the ground. Fiona had to shift her position to keep a hold on him as his sharp claws raked hideously at the ground by her feet. Fiona clutched his mane tightly, her fingers digging in it, not letting go. Maggie gripped Fiona's other hand so tightly, Fiona was sure she would have no use of either hand when all this was over.

"AAARGGHHHH!" Barabel stormed, raising her arms and lifting mother, father and child into the air. Fiona felt pressure ripping through her body and some elemental force tore her breath from her. She knew Barabel thought she had bested her, but Fiona's resolve was greater than her fear, and she rallied, holding on to her parents as they all came crashing down to the ground.

As the three touched the earth, Fiona was gasping for breath, still holding on to her parents. Maggie struggled to sit up, and Ewan, who had returned to human form, lay lifeless on the ground.

"YE KILLED ME PRIZE AND NOW YE WILL DIE, HARLOT! AND THEN ALL OF YE WILL DIE!" Creaghan shrieked and lunged towards Barabel. He grabbed her by the throat and began to squeeze the life out of her, as everyone watched in horror. Barabel's face became mottled as the monster tried to strangle her. She fought back with a vengeance, her own fingers scratching the monster's face until it bled sickening liquid.

"I'LL HAVE YE INSTEAD THEN! YE'LL SOON KEN TORTURES FROM THE VERY DEPTHS OF HELL!" Creaghan's voice reverberated.

"GO TO HELL YERSELF!" Barabel screeched, her voice rough and barely audible. The queen's eyes bulged as the creature squeezed her neck harder. Creaghan stood up tall, his hands still about the queen's throat and raised her above his head in an attempt to throw her like a discus when from the edge of the clearing a spelled arrow came sailing out, taking the fachan directly in his center, where a heart might be, if he had one. It came so fast, that those present only heard it whir by and then saw the fachan fall to the ground, dead. His hideous body began to smoke and sizzle, like a hot pan doused in water, and the smell was enough to make them all retch. Barabel lay on the ground gasping for air, her face crimson, her throat permanently scarred.

Fiona and her mother were crying and shaking Ewan in an attempt to revive him, but to no avail. Maggie pounded the ground, grabbing Fiona, hugging her hard, sobbing.

"No! Not now! This can't be! I can't take it!" Maggie screamed, her heart breaking in pain.

"I...I tried to save him... I'm so sorry, Mom," Fiona said, voice cracking.

"Fiona, dinna give up!" Rionnag and Kieran were halfway across the field, flying toward them, shaking their heads. King Niall and Queen Catriona followed behind. The king stood next to his wife, both standing guard over Barabel who was still struggling for breath.

"It's too late!" Fiona wailed.

"Fiona, ye've come this far. And this is Faerie, is it not? Use yer gift to bring him round."

"Rionnag, don't you *get* it? He's not unconscious, he's

dead."

"The fachan's dead. Yer faither...I think not. Use yer gift, Fiona."

"What are you talking about?"

"Fi, what brought ye to yer da?"

Fiona understood what her friend was talking about and felt inside her cloak for her whistle. She pulled it out and looked at it sadly. "I can't play now!"

"FIONA!" For the first time, Rionnag sounded angry. Fiona looked at her strangely and the faerie nodded her head vigorously. "Play!" she ordered.

Fiona looked to where her Irish friend stood and he nodded his head in agreement. Fiona looked at Maggie, who was watching the scene, tears streaming down her face. She too nodded her head at her daughter.

Whistle to her lips, Fiona once more called on her source to give her strength. The tune that came from the pipe had no earthly sound; it seemed to come from no physical reality. It had the quality of a heavenly air. The listeners stood in awe, Fiona herself awed by the sound, wondering what magic she possessed to allow something this sublime to come through her. Because whatever it was, it was coming *through* her, not from her.

All eyes were on the human man, the captive, the lover, the father, the friend. He lay still as a windless lake, his eyes were closed, his face a ghostly mask. Fiona wanted to see his eyes open and see her own eyes reflected there, but she knew it would never happen. Blood trickled down his cheek and his lips were white as chalk. But she played on. She played and played, the music unwavering, her fingers moving over the open holes, creating a language all their own. She ended on a long high note. She knew the piece was over, though she couldn't say how she knew. But it ended, the note lingering like a sigh on a breeze. She closed her eyes, not wanting to see the disappointment in the eyes of her friends, or the anguish of her mother, at her failure to bring her father back. She stood for a moment, listening for their laments, but all she heard were gasps and intakes of breath.

She opened one eye and then another and saw her mother cradling her father in her arms, his eyes fluttering open. Rionnag came to her and gently put her arms around her and whispered, "I kent ye could do it. I'm so proud of ye."

"I am, too, me beauty," Kieran smiled broadly.

Fiona stood between her new friends, watching her mother's face transform from sorrow to joy as her father's eyes opened and looked up into her mother's. As she stared at them, her father pulled his eyes away from Maggie's and searched the crowd. His eyes found hers and he gazed at his daughter, eyes filled with admiration and what she hoped might be love, too. Never taking her eyes off his, she walked slowly to him. Maggie looked over to her and reached out an arm. Fiona grabbed it and was pulled into a loving embrace, her father putting his face in her hair, crying quietly. Fiona didn't bother to hide her tears and the three of them laughed and cried and rocked one another until they were done. Looking up, the three humans were not surprised to be surrounded by faerie friends. Kieran extended a hand to Ewan, who took it and pulled himself to his feet, taking his wife and daughter with him. More hugging ensued until everyone was breathless.

From the ground where she lay watching the scene, Barabel screeched mightily, her voice rough, "Ewan MacDougall, I curse ye and yer loathsome daughter..."

"Barabel! Stop it! He is lost to ye as ye are lost to yerself!" Queen Catriona shook her head, paused and added, "Ye make me regret yer existence." Her sister looked at her with utter contempt but spoke no more, defeated.

King Niall glared down at Barabel, who was shrinking in her countenance. "Barabel, I place ye under arrest, to be taken to the tower of the *Sidhe* where ye will await trial for treachery and villainy against the heir to the Seelie throne, yer own niece, my daughter, Princess Rionnag." To his knights, the king called contemptuously, "Get her gone."

The knights chained her and threw her unceremoniously onto one of the Seelie horses, guarding her well on all sides.

Fiona and her parents stood fixed and stared at the scene that was playing out before them. Ewan turned to his Maggie and their child, his eyes tired, and said, "Let us go home."

Fiona nodded up at him, her eyes searching his face, never wanting to stop looking at those eyes. He looked deeply into hers and took her chin in his hand.

"Ye are the bravest lassie I've ever known. And sae proud I am to call ye my oon." A single tear slid down his cheek. Fiona reached up to wipe it away, touching his face. "Let's go home," she said, smiling, taking his hand.

"Fiona, wait!" Rionnag cried. "Dinna leave without out saying goodbye!"

"I never would!" Fiona ran over to her friend who opened her arms and wings wide, embracing her. Maggie watched as Fiona was embraced by a faerie of such elegance and beauty, she was thunderstruck. Seeing her confusion, Fiona took Rionnag by the hand and brought her to her mother. "Mom, I've been busy while you were away. This is my friend and faerie sister, Rionnag, Princess of the Seelie Court." Maggie said nothing, her confusion mighty, but her happiness grander. Rionnag looked up at Maggie and Ewan and smiled, her face glowing, "Take good care of my sister." They nodded in agreement.

"Thank you, Rionnag!" Maggie cried. "Thank you all!"

"Ye ken, I'd do anything for Fiona! For all of ye!"

Kieran went over to his friend, no longer captive, and put up his hand in the faerie way, but Ewan grabbed him in a fierce hug. "Thank ye, my friend. Ye've been more help than I can say. I wish ye well with everything," he said, winking at the young man.

"We're both the luckiest of fellows, aye, Ewan," Kieran whispered. He then embraced Fiona and whispered something. She nodded her head and said, "I knew it all along!"

"See you at Bealltainn!" Rionnag cried, as she flew off to where her parents were waiting.

"Goodbye!" Kieran called, following the princess. The three humans waved to them and turned to leave.

Ewan looked from his Maggie to his daughter, seeing his own mother reflected in her hopeful young eyes. "Take me back tae life again," he said to them both, though his eyes were on his daughter's. He held her gaze and as a thought struck him, his eyebrows rose comically in a gesture that Fiona would grow to love, and said, "Bealltainn?"

She smiled and shrugged her shoulders.

They found the ring and Fiona used her remaining strength and gripped their hands as tightly as she could. She remembered the words easily and said them to herself once before repeating them aloud. The ground shifted under their feet and then blackness came over them, so deep it seemed to have no end. They held one another fiercely as they whirled deeper into the gloom. A faint spark of light appeared in the dimness, hovering in their line of sight like a tiny white butterfly, fluttering and flickering, full of expectation. The light became constant, glowing steadily and they could make out dim shapes shimmering just out of focus. And then they were feeling chilly air on their skin and smelling sweet wood smoke. As they felt all movement cease beneath them, they came out into the light of an autumn day on a hill miles from a tiny village. Ewan dropped to the ground, pulling Fiona and Maggie with him, their hands remaining firmly joined, while he kissed the earth and wept.

Fiona put her hand on his broad shoulder in comfort and as he moved to look at her, his eyes were drawn to a figure standing close. Fiona turned to look at what had caught his eye and watched her father slowly look up, tears spilling from his blue-green eyes. For a brief moment, they all saw an image standing over them, tears glistening on a beautiful ancient face. A face Maggie had seen in a picture hanging on a wall, and one Fiona had seen in a shaft of sunlight in a faerie's bedchamber. Ewan's eyes met hers in a look so bare and filled with emotion that Fiona had to look away, feeling like an intruder. And then the image was gone. Maggie smiled through a flood of tears until Fiona threw her arms around her and then reached for her father beside her until they were all united in a single embrace and such was the energy of love surrounding them, they were all overwhelmed.

It was still mid November and the temperatures were brisk as the three hiked back the many miles to the village where they found old Hugh at home, shocked and thrilled to see them standing at his door.

"Ye made it home, lass. I kent ye would! And this must be Fiona! Welcome! And this," he said, putting his hand out to shake Ewan's, "This must be my grand uncle. Welcome home, laddie. We've been waitin' o'er long."

They entered the warm house and as Hugh led them into the kitchen, Ewan was startled when the old man flicked at something on the wall and the room was illuminated. He was about to question Hugh about this wizardry but exclaimed when he saw the picture hanging on the kitchen wall. He went over to it, gently took it down and touched the cheek of the face with love, staring into it for several long moments. Fiona came into the room and went up next to her father to see what he was staring at. Her breath left her in a gasp as she saw the illustration, the likeness remarkable. Ewan made to put it back when old Hugh cried, "Nay, uncle, ye are tae keep that! It is yer own dear mither and I drew it myself. I want ye tae have it!"

"Thank ye, Hugh. Ye are a gifted artist, the likeness is exact."

"Och, aye," Hugh said, beaming with embarrassment.

To Fiona Ewan said, "This is yer granny, child. Her name was Fiona. Like yer oon. Ye have her eyes."

"Yours, too," she said quietly.

"Aye," he acknowledged, gently petting her hair.

Maggie made a request to old Hugh, who nodded happily in response and Ewan watched in fascination as she picked up a black object from the wall, then spoke into it. He looked at Fiona questioningly, who only smiled at him, enjoying his wonderment.

"Hello, Mama! It's me, we're back...Yes, Fiona is with me. Yes, we're in Scotland! Okay, okay! Yes it really *is* me! Is everything all right? What! Kat's where? Oh my God! I'm calling there next! ...I don't know, but soon! I love you, too...I'll tell Kat! Bye!"

"Aunt Kat's *here*?"

Maggie nodded, wiping away some happy tears.

Fiona tried to explain to her father what had just occurred, but he shook his head in disbelief. Maggie made another phone call, this one even more exciting than the first. Between Agnes and Kat, Maggie could barely get a world in edgewise. When she hung up, she was shaking her head, smiling.

"Agnes will have dinner for us, and Hugh, you're invited too!" she told the older man. "We've had pretty meager rations lately."

"Not me!" Fiona said emphatically.

"Och, nay, Lassie, I dinna want tae intrude on yer first meal together as a family."

"You *are* family, Hugh," she said, taking his warm hand in hers.

"Aye, ye are, but what exactly? I canna figure it," Ewan said, looking confused.

"He's your grand-nephew," Fiona said shaking her head. "That's too weird."

"By the way, Maggie, what do ye plan tae tell Agnes aboot...?" Hugh gestured in Ewan's direction.

"The truth, Hugh. I think after all these years, she's entitled to know the truth. I think she knows it anyway," she said, touching her necklace. "And with my sister there, I'm sure there will have been no end of speculation!"

Fiona sat in the front, next to Hugh, as they rode in the wagon the short distance to the Grey Goose, while Maggie tried to explain an abridged version of modern Scottish history and the Industrial Revolution so that Ewan would get an inkling of what he would need to know about modern life. He shook his head in confusion. "One thing at a time, my love. Ye say there's a place where I can soak my bones in hot *running* water and soap myself clean? I must be a rare filthy lout." He grinned mischievously at her, his eyes full of warmth.

"Yes, my love," she said, feeling a flush coming into her cheeks at the look he gave her.

"So ye agree? Are ye sure ye want tae marry a lout then?"

"I meant yes, there's a tub. Oh, Hugh!"

"Aye, then, ye'd better be there tae show me. There's centuries of Fey dirt on my skin that need tae come off, which I daresay I canna reach, before I'll give myself tae ye as a proper husband." Maggie laughed and snuggled more firmly into his side. Fiona couldn't recall ever hearing that sound before, and she liked the way it rang out. She hoped she would hear it often. She turned to look at her parents who were oblivious to her as they sat cuddled together under their blanket, eyes fixed on each other's. She turned back to the front, not wanting to intrude, and said with a smile, "Looks like I'll be going to two weddings!"

Old Hugh stopped the wagon and turned to his friends and said, "Before we go tae The Grey Goose, I'd like tae make one stop, if ye dinna mind."

Everyone nodded in agreement. He clicked Molly and the wagon turned down a narrow, well-trodden path. After several minutes, he reined and hopped out. He walked over to a crooked gate, lifted the hinge and opened it. He got back in and the wagon jostled as they made their way through a maze of stones. Fiona looked at old Hugh as she realized they were in a graveyard. He nodded at her, smiling, and when he found the stone he sought, pulled Miss Molly to a halt.

"This is the place. Ahem, Ewan," he said to his young granduncle, reluctant to disturb him.

Ewan, who had Maggie snuggled under his chin, his eyes closed, opened them and acknowledged the older man.

"I've brought ye here tae show ye."

Ewan immediately knew where they were. They climbed out of the wagon and Hugh took the younger man by the arm and led him to a moss covered stone. The old man picked off a piece of moss, revealing carved words. Ewan's breath caught in his throat as he looked down at his mother's grave. He gave the old man a grateful smile.

Her name and date of death were hard to make out, but the words underneath were as clear as the day they were carved: "Ever Waiting." Ewan knelt before the stone and spoke softly in Gaelic, telling his mother to wait no more. He'd come home.

Chapter 49

They arrived back home just in time for the father/daughter dance, and even though Fiona told her mother it was stupid, they both knew she really wanted to go, had dreamed about it. Gram had waited and watched for them day and night for nearly three weeks, which still astounded Fiona, since for her, only a few days had passed. Aunt Kat had gone to Scotland after almost two weeks of no news, unable to do anything else. Kat had flown home as soon as she saw her sister in the flesh. Maggie, Ewan and their daughter stayed until papers were sorted (with the help of Agnes' barrister first cousin) and Ewan could fly with them to America.

Gram put Fiona's hair up in a chignon and she wore a velvet dress, deep rose with tiny gray hearts on the hem. Her father, Ewan MacDougall, wore a kilt representing the MacDougall clan, replete with sporran. When they walked into the gym, every head turned. Fiona and her father danced every dance, happily oblivious to the stares and whispers.

Maggie wore a cream colored dress, embroidered with tiny pansies and cowslips, when she and Ewan were married officially on a warm spring day in April, at the spot where Rionnag first flew from Fiona's open palm and bathed herself with morning dew. Fiona had chosen the site, telling her father that it was her favorite place in all the world. He had taken her hand, admiring the sweeping vista, the trees just beginning to flower and said, "Then, it is only fitting that we wed here, under yer beloved tree, looking out at yer cherished hills."

Under the apple blossoms, Ewan read the vows they had composed, adding to those they had borrowed from the Scottish bard, in Gaelic, and Maggie repeated them in English.

"I, Maggie Harris, will love you, Ewan MacDougall, as I have loved you for lifetimes and I will forever hold you dear to me now that we are together at last."

Together they spoke the famous Scottish bard's words, "'Till a' the seas gang dry, my dear. And the rocks melt wi' the sun; I will love thee still my dear, While the sands o' life shall run.' I will be forever yours."

Neither could speak the words clearly, so full of emotion were they.

Old Hugh, Agnes, Gram and Kat tried to contain their tears of joy as the justice of the peace asked for the rings. Fiona took them from her finger and handed them to her parents. They were gold circles etched with the Celtic knots representing love and the circle of life. The rings exchanged, they were declared husband and wife. As the two kissed a long and lingering kiss, a quiet howl was heard on the breeze and soon the hills were echoing with the sound until the kiss ended and the howl faded, a sweet sigh on the wind.

Jana Laiz

Maggie and Ewan sat at the breakfast table sipping tea, laughing together when they heard a car pull up in the driveway and the sound of voices outside the house. They waited for the customary knock on the door, but none came. The voices were getting closer and from the kitchen window they saw the slick figure of Frank Costa with two other men, holding maps and pointing animatedly. Fiona opened the window quietly and their voices sailed in. "...at least twenty five luxury condos right there!"

"Yeah, the road could be between those trees. Nah, we'll take them down anyway."

Ewan rose from his chair, his ire beginning to burn, opened the kitchen door and stood, arms crossed over his chest. "And what would ye three be wantin' on my land, then?"

The three men turned around and stared unabashedly at the imposing Scotsman, dressed in a tartan kilt, looking very much the Scottish laird.

The surprised developer muttered something under his breath and the two men strode took off toward the front of the house. Putting on his most charming smile, looking rather like a snake, Frank went up to the Scotsman, hand extended. Ewan ignored it and repeated his question, glaring down on the developer's glossy head.

The man began stuttering, "Uh, sorry... I...don't understand...I...uh...thought... Maggie...did she sell?"

At this point Maggie came and stood leaning in the doorway, arms folded on her chest. Gram and Fiona stood behind her. "Frank, I see you've met my husband, Ewan MacDougall. Is there something you want?"

"Uh, no...nothing at all...I'll..."

"Get ye gone!" Ewan said, imperiously.

"I..."

"NOW!"

He turned and ran to his SUV. They watched him speed off and they laughed heartily. Maggie walked out to where her husband stood fuming. She reached up and put her arms around his neck and said in her best Scottish accent, "Och, ma brave Scottish knight. Come and kiss me before I swoon." And he did.

Fiona stood at the doorway watching her mother and father embracing, thinking, those are *my parents*! She smiled at their happiness, sharing it.

Since her father had come home, the three of them would sit together poring over every photo album of Fiona's life, from her birth until the present. She loved watching his face light up with each page, as he filled in the missing blanks from his life. As Ewan looked at those images, he imagined himself holding his child on his knee, singing her lullabies in his own language, pushing her on the swing, rocking her to sleep. He had a young woman now, and no matter of wishing would give him back those lost years.

Fiona had similar feelings of loss and she prefaced many a sentence to him with, "I wish you could have been there when...." or "If only you saw..." Sometimes, though not often, she referred angrily to a certain queen of the faerie realm, but Ewan and Maggie both reminded her that had it not been for Barabel, she wouldn't be here at all. Ewan would have been dead these many years.

She had begun calling him 'Dad' and after an awkward start, the name seemed to roll off her tongue as naturally as if she'd been calling him that all her life.

Earlier that morning, Ewan had stood at the foot of Fiona's bed watching her sleep. He'd been coming in every morning at the break of day since their return and though the soft bed he now shared with his wife was a comfort, after more than a century of waking at dawn's arrival on his rough cot, he was unable to sleep after the sun made it's appearance. His daughter, her features so like his own dear mother's, smiled in her sleep. He watched her, feeling a combination of joy at having found her and great loss for all he had missed.

This morning, feeling his presence, Fiona opened her eyes, and smiled at him. "Good morning, Dad," she said sleepily.

"Good morning to ye, my *caileag*, my lassie."

"Dad?"

"Aye?"

"Are you interested in taking a walk? I want to show you something."

"I'm always interested in anything ye care tae show me," he said, with fatherly affection.

Fiona felt her heart swell. "Great! I'll just get dressed and I'll meet you downstairs in five minutes. Bring your whistle. Okay?"

"Okay," Ewan said, trying out this strange new expression.

Fiona loved watching the faces he made as he tried these new words, loved the way he turned on and off the lights (much to Maggie's environmental chagrin), as he awkwardly got into the truck, as he marveled at the music coming out of the strange black boxes, as he beamed with pleasure every time he opened the refrigerator and as he sang at the top of his voice in the shower, making the water as hot as he could stand.

And Ewan loved teaching Fiona the words of his language, the language of her newly found heritage, loved the way she scrunched up her eyes as she tried to repeat them perfectly. He loved talking with her about the strange, and terrible, and wonderful world where he had spent most of his life, and where she often longed to return. He loved letting her show him everything he didn't comprehend in this strange, new world.

They met downstairs, the early sunlight spreading throughout the kitchen like honey. She grabbed two apples from the wooden bowl on the table, took her father's hand and led him out into the awakening day. They walked hand and hand down the path, admiring the little plants coming to life in Maggie's garden, through the orchard where pink flowers would soon turn to fruit, until they got to a place Ewan had not seen before on his many walks of exploration. Fiona led him to what looked like a round garden, a circle of flowers, all in full bloom, though it was only early spring. And the flowers themselves reminded him of a place he'd not soon forget, so vibrant in color were they, so unusual in their intricacies. She led him inside the circle and though he hesitated at first, knowing too well the power of rings, he let her lead him in. She sat down on the cool grass and pulled him down beside her. Keeping his hand in hers, she leaned close and whispered, "Close your eyes." He looked at her, seeing her joy, trusting her, and after watching her close her eyes, shut his own. All at once, in his inner vision, a face came into view, a smiling face, creased and old, yet as dear to him as his heart, eyes the color of the sky, rings of earth in star bursts surrounding jet pupils. The wrinkled face beamed brightly until the only thing either of them could see was light. Ewan opened his eyes wide and stared in disbelief at this child of his. She looked up at him, eyes big with wonder and elation. He took her face in his two hands and held it there. Then he leaned down and gently kissed her forehead.

They rose to leave, but Ewan noticed something under the flower circle and bent down to pick it up. It sparked in his hand as he lifted it. As he looked at the object, a distant memory rushed back at him. He saw himself carving this for his Maggie and giving it to her, tears streaming down her fine face as he handed it to her, telling her its meaning. He looked at it again and then again, for the words he had carved there had changed. In the old language, the stone now read, *"Free"*. He returned the stone gently to its circle of power and the flowers covered it once more. He looked up as he heard a familiar tune and saw his daughter, whistle to her lips, playing. He took his own whistle out of his pocket and joined in a duet, the music bringing him for the moment, back to a land of craggy hills and moors, of lochs and castles, heather and thistle, and of course, faeries.

When they finished the tune on the same note, he took his daughter's hand and they made their way back to the house he would share with Maggie and Fiona for the rest of his days, home at last.

Epilogue

Fiona and Gram went through at midnight on a star filled May night, stepping from night into a clear, bright Faerie day. The moment they stepped through, Fiona felt a strange sensation in her back. She frantically reached around, trying to comprehend what it was that caused the feeling. She could feel something protruding from her shoulder blades. She turned visibly pale. Her grandmother watched her with a perplexed expression, but before she had time to ask her grandchild what was wrong, a handsome youth, green eyes smiling at them, appeared. "Me beauty! I knew ye'd come!!"

"Oh, Paddy! I'm so glad to see you. Does Rionnag know?"

"Nay, she does not and don't you say a word! Did ye bring yer whistle?"

"Yes, of course I did! Paddy, this is my grandmother. You can call her Gram."

"Enchanted I am," he beamed, taking her hand to his lips. "And ye both can call me Kieran, or Paddy is fine too."

"I'm so pleased to make your acquaintance, Kieran," Gram returned, wondering why this faerie man was as big as she was.

"Kieran, huh?"

"Well, I didn't know yer intentions when we first met, and then it was too late."

"What are you doing here? Won't Rionnag see you? Shouldn't you be getting ready for your wedding?" Fiona asked.

"Aye, I should! Give us a kiss for luck!"

Fiona kissed him soundly on the cheek and sent him on his way to ready himself for his wedding. He flew off just in time for as they watched him fly out of sight, two faeries were flying toward them, the chubby one waving her hand madly, barely able to contain her excitement. The other one swooped down and landed before Fiona, throwing her arms around her. "Och, 'tis my dear Fiona! Give yer Jinty a hug!"

Fiona put her arms around the faerie, breathing in the scent of lavender. "Oh, Jinty, I'm so glad to see you!"

"And what about me?" Mòr demanded, letting go of a gasping Gram and moving Jinty aside to embrace Fiona.

"Of course, Mòr! You look so much better! I'm so glad! I feel like I'm in heaven."

"No dearie, 'tis Faerie, really."

The castle was adorned with flowers of every color and description, some of them newly designed for this very occasion. Colorful raffia banners hung from every beam and festivity was in the air. Faeries were flitting here and there with baskets of fruit and flowers, tables were laden with delicacies, and stewards were arranging furniture to accommodate the multitude of arriving guests. Fiona turned to Mòr and said, "Where is Rionnag? Can I go to her?"

"The Queen is wantin' tae see ye first. She's been wantin' tae talk wi' ye."

"Oh, of course."

Mòr led them to the throne room where Queen Catriona was dressed in a dazzling diaphanous gown a shade of purple Fiona never knew existed. It was embroidered with tiny pansies and sparkled as if diamonds were sewn onto it. Gram curtsied and Fiona followed suit.

"Fiona, my dear, come here. And this must be yer grandmither. Please, come forward."

Fiona came forward and kissed the queen's extended cheek. Gram took her proffered hand and kissed it as well.

"Fiona, yer friend and sister is miserable. Ye must make her see reason, make her go through with it. She seems resigned, but has lost her bloom. Since ye left she's not the same. Go to her. Talk with her. Perhaps ye can bring her to her senses."

"I will, Your Highness. May we go to her now?"

"Aye, ye'll find her in her chamber."

They found Rionnag in her room before the looking glass, a wistful expression on her face. She sparkled when they walked in.

"Fiona! Gram! Thank Oberon you're here. I've been forever waiting."

There was a flurry of hugs and kisses and then Rionnag threw herself down on her bed. Gram stood by her side dumbfounded, the sight of a life-sized Rionnag almost too incredible to comprehend.

"Och, Fi, Gram, I feel I'm walking to my death this day. I so wanted to marry the way my parents did! I told ye it would be a merry day and I've tried to be cheerful, but ... oh..." Lavender tears spilled down her delicate face.

Fiona wanted to break her vow to Kieran and just tell her, but she knew she could not. "Rionnag, listen to me. Do you trust me?"

"Aye, Fiona, I trust ye with my life, dear sister."

"Then just believe that you will be the happiest bride ever, well, maybe the second happiest. My mom is pretty happy!"

"But that's the problem. I dinna begrudge her, but I want what she has. I'm glad she's happy of course, but how can ye be sure *I'll* be?"

"Is anything really sure? I promise is all, believe me. I can't say more."

"Aye, I will try."

Fiona released the breath she was holding and Gram sat down beside the faerie and patted her hand lovingly.

"Then let's get dressed and ready for this big Ceilidh," Fiona said, turning to her grandmother, "That's a celebration, Gram."

"I knew that!"

"And Ri, it's working already, the magic! Remember the cement factory I told you about? Well, it got defeated! Mom's working on getting a windmill plant to go there instead. And polar bears have been put on the endangered species list. That means we'll *have* to save them!"

"That is grand." she said, brightening slightly.

"So, what do you say, Ri? It's worth it, right?"

"Time will tell. I hope so."

"Well, I'm here now and you promised me that blue dress, remember? The one with the wing slits."

"All my gowns have a place for my wings," the faerie smiled indulgently.

"Good, because Ri, will you have a look at this?" She turned her back to her friend and lifted the back of her shirt. She heard Rionnag's gasp. "Och, so ye do have the blood for true. Fi, ye do!"

"I don't get it. What's happening to me? As soon as I

got here, I felt something strange. I didn't feel it before."
By this time Gram was looking aghast at the little wings
protruding from Fiona's back.

"What's happening?" Gram repeated.

By now Rionnag was smiling broadly, "When Fi and
I became sisters, I gave her a piece of my wing, as a token,
to connect us in some way. The only way this could be
happening is if she's got the blood. And it will happen
whenever she comes to this side, getting stronger each
time."

"Oh, my," Gram mumbled, turning pale. She shook
her head and said, "Your father told me about your other
grandmother, Fiona. He said there were always rumors
about her."

I know," Fiona gulped.

"Och, this is guid news! Remember what ye asked
me that day on the hill at yer favorite spot? Do ye? Do ye
remember?"

Fiona's mind went back to the day she had played the
recorder for her friend while the faerie dipped and glided
in the morning sky. "Yes, I do remember. Ri, no way! You
mean, I can...?"

"Fly? Possibly. I'll have to teach ye, though. Ye might
have a hard time at the beginning, ye ken. So many things
to remember about the wind and the currents, och, and of
course the birds...."

Fiona was shaking her head in disbelief, her furrowed
brow changing to a radiant smile. She began to laugh and
Rionnag began to laugh with her, the faerie's mood lifting.
Gram was behind her granddaughter, gingerly touching the
translucent wings, which were by now several inches wide.
"I want some, too," she said, feeling rather foolish that she
had said it aloud.

"Och, Gram... If I give ye some, will that make ye my

grandmither?"

"You can be my other granddaughter regardless. But you're not serious?"

"Why am I not?"

"But, I don't have 'the blood', do I?"

"I suppose not, but no matter, come, let's try."

"But I have nothing to give to you!"

"Yer love will do just fine!"

"Well, if that's the case, you've had it all along!"

"As ye had mine!"

Rionnag was about to pluck a tiny bit of new growth wing from herself but Gram stopped her with a wave of her hand. "You know," she said thoughtfully, "I think your love is enough. Just being here and knowing this is all real is plenty. We'll leave the flying to you young folks."

Queen Catriona entered the room, smiling as she saw her daughter looking considerably cheered. Mór and Jinty helped the princess into her opalescent gown, the subtle colors having a milky iridescence. The dress came to the floor, with a long train of lacy material and Rionnag's wings matched the color of the dress, shimmering like Australian opals, changing colors with the light. She spread them wide and fluttered several inches off the ground, admiring her appearance. Fiona was amazed by her friend's radiance.

Rionnag fluttered around and landed gently in front of Fiona. "Thank the goddess ye are safe and here with me again. I dinna ken how I would get through this day without ye." To her mother, she whispered, "Mither, I love ye well. Thank ye for letting my friends be with me."

Her mother held her two hands in her own and looked long into Rionnag's eyes. A tear slid down the queen's face and she kissed her daughter gently on the forehead. All the words needed were unspoken as the two embraced. The Queen left the chamber to ready herself.

The door opened and two servants entered, gowns over each arm. Mór took the gowns, dismissing the servants and said "Here are some choices for ye both. Come and have a wee look." Gram chose a soft lavender gown of the finest silk, dotted with what she thought were sequins, but she was corrected, "Nay, not sequins, dew drops."

Fiona wore the hazy blue gown she had worn before, her tiny wings just peeking through the slits. Jinty gasped when she saw them. "I told Mòr ye had the blood, I did, didna I, Mòr?" she said, straightening the garment.

"Aye, lass, ye did. And ye were right. I kent it all along," Mòr said, not to be outdone.

The two faeries fixed Fiona's and Gram's hair, adding flowers to match their gowns, sprinkling faerie dust for extra shimmer. When they were done, the two took turns examining themselves in the glass. "Goodness," Gram breathed, "I wish we had a camera!"

There was a knock on the door and a footman announced that King Niall and Queen Catriona were ready for the ceremony to begin, and were requesting the presence of their daughter in their chamber. Rionnag looked at Fiona and Gram, her face a mask of something between terror and resignation. The two nodded to her reassuringly as she left the room to face her parents.

Mòr and Jinty led Fiona and Gram to the Great Hall where the wedding would take place. Gram was given a place of honor in the family aisle. Fiona was brought to an antechamber to wait for the bride, as she would precede her down the aisle.

Rionnag entered the antechamber followed by King Niall and Queen Catriona, and then took Fiona by the arm. "My parents tell me we can stay here after we're wed. I willna have to move far. That feels better. Tell me again, sister, tell me it'll be all right."

"Rionnag, when you see your Prince standing there waiting to take your hand in marriage, everything will come clear to you and you'll see that I was right. Have a little faith."

"Aye, I could stand to learn a thing or two about faith!"

"The music begins, child. Fiona, ye first." The queen urged Fiona down the mossy path, bouquet of blue and purple pansies in her hand, her heart pounding as she made her way down the springy aisle, looking at the strange assortment of elemental beings on either side, watching her every move. There were sprites dressed gaily in yellows and reds, tiny pixies throwing miniature pansies as she passed, and from Ireland, several jolly leprechauns in their three cornered hats, winking humorously at her. She arrived at the canopy and stood to the left of Kieran, leaving a space for Rionnag. He held a mask over his face, with only his eyes visible, but Fiona could make out the merry twinkle of those warm eyes. She smiled at him and then a hush fell over the gathering as everyone turned to look at the bride, her face covered by a lacy veil, gliding down the aisle escorted by both her parents. Gasps and sighs could be heard from the guests as they gazed at the hidden princess, her loveliness ethereal, despite her veil. Had Rionnag cast a glance at her bridegroom, she might have made out "Paddy's" eyes from behind his mask, but her eyes were cast down. She handed Fiona her bouquet and with a grateful smile for her friend's presence, stepped forward to meet her groom. Her parents kissed her cheeks encouragingly and urged her forward to fulfill the promise made long ago.

She stepped up to the platform and looking straight ahead, gave her hand to her betrothed's outstretched one, as he stood by her side. At the touch of his hand Rionnag felt a spark. It had a familiar feeling. Nay, impossible! her mind screamed. She breathed harder, not daring to look at him for fear she was mistaken.

A beautiful woman stood before them speaking in the oldest of all tongues. She wore a flowing robe that sparkled majestically, and on her long white hair she wore a wreath of sweet myrtle and lavender. She placed a silver cord over the heads and shoulders of the bride and groom and fluttered around them three times, gesturing with her hands. As they stood there, newly joined in wedlock, the priestess flew up above their heads and sprinkled them with stardust and flower petals.

Fiona watched as the room began to glow with warm intensity and the couple rose off the platform, floating. Hands intertwined, cord uniting them, they slowly spun around three times and then floated gently back to the altar. The white-haired officiating faerie removed the cord and gestured to Kieran, who with trembling hands slowly lifted the veil from Rionnag's face. He whispered something inaudible, but the feeling in it was plain. Fiona straightened the veil as it fell down Rionnag's back, and moved a little closer so she could see what she had been waiting for. For the first time, Rionnag dared look at her husband. She could not make out the face under the mask but she could feel the warmth in the look he was giving her. She closed her eyes and with fingers visibly trembling, she removed his mask. She stood there for a moment; her eyes still shut and then ever so slowly opened them. There before her was her own dear Paddy, green eyes shining with love and a smile for his beloved, for *her*, filled with such exultation that she let go a sob of joy. She felt herself explode with such enormous feelings of love for him she could barely contain herself. She turned to look at Fiona who stood next to her, smiling, tears streaming, head nodding, and reached out her hand for her human sister, who grabbed it and squeezed it tightly.

The mistress of ceremonies said something that only

one small faerie boy heard, for everyone else was lost in the moment. The child flew up to the altar and removed two shimmering rings from his pockets, handing them to Fiona. Taken aback, she stared at the gold rings, each etched with the Celtic symbol for love within the circle of life, exactly like her own parents' rings. She handed the larger of the two to Rionnag, who placed it lovingly on Kieran's finger. She then handed the tiny one to Kieran who knelt down, taking Rionnag's hand first to his lips, then with a gentle caress, slipped the ring onto her finger.

The audience applauded and Fiona looked over to see Gram being embraced by the king and queen. The priestess said something that caused the guests to stand and cheer, freeing hundreds of tiny butterflies into the air, and Kieran leaned forward, took Rionnag in his arms and kissed her. And she kissed him back ardently, in a kiss that would go down in Faerie history as being the sweetest, most transcendent kiss ever.

Fiona pulled her whistle from a bag she carried on her arm and began to play a tune she had composed for the occasion; an air so filled with passion and rapture, it had the audience weeping and swaying in the aisles, holding their hands to their hearts. Rionnag and Kieran turned to her, eyes shining with the emotion of the moment as she played her wedding gift to them.

The wedding *Ceilidh* was unlike any that had gone before or since, so filled with gladness and merriment that everyone knew it would be talked about for centuries to come. Fiona and Gram danced all night with a variety of handsome Scottish and Irish faeries. Gram was shocked when the king himself asked her for a dance. She graciously accepted and the two whirled about the hall. Kieran and Rionnag barely let go of each other the entire night, except for one dance, which Kieran gave to his new dear sister. He spun Fiona about the room in a fast-paced jig, whirling and stomping before carrying her up into the air. For a second, she lost her balance and began to drop through the air. Yet before Kieran could catch her, more to her amazement than anyone else's, her wings fluttered keeping her airborne until Kieran could grab her and bring her gently to the floor.

"Well done, me beauty! I knew ye had it in ye!" he kissed her soundly on her flushed cheek. Then more seriously, he added, "Ye've brought me and me love happiness this day." She smiled at him and joking once more, he rolled his eyes heavenward and held his hand dramatically over his heart, saying, "Did ye see her face when me cover came off me head? I thought I'd died and gone to heaven, I did!"

Fiona and Gram left the next day, as Rionnag and her 'Paddy' went off to take their honeymoon. The kingdom was bursting with happiness as they said their farewells to one and all. "Ye'll both come back at *Samhain*, won't ye?" Rionnag reminded them as they made to leave.

"Of course we will, dear. We'll come as often as we can. And you two come to visit us. You know you are always welcome!" Gram said, kissing the two goodbye.

Fiona came forward, brimming with emotion as she said goodbye yet again to her friends. "*Samhain* seems so far away!" she said.

"Aye, 'tis, but remember, me beauty, *ye* can come whenever you like!"

"And ye can always call me. Just say this..." And Rionnag whispered into Fiona's ears a spell that would have them chatting anytime they liked!

Fiona's eyes widened as she thought about the possibilities before her.

"Och, Fi, I almost forgot. Yer friend Kumsah..." Rionnag stopped, smiled and pulled Fiona next to her, whispering something in her ear.

"Dancing? With me?" Fiona blushed ever so slightly, then smiled.

Kieran took her in his arms and lifted her off her feet. "Give me best to Ewan and Maggie when you return home! We'll see ye before too long, me beauty. I've no doubt!" He put her down, bowing theatrically to her. Rionnag took her hands and looked into her eyes. "There can be no goodbyes between us, ye ken, only Godspeed." The faerie kissed Fiona and her grandmother and sent them through the crossing and home. Home to a life that was now very full.

The coyote stood below the window, gazing up until her light went out. She stood by the slightly moving curtain, half hiding in its shadow, and looked out into the night. She saw him standing there like Romeo or Cyrano under the waning moon. Their eyes met briefly, his reflected in the moonlight, and then with a lift of his head, he bared his teeth in his coyote smile, howled softly and loped back into the shadows. She watched his gray figure disappear until the world held no trace of him whatsoever.

THE END

The Twelfth Stone
Gaelic Glossary & Pronunciation Key

Words:

Banais: (<u>ban</u>-eesh) wedding

Ban Righ: (bahn <u>ree</u>) Queen

Belltainn: (bel-tane) In Celtic religion, a festival held on the first day of May, celebrating the beginning of summer and open pasturing. Bealltainn was one of two turning points in the year, the other being Samhain, the start of winter. At both, the bounds between the human and supernatural worlds were erased. On May Eve, witches and fairies roamed freely, and measures had to be taken against their enchantments.

Cairdean: (car <u>jeen</u>) friends

Daoine Sidhe: (deena <u>shee</u>) faerie folk

Fachan: (<u>fa</u>-kun) beast, monster

Fir Darrag: (fear dare-ek) a nasty faerie

Ghillie Dhu: (gilly doo) a faerie made of rustling leaves

Leig as mi: (leek gas me)

Mither: mother

Mnathan: (<u>mnah</u>-hun) lady wife

Samhain: (<u>saw</u>-ween) the festival on the eve of
    November - Halloween

Names:

Barabel: (baar-ah-bell)

Catriona: (ka-trina)

Celllach: (kee-al-ak)

Creaghan: (kree-ah-gen)

Fearghas: (fer gus) Man's name

Keiran: (keer-ran) Irish for Charles

Mòr: (more) meaning big/senior, woman's name

Niall: (nee-ahl) Neil

Rionnag (Ban): (<u>ree</u>-oh-nek) (bahn) fair star

Phrases:
Aye: yes
Bairn: baby, child
Bonnie: pretty
Couldna: couldn't
Canna: can't, cannot
Daft: silly,
Dinna: don't
Doesna: doesn't
Fair fashed: exhausted
Faither: (fayther) father
Guid: good
Hasna: hasn't
Ken: know
Kent: knew
Kirk: church
Lassie, lass: girl
Lang: long
Nay: no, as in NO!
Naiver: never
Noo: now
Och: expression as in "oh"
Oon: own
Oor: our
Oot: out
Puir: poor
Tak: take
Verra: very
Wasna: was not
Wee: little
Weel: well
Willna: will not
Ye: you
Yer: your, you're

Jana Laiz

ACKNOWLEDGMENTS

This book has been a lifelong labor of love and there are many people to thank for all their support, help, and encouragement. I will try to name them all, but this book has had so many incarnations and has taken so long to write, you must forgive any omissions. I will start by thanking the most encouraging person of all; the one who was there when I had my first o/o/b experience (looking out the window in Social Studies class,) the one who was there when the idea was conceived and who has listened to every chapter, every change, every idea and never ever wavered in her encouragement – Mom, thank you for your belief in me and this story. I love you more than words can say. Dad, my love and thanks to you for pushing and pushing me up the hill and for your contagious enthusiasm. And for your boundless, unbridled energy, from where I undoubtedly get mine. To my daughter Zoë, to whom this book is dedicated... for your unwavering belief in me and the faerie world, for your unerring editorial insights and suggestions and your loving support. You've grown up alongside this story. To my beautiful son Sam, for your extraordinary adolescence, which enabled me to not only write Barabel and Creaghan, but to become them. And for your inner and outer beauty whence my lovely coyote boy, Kumsah was created. I love you madly! Sincerest thanks to Nancy and Bob Tunnicliffe my Gaelic and Scottish consultants. Your dialect guidance was invaluable, your magical spell help sublime. The best virtual tour guides ever! Nancy, your steadfast friendship and loving support throughout the writing and beyond have sustained me in more ways than I can express. Godspeed and tuppence, Bob. My loving thanks to: Joe for your love of this story and your good red pen; to WindRose, not only for introducing me to Tamlin and his Janet but for being my picture of Rionnag; to Marion for your sweet friendship and happy praise; to Ann-Elizabeth & Richard for your unyielding love and support; to Ariana & Laura Marie for your belief in me and for showing me the Magic; to Heidi & Jess, steadfastly there for me since the beginning; to my dear Irish friend Deirdre for your sublime music and your enthusiastic endorsement; to my new friend and kindred spirit Alison Larkin for your sincere praise and wacky zeal; to Jackie for your wonderful insights; and to Pam & Toni, my ever-encouraging sisters for their excitement for me! And thank you to all my editors, readers and critics young and old: Kayla, Rachel, Danielle, Maddie, Gwen, Nathan, Mari, Elizabeth, Irena, Kate, Laura, Sheena, Elaine, Emma and also to Kat for her unerring advice. And to Sean for listening with such love. Special thanks to Adam Michael Rothberg for putting it all together. For the music of Solas, Mick Mcauley, Lunasa, Old Blind Dogs, Dougie MacLean, Clannad, Altan, Davy Spillane, and so many others, without which this book could never have been written. I hope you hear it within these pages.

And last but certainly not least, to my 6th grade Social Studies teacher who interrupted a most whimsical dance in the schoolyard (thus lodging it into my psyche) and to the Luna Moth that lighted on the screen door and put the whole idea into my head in the first place.

JANA LAIZ has been writing for as long as she can remember. In addition to writing the Award Winning novel, *Weeping Under This Same Moon*, she is the author of *Elephants of the Tsunami*, and the co-author of *"A Free Woman On God's Earth"*, The True Story of Elizabeth "Mumbet" Freeman, The Slave Who Won Her Freedom. Fascinated by other cultures, Jana studied anthropology and Chinese language at University. She is a teacher, a writer, an editor, a publisher, a photographer, a mom, an animal lover and keeper of pets, a sea glass collector, a jeweler, a musician and a dreamer. Jana was a caseworker at The International Rescue Committee working in refugee resettlement. She is passionate about our beautiful planet and endeavors to make a difference in the world and to work with others who feel the same. She lives in The Berkshires, Massachusetts. Visit her at www.janalaiz.com